Nate the Texas Story

Also by Mark Warren

The Westering Trail Travesties
A Last Serenade for Billy Bonney

Nate the Texas Story

Nate Champion Duology

Part One

Mark Warren

WOLFPACK
PUBLISHING
— EST 2013 —

Nate the Texas Story
Paperback Edition
Copyright © 2024 Mark Warren

Wolfpack Publishing
1707 E. Diana Street
Tampa, FL 33610

wolfpackpublishing.com

Image of Nate Champion Courtesy of the Jim Gatchell Memorial Museum

Paperback ISBN 978-1-63977-533-0
eBook ISBN 978-1-63977-532-3
LCCN 2024939091

To Nathan David Champion

Nate the Texas Story

Late Summer 1871

Round Rock, Texas

Chapter One

B efore the noon hour, the two brothers had erected six new fenceposts along the north line of the Champion pastureland. Throughout the morning, John Thomas had carped about the heat, placing the blame on the size of Texas or its proximity to Mexico, neither of which made sense to Nate.

Nate had resigned himself to the usual litany of complaints. As the younger brother—by two years—he had no choice. But he knew that grumbling about something that could not be changed was wasted energy. Nate considered their assigned work to be something that simply had to be done, whether it be in heat, rain, or the freezing cold. Over the years, his father had made that clear. What was important was the job. And its part in making the Champion ranch a growing operation. A ranch depended upon people—each person doing his share—and Nate was not going to disappoint his father.

John Thomas retreated to the buckboard parked in the shade of the trees. There, he dawdled as he drank from his canteen and selected the next post from the stack of quartered staves in the bed of the wagon. Nate paced off the distance for the next posthole, stabbed the auger into the ground, and looked up to see a rider approaching from the east.

"Ain't that Naomi?" he called out to John Thomas.

They watched their little sister come on at an easy gallop. She was the only female in Williamson County to wear denim trousers under her dress. Arriving at the work site, she reined up, looked from Nate to John Thomas, and sized up the situation with a snort.

"So, Nate does all the work, and you lollygag in the shade? Is that how it works?" Her voice could be like a knife edge, and today it, was well-honed.

"Whatta you want, Naomi?" John Thomas demanded with the typical whine in his voice.

"There's a rattlesnake in the well house," she reported in her brusque way, undoubtedly annoyed at having to ride out here to find them. "Our stepmother says to come git it out."

"Now?" John replied, his voice rising.

Naomi's face squeezed down as if she had detected a disgruntled skunk in the area. "Well, I didn' ride all the way out here to tell you to come'n git it tomorr'!"

John's brow lowered over his eyes. "Why cain't James do it?"

"Well, he could 'xcept he ain't there. He's gone with Daddy into town."

"I can come," Nate said. "I ain't afraid of 'em."

John shot Nate an indignant look. "I ain't afraid! I'll go 'cause I'm older. You just stay an' work on the posts!"

Nate shrugged. "I caught that one in the barn coupla months ago. 'Member?"

"Yeah." John Thomas laughed. "An' Daddy d'livered a sermon 'bout the foolishness o' not killin' the damn thing." He leaned toward Nate and mimicked his little brother's quiet and earnest voice. "'Member?"

Naomi Jane, as usual, had the last word. "I think the reason she wants John Thomas is, if anybody's to git bit, it oughta be *him*." When John turned away to indulge in one of his pouting frowns, she gave Nate a wink.

John Thomas unhitched the Morgan and rode off bareback, kicking his boot heels into the horse's ribs as he tried to keep up with Naomi. Nate watched them until they disappeared behind the trees at the sharp turn of the creek. The quiet that settled in after their departure was much to his liking. He took a strong grip on the auger handle and began to rotate the tool as he leaned in with his weight.

The tricky part was getting started, trying to turn the wide haft until the auger took a bite and could stand up on its own. Once he had dug down about a foot, the going was easier for not having to balance the tool...but harder due to the stubborn layer of rocky soil below. The formula then became redundant. Drill down six inches, wrestle the auger out of the earth, pour water into the hole, and then, while the soil soaked, he cleaned the curled slices of dirt off the spiral blade. And so it went.

———

After tamping in two news posts, Nate lifted the bucket and emptied what little water was left over his head. Then he carried the empty bucket down the tree-shaded slope to the creek. Setting bucket on the sand, he sat on a crate-sized boulder to pull off his boots, socks, and gloves. Then, after hanging his hat on a broken-off sycamore branch, he waded out into the cool water, where it was deep enough to squat down and submerge his whole body.

When he came up, he lunged for the flat slab of lime-stone that parted the water at midstream. The warmth of the rock was a welcome antidote to the chill bumps that now covered him, and so he stretched out with his chin resting on the backs of his hands at the boulder's edge.

Just inches beneath his nose, the creek water slid by like the passage of time. Effortless, indifferent, and never-ending. It was this thought of water and time that reminded him of Billy Hill's wager. Until this moment, he had never really considered taking up the bet. Now he did.

Rolling to his back, he found the sun too bright on his closed eyes, so he draped the crook of his arm over his face and thought about the possibility of winning that bet. If he could do it, he might substantially increase the cache of money he kept in the cigar box under his bed. Twenty-five dollars was his last count, all of it earned on his off time working with neighboring ranchers who had acquired troublesome horses that needed Nate's special touch.

Billy had thrown out the challenge to everybody in the schoolhouse, claiming that he had stayed underwater for a minute and a half. He dared anyone to beat it. To all who refused to believe him, Billy referred those skeptics to Lindy Hildebrand, who had supposedly witnessed the feat. Billy told anyone who would listen about how he had worked up to the task over several weeks, learning how to increase his air intake and to slow down his heart rate. That's what he claimed. Billy insisted it was no different than a turtle burrowing into mud for the winter.

But Nate knew Billy Hill. He knew those shifty eyes that looked away whenever Billy stretched the truth about something he'd done. Nate suspected the conniving boy had sped up the count in his favor and talked Lindy into believing him. Billy could be persuasive, especially with girls, who seemed to want to believe him about anything, based on his roguish smile alone.

It didn't matter now whether or not Billy had lied. What mattered was the bet and the money it could bring in. The wager was on the table, and Billy was letting all takers name the stakes. If Nate could stay underwater long enough, he could collect on that bet and be that much closer to buying the used saddle that waited for him at Mr. Cooke's blacksmith shop.

Flipping onto his belly, Nate pulled himself to the edge of the rock again and watched the water glide beneath him like a universe in motion, its specks of sand and mica shining like stars blinking on and off in random order. The surface of the creek was but a thin skin separating two worlds, a membrane ever moving and yet, somehow, seeming never to change.

On one side of this skin was air and life. On the other, a choking death. Just a year back, a young girl had drowned in the Brazos while her family had picnicked. And a year before that, Nate had lost a schoolmate to Brushy Creek in the spring when it had flooded out of its banks. It was events like these that wrote an eerie mythology about certain streams, stories that people liked to repeat in whispered tones, as if these creeks and rivers had an evil will of their own. But Nate knew better. Those stories said more about people than they did about moving water.

There was, Nate had learned, a flip side to everything. If he thought about a catfish or a crawdad, the formula was reversed. Life and death traded places like a do-si-do at a barn dance. A fish flopping on land was no different than a child flailing underwater. Life was life, and death was death. Nate wondered how the two could be so close together here at the creek, sharing a common boundary so fragile that a finger could poke right through it.

He knew he should get back to work, but on an impulse, he wanted to know how he might fare against Billy Hill's challenge. Priming himself with five deep breaths, Nate filled his lungs on the sixth, eased his head under the water, and calmed himself as if he had laid his head upon a pillow in a dusky room. As soon as his ears dipped beneath the surface, all sounds were reduced to a dull, otherworldly murmur in the murky creek. Furtive conversations between moving water and unmoving stone. From the moment his head was enveloped by the cool water, he began a silent count.

One...two...three...

Reaching down to the streambed, Nate gripped a melon-sized stone, not so much to anchor himself against the current but to connect to something that so effortlessly defied the need for air. His hands splayed lightly on opposite sides of the smooth stone, his grip as gentle as a mother's hand cradling the head of her baby.

...Nine...ten...eleven...

He concentrated on relaxing and let the counting take on its own tempo, keeping the cadence true by his familiarity with the steady tick of the grandfather clock at home. With his eyes closed, Nate settled in and thought about that saddle.

...Twenty-one...twenty-two...

Two older boys at school had already taken up the bet with Billy. Both had failed, each lasting little more than a minute. Those two had been big, stocky boys with long legs and muscular arms. Nate figured their bulk had caused their bodies to scream out for air too quickly, while someone with less weight might fare better at this breath-holding business. Someone like himself. And it also probably helped to have the right inspiration. Most folks would think of the money. Nate kept thinking about that saddle.

It was a russet, drover's outfit, fully rigged and showing a few scratches but soaped to a mirror finish that made it shine like new. Wide pommel and straight-back cantle. Mr. Cooke, one of two blacksmiths in Round Rock, had taken it as payment for a debt and then put it up for sale. He had told Nate he would let it go for forty dollars—a fortune for a boy his age.

If Nate could build his cache to thirty dollars, he might be able to borrow the rest from his aunt Hattie, once she returned from her cattle drive to Kansas. He figured to work that off by training whatever horses she and Uncle George might bring back with them.

Of course, this meant that Nate was going to *have* to break that minute-and-a-half record. That or die trying. Losing all his saved money was not an option. If he came out on the short end, he would never be able to face his father's righteous eyes. That was the thing about gambling. It was the flip of a coin. Somebody was going to win all right...but somebody had to lose.

...Thirty-nine...forty...forty-one...

Normally, Nate did not favor games of chance. He was accustomed to working his way toward a goal in a straight-ahead fashion. Sweat and muscle. Dedication and stamina. But the idea of owning that saddle had taken a fierce hold on him until thinking about it made him ache.

...Sixty-three...sixty-four...

The creek swirled easily around his head, but time seemed to drag. For over a minute, the cold had been creeping into Nate's skull, and now each of his eyes felt as if an icy finger were pressing deep into the socket. The pain was bright. But so was the image of that saddle.

...Eighty-four...eighty-five...

Almost there! Now, the need for air was like a fist thrust deep into his chest, squeezing all the blood from his heart.

Ninety! A minute and a half! Deep in his chest, his lungs silently screamed, but instead of surfacing, he tightened his grip on the stone, wanting to see how far he could push through the pain.

...Ninety-five...ninety-six...

9

The ache in his eyes was nothing now. The need to breathe trumped everything else. Every part of his body was demanding that he surface. It was like a weight that got heavier and heavier, and it wanted to crush him.

...One hundred...hundred and one...

At a hundred and five, his head jerked up from the water, droplets sluicing a circular waterfall around the sides of his face. With a loud sucking sound, he drew in a long, gasping breath to bathe his lungs with the delicious air hanging over the creek. His ears opened to the world again, and a cardinal whistled its sweet, plaintive song from the trees behind him, notes so clear he could have thought himself reborn from the womb of Brushy Creek.

"A minute...and forty-five...seconds," Nate whispered between breaths. When his heart settled and his breathing calmed, he turned, lay on his back on the smooth, hard stone, and smiled, tasting the air like a holy meal delivered to him by a host of angels. The shades of green in the sycamore above him were so vibrant that the colors appeared to tremble slightly, even though there was no breeze.

After a time, he pushed up onto his elbows and saw the bucket waiting for him on the creek bank. Next to it, his boots stood upright with his socks and work gloves stuffed inside. Sitting up, he crab-walked on all fours across the rock and slid feet-first into the water. After wading to the bank, he sat to pull on his socks and boots and gloves, and then he plopped his hat onto his head. Gripping the bucket by its bail, he scooped up enough water to finish the day's work.

Carrying a load that would have outmatched most boys his size, he climbed up through the deep shade of the oaks, ashes, and hickories without a spill from the bucket. When he broke out into the pasture at the top, he set down the bucket at the site of the next hole and looked back at the progress that John Thomas and he had made. The fenceposts lined up like soldiers standing at attention, the line perfectly straight across the rolling terrain.

Using his teeth on the leather fingertips, Nate tugged off one glove. Stretching his arm to the west, he hinged his hand at the wrist, palm toward his eyes, fingers together. This was the way his uncle George had taught him to measure the working hours left in a day. With his hand positioned to rest on the distant horizon, Nate measured one and a half hands up to the sun. An hour and a half of daylight remained.

He walked back to the trees at the edge of the meadow, where the wagon was stranded without its draft horse, the traces sprawling in the mix of bluestem and buffalo grass.

Taking up the work shirt he'd hung over the sidewall of the wagon, he wiped the sweat from his eyes and then draped the shirt over the boards again to dry. He drank several big gulps of water from his canteen and then studied the wagon bed as he capped the mouth of the bottle. The bed was half filled with quartered posts, split from stout sections of juniper and locust and Osage orange—all woods that would not rot when planted in the ground. He chose one he liked and carried it out into the sun.

Nate would much rather have been assigned the heavy work of splitting these tough posts with metal wedges and sledgehammer, but there was a tacit hierarchy in the ranch work. All tasks that required raw strength fell to James, who, at eighteen years, had taken over as the oldest brother ever since William had departed for California. Nate, just days away from his fourteenth birthday, had been assigned to help John Thomas plant the fenceposts along the boundaries of the north pasture. It irked Nate some, but only because it meant he would not be working from horseback for a while.

"We'll be settin' up these stinkin' posts for most of a year!" John Thomas had moaned earlier that morning.

John was not far off in his calculations, Nate knew. Once the north line was complete—with posts spaced at ten paces apart for half a mile to the northwest corner— they would make a quarter turn to the south and continue digging holes for another half mile. At the southwest corner, they would angle east and hook up with the fence line already in place at the south pasture. And that was just the beginning. Once the posts were secure, the two brothers would return to their starting point and cover the same distance, this time stretching three strands of barbed wire as tight as the strings of a new banjo.

Whether for a day or a month or a year, Nate would stick to his assigned job, simply because it was in his nature to do so. "Nate don't know *quit*," brother William had once told their daddy. "An' he don't grouse about the work like John Thomas does."

Nate had been within earshot of those words from his oldest brother, and he never forgot them. His daddy had made no reply, but that was no surprise. Jack Champion expected nothing less from his brood than loyalty and obedience and hard work. His rules were clear: You did what you were told, and if you failed at it, you learned how to do it right, and you did it again.

Because he was small for his age, Nate figured he had more to prove than the others did. Even Dudley, who was two years younger, stood almost as tall as Nate and already outweighed him. Last Christmas, Dud—the prankster of the lot—had given Nate an iron logging chain that must have weighed sixty pounds. With a straight face, he had presented it wrapped in brown paper and tied with a red ribbon as he offered instructions.

"Nate, if ever you should be taken unawares out on the prairie when a high wind whips up, I want you to knot one end o' this chain around your waist and the other end to the closest boulder you can find. I'd hate to have to ride all the way down to the Nueces to fetch you."

Nate smiled at the memory and returned to his work. It took almost twenty teeth-clenching turns to lower the white paint mark on the auger's shaft to ground level. Having reached the proper depth, he strained to pull the blade out of the hole, but this time, it was like trying to uproot a thick sapling.

Nate stepped back, frowned at the auger, and dropped his hat onto the grass. Bending at the knees, he got his shoulder under the handle and pushed with his legs. The auger didn't budge.

As he prepared for a third try, he heard horses down below in the creek, snorting and clacking shod hooves on the rocks. Then came voices and a laugh he recognized. The party climbed the hill and came out of the woods near the wagon. A sorrel and a buckskin. Half brothers John and Martin Tisdale took their horses at a walk and reined up ten feet away from Nate.

Chapter Two

"**D**amn, Nate!" Martin laughed. "Yore daddy got you puttin' up fence by yoreself?" He twisted in his saddle to look down the long row of bare posts that ran true as a surveyor's line. When Martin turned back, he wore the crooked smile he used whenever he was having fun at someone else's expense. "Son, you know you ain't much bigger'n one o' those posts yourself, don'cha?"

Nate couldn't help but smile. He pulled off his gloves and stacked them together on his shoulder.

"John Thomas and me was workin' together, but he had to go back to the house."

Martin threw back his head and laughed to the sky. "Poor ol' J.T.! He's prob'ly sittin' in yore kitchen samplin' some cool lemonade 'bout right now."

Nate looked east toward the ranch. "I reckon he'll be back purty soon."

John Tisdale narrowed his eyes as he studied the top of Nate's head. "I believe you've got a tenant upstairs, Nate." He pointed. "Something's crawling in your hair."

Nate lightly fingered the top of his head until he felt a

shape like a seed pod tangled in his hair. Carefully caging it inside his fingers, he combed the object from his hair and held it in his open palm to study it.

"That's a water beetle, isn't it?" John said.

Nate nodded. "I's just down at the creek coolin' off."

John glanced at the blistering sun. "Don't blame you. Good day for a swim."

Nate set the beetle in the bucket and watched it swim circles. "Didn' really swim," he explained. "Just put my head in."

Martin chuckled. "Well...looks like you managed to fish it back out just fine. Your head, I mean. I see you're wearin' it again."

Nate met John's earnest eyes. "I was seein' how long I could hold my breath."

John nodded as if this were common fare for every citizen of Williamson County. "How'd you come out?"

Pushing out his lower lip, Nate shrugged. "Purty fair, I reckon. Didn' have a watch."

"So, what's the point?" Martin laughed. "You plannin' on becomin' a crappie or a bullhead?"

Nate wrinkled his nose and shook his head. "Billy Hill claimed he stayed under for a minute and a half. I was tryin' to decide if I believe 'im."

Cocking his head, Martin—or "Tiz," as he liked to be called—squinted at Nate's hair. "Reckon we oughta check for other critters? Hell, son, you might be hostin' a family o' beaver up there."

Both the Tisdale boys were neighbors and several years older than Nate, but for a short while, they had all been in the same mixed-age schoolroom. During that time, Nate had ample opportunity to learn the differences in the two. John was a serious student and courteous to all. Tiz was a hot pepper that had attached to the family tree.

John always looked a man in the eye and spoke in an

earnest way. There was not a person in Round Rock who did not trust and respect him. It was common knowledge that he planned to attend the college in Georgetown, and there was plenty of speculation as to what he might become: a lawyer, a doctor...or maybe a teacher.

Tiz usually carried a spark of mischief in his eye, but there was no meanness in him. For Tiz, drawing laughter out of an audience was reason enough to act the clown as he did. He held no aspirations for more schooling. He seemed content to work as a top hand on his family's well-stocked cattle ranch, and when he wasn't doing that, he frequented the saloons in Round Rock and caroused with his drinking buddies.

Tiz laughed. "So, J. T. abandoned you, did he?"

Nate nodded and stooped under the auger handle to give it another go. "He was needed at home. He'll be back." With the padding of the leather gloves between the handle and the sloped muscle beside his neck, Nate pushed again with his legs, straining until his face felt like a branding iron ready to singe hair. The auger would not give.

Tiz showed all his teeth in a festive smile. "How long you been fightin' that auger, Nate? Looks like it's gittin' the best o' you."

John nudged his sorrel closer. "Step aside there, Nate, and we'll give it a pull." John looked back at his half brother. "You going to help or just sit there and smile?"

Tiz pretended a thoughtful look. "Well, let's see," he quipped, "it *is* easier to smile." With a quick laugh, he prodded his buckskin forward, and Nate stepped back out of the way.

The two brothers positioned themselves on opposite sides of the auger. Without speaking, they leaned from their saddles, each taking a one-handed grip on an end of the handle. John nodded, and they jerked in unison. The auger held fast, but the horses shied at the effort.

Getting their mounts under control, the Tisdales flanked the handle again for another try. John's face was set with determination, but Tiz looked downright insulted by the obstinate tool.

"Ready?" John said. "One...two...*three!*"

This time, they pulled with an explosive tug, and the auger popped free. The horses spooked again, but John quickly calmed his mount. Tiz's buckskin mare—wall-eyed and splay-legged—scrambled backward and reared up, whinnying and clawing at the air with her front hooves. Tiz slid sideways off the horse's rump but freed his boots from the stirrups in time to land on his feet.

"*Damn!*" Tiz snapped. Still holding the reins, he swept off his hat and swatted the buckskin's muzzle, which only set up a pulling contest between man and horse. "You damned ol' outlaw!" Tiz laughed. "I oughta skin yore hide!"

John shook his head and turned to Nate. "How many posts you boys puttin' in?"

Nate kneeled and cleaned dirt from the auger blade. "A lot," he replied. "Prob'ly be plantin' poles come next spring. After that, we'll stretch wire. Till Christmas next year, I reckon."

John turned in his saddle to look back at the wagon full of staves. He removed his hat and wiped his eyes on his shirt sleeve in the crook of his arm.

"Looks like your brother took your draft animal. You need a ride back to your house?"

Nate smiled his thanks but shook his head. After dropping the post into its hole, he began pushing in handfuls of dirt and packing it down with the tamping rod.

"We're going right by there," John said.

"You boys go on ahead," Nate said. "I got two more posts to lay in after this'n."

Tiz mounted his horse and laughed. "Hell, son! It'll take you a hour to walk home."

Nate paced off the next distance with the auger in hand. "I can always run," he told them in his guileless voice. "Prob'ly make it in half that."

John nodded, taking Nate's reply as fact, but Tiz appeared confounded. "*Run*?! It's hot as hell, son! What are you? Part-Comanch'?"

John crossed his arms over his chest and raised an eyebrow at his brother. "I've seen Nate run. It's like watching a deer. He's practically the Pheidippides of central Texas."

Tiz blew a spurt of air that made his lips flutter. "Well, I don' know who your Mr. Fa-dippity-dee is, but Nate ain't built to run like no deer. There just ain't enough meat on his bones."

John smiled. "I'll bet you that Nate—on foot—can outrun you—on your horse—to that dead tree." He pointed fifty yards away to a barkless oak leaning at the edge of the pasture.

Tiz took measure of the distance. "Well, hell, that ain't much of a race!"

John shrugged one shoulder. "It's like any other race. It'll have a winner and a loser."

Tiz was shaking his head in mock pity. "Seems a shame to embarrass the boy like that." He patted the neck of his buckskin. "This old girl has got a lotta *go* in 'er!"

They turned to Nate for his final say on the matter, but he raised the auger, stabbed it into the ground, and began wrestling a new hole out of the pasture.

"Well, whataya say, Mr. Fa-dippity-dee?" Tiz goaded. "Think you can beat me?"

"Prob'ly could," Nate replied, "but I got two more posts to lay in before I lose daylight."

Tiz studied the distance again. "Well, how 'bout we put some value to this bet?"

As he worked the auger, Nate glanced at the skittish buckskin, noting the muscles in her haunches and the strong, tendon-streaked legs. She was a good cow pony. Nate had seen her at work. In the last Fourth of July celebrations, Tiz had beaten out Tom Gardner's quarter horse in an impromptu race.

"I ain't really got nothin' on me to bet with," Nate said with a shrug.

Tiz worked up his bargaining voice. "Aw-right then...I tell you what! You know the girl works at the Kirkpatrick Hotel, right?"

Nate looked toward town and narrowed his eyes. "You mean Sarah?"

Tiz smiled. "That's the one," he said, putting some melody into his words. "She seems to think purty highly o' you."

Nate shrugged. "I know 'er some. I helped 'er with some heavy crates one time."

"Okay," Tiz said, getting down to business, "maybe you could help *me* out with *her*."

"How do you mean?"

"Well, say we make this bet an' I win. I'm guessin' you could talk 'er into goin' with me to that dance in October at the Mason's Hall."

Nate narrowed his eyes. "She ain't gonna listen to me 'bout somethin' like that. You oughta be the one to do the askin'."

"Yeah, well, I tried that, and she don't seem to favor the idea. 'Course she don't really know me. Seems she's got some notion 'bout the people I hang out with bein' unsav'ry."

Mark Warren

Nate was shaking his head. "I don' know how *I* could do any better than you did."

"People *like* you, Nate," Tiz pressed. "They listen to you. You could try, couldn' you?"

Nate frowned out into the pasture. "I cain't promise nothin'. She's the one gotta decide."

Tiz nodded deeply. "I understand that."

"But what if *I* win this race?" Nate said, changing course. "What would *I* git?"

Tiz laughed. "Hell, I'll drill those last two holes for you myself, stab a coupla posts into the ground, and tamp 'em down tight as fat lady stuffed in a cedar chest. How 'bout that?"

Nate looked down at the grass for a time. "How 'bout a dollar?"

"'A *dollar*'?!" Tiz balked. He turned to his brother. "He wants me to bet a dollar!"

John Tisdale leaned forward with both hands on his pommel. "Sounds fair to me. Put your money where your mouth is, brother. Isn't that what you're always telling me?"

Tiz lifted off his hat and scratched the top of his head as he eyed the racecourse. He spat off to one side and put on a defiant face.

"Aw-right, damnit! Hell, I'll put up a dollar *and* two posts to boot! How's *that* sound?"

Nate nodded once. "But you gotta do a good job with the posts. And you gotta do it as soon's we've raced. I wanna get it done tonight."

Tiz flashed a toothy smile at his brother. "He's a cocky one, ain't he?"

When Nate laid the auger in the grass, sat, and began pulling off his boots, the skin on Tiz's forehead creased like a freshly plowed field. "You ain't gonna race in the buff, are you? That might distract my horse." Tiz brayed a laugh and smiled at John. "How 'bout you startin' us, brother?"

John shrugged. "Just remember I warned you." He tilted his head sideways toward Nate, who now stood barefooted in the grass. "Like a deer," John reminded. Then he dismounted.

John walked his sorrel to the wagon and tied her off to a rear wheel. After sliding his carbine from its saddle scabbard, he levered a round into the chamber.

"Whoa!" Tiz laughed. "You ain't gonna shoot the loser, are you?"

John smiled. "I'm going to give you a proper start. Any objections?"

Tiz laughed again. "Hell, no! Let's have some fireworks for the occasion!"

Chapter Three

J ohn tossed his pearl-gray hat into the grass. "You boys line up here on either side of this. I'll start you from behind." He stepped back a few paces and raised the muzzle of his rifle to the sky.

Nate took his place beside the hat and waited for Tiz to coax the buckskin to its starting position, but the horse was testy and kept up a nervous changing of direction as if unsure of which way to stand.

"Ready?" John called out.

"Well, wait a damn minute!" Tiz growled. "Lemme get this beast to stand still!"

Leaning forward slightly, Nate stood poised with both legs bent, one foot in front of the other. His arms extended downward like two lowered wings, his hands flattened out, the fingers splayed. With his eyes fixed on the dead oak, he nodded once to show he was ready.

When the buckskin finally sidled next to the hat, Tiz lowered his chest to within an inch of her dark mane. With both his hands gripping the reins, he leveled his forearms before him, his elbows pointing north and south.

"Aw-right!" Tiz called out. "Let 'er rip!"

When the rifle shot cracked and blossomed into the open sky, the buckskin whinnied and crow-hopped toward the forest. "*Hyawww!*" Tiz screamed. "*Run*, damn you!"

Nate flew over the grass like a bird flushed from its nest. His bent arms pumped in a steady, relaxed motion as his legs churned like the driving rod of a locomotive. He felt so light and fleet, his feet seemed barely to touch the ground.

By the time Tiz got his buckskin moving and had covered half of the agreed distance, Nate was coasting to a jog beyond the finish line. John Tisdale was laughing so hard, his voice had climbed an octave, and tears shone in his eyes.

As Nate tugged on his boots, Tiz returned with a scowl on his face. "I guess you know the damned gunshot spooked hell outta my horse! Let's try 'er again without burning powder!"

John was still chuckling as he walked his rifle back to his horse. "Nate was gone before that mooncalf mare of yours knew which way was up." He pushed his Winchester into its scabbard and turned. "Hey! Nate could have flinched, too! But he didn't! He just ran like... well, like a deer!" He smiled. "I believe I already mentioned that, didn't I?"

Walking back with his horse, John scooped up his hat from the grass and settled it on his head. Tiz leaned and gave his brother a dark glare.

"I guess you'll be talkin' this up all over the county, won't you, Mr. Chatterbox?"

John pretended to think about it as if the thought had never occurred to him. "If you pay up as promised, I might be persuaded to forget about it." He winked at Nate. "Give this man his dollar, set his last posts of the day, and let's get home."

Tiz gazed south across the pasture as if he were facing

a crucial decision in his life. "Aw, hell!" he grumbled and swung down from the saddle. After handing his reins to his brother, he dug into his saddlebags, marched over to Nate, and doled out four coins. "There you go, you damned barefoot antelope! One dollar!" He walked to the auger and set it upright. "How deep d'you want this damned hole?"

The three of them worked together and had both posts tamped in place while the sun was still half a hand above the horizon. After the tools were laid in the wagon, Nate picked up the bucket and started down the hill for the creek.

"Where the hell're you goin', Nate?" Tiz yelled. "Come on! We'll give you a ride home!"

"I'll be right back!" Nate called out.

Before a minute had passed, he was back up the hill, breathing hard from his quick ascent. He set the empty bucket in the wagon bed and pushed his hat down tighter on his head.

"You forget the water?" Tiz laughed.

Nate shook his head, took John's wrist, and swung up on the sorrel's rump behind the saddle. "Didn' want no water," Nate returned.

John twisted at the waist and tried to look Nate in the eye. "You took that beetle back to the creek, didn't you?"

Nate nodded and snugged himself up to the cantle. "Seemed like the right thing to do."

Tiz stared at Nate with bulging eyes. "You climbed down there and back for a *bug*?"

Nate shrugged. "If I was that little feller, that's what I'd'a wanted. So would you."

Tiz's mouth hung open as his eyes narrowed. "But it's a *bug*!" he said in a breathy voice.

John reached back and patted the side of Nate's left knee. "You're a good man, Nate."

Tiz let out a hissing laugh. "Yeah...good to bugs!"

With the blood-red sun painting their backs, they rode east through the pleasant cool of the early evening. Nate sat behind John, rocking with the shifting rhythm of the sorrel and listening to Tiz present an unsolicited discourse on fair play concerning informal horse races.

When, after a mile, Tiz ran out of complaints, they rode without talking and listened to the yip of a coyote somewhere off to the south. Soon enough, several more coyotes answered the call, and then, altogether, they howled in eerie, high-pitched phrases that seemed to intertwine into a common song of chaos.

"Isn't that one of your brothers up ahead?" said John.

Leading Nate's paint behind him, John Thomas rode toward them at an easy gallop on his bay mare. When he reached the trio, he circled behind them and came up next to John Tisdale's sorrel, where he handed the reins of the paint to Nate.

"Well, if it ain't Johnny-come-lately!" Tiz sang out. "How ya doin', J. T.?"

As was his habit, John Thomas ignored Tiz. "Supper's a-waitin', Nate." Then he plucked at the brim of his hat to greet John Tisdale.

Nate made the transfer, slipping easily onto the bare back of the paint he had named "Peaches." "You find that rattler?"

John Thomas nodded. "Kilt and skinned and scraped. Twelve buttons."

"How big?" Nate probed.

John Thomas chuckled. "Well, I'll describe it the way Dudley did: 'Fat as a stovepipe and twelve feet long.' I let Dud kill it. Took 'im four shells o' the ten-gauge to put it to rest."

"You know," Tiz butted in, "they say a day-kilt rattler don't really die till nightfall."

John Thomas looked straight ahead to comment. "That makes no sense at all."

Tiz laughed. "I heard of a man in Laredo thought he kilt a rattler an' skinned it too early. When the man weren't lookin', the damned snake crawled back into its skin an' got clean away."

John Thomas just shook his head. It was clear he had no intention of continuing the conversation. And it was just as clear that Tiz was not going to let it go.

"I heard a similar story 'bout a steer over to Del Rio. Man kilt an' skint it an' hung it in his ice house to butcher the next day. Damn steer lit out to Mexico, come back one night, and gored the man who'd skint it. He bled out...by all accounts, it was a painful death."

The muffled clopping of the horses' hooves in the soft dirt and the creak of leather were the only sounds for half a minute. Then John Thomas cleared his throat and broke the silence.

"I guess the man got un-gored and came back to life, too?"

Tiz took his time answering. "No...didn' work out so good for him. His wife butchered him for meat and married the steer. She said the steer didn' have no balls either, but it was the most satisfied she'd been in twenty years."

John Thomas put a sour look on his face and turned to Tiz. "That s'posed to be funny?"

Tiz spat off into the weeds and changed his tone to a surly growl. "Only if you know how to laugh."

The four horsemen rode on without speaking. Now, the silence was not as comfortable with the friction between Tiz and John Thomas let out of its box.

When the horse path joined the Old Shawnee Trail, Tiz tapped his brother's shoulder. "So, who's this '*Mr. Fa-dippity-dee-do*' feller you was talkin' 'bout?"

"Pheidippides," John said, enunciating the word. As he held the group in the thrall of his storytelling skills, he related the military maneuvers used at the Battle of Marathon and the historic run that announced the Greek victory. When it was done, they were quiet for a while as they digested the story. Once again it was Tiz who finally broke the silence.

"Well, damn!" he said in whispery awe. "That boy could run, couldn' he?"

"'*Like a deer*,'" John replied and turned to wink at Nate.

Tiz chuckled. "I do believe there's an antelope somewhere in the Champion family tree."

John Thomas snapped a quick reply. "What's that s'posed to mean?"

Tiz laughed. "Don't git your feathers up, boy. I'm payin' you a compliment."

"How's that?" John Thomas asked, his voice still hard.

John Tisdale spoke up before his brother could reply. "We had a little footrace. Man against horse. Your little brother on his own two feet outran Tiz on his buckskin."

"Not much of a race!" Tiz was quick to add. "'Bout as far as you could throw a mule."

John Thomas smiled. "Nate take his boots off?"

John Tisdale chuckled. "Sure did. He ran unshod and almost set fire to the grass. Cost a dollar to be a witness to it."

John Thomas laughed. "You bet against Nate?"

John shook his head. "Not me. Martin."

"He pay up?"

"'Course I paid up!" Tiz broke in.

No more was said on the subject, but Nate was glad to see that his brother's mood had lightened. The dark settled over the land, and the stars spread across the sky like a sack of white jewels emptied over a black blanket.

When the riders saw the lighted windows of the Champion house, Tiz spoke up in a voice that carried the soft timbre of a plea.

"Say, Nate...would you consider doin' me that little favor 'bout the dance anyway?"

"Now, wait!" John Tisdale interrupted. "That's not how it works! You lost the bet!"

"Aww," Tiz groaned. "Don't hurt to ask, does it?"

John shook his head. "It's not the honorable thing to do, brother."

Tiz laughed it off and tried for a lighter tone. "You goin' to that October dance, J.T.?"

"Yep," John Thomas replied.

Tiz looked a little surprised. "You aw-ready corner a girl into goin'?"

"Yep."

They reached the gate to the main yard and stopped as if by a common signal. "Well, do we git to know who it is?" Tiz pressed.

At first, it seemed that John Thomas would not supply an answer. But when his bay nickered and began to shuffle its hooves in the dirt, John Thomas sniffed and spoke in a brusque tone as though he were in a hurry to part ways with the Tisdales.

"Girl that works down at the hotel," John Thomas said.

Frowning, Tiz turned in his saddle, the leather creaking like a lament. "Sarah?"

Now, John Thomas turned to face Tiz. "Yeah? What about it?"

When Tiz did not answer, his brother began to laugh quietly. "We'll see you boys later," John said and pointed at Nate. "Spend that dollar on something special, Nate."

The Tisdale brothers peeled away and continued

down the trail side by side. Their two horses seemed as companionable as the oldest of friends.

"G'night, John," Nate called. Then, a little louder, he yelled, "G'night, Tiz!"

The two Champion brothers took their horses at a trot into the yard. The old hound, Checkers, came out to meet them, his tail wagging, and his body squirming like a worm. The lighted windows of the house welcomed them like prodigal sons, always sure to return for the next meal.

Chapter Four

On the day following, a Sunday, after the twelve members of the Champion family had returned from church and partaken of their noon meal, John Thomas and Nate saddled up at the stable for their ride out to the work site. Like the day before, the hot sun was unforgiving. There was no wind, and the yard was quiet but for the muted clucking of the chickens as they pecked in the weeds for bugs and scorpions. The windmill stood tall and idle, its latticed frame casting a compressed shadow at its base, as if the boards and timbers had shed a blackened skin that had fallen into a flat pile beneath it.

As the two brothers led their horses to the well house to fill their canteens, Checkers trotted out toward them from under the porch. Halfway across the yard, the dog stopped and stared intently out the front gate.

From far up the north road came the sound of a horse at full gallop. "Who the hell is that a-burnin' up the road on a Sunday?" John Thomas mumbled.

In the distance, a rider on a big dapple gray approached, tearing up the road as if it were on the home stretch of the Fourth of July races. A lean rider hunched over the gray's withers, the brim of his hat flattened against the crown as if he were facing into a stiff wind.

"That stud belongs to Billy Hill's daddy," Nate said. "Looks like Billy in the saddle."

The screened door at the front of the house slapped shut, and Nate turned to see his father come out onto the porch in his white shirt and Sunday trousers. Stopping at the edge of the planks, Jack Champion stood like a preacher about to deliver a sermon. His rounded gray-and-white beard and mustaches all but swallowed the lower half of his face. His scalp hair was combed flat and shone with oil like it did every Sunday. With one hand on an awning post, the old man watched horse and rider approach as if he had expected company.

Checkers barked as Billy Hill charged into the yard past Nate and his brother and reined up a few yards from the house. A pink-gray cloud of dust trailed him through the gate and hung in the air without a breeze to disperse it. Tiny blinks of sunlight sparkled in the cloud as it slowly came apart and tried to settle back to earth. The dog made a ruckus as Billy stroked his mount's neck. The dapple gray snorted and stomped in the dirt until John Thomas yelled at the dog to leave off on pestering the visitor.

The three other Champion brothers—James, Dudley, and Ben—came outside onto the porch with Naomi Jane squeezing through their legs to get in front. When she stood beside her father, she wrapped one arm around his leg and watched wide-eyed as the visitor reached back and slipped the knot on a saddlebag. Nate could not make out the words, but he recognized the excited tone in Billy's voice. It was the same way the boy sometimes tried to impress his friends when he was privy to some news that others were not.

Billy leaned and handed a paper to the elder Champion. After a brief exchange of words, Billy reined his horse around and started back across the yard at a trot, heading for the well house. Checkers followed at a cautious distance.

"Hey, Nate!" Billy called out as he reined up. "I brung a letter out for your daddy."

Billy sat his horse straighter than usual, his shoulders back and a triumphant smile pasted on his face. He glanced at John Thomas only long enough to give him a nod, and then his eyes filled with the twinkle of a grand secret as he fixed his attention on Nate.

"I figured it was important. Your daddy's deputy in town sent me out with it."

"He ain't my daddy's deputy," Nate said through the well house's open door. He began feeding out the rope to lower the bucket into the dark shaft. "Daddy ain't sheriff no more."

"Well," Billy whined defensively. "*Used* to be his deputy."

John Thomas's brow rippled as if three strands of wire had pressed into his forehead. "Well, who's it from?" he asked.

Billy shrugged. "I don' know. It's from some hotel in Kansas. Deputy just tol' me to git it out here, so I rode like the wind."

John Thomas nodded at the unmoving windmill blades. "There ain't no wind," he said.

Billy shot him a look. "Aw, you know what I mean."

John Thomas snorted. "Post office ain't even open on Sundays."

Billy leaned in and lowered his voice. "Well, it arrived yesterday, and the mail carrier left it at the sheriff's office. The deputy didn't find it till this mornin'." Billy smiled. "He give me a five-cent piece to deliver it." Then Billy's face turned somber. "Hey, Nate, how come your daddy talks different from the rest o' y'all?"

"Daddy's from South Car'lina," Nate said. "*We* was all born in Texas."

Billy pushed out his lower lip and nodded as if he'd heard the moral to a good story. Then, his eyes filled with light as he watched Nate feed out the rope.

"Hey, Nate, I hear you might wanna take me up on my bet. Let's you and me go out to the round rock. I'll bring my granddaddy's old pocket watch."

When the bucket hit water, Nate jerked on the rope a few times until he felt the rim of the bucket take a bite under the surface. Raising it by one pull, he gauged the bucket to be more than half full and began pulling the rope hand over hand, making the pulley squeal like a hungry shoat.

"Who tol' ya that?" Nate asked.

"I run into John Tisdale's brother," Billy reported. "He tol' me."

Nate shook his head, both at Billy's offer and at Tiz's loose tongue. "I got to work now," he explained. "We're layin' in some new fence."

Billy's eyes narrowed. "On a Sunday?"

John Thomas scoffed at the boy. "It ain't Sunday no more, son," he said flatly. "After church and dinner, the rest o' the day is considered real early Monday on this ranch."

Billy raised his eyebrows. "Ain't that contrary to the Good Book?"

Nate had filled his canteen and now started pouring for his brother. "Daddy says it ain't," Nate explained. "And since he was the sheriff—" He glanced at Billy and raised his eyebrows as if that were answer enough. When the canteens were full and capped, Nate looked Billy in the eye. "You really stay under for a minute and a half?"

Billy frowned and looked away. "Ask Lindy Hildebrand if I didn'!"

"You use a watch?"

Billy's frown deepened, and he fiddled with his reins. "I didn' have one that day, so she counted for me. It's hard to count when you're holdin' your own breath, you know."

John Thomas huffed. "Well, who the hell else's breath are you gonna be holdin'?"

Billy seemed unable to conjure up a proper reply to that. When he looked back at Nate, his face turned hopeful.

"We could go down to the creek tomorr' after school. I'll time you...fair and square."

"Got to work after school," Nate said.

Billy nodded. "Well, guess I'll see you tomorr' then."

As Billy lifted his reins, Nate stopped him with a hand on Billy's knee. "How much are you puttin' on that bet, anyway?"

Billy pushed out his lower lip and squinted. "Well, when Lee Moore tried it, he put up four bits. But I think it oughta be more." He hitched his head to one side. "I mean, considerin' how hard it is." He nodded at his own sense of reasoning. "And *I* oughta know!"

John Thomas tied his canteen to his saddle. After mounting his bay, he did his best to look like a big brother who had run out of patience.

"We gonna be leavin' anytime soon, Nate?"

Nate nodded toward the porch where the family listened to Naomi Jane read from an unfolded piece of paper. "Don't you wanna know what the letter says?"

John Thomas leaned forward on his pommel. Tilting his head down, he appeared to study his hands, one stacked upon the other.

"What I want is to git five posts laid in b'fore dark."

Billy lingered as if he, too, was curious about the letter.

Nate carried his filled canteen to his mare and strapped it to his saddle. When he noticed a dark knot of hair in Peaches's tail, he examined the lump and found a cocklebur tangled in the hair.

From behind his right hip, Nate pulled out the new sheath knife he had carried for only a few months. Its polished blade was like a mirror interrupted by a pattern of concentric swirls that hinted of violet and blue. The antler grips felt as smooth as river stone.

"That what you won at the Fourth of July horse race?" Billy asked.

Nate nodded. "Yep. Second place." Sorting through the tail hairs, he singled out the strands that were tied up with the bristly seed. With one smooth stroke, he sliced through the hairs above the knot and tossed the tangled strand out into the yard.

"That damn blade looks sharp," Billy said.

Nate nodded again. "It is. I work on it 'bout ever' night." He held up the knife on display. "Damascus steel and elk horn handles. They say the elk is from up Wyomin' way."

"Bet that would'a cost you a bundle." Billy laughed. "Can I hold it?"

Nate reversed his grip and gave it over, handle first. "I looked it up in the catalog at the hardware store," Nate admitted. "Cost more'n four dollars brand new. Plus, the mail order."

Billy turned the knife and made a little whistling sound through his teeth. "Hey, maybe you could put this up for the bet." Billy tested the blade by scraping his thumb across its edge. "Damn, Nate. That's 'bout as sharp as the barber's razor."

Nate nodded. "It'll shave the hairs off the back o' your arm in one clean stroke."

Billy returned the knife and leaned to watch Nate slip

the blade into its sheath. "How the hell do you keep it on?"

Nate twisted at the hips. "Got Naomi to sew this lil' piece o' cord to my trousers."

Billy pursed his lips and nodded. "So, whataya say? Wanna put it up for the bet?"

Nate pulled out the knife again. Studying it in his open hand, he made a pained look. It was a handsome tool with a good weight, and he'd miss it if he lost it to Billy. Returning the knife to the sheath, he shook his head.

"I don' know...I've gotten right attached to it."

Billy squirmed in his saddle. "Tell you what. I might can allow four dollars for it."

Nate frowned. "You mean to buy it?"

Billy laughed. "Nah, I mean that's what it'd be worth for the bet."

With the stakes raised that quickly, Nate studied Billy's face, trying to read it for sincerity or exaggeration. "So, you're sayin'...if I win...you pay me four dollars?"

Billy laughed. "That's the way it works, Nate." Arching one eyebrow, he smiled. "But you got to agree to the other possibility, too. If you cain't make it past a minute and a half—" Billy pointed to the knife at Nate's hip. "...Then that there becomes *mine*."

Nate checked the cinch of his saddle. "I'll think on it."

From the porch, the soft drawling voice of Jack Champion spilled out into the yard. "John Thomas! Come he'ah, son!"

John Thomas turned in his saddle. "I'm just waitin' on Nathan, sir!" he called out.

With a come-hither gesture with one hand, the father beckoned his son again. John Thomas kicked his heels into his bay and trotted off for the porch.

Nate gripped his pommel and cantle, jumped up, and nimbly poked the toe of his boot into the stirrup, and

Peaches stood for it without shying. Nate swung his free leg over the horse's rump and toed into the other stirrup. The paint snorted, nodded her head, and began to shuffle her hooves in anticipation of leaving the yard.

"Uh-oh!" Billy chortled as he watched the conference on the porch. "Looks like yore brother's got hisself into some hot water."

Nate turned and saw the last of his younger siblings filing back into the house. John Thomas jerked at his reins and started his horse back toward the well house, his face set with anger or resentment or simply disappointment at his lot in life. When his horse nickered and tried to pick up its pace, he held it to a walk. Reining up beside Nate, he stared straight ahead at the front gate. All the while a muscle in his jaw flexed as steady as a heartbeat.

"He wants to see you now," John Thomas mumbled without looking at his brother.

"What about?" Nate asked.

John Thomas looked down at his hands as he sorted the reins. "You can hear it from him." Without another word, he kicked his bay into motion and headed toward the gate.

"John?" Nate called. "You ain't gonna wait on me?"

"No, I ain't," he replied over his shoulder. Then, he growled something at the bay and whipped the tails of his reins against the mare's haunches. The horse picked up its gait to a trot and passed through the front gate. Turning west on the road, John Thomas coaxed his horse into a relaxed gallop and never looked back.

"Uh-oh," Billy whispered. "Looks like it's yore turn for trouble. Reckon I'll git goin'." Billy winked. "Good luck," he said and made the barest of nods toward Nate's daddy. "If yo're still alive, I'll see you at the schoolhouse tomorr'."

Nate reined Peaches around and started her at a walk for the house.

Chapter Five

Standing alone on the porch, Nate's father spread his feet and folded his arms across his lean chest. It was the same stance he had used as a sheriff when questioning a man about a crime.

"Got a lett'ah from yo'ah aunt Hattie," his father began in his soft, unhurried drawl. He held out the envelope for Nate to see. It was addressed to "J. C. Champion and family."

"Are they on their way back from Abilene?" Nate asked.

Jack Champion shook his head. "She's with child. Due in less than a month. They plan to stay in Kansas until the baby can travel."

"Did they sell all their cattle?"

The father smiled with his eyes. "She says they'ah rich as thieves. Said to tell you she's sorry to miss yo'ah bi'thday."

Nate frowned. "I don' 'xpect people to plan their lives 'round my birthday."

His father chuckled. "Well, she says she's got you

somethin' and will save it fo' you. They should be back come late spring."

Nate began turning Peaches. "I better catch up with John Thomas."

His father held up his hand to stop him. "I need you to ride out to George and Hattie's place, son. The Bolen girl and her husband have been lookin' aft'ah it. Ask 'em if they can stay on till spring. If they cain't, we'll need to find someone who can get ov'ah to the house and tend to the chickens and the milk cow. Hattie's gonna want a garden laid in, too. I figure you and Dudley and Ben fo' that. An' maybe yo' little sister can go with you an' help."

"Yes'r," Nate said and hesitated. "You want me to go out to their place now?"

"I do," his daddy said. "Reckon that'll balance things out fo' yest'ahday."

Nate frowned. "How do you mean?"

Nate's father scanned the grassland that stretched to the east. Beneath his unruly beard, his jaw was set like a steel trap. Raising his arm, he pointed at the well house.

"Looks like yo' brother spent half o' yest'ahday coaxin' a snake out the well house."

"I didn' mind workin' alone," Nate said.

The man almost smiled. "No, you prob'ly didn'. But *I* mind." He turned an amused eye on Nate. "How many posts did you sink aft'ah he left you yest'ahday?"

Nate curled the tip of his tongue to his upper lip as he recalled the count. "Five." He decided not to mention that the Tisdale brothers had helped him with the last two.

"And how many fo' the two o' you that mo'ning?"

Nate looked down at his hands and considered whether or not his answer might make trouble for his brother. "I think it was six...maybe seven."

The father's eyes remained fixed on the horizon as he

grumbled deep in his chest. It was an all too familiar sound of discontent from Jack Champion.

"Go on out to George and Hattie's place and see what the Bolens say. Then stop by the Snyd'ah ranch and bring back that little black colt with the blaze on its fo'ah-head." He held up the letter like a piece of evidence. "Mist'ah Snyd'ah wants you to train it. Said he'll pay you the usual amount. An' you'll need to tell the Mexican boy out that way, he don't need to go feed the colt no mo'ah."

"Yes'r!" Nate replied. "Then I'll go out an' join John Thomas."

His father held up a forefinger. "Yo' aunt Hattie wrote somethin' else in the lett'ah. Said yo' Uncle George talked to that Hickok fellah you like to read about in the dime novels."

Nate swallowed. "He met Wild Bill?"

The ex-sheriff leaned a shoulder into the awning post. "He's the marshal in Abilene now." Jack Champion showed one of his rare smiles. "Yo'ah catchin' flies, son."

Nate closed his mouth and swallowed again. "Well, what'd he have to say?"

The old man shook his head. "Don't know."

Nate leaned and patted Peaches's neck. "Well, I reckon Uncle George'll tell me all 'bout it when he gits back."

A breeze picked up out of the north, and the windmill blades stirred for the first time in a week. Father and son watched a small dust devil whirl like a child's toy and make its way across the yard and veer toward the east meadow, where it lost its momentum and then disappeared altogether.

The father pushed off from the post and strode to the front door. "Be back in time for supp'ah tonight, son."

"I will, sir!" Nate replied.

———

After talking to the Bolen couple, Nate rode for the hills to the north and into the wide valley where Dudley Snyder's ranch lay in a lush pocket of buffalo grass surrounded by several springs. The sky was a hard metallic blue, and the blazing sun was oppressive. The air was so still that the chirr of crickets in the grass sounded as crisp as the inner workings of a roomful of clocks.

When he passed through the front gate of the Snyder ranch, Nate saw a cloud of yellow-ochre dust rising from the paddock behind the barn. Two lanky cowhands sat on the fence watching a third man work a frisky chestnut mare from the snubbing post. The mare tried to back away from the man, fighting against the pull of the rope tethered to the post.

The man at the snubbing post laughed. "This damn horse ain't got no more sense than a bucket o' bent nails!" he yelled to his companions. Taking a two-handed grip on the rope, he jerked with a violent tug, but the horse did not budge. "You damned mule-brained slacker! You wanna feel my bite?"

Nate took his horse at a walk past the idle windmill to the back of the barn, reined up, and watched the scene of conflict inside the paddock. Next to him, draped over the top rail of the fence, were a blanket, saddle, and bridle waiting for a moment that Nate knew would not come on this day.

The young man fighting with the mare wore faded denim trousers and a dark-blue shirt. The crown of his black hat was ringed with a showy band of silver conchos, and his black boots followed a similar theme with a column of bright silver buckles running up the sides. Strapped around his narrow waist was a black cartridge belt, its loops filled with ammunition that gleamed like the teeth of an alligator gar. His holstered gun showed white grips of bone or ivory. Everything about his manner of dress seemed calculated and excessive.

At the man's feet lay a braided whip that sprawled in lazy loops on the hoof-marked hardpan. When he bent and picked it up, the whip uncoiled itself like a dead snake come back to life. The horse kept tension on the rope, snorted, and clawed at the earth with a front hoof.

The young man swung the whip in a wide arc over his head and snapped it at the mare's flank. The sharp *crack* of the leather threw the horse into a panic, her eyes showing a lot of white. An old gray halter had been fitted over her head, but the rope was not attached to it. Instead, the noose wrapped around her neck and tightened behind her jaw bones as she pulled.

With her ears laid back, the mare reared up on her hind legs and pawed at the air like a boxer. The man raised the whip again and delivered a vicious *crack* to the animal's churning forelegs. When the next blow came, the tip of the whip snapped against the horse's ribs, and a squealing, high-pitched cry tore from her throat. Her front hooves came down hard on the dirt, and she threw her head up and down and reprised a deeper version of the same scream.

"You ain't gonna git nowhere that way!" Nate called out.

The man turned with insult written all over his face. His two companions pivoted on the top rail of the fence. Only then did Nate recognize Martin Tisdale perched next to a man half again his age. The older man's face was cratered with scars, looking as abrasive as a farrier's rasp. Both carried holstered revolvers, and their belt loops were heavy with ammunition.

Tiz wore a new, dark-red blouse that still showed the creases lines where it had been folded and stacked on the mercantile shelf. Uncharacteristically quiet, Tiz barely raised his chin as a greeting and then lowered his gaze as he began rolling a cigarette.

"Whatta you want, boy?" called out the young man at the snubbing post. Dragging the whip behind him in the dirt, he took three steps toward Nate, stopped, and waited for an answer.

Not wanting to yell, Nate coaxed Peaches closer to the paddock. "Mr. Snyder says I'm to take the black colt over to our place."

The one with the whip was not much older than Nate's brother James, but the emotions that flashed across his face made him appear as quick-tempered as Naomi Jane. When he turned and spat a dollop of brown tobacco into the dust, Nate recognized the small features of his profile: a short, upturned nose and a sharp chin that jutted forward. His dark blond hair was streaked with summer gold, and it hung to his shoulders, silky and loose as a girl's. A tawny arch of fuzz struggled to be called a mustache above his upper lip.

Dixie Brooks had been in school with William, and Nate recalled that the boy had dropped out at the suggestion of the school superintendent. Nate also remembered Dixie getting into a fight at the Fourth of July festivities a few years past, when Nate's father had been sheriff.

Dixie wiped his mouth with his shirt sleeve, and as he did, the whites of his eyes seemed to glow in the shadow of his hat brim. Lowering his arm, he glared at Nate.

"How do I know he told you to take the colt?"

Nate leaned forward on his pommel, his manner relaxed. "Got a letter with Mr. Snyder's instructions."

Dixie stared at Nate and pushed the bulge of tobacco from one cheek to the other. He spat again and raised his chiseled chin to point at Nate.

"Lemme see the letter."

Nate shook his head. "Ain't got it with me. It's at home."

Dixie laughed. "So, what're you? 'Bout ten years old and a famous bronc buster?"

Nate straightened in his saddle. "I never said that. An' I'm fourteen...just about."

"Hoo-whee!" Dixie howled. "All of fourteen, are you? No wonder yo're famous!"

Nate leveled his voice to a monotone. "Pedro Ramirez is in charge of this ranch. You got his permission to be here?"

Dixie whirled the whip above his head and snapped it in the air before him, the sharp *crack* like the report of a small caliber pistol. "Once I break this bone-headed mare, Snyder will be thankin' me. Might even pay me for it."

The older man slid down from the fence and eased his boots to the ground. Still seated on the top rail, Tiz remained as still as a propped-up corpse as he stared down at his unlit cigarette.

"Let's head out," the older man called to Dixie. "I wanna git to the caverns b'fore dark."

Dixie gave the man a sharp look. "Hang on to yore bloomers! I wanna git a saddle on this crazy nag." He turned and lashed the whip into the ground, sending up a wispy cloud of dust.

"You ain't gonna git nowhere with that whip," Nate said.

Dixie turned slowly, his mouth tightened into a false smile. "That so?" He coiled the whip and held it out before him. "Here, let's see what *you* can do."

When Nate made no move to take the offered whip, Dixie dropped it in the dirt and, laughing, walked to his friends. Nate swung down from the saddle and tied his horse to the black cherry tree, which provided the only shade in the main yard. Hooking his hat on the pommel of his saddle, he studied the three saddled horses tied to the same iron ring at the back wall of the barn. A bay gelding, a gray stallion, and Tiz's buckskin. Each rig included a rifle scabbard and bedroll.

Nate took a lead rope and a red bandanna from his saddlebag and then sidestepped through the fence into the paddock. Shouldering the coil of rope, he glanced at the three men standing by the fence. Dixie and the older man watched to see what he would do with the horse, but Tiz still had not acknowledged him.

"I see you left yore hat," Dixie taunted. "What's the matter, chief? 'Fraid you'll lose it when she tries to kick yore brains out?"

Nate nodded toward the mare. "I'm tryin' to show 'er I ain't you." As he walked closer to the frightened horse, he lowered his voice to a gentle tone. "'Preciate it if you'd stay there by the fence. I'd like to keep this simple for the horse."

Dixie hissed a laugh through his teeth. "Why sure, chief, we'll just stand right here an' watch you break yore fool neck."

Nate bent and picked up the whip, using the bandanna to keep its scent from his hand. Then he turned for the barn, letting the braided leather trail behind him in the dirt. Stopping short of the fence, he tossed the whip over the rails where it landed in the soft dirt of the barn's entrance. Then he hung the bandanna on the rail and retraced his steps to the mare.

"This oughta be good!" Dixie sniggered.

Tiz remained silent, but the scarred saddler spat into the dirt and spoke out of the side of his mouth. "Whyn't you try shuttin' up for a while," he growled.

Tiz struck a match, lighted his cigarette, and spoke into the bowl of his hands as he cupped them around the flame. "Keep yore eyes open, Dixie. You might learn somethin'."

Dixie jerked his head around as if to challenge the remark, but Tiz ignored him, tossed the spent match into the dirt, and took a draw on his cigarette. Then the three men settled in to watch Nate's every move.

Chapter Six

The mare eyed Nate and backed away splay-legged, her neck stretched forward as the rope pulled taut with little ticking sounds. From her constricted throat came a wet, wrenching growl like a man straining to lift a weight too heavy for him.

"It's aw-right, girl," Nate began in a low, soothing voice. He lifted his arms away from his sides to show that his hands were empty. "Ain't nobody gonna beat on you no more."

Taking a light grip on the stretched rope, Nate approached the mare slowly, his hand sliding along the rough hemp, his legs moving with the patient precision of a man feeling his way through a dark room. The chestnut whinnied and shuffled her hooves, kicking up a cloud of dust. The whites of her eyes shone like bright quarter moons above her amber irises.

"We're just gonna git to know each other a little bit," Nate whispered, his words less important than the gentle tone of his voice. "You an' me are gonna git along just fine. You can ask ol' Peaches over there. I prob'ly like horses better'n I like most people."

"Hey, boy!" Dixie called out. "You reckon that nag understands Amer'can? She might'a come outta ol' Mexico."

Nate paid the ribbing no mind. When he moved closer to the mare, she flattened her ears.

"I can see yo're gonna make a fine cow pony," Nate whispered. The mare's ears shot up and remained erect. She nickered. "I'm just gonna help you git there. You work with me a little bit, an' I'll work with you. How's that sound?" He let go of the rope and let his arms hang naturally.

Now, the mare seemed more interested than alarmed. Nate knew that the horse was curious about him, and curiosity was a big step up from fear.

"Hey, kid!" Dixie yelled. "Whyn't you juss ask 'er to marry you? One o' us boys here could ride into town for the preacher an' be back in no time." He broke into a braying laugh.

Nate waited for him to quiet and then slowly turned his head to let his voice carry to the men at the fence. "If you'll just be quiet," he said in the same tone he had been using with the mare, "we might git somethin' done here. It ain't helpin' if this horse has to listen to both o' us."

"Aw-right, boys, let's simmer down!" Dixie ordered in a mock command. "We got us a *gen-u-ine* horse trainer at work here!"

Staring at the cigarette in his hand, Tiz shook his head. The older man spat again.

Nate slowly extended his free arm, his hand hovering before the mare's nostrils. She sniffed and nickered and shifted her weight, but still, she kept the tension on the rope. Nate lowered his arm. For a long time, nothing happened. Then he leaned forward to breathe into the mare's muzzle. She stood for it and drew in the scent, her nostrils pulsating like a heartbeat. When Nate took one step backward, the mare followed, and the rope loosened to a shallow arc.

"You can smell a friend from a enemy, cain't you, girl?"

The mare nickered again, this time a calmer sound, without the rough stutter of urgency. Her eyes had lost the shine of panic, the lids lowering to cover most of the white.

Using the backs of his fingers, Nate made downward strokes along the soft, velvet section of the muzzle between the nostrils and the mouth. The mare threw her head up and down. Then she calmed and allowed Nate to stroke her again. With his other hand, he began scratching the bristly hair around the base of the mare's ears. Finally, he moved in close enough to press a hand flat against her neck. Three times, he stroked the long, rounded muscle beneath the mane. On the fourth, the mare took a half step forward and snugged her muzzle against his chest. Then she raised her head and blew a stream of air that poured across his ear like warm bathwater.

Dixie laughed. "I b'lieve that nag has gone an' mistook you for a het-up stud, son."

"Here," Nate whispered to the mare, "let's git that choker off you." With gentle tugs on the halter, he coaxed her closer and let the coil of lead rope slide from his shoulder to his hand. When there was enough slack in the lariat, he slipped the noose from the horse's head and let it drop to the ground. Then he threaded one end of the lead rope through the halter ring and tied it.

"Don't reckon I'd wanna rope 'round my neck neither," Nate said, keeping up a running monologue just to let the animal hear his voice. The mare blew, the flapping of her nostrils like the snapping of a flag in the wind. When she raised her head and blew again, Nate felt her warm breath wash over his face.

"Let's you an' me walk over by the barn an' git away from these three jaybirds."

Guiding her by the lead rope, Nate walked the chestnut to the far end of the paddock. There, he began walking her along the perimeter of the fence, short-cutting the side where the three spectators clustered together. Soon, Nate and the horse were trotting side by side. Once, she broke loose from him and doubled back, but when he approached her, she stood still and let him pick up the lead rope to guide her back to the fence. There, they resumed the repetitive laps.

When Nate played out the rope to its full length, the mare began to canter in a circle around him as he controlled her from fifteen feet away. Sidestepping his own smaller circle around the snubbing post, he kept up words of praise for her smooth gait. After a dozen circuits like this, he got behind her and began putting tension on the rope.

"Whoa, girl! Whoa!" He leaned back on the rope. "Whoa, now!"

When she stopped, he walked toward her, gathering the rope into loops as he did. After untying from the halter, he returned the rope to his shoulder and stepped empty-handed before the mare. Leaning, he breathed into her nostrils and watched her take in his scent as if she were sucking up water from a stream. Then he turned his back to her and walked away five paces.

At first, nothing happened. Nate and the horse stood still for so long that Dixie snorted and began mumbling to his friends in a sneering tone.

"Hey, chief!" Dixie called out, his voice full of mockery. "Ain't you gonna—"

Cutting off Dixie's question, the chestnut filled the paddock with a high-pitched whinny and swung her head up and down in a deep nod. Nate continued to look straight ahead at the barn. The mare walked forward, clopping one hoof at a time, until she stopped so close to Nate that he could feel her breath on the back of his neck.

He repeated the exercise, this time walking all the way to the fence. As soon as he stopped, he heard the mare snort and follow again, her pace now steady and relaxed. When the sound of her hooves quieted behind him, Nate felt her muzzle brush the back of his shirt. She nickered, and the sound of it was as sweet as the warble of a meadowlark.

Nate turned and gently placed his hands on the flat, platelike cheeks of the curious animal. "Come on now, girl," he whispered. "Let's you an' me go for a little walk. Nice and slow around the paddock, whatta ya say?"

When he turned and started away, the untethered mare whinnied, shook her head, and then slowly trailed him around the inside of the fencing, dipping her head with each step of a forefoot. When Nate broke into a jog, she transitioned into a crisp trot. On the third time around, as they approached the three men, Dixie stepped out behind Nate and held up both arms at the horse, bringing her to a sudden halt. She snorted and backed up, her hooves stamping at the hardpan.

"Aw-right, you've had yore time!" Dixie growled. "Now I wanna git a saddle on 'er and ride some o' that sass out o' 'er."

The mare continued to back away, and Nate watched her go wild-eyed again. "Yo're a damned fool," Nate said, the words spilling out of their own accord. "She ain't ready for a saddle. Don't you know nothin' 'bout horses?"

Dixie spat off to one side and then glowered at Nate. "A horse has gotta be ready for a saddle when a man needs it to be! You don't ask 'em! You tell 'em!"

For the sake of the nervous mare, Nate stepped forward and lowered his voice. "Looks like all your *tellin'* weren't workin' out so good. You got to' give 'er more time."

Dixie put on a crooked smile and turned to his friends. "Y'all hearin' all this shit?"

The older man gave Dixie a hard look. "Yeah, an' it's all comin' from yore mouth."

For just a moment, Dixie's face went slack with hurt. Then he looked off toward the hills to scowl at the world. He reminded Nate of a headstrong child who refused to take his medicine.

"Did Mr. Snyder ask you to work with this horse?" Nate asked.

Dixie spat and wiped his mouth with his shirt sleeve. "Didn' say *not to!*"

Tiz flipped his cigarette into the dirt and dropped down from the fence. "For Christ's sake, Dixie! What the hell're we doin' here?"

Nate started past Dixie toward the mare. "I'll take 'er with me along with the colt."

"The hell you will!" Dixie snapped.

Nate stopped and turned to see Dixie's face full of challenge. "You ain't gonna be beatin' on this horse no more. I'm speaking for Mr. Snyder. That's the end o' it!"

Nate and Dixie locked eyes for a long five heartbeats, until the scar-faced saddler spoke up. "I'm tired o' yore act, Brooks. I'm leavin'."

Dixie made a quick pivot to face him, but the man had already started for his horse. Putting on a pout, Dixie gazed out at the valley again, adjusted his hat up and down on his forehead, and then forced an unconvincing laugh.

"Go on an' take the damn things then!" he snapped at Nate. "I don't give a rat's ass. Less trouble for me."

Nate walked to within six paces of the chestnut and spoke to her quietly. When she relaxed and nickered, he eased up to her, stroked her neck, and attached the lead rope again. Walking her to the gate, he opened the latch and guided her to where Peaches stood. There he tied the mare to the slit in his saddle skirt. Then he walked to the barn.

He found the white-blazed colt in the last stall and introduced himself with a palmful of grain from the feed barrel. Rummaging through an array of tack, Nate searched for a halter small enough to fit the young horse's head. Finding none, he fashioned a hackamore from a length of soft hemp rope, attached a lead, and brought the colt into the main bay of the barn. There, he brushed specks of dried dung off the shiny coat and listened to harsh words bandied back and forth among the men outside.

When Nate walked the gangly colt out of the barn, all three men were gathered at their horses. Only Dixie was mounted. Wearing a devilish smirk, he laughed at Tiz.

"Aw, come on, boys," Dixie chortled. "Don't you know how to have some fun?" He began pulling on his gloves and whistling a tune as if he hadn't a care in the world.

When Nate reached Peaches and the chestnut mare, he tethered the colt beside them. That was when he saw that his saddlebags were missing. The leather laces behind the cantle were cut cleanly in four places. Nate felt the skin on his face warm like a flash of fever. Keeping his anger in check, he walked back to the trio of men and said nothing as he examined Dixie's rig and the fence rails around them. His saddlebags were nowhere to be seen.

The older man jerked on the pommel of his saddle, grunted, and hoisted himself atop the bay. Then Tiz mounted and stared down at his horse as if he were counting the hairs on the buckskin's mane. Nate waited for Tiz to meet his eyes, but his friend would not look at him.

"Who took my saddlebags?" Nate said, his voice flat and hard.

The three men sat their horses as if they had not heard him. Dixie tightened the fit of his gloves by forking the fingers of one hand against the other. Then he turned to Nate.

"Ain't nobody here got yore saddlebags, son. You oughta think twice b'fore accusin' a man o' stealin' from ya." He slapped a gloved hand to his holster and held it there. "That's how some people git theirselves shot."

Unblinking, Nate stared at Dixie's taunting eyes. The only sound in the yard was the occasional shuffle of the horses' hooves in the sunbaked dirt.

"Where're my bags?" Nate said.

"Hell, son," Dixie crowed and swept a hand toward the grasslands that stretched toward town. "You prob'ly lost 'em on the ride out here."

Nate clenched his teeth. "The laces are fresh cut."

Then, he remembered the word that William had used to describe Dixie from their school days. *That trickster is gonna git the wrong end o' the stick one day,* William had said one night as they talked on the front porch. That was the day that Dixie Brooks had loosened the wheel nut on the schoolteacher's carriage.

Scouring the yard with his eyes, Nate searched for a place where someone could have hidden his bags. The land was open all around the barn and paddock, and then his eyes locked on the cherry tree where the horses waited. It took only a quick glance to spot the dark leather bags hanging up in the branches among the green boughs. They had been slung high into the canopy, where they had snagged on a limb thirty feet from the ground. When

Nate turned back to the men, he caught Dixie glancing up at the tree.

Reaching behind his hip, Nate slipped his knife from its sheath, and before Dixie could react, he sliced through the leather thongs that lashed the saddlebags to the top skirt.

Dixie spat his entire wad of tobacco into the dirt and swiped his sleeve across his mouth. "Hey, goddamnit! What the hell're you doin'?!"

Marching to the tree with Dixie's bags swinging in one hand, Nate stopped beside Peaches's hindquarters and laid the bags over the rump of the paint. "We'll just call it an even trade," Nate announced. Pulling out a section of the cut lacing, he secured the bag with a single knot. After untying Peaches's reins, he mounted and reined the paint around to face the three men. Dixie's face was dark as a thundercloud. His hand gripped his holstered pistol, but the older man's hand covered Dixie's like a hawk's talons wrapped around a mouse.

"What'd you say your name was, boy?" the scarred man called out.

Nate glanced at Tiz before answering, but Tiz looked away as if someone had called his name from out in the grasslands.

"It's *Champion*," Nate replied.

The man's eyes were like ice. "Your father was the sheriff here a few years back?"

Nate nodded. "He was."

Pushing his brow low over his eyes, the man turned to Dixie, but the trickster was too busy glaring at Nate to acknowledge the message. Tiz continued to stare at the distant hills.

"If you wanna trade back," Nate called out to Dixie, "bring my bags out to our ranch."

When the older man whispered something to Tiz,

Dixie turned to him and snapped, "I got money in them bags, goddammit!"

Nate reached back to his left, raised the flap one-handedly, and blindly rifled through the bag. Finding two heavy boxes, he shook one and heard the distinctive rattle of live cartridges. Searching the other bag, he pulled out a folded flannel shirt with a checkered pattern of black and blue. Inside its folds, he found a cracked leather wallet stuffed with a few bills.

With a *chick, chick* from the side of his mouth, Nate coaxed the paint forward, and the two horses tethered to him followed. Leaning, he propped the bundle of shirt and wallet on a fencepost. Then he straightened to meet Dixie's hostile eyes.

"I got some personals in my bags, too," Nate informed him. "When you come out to the ranch, I'll expect to receive 'em. Till then, I'll hang on to your ammunition." He pointed up into the branches of the cherry tree. "'Course, if you wanna trade now, I'll just wait while you climb up an' fetch what's mine."

Dixie's face soured. "You go to hell!" he said, pushing out the words like the snarl of a dog. His hand on the butt of his gun showed bone-white beneath the older man's grip.

"Go on home while you can, boy," said the older man. "We'll just call it an even trade."

Dixie's head jerked around to face the man again. "I just bought them bags!"

Using his other hand, the man gripped Dixie's arm and shook so hard that the fancy hat with the silver band fell to the ground. Dixie's yellow-streaked hair caught the sun and shone like threads of gold.

When Nate made no move to leave, the older man released Dixie and coaxed his bay forward and reined up a few feet away from Nate.

"Son," he said, "yo're gittin' too close to the rattlesnake, if you know what I mean."

"Who *are* you?" Nate asked. "Why are you here at the Snyder ranch?"

The man's eyes showed a twinkle of amusement. "You got some sand in you, don't ya, son?" He leaned to one side, spat a dollop of tobacco into the dirt, and shook his head. "It don' matter who I am. What's important here is that you better head for home now." He jerked his head at the two behind him. "This jackass back here is anxious to show me what he can do with that fancy pistol o' his."

"Was Dixie the one took my bags?"

"'Course he was. An' that's one o' the reasons I'm ridin' outta here alone." He raised his eyebrows. "You'd best do the same right now."

When Nate did not answer, the scar-faced man closed his eyes slowly and then opened them. "Cain't you see I'm tryin' to help you here, boy?"

"I don' need no help."

The saddler took in a deep breath and let his head sag forward as he exhaled. When he looked at Nate again, he cracked a half smile, and a twist of light turned in his eyes.

"Look...I know you ain't afraid o' him, but you need to respect a gun in the hand of a man who's tryin' to be some-thin' he ain't. I don't wanna have to kill 'im an' answer questions 'bout that with yore daddy. You'd be doin' me a favor if you'd leave."

"You know my father?" Nate asked.

"Know *of* 'im. Don't wanna git to know 'im too well."

"He ain't sheriff no more," Nate pointed out.

The drifter huffed a laugh and shook his head. "Don't matter. Once a sheriff—" He shrugged a shoulder, letting the gesture finish his sentence.

Nate patted the saddlebag behind his cantle. "Reckon I got all I need. Only thing in my bags was a wore-out pair o' gloves and half-broke pliers." He nodded to the man and then looked past him to give Tiz the same farewell, but Tiz looked away and pretended to study the horizon. Nate reined around his paint and led the other two horses out the front gate.

"I'll be seein' you ag'in, chief!" Dixie called out. "You can count on that!"

Chapter Seven

Nate could think of half a dozen reasons to go straight home, but he needed only one reason to detour through town. Dismounting outside Cooke's livery barn, Nate led the horses into the alley where he tied them to hitching rings bolted to the side of the building. With the animals secure, he returned to the street and entered the barn through the double-door front entrance.

The cold, hard ring of a hammer banged four times from the back of the building. Then four more. Nate walked past the stalls where the horses of customers awaited their turn with the farrier. In the dimly lit back room, the rhythm of the hammer started up again. Stopping in the doorway, Nate waited for a lull in the pounding and watched the broad back of the squat blacksmith as he swung a one-handed sledge against his anvil. A bed of hot coals glowed next to him, sending up a wavering sheet of heat that distorted the tools hanging on the wall.

"Mr. Cooke?"

Cooke half turned, one hand clutching the heavy

hammer and the other squeezing the end of a pair of long-handled tongs. The smithy's pale, rounded face broke into a toothy grin.

"Nate Champion!" He nodded to the coals. "Give the bellows a few pumps, would you?"

Nate walked around the anvil and put all his weight on the treadle six times. With each pump, the coals roared louder and glowed brighter.

"That enough?"

Nodding his approval, Cooke placed an L-shaped piece of metal on the enlivened coals. Then he balanced hot tongs on the anvil. The hammer followed with a heavy *clunk*!

"Workin' on a Sunday, are you?" Nate said.

Cooke gathered up the front of his apron and wiped his hands as he shook his head. "Well, it's for me, you see... a shelf bracket for my wife...so I guess, stric'ly speakin', it ain't really work. I cain't rightly charge 'er for it, can I?" He raised his chin and narrowed his eyes. "And what brings young Nate Champion into my shop on a Sunday afternoon?"

"You still got that rust-colored saddle for sale?"

Cooke crossed one meaty forearm over the hard swell of his belly and propped the other elbow upon it. Like an amateur actor, he angled his eyes to the corner of the ceiling and cupped a hand under his chin. Then he pulled at the sides of his face with his soiled thumb and fingers.

"Let's see now. A saddle for sale, you say?" He frowned until his face was etched with so many lines it looked like the cracked mud of a parched waterhole. "Got a Mexican saddle...a vintage McClellan cavalry model...a Somerset from a stranger who died here without any papers to show who he was...and I got a ol' Californee style with silver conchos on the skirt."

"Nos'r," Nate said, offering his part in the game. "You know I ain't int'rested in them."

Cooke stopped tugging on his chin and lowered his gaze to the ground. "Let's see now." Then he looked up. "Oh! You must mean that purty little drover's saddle I got out back!"

"Yes'r," Nate said, cracking the obligatory smile.

The smithy took on a pained expression. "Sorry to tell you, Nate, but a man come by this week to talk to me 'bout that saddle."

Nate's skin went cold, and his gut tightened as if he were expecting a punch to his belly. "He ain't put down no money, has he?"

Cooke closed his eyes as he shook his head. "Not a cent."

Nate stared at the bed of glowing coals and raked his upper teeth over his lower lip. "Well, how much would I need to put down so you can hold it for me?"

Cooke chuckled, and this time, his laughter was casual and unaffected. "Nate, I been holdin' it for you for three months."

Nate swallowed. "You have?"

Cooke made a tight smile that carved dimples into his fleshy cheeks and narrowed his eyes to friendly slits. "I don' reckon that saddle wants to belong to nobody else, do you?"

Embarrassed, Nate's cheeks flushed with heat. "Maybe I should pay you somethin' to hold it for me."

Cooke picked up the tongs and lifted the angle iron from the coals. The metal glowed orange and sparkled with tiny specks of brilliant red and incandescent white. When he set it on the anvil and struck it with his hammer, yellow and red sparks flew off in a shower. With each blow, fewer sparks appeared, and the color faded from the metal.

Holding the bracket high above the anvil, Mr. Cooke tilted his head to appraise his work. Satisfied, he lowered the heated metal into the barrel of water. A sharp hissing sound shot through the air and was suddenly sucked away by the water.

"That ol' Kilgore you strap to yore paint," Cooke said. "It b'long to you?"

"Yes'r. My brother, William, give it to me b'fore he left for California."

Cooke set down his tools and crossed both thick arms over his chest. "Tell you what...if you was to throw in that Kilgore, I could let you have that saddle for maybe thirty."

Nate perked up. "Mr. Cooke, I can just about do that right now!"

Cooke smiled at the boy's enthusiasm. "How much do you lack, Nate?"

"I only need 'bout five more dollars."

Cooke nodded. "Next time you come in, bring in what you have. We'll make the swap, an' you can make up the diff'rence later."

"Yes'r," Nate replied in a breathy voice. "Long as I'm here...if you don't care—"

The blacksmith laughed and waved Nate toward the storeroom. "Have at it, son!"

———

It was after three o'clock when Nate crossed the bridge out of town and rode into the shade of the cottonwoods along Brushy Creek. As he approached the round rock for which the town was named, he pulled back on the reins and tried to sort out the voices coming from the swimming hole up ahead. Over the hushed, airy sound of the water, a high-pitched, jubilant squeal of laughter was punctuated by a heavy splash. More laughter followed. Male and female.

At a break in the trees, Nate caught sight of a slender girl in a blue dress standing on the rock. Next to her, a boy crouched on the stone as he reached out for another girl who was in the water. The boy and the swimming girl were laughing up a storm and talking a mile a minute.

When the boy got to his feet to pull the girl out of the water, Nate recognized Billy Hill. The girl climbed up, dripping wet in her undergarments, her light hair flattened to her skull and hanging straight down around her face like a stiff veil. Nate knew Lindy Hildebrand by the way she leaned forward with her fists on her hips and yelled at Billy. Lindy shook her head like a dog as she tried to fling water on him. The smaller girl in the dress stood by and watched.

Nate led his horses at a walk and reined up where a brown and white calico dress was neatly folded on a bench-sized boulder. Next to the rock were two pairs of black button-up shoes and short stockings. Closer to the creek, a hat, a gray shirt, and two ragged socks hung from a willow branch, and beneath it lay two scuffed-up boots, lying on their sides like an invitation to scorpions.

"Hey, Nate!" Billy yelled. "Come on out!"

Nate pointed down the road. "I got to go and help John Thomas with the fenceposts."

"Awww!" Billy groaned. "I thought maybe you'd changed your mind 'bout our bet."

Lindy raised a hand and waved by bending her fingers over her palm. "Hey, Nate! Billy says you're gonna put your knife up for the bet."

Wearing his cockeyed grin, Billy just shrugged and raised his palms in a helpless gesture. Even from the creek bank, Nate could see the mischief in Billy's eyes.

"I told 'er you *might*," Billy corrected. "You wanna swim with us?"

Nate watched the three on the rock for a time. The little girl in blue sat and wrapped her arms around her shins, one bare foot crossed on top of the other. She was new to school that year, but Nate knew that she was Lindy's little sister.

"Don't look like you're doin' much swimmin' to me," Nate observed.

"Hey!" Billy called out and pointed toward the shore where Nate stood. "Look inside one o' my boots an' bring the lil' pouch with you."

Nate dismounted, found the small leather bag, and held it up.

"That's it!" Billy yelled. "Shake it an' see what kind o' sound it makes!"

Nate jiggled the bag and heard the jangle of heavy coins.

"Four silver dollars!" Billy announced. "Just like we talked about! For the bet!"

A breeze swept through the trees, and Nate removed his hat to face into it. Closing his eyes, he pictured the russet saddle perched atop Peaches's back like a crown set upon a queen.

Nate brought his head around quickly. "You got a watch?"

Billy shook his head. "But Lindy's real good at countin'. I tested 'er once 'gainst my granddaddy's pocket watch. She was right on the money."

When Billy tapped Lindy's elbow, she chirped up on cue. "We'll count it for you, Nate."

"Come on!" Billy prodded and waved him over. "This's better'n diggin' postholes!"

Nate hung his hat on a nub of willow limb. Sitting beside the folded dress on the boulder, he tugged off boots and socks. Then he stood, pulled off his cotton blouse, and draped it next to Billy's shirt on the branch.

The rocks on the creek bed were slick, so Nate waded his way out to midstream as though tiptoeing through his stepmother's garden. When the water level crept up to his thighs, he lunged for the rock and did a half pivot on stiffened arms, landing on his seat right next to Lindy's sister.

The little girl's big brown eyes had followed his every move, but now she fixed her gaze on the water parting around the rock. Nate looked her over from summer-streaked blonde hair to pale bare feet. Her blue dress shone in the sun like a field of bluebonnets. She was bone dry.

"How in the world did you git out here without gittin' wet?" Nate asked.

The young girl pulled in her lips as she considered the width of the creek Nate had just crossed. "Billy carried me on his back," she replied so quietly that her voice could barely be heard over the murmur of the creek. "I used his hands like stirrups."

Nate nodded, as if she had confided something personal to him. Her face seemed frozen in an awe-struck uncertainty, as she stole glances at him.

"That was smart," he said to the girl. "How'd you talk 'im into it?"

Her shoulders lifted and fell. It was the most subtle shrug Nate had ever witnessed.

"That's my little sister, Nate," Lindy announced. "Her name's *Dory*."

Nate nodded to the girl, but her eyes remained fixed on the water. "Well, Dory," Nate said, "I'd offer you a ride back, but you know what they say 'bout changing horses."

She smiled at that, and her eyes cut to Nate. "In the middle of a stream," she whispered.

"So, you gonna give it a try, Nate?" Billy prodded.

"Minute an' a half! All you gotta do is stay under one more second than that." His eyes took on that shifty look that Nate knew so well. "You still got the knife on ya?"

Nate lifted his feet from the water and pivoted on his seat to face Billy. Leaning to one side, he patted the sheath knife. Billy's eyes locked on it as if it were a ten-ounce nugget of gold.

Nate untied the cord and offered the knife to Dory. "I'll let *her* hold on to it till we see how this goes." He lowered his head to pull up her eyes. "That okay with you, Dory?"

The little girl nodded, took the knife in her slender hands, and cradled it in her lap.

Nate turned to Lindy. "Let me hear this count you're gonna be callin' out."

Lindy struck the pose she must have deemed correct for an official counter. Nate thought she looked silly standing upright in her underwear, every part of her dripping water. She cleared her throat and began, tapping one hand against her leg to keep the rhythm.

"One...two...three...four—"

"See what I mean?" Billy interrupted. "Steady as a clock!"

Nate stood and looked upstream, watching a few leaves float toward him on the water's surface. "Dory?" he said and squatted beside her. "Would you hold Billy's money, too?"

When she nodded, he handed over Billy's pouch. Crossing her legs Indian style, she deposited all the valuables into the nest of her blue dress. Then she covered it all with her hands.

Nate stood, spat into his hand, and held it out to Billy. "Swear on Sam Houston's grave?"

Billy spat into his own hand. "Swear on his grave," he said, and they clasped hands.

Nate moved to the side of the rock where the water was deepest. There, he sat and eased into the cool water, probing the creek bed with his feet. When he found a submerged rock to his liking, he started taking deep breaths, expanding his lungs with each inhalation.

"You gotta stay where we can see you now!" Billy insisted.

Nate nodded. "I ain't goin' nowhere," he said between breaths. He turned to Lindy. "Don' slow down just 'cause the numbers take longer to say."

Lindy's face squeezed down into a question. "What?"

"Takes longer to say *twen'y-nine* than it does *nine*, don't it?" Nate explained.

"I won't slow down!" Lindy insisted, a little irked at his inference.

"I'll be countin', too," Nate assured them. "Be sure to start soon's I go under."

After three more deep breaths, Nate sucked in a gasping volume of air, the sound like cloth tearing. Submerging into the muted dark of the water, he felt for the rock and gently hugged it with both arms, his chest resting lightly on top and his legs trailing downstream. The dull murmur of moving water filled his ears, and the cold prickled his skin. He could hear Billy's voice from above, but the words were too muddled to make out. He could not hear Lindy's count, but he had started his own count, the numbers advancing of their own accord as he settled in for the ordeal.

At "sixty-one," someone yelled down to him. Nate looked up and made out Dory's blue dress through the wavering water. He could only guess that she was letting him know that a minute had passed. Closing his eyes, he fought the deficit of air in his lungs. The pain hit him to the core.

At "seventy-five," the pain had spread to the outer

reaches of his body. At "eighty-five," the pressure was overpowering, screaming at him to surface. A cold darkness began to leach through his head, like an ink drop sending out tendrils of black on wet paper.

At "ninety-one," a stream of bubbles escaped his lips, and he growled, the sound of it more animal than human. At "ninety-five," more bubbles involuntarily raced from his mouth, and he felt light and dizzy. Gathering his legs beneath him, he pushed off from the creek bed with what little strength he could muster. When he surfaced, it was like plunging face-first through the glass of a window to escape a room filled with smoke. Someone grabbed his wrist and kept him from drifting downstream, but all Nate cared about were the delicious volumes of cool air he drew into his body. The dark void that had opened at his core began to fill with light.

Chapter Eight

The first thing he saw was Dory. Standing on the rock in her blue dress, she stared back at him, her face frozen in a mask of horror, as if she were witnessing a corpse rising from a grave. Then, as he lay on his back on the rock, Billy's worried eyes hovered above him, looking intently into his own for signs of life.

Nate closed his eyes and soaked up the warmth of the stone. As his breathing settled, he felt the tortured parts of his body resurrect until his presence among the living was assured.

"Dang, Nate!" Billy said close to his ear. "You almost made it! Two more seconds and you'd'a won!"

Nate opened his eyes to the brightness of the day. Billy was kneeling down beside him now, his freckled face squeezed down as though he were sharing in Nate's pain.

"You made it to eighty-nine! You almost clipped my record!"

When Nate spoke, his words came out in a ragged whisper. "I *did* clip it."

Billy produced the forced smile he was known to use. "Eighty-nine," he said again. "That was the count." He turned his head to Lindy, who sat on the rock, her pinched eyes fixed on Nate. "Ain't that right, Lindy?"

Lindy turned away and stared downstream, her feet in the water, her hands gripping the rock's edge, and her back slumped. Dory stood beside her, watching Nate carefully.

"Lindy?" Billy called a little louder. "Wasn't it eighty-nine?" He kept staring at her, but she would not look at him.

"Yeah," she finally said in a lackluster voice. Then she mumbled, "I guess."

Nate propped up on his elbows. "I counted *nine'y-six*," he said, his words quiet but deliberate. "I beat you by six seconds."

Billy snorted a short, nervous laugh. "Well, it's easy to speed up yore countin' when yo're the one under there with no air. But it was close, Nate! You done real good!"

Nate lay back on the stone and met Billy's skittish eyes. "I done better'n that."

Billy Hill tried to look amused as he shook his head. "Now, Nate, you cain't go crawfishin' on a bet just 'cause you come out on the losin' end."

Nate sat up, propped his forearms on his bent knees, and threaded his fingers together. Billy squinted upstream as if he had taken a sudden interest in the moving water.

"Thing is, Billy, I ain't the one on the losin' end o' this deal."

Billy turned and retracted his head an inch, pretending to be surprised. "Well, you ain't sayin' Lindy cheated, are you?"

Closing his eyes, Nate shook his head slowly and then fixed his gaze on Billy. "This ain't 'bout Lindy. This is 'bout you and me...and what's right and what ain't."

Billy stood, threw his arms out from his sides, and let them fall so that his hands slapped against his wet trousers. "Well, then, just ask *her*. She's the one done most o' the countin'."

The sound of water parting around the rock seemed to grow louder as Nate studied the profile of Lindy's face. She remained as still as the rock and just as mute.

"*Most* o' the countin'?" Nate said. "Lindy?"

It looked as though she was not going to respond, but then she cleared her throat and spoke out to the creek. "I just counted like Billy said to."

For about a dozen heartbeats, Nate waited to see if she would say more. Dory squatted beside her, took her sister's arm, and gently shook her enough to make Lindy's head bobble. Lindy jerked her arm away and mumbled something that Nate could not hear.

"And how was that, 'xactly?" Nate asked.

Lindy shrugged. "You know...just steady...like a clock."

Dory put her lips against her sister's ear and whispered, but Lindy shook her head.

"How long do you say I stayed under, Lindy," Nate asked with a tenderness in his voice.

When Lindy would not answer, Dory looked quickly at Nate and spoke in a rush. "When she got to eighty, Billy told her she was countin' too fast and to go back, but she wouldn' do it. So, Billy took over the countin' and started at seventy."

When Nate looked at Billy for confirmation, the boy's face reddened, and his hands balled into fists. "Well? She *was* countin' too fast! I had to keep it fair, didn' I?"

Lindy lifted her feet from the water, spun around on her backside, and glared at Billy, her eyes on fire. "*Fair!*" she chirped. "You don' know the meanin' of *fair*, Billy Hill! You just want that knife o' Nate's, is all!"

Still glaring at Billy, she now looked somehow regal in her undergarments. Slipping into the water, she started toward the bank, her arms bent at the elbows and level with her shoulders, her torso rotating back and forth as she barged her way through the water.

"Come on, Dory!" she snapped over her shoulder.

Dory stood with Nate's knife clenched in one hand and the bag of coins in the other. She watched as Lindy waded to shore and climbed out on the rocks. When her sister disappeared into the shadows of the trees, Dory turned to Billy and waited for him to meet her eyes.

"Lindy don't like to lie. And she don't like being told what to do. She thought you might ask 'er to the October dance if she helped you." Dory tightened her lips into a knot. "I doubt she'd go with you to a hog killing now."

Billy turned away, scowled down at the water, and sulked.

"How 'bout it, Billy?" Nate said quietly. "I cain't see no reason Dory would lie."

"I'm *not* lying," Dory assured Nate.

Nate smiled. "I know you ain't." He nodded toward Billy. "He knows it, too."

The skin on the back of Billy's neck darkened to the shade of a ripe prickly pear. Then, without a word, he jumped into the creek and began slogging his way through the waist-deep current. Slipping, he cursed and slapped at the water. After following Lindy's wet path up the bank, he snatched up his boots, shirt, and hat and marched into the trees.

Dory walked to where Nate sat and laid the knife and bag on the rock next to him.

"Did Billy really stay under for a minute and a half?" Nate asked.

She pressed her lips into a thin line and shook her head. "Didn't even make it a minute."

Nate put on a sad smile. "What I figured," he said. He tied the knife to his side and stuffed the bag of coins behind the waistband of his trousers. "Come on," he said and got to his feet. "I'll give you a ride back over."

He eased over the edge of the rock, patted his hand on the top of his shoulder, and waited for her to climb on. Her slender legs slipped into place around his neck with the dress bunched beneath her like a saddle blanket. Her slender feet dangled before him.

"How'd you git that scar on yore right foot?"

"A horse stepped on me when I was six," she said. "How do I hold on, Nate?"

"Grab my hair if you need to."

Dory laughed. "You don't have enough hair to hold on to!"

Nate chuckled. "Well, we could wait here till it grows out, or we could go ahead and give 'er a try. Whatta ya think?"

Dory was quiet for a time. "Can I hold your ears?"

Now, Nate laughed outright. "I might could stand havin' some hair pulled out, but I'll prob'ly be needin' both my ears. Just hold on the best you can."

The crossing went smoothly. When they stepped into the little clearing where Billy and Lindy had left their clothes, only Dory's little black shoes remained on the boulder. Nate backed up to it and waited as she climbed down. As she sat, he pulled his blouse off the branch and offered it to her.

"Here...dry yore feet off with this."

She shook her head. "I don't mind being wet."

While she laced up her shoes, Nate slipped into his shirt, tugged on his stockings and boots, and pushed his hat down on his head. Then he secured the bag of coins in his saddlebag.

"I'd offer you one o' these other horses to ride," Nate said, "but the colt's too young, and the mare's not ready. You can ride on Peaches with me."

Dory stood on the rock and waited for Nate to mount the paint. When he sidled Peaches closer to her, she eased nimbly behind the cantle and sat there, careful not to touch him.

"Better hold on," Nate said and started the three horses back toward town along the creek trail. As their bodies shifted in unison with the relaxed gait of the paint, he felt Dory take a grip on his shirt at either side of his ribs. They rode for five minutes without a word.

A fat bull snake slithered across the road. Nate pointed, and she leaned in time to see it slither into the switchgrass. Neither rider remarked on it, but the snake's appearance seemed to open up a space for conversation.

"I reckon I owe you for speakin' up like you done, Dory. I 'preciate it."

She was quiet for so long that it surprised him when she finally replied. "Maybe you'll take me to the October dance," she said, her voice little more than a whisper.

Nate frowned and turned his head. "How old are you, Dory?"

"Twelve...in December."

Nate laughed quietly. "I doubt your mama and daddy would care to see that happ'n." He shook his head. "B'sides, if you'd'a ever seen me try to dance, you'd know to avoid me."

The paint settled into an easy lope, its hooves chopping at the dirt in a steady rhythm. The other two horses shuffled along behind them, their gaits melding into a jumbled pattern.

"Is it because I'm so much younger?"

Nate chuckled. "Maybe it's 'cause I'm so much older."

"Well, isn't that the same thing?"

Nate turned his head to talk over his shoulder. "I wasn't really plannin' on goin' to the dance." When, after half a minute, she'd made no reply, he added, "If I did, I might could try one dance with you." Surprised at what he had said, he added, "But I cain't see me goin'."

When they arrived at the hill where the Hildebrand home perched high over the town, Nate lowered Dory to the ground with one arm and watched her back away from the shuffling hooves of the three horses. She stood with her hands clasped before her and smiled up at him.

Nate looked down at the reins in his hand. "Tell Lindy I'm sorry how Billy treated 'er."

Dory shook her head. "You oughtn't be sorry. She just gets plain stupid around boys."

Nate chuckled. "Well, I guess we all git stupid sometimes."

Dory smiled. "Like you believing Billy stayed underwater for a minute and a half?"

He laughed as he nodded. "Yeah...an' maybe half-drownin' myself over four dollars."

Dory tilted her head to one side. "Why did you want to make that bet anyway?"

"I'm savin' up to buy a saddle. I'm only one dollars shy now."

She shifted her gaze to the saddle on which he sat. "Why do you need a new one?"

With a quiet chuckle, he shook his head. "Reckon my mind just got set on it. Soon's I laid eyes on that saddle, I knew it was s'posed to be ours." He patted Peaches's neck.

Dory waited for Nate to look at her. "Sometimes you just know, don't you? You see somethin' that oughta belong to you...and you to it."

Nate felt his face flush, and he looked down as if checking on his stirrup, hiding his face under the brim of his hat. When he straightened up, he narrowed his eyes at the horizon.

"Reckon I better git home an' listen to my brother complain 'bout workin' by hisself." He plucked at the brim of his hat. "So long, Dory." He turned the horses in a wide arc.

"Hey, Nate?" she called out, stopping him. "I'd give you the dollar if I had it."

He waved away her gesture. "You aw-ready done plenty for me today. Take care now." He tapped his heels to his pony's flanks and started his little remuda for the Champion ranch.

Chapter Nine

By the time Nate and John Thomas had cleaned up for the evening meal, the rest of the siblings—all eight of them—had gathered at the long, pecan-wood table that dominated the dining room. Whenever the entire Champion family crowded into this space, the current of mixed conversations usually ran together like the whispery shoals of a river, but on this night, as Nate sidled along the wall toward his chair, all was quiet but for the scuff of his boots on the floor.

There was no food on the table, only plates and flatware. Nate looked at his siblings, but they just stared back at him, each with the same impassive expression.

"Sorry if we're late," Nate said. No one seemed to hear him. Even his young stepbrother and stepsisters were unnaturally still. Standing behind his chair, Nate hesitated. "What's ever'body lookin' at? We ain't *that* late, are we?"

"Well, there's a reason we're late!" John Thomas was quick to say. "You know how skinny Nate is. Well, he fell down into the bottom of a posthole, and I didn' know what happ'ned to 'im. I looked around for 'bout a hour b'fore I found 'im."

Because this yarning was young Dudley's kind of game, Dud joined right in. "Well, how come you didn' yell out, Nate? Did you go in headfirst an' git a mouthful o' dirt?"

Knowing there would be more, Nate smiled and sat down. There was nothing he could do or say to stop the momentum of John Thomas and Dudley once they got started.

"He was upside down all right," John went on. "Lucky I spotted his boots when I did. He was tryin' to dig out the wrong way." John Thomas leaned forward on his forearms and put a little mystery into his voice. "By the time I managed to git a rope looped 'round his feet, I swear I heard some *stra-a-a-nge* voices down below. And danged if it didn' sound like Chinamen." He shrugged. "'Course I cain't be sure, since I don' speak no China words."

Naomi Jane held baby Corelia in her arms, as was her duty as the oldest sister. "You don't hardly speak much American neither," she mumbled.

Everyone laughed except John.

"It's called *English*, Naomi," James reminded.

Naomi looked insulted. "I ain't talkin' 'bout England. I'm talkin' 'bout Texas."

Dudley slathered his words with a comic drawl. "Lil' sister, I'd say ol' John Thomas speaks Texan purty dang good."

"Aw-right, aw-right...quiet down," came a soft Southern voice from the kitchen doorway. All heads turned to watch Jack Champion enter the room and take his seat at the head of the table. The sleeves of his white Sunday shirt were rolled halfway up his tendon-streaked forearms. Behind him, Nate's young stepmother stood in the doorway wearing a crooked smile that looked out of place on her usually stoic face. When the father turned his head and nodded, she spun around and disappeared into the kitchen.

"Nathan?" his father said. "What did the Bolens have to say?"

To meet his daddy's eyes, Nate leaned forward to look past the flank of siblings beside him. "Said they'll stay an' take care o' things at Aunt Hattie's place till she gits back. I think it was a relief to 'em to know they didn' have to move out."

Jack Champion nodded. "That's good." He unfolded his napkin and stuffed one corner behind his enormous beard, where it would do little good. "Ever'thin' aw-right out at Snyder's?"

Nate squared his fork to the knife beside his plate as he decided what to leave out of his report. "I brung back a mare along with the colt. Figured I'd work 'em both."

The father nodded, placed his hands on the table, and threaded his fingers together like the weave of a basket. "His livestock lookin' aw-right?"

"Yes'r," Nate said and pushed back the image of Dixie Brooks and his whip.

"How many posts did you boys sink today?"

Nate glanced at John Thomas before answering. "John put up three by hisself. I didn' git there till late afternoon. Together, we put up three more."

Jack Champion leaned forward on his forearms. "You ready to dig some mo'ah tonight?"

Nate looked around the table at his siblings, all of them trying to hide the smiles that played on their faces. Even the youngest children—Fannie, Mary Lou, and Calvin—appeared to be a part of a conspiracy.

"Diggin'?" Nate said. "Tonight?"

The father turned his head and called to the kitchen. "Mary? I think we'ah ready."

Nate's stepmother came through the doorway carrying a cake topped by a constellation of small, burning candles. As she carried it around the table, the teardrop flames angled toward her and flickered. She laid the platter before Nate, and he made a quick count. Fourteen.

On a cue from Dudley, everyone chimed in together with a collective, "Happy birthday, Nate," but their voices were staggered and unrehearsed, each trying to be louder than the others.

Nate met his stepmother's slate-gray eyes. "But it ain't my birthday for two days yet."

"Your father is leaving for Milam County, so we thought we'd celebrate tonight."

Nate stared into the dazzling shine of the candles and the reflection glowing off the rich-brown icing. It was his favorite—caramel—and Dudley's favorite, too.

"Nate," Dud chimed in with a straight face, "you git the first slice, but you better make it a big'n. By the time that cake gits 'round to me, I will show no mercy."

John Thomas shot Dudley a hard look. "If that platter comes 'round to me empty, you can 'xpect comp'ny over at yore plate right quick."

Dudley started to reply until his father set down his coffee cup and cleared his throat. "Any o' you boys get sick eatin' cake, you still got to go to school tomorr'. Undah'stand?"

Nate sucked in a long breath to extinguish the candles, but Naomi slapped her palms flat on the table. "Ain't you gonna make a wish?"

Mary Champion cleared her throat. "Not *ain't*, Naomi. *Aren't!*"

Naomi waggled her head from side to side and delivered the exasperated sigh she had perfected for all things having to do with grammar. "Well? *Aren't* you gonna make a wish?"

Nate pulled up a mental image of the drover's saddle that hung in Mr. Cooke's backroom. Then, taking a deep breath, he leaned forward and blew in a sweeping motion across the candles. The flames gave way to a skein of gray smoke that swirled and rose above the table.

Mary laid down a large kitchen knife next to the cake. "Use that, Nathan," she said.

"What about supper?" Nate asked. "Ain't we...*aren't* we having that first?"

"We're doin' things a little backward this evening," Mary announced. "Your father is leaving tonight. He's already eaten his supper, so we're having the cake now."

"Yes, ma'am," Nate replied and nodded at the cake. "This is real nice. Thank you."

"You do the cutting," Mary ordained and then glanced at Dudley. "So that all get a fair share."

A flotilla of plates were pushed across the table to surround the cake platter. Laughter and talking filled the room as Nate sectioned the cake and served each plate.

It did not take long for the cake to disappear. Even baby Corelia was allowed a tiny sample. A glass pitcher of fresh milk was passed around, and by the time it had made a full circuit around the table, the pitcher was empty.

Jack Champion rapped the table quietly with the knuckles of one hand, and the room quieted. "Nathan, we all chipped in on this." He set down a tiny pasteboard box no bigger than a deck of cards. "This's for you, son." He slid the box to James, who relayed it to John Thomas. Naomi took it from John, and when she set it down before Nate, a sharp, metallic *clink* came from inside the box.

"It's a new pair o' boots, Nate!" Dudley crowed. "We hope they ain't too small!"

And that started everyone else fabricating a guess, each one more absurd than the one before it. "A new hat"..."a Winchester rifle"..."a thoroughbred racehorse."

When Nate opened the box, he beheld a stack of five silver dollars nestled into a bed of cotton. With his mouth hanging open, he tore his eyes from the gift and turned to his father.

"Look about right?" his father asked.

Nate wrinkled his forehead. "Whatta you mean?"

The elder Champion pulled his napkin from his shirt front and wiped his mustaches and beard. "James rode in to see Mr. Cooke last week 'bout a new brandin' iron. Said that's what you lacked fo' the saddle...five doll'ahs."

Nate pointed at James. "*You're* the one Mr. Cooke said was askin' 'bout it?"

James smiled. "It's a dandy of a saddle, Nate. Gonna look real fine on Peaches."

The father pushed away from the table. "I've got to be goin'," he mumbled to his wife.

With a quick touch to his arm, she kept him in place. "Wait," she said and hurried into the kitchen. Right away, she returned carrying a reed basket by its large hoop handle.

"I packed you a biscuit and a slice of meat if you get hungry. And there's some cheese, too."

He lifted a folded blue cloth from the basket. "Thank you, hon. I'll just take it like this." Turning to Nate, he pointed toward the front door. "Nathan, walk with me out to the barn."

"Yes'r," Nate replied and forked the last of his cake into his mouth.

They were quiet as they crossed the yard. Checkers crawled from under the porch and followed. When father and son entered the shade of the barn, Nate took down a bridle from the wall and entered the stall where his daddy's big bay stud stood idly in the crepuscular light. After leading the bay into the yard, Nate began brushing the animal from the withers back, making quick, overlapping strokes that sent wisps of dust into the air.

When his father brought out blanket and saddle, Nate took the blanket and squared it on the bay's back. Jack Champion lifted the saddle into place, and Nate crouched to strap the cinch.

"Do you like to gamble, Nathan?" his father asked.

Nate straightened and frowned. "Sir?"

"Do you like to gamble?" he repeated with a hint of irritation. "Is it a new habit o' yo'ahs?"

"Nos'r," he replied, hoping his answer might suffice for both questions.

His father stuffed the wrapped food in a saddlebag and buckled it. Then he gripped the cantle and the pommel and gently rocked the saddle to test its fit.

"When I was she'iff, people liked to tell me things." He arched his eyebrows. "Still do."

Nate nodded. "That how you learned 'bout me wantin' that saddle?"

Jack Champion shook his head. "That's not what I'm talkin' about." He turned to face Nate squarely. "I he'ah you made some money on a bet with the Tisdale boy."

Nate swallowed. "It was just a footrace, sir."

The former sheriff's eyes turned cold. "Was there money at stake, son?"

Nate wanted to look away—at anything other than his father's judgmental frown—but he could not add cowardice to the old man's list of grievances toward him. "Yes'r, there was."

The old man gazed out at the twilit yard, sucked in his cheeks, and nodded once. When he turned back to Nate, some of the hardness in his eyes had softened.

"Do you rememb'ah the talk I had with all you boys about gamblin'?"

"Yes'r," Nate replied. Then he lowered his voice to a

whisper and allowed for some hope. "Weren't me that put up any money, Daddy."

His father eyed him for a time. "And you think that makes it aw-right?"

Nate looked down at his own boots but remembered that his father did not like to talk to the top of his head. He brought up his guilty face and cleared his throat.

"Nos'r, I know it's still gamblin'."

His father inhaled deeply and let his breath ease out in a long sigh. "And what if you'd lost? What were *you* to give up?"

Now, Nate felt so embarrassed, he wondered how he had ever agreed to the bet. "I was s'posed to prod Sarah Netherlin into goin' with Tiz to the October dance."

"*Tiz?*"

Nate shrugged. "*Martin.* He likes to go by *Tiz.*"

The tendons in Jack Champion's jaws flexed. "Son, you wouldn' be doin' a girl any fav'ah by introducin' her to Mah'tin Tisdale."

"Why not, Daddy?"

"Because he is hangin' 'round with the wrong crowd. I predict that boy is headed for trouble. I don't want you associatin' with 'im."

Nate swallowed and licked his lips. "Does that go for his brother, too?"

Without hesitation, his father shook his head. "John Tisdale is as good a man to come out o' Williamson County as anyone I know. But Mah'tin—the one you call *Tiz*—is not cut from the same cloth. You be a friend to John, but I want you to stay away from Mah'tin, undah'stand?"

Nate nodded. "Yes'r."

"As fo' gamblin', that is not on the list of things fo' you to do. It has been the ruin of many a man. Since I was in the ah'my, I've seen three men kilt, Nathan. One was Doc

Black when he got shot. The othah two died in saloons while gamblin'. Ah ya listenin' to me, son?"

"Yes'r." Nate held his father's stare to show the man that he could be trusted.

"How much did you take from 'im?"

Nate cleared his throat. "A dollar."

Jack Champion mounted the bay, took up the reins, and looked straight ahead out the door. "I want you to put that doll'ah on my bedroom dress'ah. When I git back, I'll retu'n it to the Tisdale boy."

When the old man started to depart, Nate placed a hand on his leg and stopped him. "Daddy, I won some money off o' Billy Hill, too."

The father closed his eyes and bowed his head. "Anoth'ah bet," the ex-sheriff said, not bothering to pose his reply as a question.

"Yes'r. I won four dollars from 'im."

The father raised one eyebrow. "And is he still a friend? Aft'ah losing that money to you?"

"I reckon," Nate said, but as the words came out, he knew he could not be certain.

Jack Champion thumbed up the front of his hat brim and stared off into a distance that seemed to displease him. The bay stood absolutely still, as if it understood that the father and son had more to work out between themselves.

"Anoth'ah footrace?"

"It was...a diff'rent kind o' race, I guess you'd say."

"Son, is this the way you want people to know how you make a livin'?"

Nate thought about how hard he had run to outrace Tiz's buckskin. But that effort had paled compared to the ordeal at the round rock. He wanted to explain to his father that he had earned the money both times, but he didn't know how to begin that argument.

Jack Champion sniffed. "You put *that* money on my dress'ah, too."

Nate tightened his grip. "Daddy, it oughta be me to do the returnin'."

The man nodded, and Nate thought he saw a glint of admiration in his father's eye. "Yo'ah gettin' to be a man now, son. I want you to think about how you carry yo'self among the people you know. Think things through till you see the right and the wrong of it."

Nate stepped back, letting his hand slide from his father's leg. "Yes'r, I will."

He watched his father ride out the front gate into the gloaming hovering over the grasslands. The sound of the bay's hooves faded beyond the cattle trail, leaving only the dry chirr of crickets. Checkers whined, and Nate turned to see the dog sitting behind him, eyes alert, ears up, waiting.

Nate kneeled and stroked both hands along the sides of the dog's face, flattening the ears and narrowing the eyes. "You know what, Checkers? I'm gonna earn me some money the right way an' git me a new saddle."

Chapter Ten

During the noon break, the youngest children were chasing each other in the front yard of the schoolhouse. Of the older students, Nate was the first one out and free to choose his place in the shady spot where the boys ate at the edge of the trees. The best seat was a flat-topped rock that could accommodate four or five, but it was the tacit territory of the older boys. Nate took a seat between the thick roots of the largest oak, leaned back against its trunk, and opened his food bag.

The girls, as always, began laying out blankets on the grassy ground at the back of the schoolhouse. Within minutes, the yard would look like a huge, colorful quilt covering the grass.

"Hey, Nate."

Nate looked up from the biscuit he was loading with a slice of beef. Wearing a bright yellow dress, Dory Hildebrand stood before him, her feet together, both her hands gripping a cloth bag that hung to her knees. Reaching into the bag, she brought out a small package wrapped in newspaper and tied with a simple bow of brown string.

Behind her, Mrs. Boyce—her scarecrow of a teacher—

clanged a hand bell to call her young students inside, but Dory paid her no mind.

"Hey, Dory," Nate said quietly. "Whatcha got there?"

She held out the package. "It's for you."

Three of the older boys approached from the school building and looked curiously at the young girl as they climbed up on their privileged rock. Two more boys arrived and sat on the ground beside Nate. All of them began wolfing down their food in their hurry to play a ballgame before having to go back inside. The boys on the rock made sidelong glances at the audacious little girl who had trespassed into their lunch area.

Nate unwrapped his present and found a shortbread cookie almost an inch thick. "You make this?" he asked.

Before she could answer, Henry Kirkpatrick piped up from the rock. "Y'all gittin' hitched, Nate?" He broke into the high-pitched giggle that made him sound like a canyon wren.

Dory took a step closer to Nate and lowered her voice. "I heard it was your birthday."

Nate shrugged and smiled at the same time. "It ain't till tomorr'...but thanks."

"*I heard it was yore birthday, Nate!*" Henry sang in a mocking tone. Sitting on the edge of the rock, he showed his teeth through a smile that cut deep dimples into his plump cheeks. "You bring one for me, too? I got a birthday next month."

"No cookies for you, Henry. You're so fat you can barely fit into the schoolhouse."

Nate turned to the familiar voice to see Naomi standing alone, a book in her hand.

Henry's eyes narrowed to mean little slits. "Whyn't you eat a fresh cow patty!"

"If only I could find one," Naomi returned, "that you ain't aw-ready took a bite out of!"

The Kirkpatrick boy cocked back his arm and threw a half-eaten peach at Naomi. It hit the oak tree and burst into pieces that rained down on Nate and the boys near him. Dory had tried to dodge the throw, caught her heels on a root, and tripped. Spilling his lunch, Nate tried to catch her, but she sat down hard on the packed earth. Henry slapped his fleshy thighs and cackled.

Nate got to his knees to help Dory up. "You aw-right?"

Tears welled in the girl's large brown eyes, but she set her jaw and nodded. Naomi laid down her book and picked up half of the peach off the ground. After wiping it on her dress, she examined it from several angles. Then, with her eyes fixed on Henry, she stuffed it in her mouth and chewed, surprising everyone. All the boys broke into laughter as her cheeks filled and made her look like a chipmunk. But when she marched up to the rock and stood before Henry, all went quiet.

Naomi mumbled something through the mouthful of food, but the words were impossible to decipher. Henry frowned and leaned forward to hear.

"What?" he said.

Naomi held up a forefinger as she finished chewing. Then she arched her back, leaning away from Henry, took a deep breath, and lunged forward from the waist as she spat an explosive spray of food and saliva. Henry's eyes snapped shut as he leaned back, his face and shirtfront covered with peach debris. In the quiet that followed, Naomi spoke with perfect clarity.

"I said, 'Thanks for the peach but I cain't eat 'em 'cause they make me spit up.'"

The roar of laughter from the other boys drew the attention of everyone else in the schoolyard. Henry sputtered and wiped at his face, flinging wet debris in every direction. The boys next to him abandoned the rock, leaving their lunches behind.

"Dory? Naomi?" Mrs. Boyce called from the front yard of the schoolhouse. Nate turned to see the teacher standing by the corner of the building, her stick-like arms crossed over her flat chest. "Get inside now, before I mark you *late!*"

With a triumphant grin, Naomi spun around and walked to Dory, where she helped the girl to her feet and brushed off the back of her dress. Together, they marched to the schoolhouse, neither of them looking back.

Henry was so mad he was shaking. The boys standing around him tried to muffle their laughter, as they watched him pick at specks of fruit clinging to his shirt.

"Snotty little bitch!" Henry blurted out. A few of the boys looked at the teacher to see if she had heard, but most looked at Nate.

Still on one knee, Nate closed his eyes. The pressure gathering inside his chest was like a ball of heat trying to burst into a flame. He got to his feet and walked to Henry, who was still busy swiping at his shirt with his stubby, sausage-like fingers.

"You're gonna skin that back...to both o' them girls," Nate said.

Henry fixed his beady eyes on Nate. "Or *what?!*" he snorted and curled his upper lip. "Yore sister's a bitch an' yo're a sonovabitch!" Henry raised a finger and poked at the air toward Nate. "I oughta climb down there an' whip yore ass for what she done."

Nate took his time answering. "You need help in gittin' down to do all this whippin'?"

A muffled laughter made its way around the lunch area. Someone gave Henry a shove from behind, but he clamped his pudgy hands to the edge of the rock and resisted.

"You don' wanna mess wi' me, Champion! I could break you in half like a matchstick."

Nate waited for ten seconds before replying. "I see yo're still a-settin' on that rock?"

Billy Hill sauntered out from the schoolhouse, making his way to the lunch rock. With his head down, he swiped his palms together, sending little puffs of white chalk dust into the air.

"Hey, Billy!" someone called out. "You're just in time to see David an' G'liath go at it!"

Billy stopped and frowned. "What's goin' on? Ain't we gonna play ball?"

Lee Moore—the best ballplayer in school—downed the last of his food and laughed. "Hell, this'll be better'n a ballgame...if Henry ain't afraid to tussle wi' little Nate here."

"I ain't afraid!" Henry huffed. "But I'd git in trouble for beatin' up a kid half my size!"

"You mean *a tenth your size*," Lee corrected. "Henry, Nate's so quick, I doubt he'll be in one place long enough for you to try an' set on 'im."

Billy stared at the side of Nate's face. "What's got y'all riled up?"

Ignoring the question, Nate took a step closer to Henry. "You can sit there like a cow'rd or git down here an' fight. Either way, yo're gonna 'pologize to both of them girls."

"Aw, they didn' hear nothin'," Henry whined.

"*I* heard it," Nate replied, "so you're gonna—"

With a sudden grunt, Henry stiffened his arms on the rock and tried to lift his hips to kick out at Nate. Dodging the clumsy ambush, Nate grabbed Henry's stout ankle in both hands and lunged backward with all his strength. Henry came off the rock flailing his arms and unbalanced. He landed hard on his back, expelling a wheezing rush of air.

Holding Henry's boot in one hand, Nate looked down

at the boy's pale, rubbery face as it tightened with a grimace of pain. "You gonna skin it back?" Nate said.

Stretched out on his back, Henry began to draw in deep breaths and expel them through inflated cheeks. His eyes fluttered and then squeezed shut so tightly that his eyebrows touched the bridge of his nose.

"Damn you, Nate! I weren't ready!"

Lee laughed. "There ain't no referee to ring a bell here, Kirkpatrick. This here altercation started when you opened your big mouth. B'sides, you threw the first punch with your boot, which—by the way—you have surrendered to your opponent."

The boys around the rock broke into laughter. Henry sulked.

"Yo're gonna 'pologize to both them girls," Nate said again.

"The hell I will! Gimme my damn boot!" With an effort, Henry sat up.

When Nate tossed the boot aside, Henry got on all fours and used his hands on the boulder to stand. Turning to Nate, he pointed at the boot.

"'Less you wont yore face rearranged...pick that up an' hand it to me!"

Nate realized that Naomi had reappeared and was standing beside him, glaring at Henry. "Naomi, what're you doin' here?"

As an answer, she bent down and picked up the book she had left.

Henry scowled. "Now I gotta look at *her* again?"

"You can 'pologize to 'er right now and be half done with it," Nate said.

Henry smirked. "I'm sorry...that I didn' spit on yore ugly face first!"

Naomi picked up Henry's boot and marched toward the schoolhouse. Instead of heading for the front door, she stopped a few paces from the side of the building and turned to gloat.

"You gonna 'pologize, Henry the Hog?" she sang out.

Henry glowered. "You better gimme my boot, you lil' shit!"

In one smooth motion, Naomi slued around and swung the boot underhanded, arcing it high over the eave of the building. It landed with a soft *thud* halfway up the pitch of the roof.

A raucous chorus of laughter erupted from the side yard. Behind the building, the girls seated on their blankets turned to see Naomi as she stuck out her tongue at Henry.

Nate took two steps toward his little sister, stopped, and pointed to the schoolhouse. "Naomi! Git on inside! This ain't got nothin' to do with you!"

She crossed her arms over her skinny torso and then spread her feet in a defiant stance that Nate knew only too well. She was not going to budge.

"How am I gonna git my boot down?!" Henry whined.

Lee laughed. "Maybe you could sprout wings, and we'll finally see pigs fly!" The roar of laughter darkened Henry's face. "Come on, Kirkpatrick!" Lee needled. "Git your fat ass to fightin'! Why, young Nate there...he ain't much bigger'n a grasshopper compared to you."

Henry struggled to reach back and stroke himself. "I hurt my back!" he complained.

Lee laughed. "Only thing wrong with yore back is the yellow stripe runnin' down it."

Henry bared his teeth at Nate. "I'm gonna kick the shit outta you!"

"Well," Lee mused, "if you *was* to try, you'd have only the one boot to kick with."

While the boys laughed, Henry glared at Nate and began sucking in deep breaths. He looked as if he were about to step off a cliff and plunge into water on a dare. When he ran at Nate, his cumbersome body seemed to move in a slow, dreamlike fashion. Nate skipped sidewise and kicked at the boy's bootless foot, so that it caught the back of his other leg. Henry fell like a side of beef, hitting the ground on his face and belly and letting go with a deep grunt.

While most of the boys winced, Lee Moore laughed. "That, ladies an' gentlemen, is what a two-hun'erd-pound chunk o' blubber sounds like droppin' outta the sky."

Pushing up to his hands and knees, Henry jerked his head around. "I ain't no two hun'erd pounds!"

Lee pursed his lips. "Yo're right. Without the boot, might be closer to one-nine'y-nine."

Grunting, Henry got to his feet and squeezed his fleshy hands into fists. "I'm gonna crush you like a egg, Champion."

Chapter Eleven

This time, Henry approached slowly, his face set for battle. Nate bent at the knees, raised his fists before him, and began to move lightly on the balls of his feet the way his uncle George had taught him. The only time Nate had employed his pugilistic lessons was when he sparred with his older brothers for fun, each trying to tag the other with a light, open-handed slap on the face. But today was different.

As soon as he was close enough, Henry threw a round-house punch, one so sluggish that he telegraphed it from the moment he shifted his weight to begin the blow. Nate ducked it easily and drove his fist into the bigger boy's belly. His fist sank into the softness of Henry's stomach, never finding a firm target to take the impact of his punch. Right away, Nate swung upward with an uppercut to the chin, producing a loud *clack* as Henry's teeth snapped shut.

Henry sat down hard, his eyes glassy and his mouth hanging open. He reminded Nate of the men his daddy had once thrown into a jail cell to sleep off a Sunday-morning drunk. Henry carefully inserted a finger into his mouth and probed along his gum. When he removed it, a bright-red smear of blood covered the fingertip.

"You 'bout broke my damn tooth, Nate!" He said this in an oddly personable tone, as if the two of them together had discovered something unusual here in the schoolyard. But then a change came over him. Grunting loudly, he got to his feet, took three deep breaths, and charged at Nate like a bull.

After making a feint to the right, Nate darted left, and Henry tripped over himself, trying to keep up with Nate's gyrations. Again, Henry fell onto his face. When he pushed himself up on his hands and knees, rivulets of blood dribbled from his nose.

"Don't let 'im git a hold o' ya, Nate!" Billy Hill called out. "He'll fall on ya an' flatten ya like a flapjack!"

To counter that possibility, Nate jumped on Henry's wide back while he was still on all fours, and for Nate, it felt like hopping bareback onto a draft horse. Unable to reach around Henry's girth with his legs, Nate locked his arms around the boy's thick neck and held on.

"Watch out now, Nate!" Billy advised. "He can still crush ya!"

Even with the extra weight on his back, Henry heaved himself to his feet and charged the wall of the school-house. Just before making contact, he turned awkwardly in mid-stride and crashed backward into the logs, using Nate as his cushion.

The impact flashed a searing red light behind Nate's closed eyes. His grip loosened of its own accord, and he found himself leaning against the wall of the building. When Henry stepped away, Nate's knees buckled, and he crumpled to the ground.

Henry wiped his nose with his forearm and then inspected the blood streaked on his skin. "I tol' ya I'd crush you, didn' I, Champion?"

Lee Moore laughed. "Wouldn' count 'im out yet, Henry the hog. Nate don't quit easy!"

Henry charged again, and Nate tried to get to his feet. But it was too late. Henry wrapped him in a bear hug from behind. Wrapping one bloated arm around Nate's throat, Henry strained to tighten his hold. All Nate could hear was Henry's hot breath huffing in his ear like a bellow.

"Break free of 'im, Nate!" Billy Hill called out. "Bite 'im! Do *somethin'*!"

Henry swung around to show off Nate's reddening face. "Say it, Nate! Say you quit!"

Nate pulled at the suffocating arm with both hands and managed to squeeze out a raspy reply. "First... you...'pologize!"

With a vicious jerk, Henry tightened his hold. "You give, Nate?"

Nate could feel the soft mound of Henry's belly pressing into his back as the boy widened his stance to keep his balance. Raising his right knee to the height of his waist, Nate stomped hard where he estimated Henry's bootless foot to be.

"*Oww!*" Henry squealed, and just like that, Nate was free.

Hopping on one leg, Henry tried to raise his stockinged foot within reach of his hands, but he could not manage it. Nate took two big breaths and then ran at Henry with all the power he could muster, heaving the boy into the log wall of the schoolhouse with such impact that something inside the building fell and shattered. Nate backed away and watched Henry lie dazed in the weeds.

"You gonna 'pologize now?" Nate said.

Henry rolled to his back, blinked a few times, and concentrated on breathing.

"*Boys!*" The strident voice turned every head to the corner of the building. Mr. Boyce's hawk-like face pinched as he peered down at Henry. "Who is banging on the building?!"

Lee Moore spoke up loud and clear. "Henry, here, was showin' us a new dance step, Mr. Boyce, an' his boot flew off an' then down he went...right into the side o' the buildin'."

The teacher lowered his eyebrows. "Are you all right, Mr. Kirkpatrick?"

Henry sighed. "I guess."

Boyce turned his attention to Nate, who was tucking his loosened blouse into his waistband. Frowning, the teacher pulled his watch from his pocket and opened the cover.

"If you boys are going to play ball, you've got twenty minutes before I ring the bell." He considered Naomi. "What about you, young lady? Aren't you supposed to be inside with your classmates?"

Naomi held up her book. "Mrs. Boyce sent me to find my speller."

"Go inside then," Boyce told her. Then he eyed Henry. "You come inside, too. You're bleeding. I'll have Mrs. Boyce take a look at you."

When the teacher led a limping Henry inside, the other boys started for the ballfield, running and laughing as though loosed from a cage. All but Nate, Billy, and Lee. Lee wandered off alone toward the small branch in front of the school where he tied up his horse each day. Billy stayed behind and began looking through the abandoned lunch bags at the rock.

"You didn' bring nothin' to eat today?" Nate asked.

Billy scowled. "Aw...I was late gittin' started an' forgot to pack somethin'."

"I got half a biscuit you can have," Nate offered.

Billy followed as Nate returned to the oak and gathered up the remnants of his meal. "How'd this ruckus git started, anyway?" Billy asked.

Nate brushed away a few ants from the pieces of his biscuit. "He was mouthin' off." He handed the largest piece to Billy. "Might be a little grit in there. Ants, too."

"I ate two big, black ants on a nickel bet one time," Billy admitted. "Kinda sour an' tangy."

They walked toward the field where teams were being chosen. Nate broke the shortbread cookie and gave half to Billy. When Billy started to run to the players, Nate grabbed his arm.

"Here," Nate said, digging into his food bag. "Take this."

Billy looked hopeful. "You got another biscuit in there?"

Billy's eyes lit up as Nate dropped four silver dollars into his hand. "What's this?"

Nate took in a deep breath and sighed. "Daddy says gamblin' ain't no way for a man to make his money." Nate shrugged. "No way to keep a friend neither."

Though he seemed to try for indifference, Billy could not hide his delight. He clenched the coins in his fist and nodded as if it were his due.

"That mean I win the knife?" Billy said.

Nate shook his head. "We're just callin' off the bet. Nobody wins...nobody loses."

Billy dropped the coins into one of his boots. "Let's go play ball!"

Nate shook his head again. "You go ahead. I'll see if I cain't get that boot off the roof."

Billy waved and ran off to join the players. Nate headed back to the schoolhouse and found Lee Moore standing in the side yard, head down as he gathered a long rope into even loops. Then he took a wide stance and fixed his eyes on the roof.

"Mind if I do that?" Nate said.

Lee relaxed and turned to face Nate. "Don't matter to me. I'm just tryin' ta keep your little sister outta trouble."

Nate laughed. "There's a hopeless mission...but I 'preciate the thought."

When Lee handed over the lariat, Nate played out a running loop through the honda, took his grip at the knot, and began a diagonal whirl above his head, his wrist rolling with the action to keep the loop open as it cut a soft, whispery circle in the air. At the release, the coils fed out from his hand, and the loop sailed atop the roof to land neatly around the boot.

"I done that much," Lee allowed. "The next part's kinda tetchy."

Nate flipped the rope with a quick, up-and-down whip of his arm, causing a wave to travel smoothly up the line. Just as it reached the boot, Nate gave the rope a little jerk that caused the high side of the loop to jump up and land on top of the boot's leather upper. Then he began a series of short tugs, tightening the loop, until the boot started sliding on the layered shingles.

"Damn, son." Lee chuckled. "You must be a old hand at roundin' up stranded footwear."

Nate cracked a smile. "It ain't my first throw, but it is my first at ropin' a boot on a roof."

Lee laughed. "That sister o' yores is a firecracker, ain't she?"

Nate gave one more tug, and the boot dropped to the ground with the rope following it. Lee picked up the boot as Nate wound the rope into even loops and tied off the finished coil.

"Well, I reckon Henry the hog will be glad to reunite with this," Lee said. "I guess you wanna deliver it?"

"I do," said Nate. They exchanged rope for boot, and Nate raised his chin to Lee. "How come you was to git involved in this with me an' Henry? It weren't none o' yore business."

Lee smiled and looked off toward the ballfield. "Aw, Henry's the kind that needs his high opinion of hisself cut down to size now an' then," Lee explained. "I figured he was overdue."

Nate shook his head slowly. "Ain't sure anybody got cut down to size today."

"Well," Lee chuckled and nodded at the boot in Nate's hand, "Henry's got one leg shorter'n the other, don't he? I'd say that counts as cuttin' down a little." He slapped the coil of rope lightly against his leg. "You're a tough ol' waddy, Nate. I seen you ride mustangs that ain't hardly saddle-broke. An' I ain't never seen you quit nothin' you started."

Nate made a quiet laugh. "I just 'bout quit breathin' with Henry a-chokin' me."

"But you didn' quit, did ya?" Lee slipped the coil of rope over his shoulder. "Ain't you gonna play some ball?"

Nate shook his head. "Think I'll git this to Henry. See if I cain't square things with 'im."

"Why bother?" Lee laughed. "He's gonna be the same ol' *Henry the hog*, ain't he?"

Nate shrugged a shoulder. "Don't seem sensible to make a enemy if you don't need to."

Lee arched his eyebrows and chuckled. "Person'ly, I think there ain't much to recommend 'bout a feller who weighs more'n the horse he rides. Wouldn' you agree?"

Nate smiled. "I reckon his horse would agree. But I ain't his horse."

Chapter Twelve

After five days of fence work and ranch chores, Nate finally had a chance to ride into Round Rock when his father sent him into town to see about repairing the auger. Its spiral blade had broken when John Thomas, using the tamping rod, had tried to loosen its hold on a stubborn section of rocky soil.

For his impatience with the tool, John Thomas was sentenced to work with James in castrating twenty-nine, three-month-old calves. It was the one job on the ranch nobody wanted.

As for his own assignment, Nate was glad to be bouncing along in the buckboard on his way to town rather than slicing off the testicles of bewildered young beeves. William had once told him that the innocent calves mewled and bawled and made such awful screams that the sounds had stayed with him for months as he lay in bed at night and tried to sleep.

The sky was a cloudless deep blue, and the early morning air carried the first cool hint of autumn. The wagon rattled and jolted behind Rube, the gentle, old Morgan who was blind in one eye. When the road to town forked off from the hoof-scarred cattle trail, the ride smoothed out considerably, and Nate could now hear the riffles from Brushy Creek off to his right.

When he passed the round rock, his thoughts ran to the day he had accepted Billy Hill's bet and relieved him of those shining silver dollars. Nate now realized how foolish he had been to trust Billy with the timing. The smart thing would have been to challenge the boy to submerge with him. That way, the count would not have mattered. The bet would have hinged upon who surfaced first...and who last.

But such considerations were meaningless now. What was more important was that he had acted against his father's principles. Nate knew that he was expected to adopt his father's set of rules as his own, at least until, like brother William, he was grown enough to leave the Champion ranch and forge his own set of rules.

As he reached the outskirts of town and recognized several of the people lounging on the boardwalk outside the grocery store, Nate resolved never again to enter into a wager with another person. A reputation of high character was more valuable than a pocketful of silver eagles. Even more important was his opinion of himself. That's what his father had tried to teach him all these years, and now the lesson was beginning to make sense.

At the blacksmith's shop, Mr. Cooke was ringing his heavy hammer against the curved horn of his anvil as he shaped a narrow steel rim for a carriage wheel. Briefly looking up when Nate entered, Cooke struck the metal in a steady rhythm and ran the rim by increments around the horn. Clanking down the hammer on the workbench, he lowered the rim into the water barrel, where it hissed like a riled-up snapping turtle and then quieted. Then, he hung it on the wall template to compare its form to the one drawn on paper.

"What we got there, Nate?" he said, still eyeballing the rim.

"Auger's got a broke blade."

Mr. Cooke's brow lowered when he turned back to Nate, his sharp focus now on the auger. For several seconds, he stared at the tool the way a doctor might examine a patient with a broken bone.

"Mm-hmm," Cooke hummed, and by the sound of this reply, Nate prepared for bad news. "Set it on that bench there," the burly man said and pointed to an empty work-table against the wall. After the smithy marked two spots on the wheel rim with a nub of chalk, he gave all his attention to the auger. He examined it from several angles and then faced Nate.

"Blade's cracked aw-right, and it's broke away from the axle in two places. I could patch it, but it'll break again in almost the same places." He pointed out the cracks and then turned at the waist to show Nate the certainty of his conviction. "I was you, I'd consider buyin' a new one."

Nate leaned against the table and frowned at the damaged tool. "My daddy give me two dollars to spend on fixin' it. How much do you reckon a new one would cost?"

Mr. Cooke looked back at the auger and chewed on the inside of his cheek. "Davis has got one over to his store. He's askin' nine dollars for it. Looks a little stouter'n this'n, so it oughta last you." He smiled and squinted one eye. "You break this'n?"

Nate shook his head. "John Thomas took a iron rod to it. He was madder'n a wet rooster an' determined to knock it loose."

The smithy leaned in and touched the crack in the blade. "Well, I could try'n shore it up, but in my opinion, you'd just be throwin' yore money away. You oughta go on down to Davis's an' have a look at what he's got." He patted the main shaft of the auger. "I could prob'ly give you a dollar for scrap. This axle is still in good shape...even if yore brother did try to kill it."

Nate nodded. "I'll keep the wood handle. It's sycamore. I carved it myself."

Taking a grip on the axle, the blacksmith began working the stout handle free by twisting it back and forth inside its ringed housing. When the shaft slid out, the smithy ran the heavy handle through his calloused hand, feeling the smooth surface of the wood.

"Nice work," he said and passed the handle to Nate.

They walked to the front room, where Mr. Cooke opened a metal lockbox. "There you go, Nate. One dollar." He counted out four quarters into Nate's hand.

"Mr. Cooke," Nate said, "I brung the thirty dollars for the saddle you been holdin' for me, but I might need to use some of it on the new auger."

Cooke nodded. "Well, I reckon I can keep holdin' it for you a little longer."

"I'll go down to the hardware store now an' have a look at that auger."

Mr. Cooke winked. "See if you cain't talk Davis down a dollar. Just tell 'im you don't need no handle." The burly man sniffed. "Ask me...his mark-up is too high anyway."

Nate propped the sycamore shaft over his shoulder. "I'll see what he says."

After walking the boardwalk to the end of the block, Nate started diagonally across the intersection toward Davis's store. In the middle of the dusty road, he heard his name called out. Lindy Hildebrand stood in the doorway of her father's insurance office. She wore a faded-blue apron and rubber boots. In one hand, she held a soiled rag, in the other, a pitcher of sudsy water. Her blonde hair was pulled back over her scalp and tied in back.

"Hey, Nate! You look like a soldier marchin' off to war."

He lowered the wood shaft from his shoulder. "Just goin' to see if I cain't buy a new auger for a decent price."

Lindy's face took on a blank expression. "What's an *ogger*?"

Nate backtracked to the edge of the boardwalk, where Lindy stood above him. "It's a tool for makin' holes in the ground," he explained. "We're puttin' up new fencin'."

"Billy said you gave back the money you won off 'im. How come you was to do *that*?"

Nate shrugged. "Guess it don't suit me to gamble. It sure don't suit my daddy."

Lindy made a sour face. "Billy didn' deserve that money. He cheated, you know."

Nate nodded. "Yeah, I know." He looked down at the rag in her hand. "You workin'?"

"Every Saturday mornin'," she said. "My father pays me a quarter each time."

Nate leaned on the sycamore shaft and figured the numbers. "That's a dollar a month!"

"Twelve dollars a year!" she added. Then her face drew tight. "But don't you go tellin' Billy Hill, you hear? He's always tryin' to wheedle money out o' somebody."

Nate nodded and shouldered the shaft again. "Guess I better go see 'bout this—"

"Did you really ask my sister to go with you to the dance?"

Nate had half turned, but now he pivoted to face her. "What?"

"Dory said you asked her to the October dance."

"I told 'er that if I went at all, I'd dance with 'er just the once't. I didn' invite 'er."

Lindy set down the pitcher and began folding the rag. "That's what I figured," she said, "but you might wanna explain that to her yourself. She'd just think I was bein' bossy."

Nate frowned at the ground and began to nod. "I'll talk to 'er on Monday."

Lindy pointed. "She's up at the milliner's shop with Mother right now."

Nate stared up the street and sighed. "Reckon I better go do it now."

When he reached the hat shop, Nate propped the auger haft against the wall, leaned into the window, and cupped his hands around his eyes to darken the glass. Inside, he saw every manner of women's hats, few of which would provide adequate shade from the sun.

Beyond a display table filled with handbags, jewelry boxes, and gloves, he saw Mrs. Hildebrand at the back of the room talking to Miss Mayweather, the owner. Another woman sorted through an array of scarves that hung on a revolving rack near the counter where sales were settled up. There was no sign of Dory. Nate opened the door for a better look.

Right away, he was assaulted by a reek of flowery fragrances. He recognized the scent. His stepmother smelled like this on Sundays when they took the wagon into town for church. Lingering at the door, Nate took a last breath from outside and then resolved to get his business here done as quickly as possible.

Miss Mayweather continued to talk to Mrs. Hildebrand, but her eyes tracked Nate, following his every move as he strolled around the front of the room and peered down the aisles. Dory was nowhere to be seen. Starting for the door, he heard the sharp tap of footsteps on the floorboards behind him. Turning, he saw Miss Mayweather approaching, a soulless smile fixed on her face and her pale-green eyes pinched with lines that spread across her temples.

"Is there something in particular you are looking for, young man?"

Nate removed his hat. "I thought a friend of mine might be here, but she ain't."

The woman's smile cut dimples into her powdered cheeks. "And who would that be?"

Nate shrugged and looked past her. "I just made a mistake, is all." He poked a thumb over his shoulder. "I better git over to Mr. Davis's hardware store."

From a curtained doorway at the back of the room, Dory appeared wearing a white dress with ruffles at the sleeves. When she caught sight of Nate, she went as still as a statue. Then, like a flower opening, a gentle smile blossomed on her face.

"There she is," Nate mumbled to Miss Mayweather. "Is it aw-right if I talk to 'er?"

The woman glanced at Dory and then gave Nate a different kind of smile that made his face grow warm. "Of course," she said, "and let me know if I can help you find something."

The woman stepped aside, but Nate did not move. "Well, go ahead," she prodded.

Nate walked haltingly down the aisle, watching Mrs. Hildebrand bend at the waist to put her face before Dory's. She appeared to be delivering a lecture, so Nate stopped short of interrupting. Turning to a display table at his right, he found himself standing before an array of stacked white undergarments and tins of bath powder.

"Listen to me, young lady!" Mrs. Hildebrand whispered. "Dory, look at me!"

Nate could not help but glance at mother and daughter. Dory stared back at him with that serene smile still on her face. The mother turned and glared at him.

"Aren't you one of the Champion boys?"

"Yes, ma'am," he said quietly. "I'm Nathan."

"Hey, Nate," Dory said, her voice as relaxed as if they were alone in the room.

Nodding to both, Nate cleared his throat to get some bottom to his voice. "Hey." He raised his hat a few inches, fanned the air with it, and let it hang again beside his leg.

Dory giggled. "Are you buying some bath powder for Peaches?"

Nate looked to his right at the red tins of talc as if they might speak for themselves. "No," was all he could think to say.

"I heard you had a new baby sister," Mrs. Hildebrand said. "Is that her name?"

Nate felt the skin on his forehead tighten. "Ma'am?"

"*Peaches?*"

"Oh...no, ma'am. Peaches is my horse."

"Nate trained her himself," Dory explained. "She's the prettiest horse in the county."

The woman forced a smile. "That's nice," she mumbled. "Are you picking up something for your mother?"

Nate was inclined to correct people when they referred to Mary Champion as his mother, but his daddy said it was disrespectful to label her with "stepmother" when talking to others.

"Can I talk to Dory?" He waved his hat toward the door. "Outside?"

The woman looked like she had swallowed a frog. "What about?"

Nate shrugged and said the first thing that came to mind. "It's just personal, is all."

Mrs. Hildebrand raised her chin and looked down her nose at him. "How old are you?"

"Just turned fourteen, ma'am."

Her eyes turned frosty. "You do know that Dory is only eleven, don't you?"

Dory spun to her mother. "I'm almost twelve, Mother!"

Mrs. Hildebrand crossed her arms over her midsection. "I think that whatever it is he wants to say to you, he can say it in front of me." She turned a defiant face to Nate.

Nate looked down at his scuffed boots and licked his lips. "I guess it ain't all that important," he said and slapped his hat to his head. "Sorry to bother y'all."

Before he had taken two steps, Mrs. Hildebrand stopped him with a high-pitched voice. "Well, now I think I *do* need to hear what it is you want to say to my daughter!"

Dory's face colored as if all her blood had rushed to her head. "*Mo-ther!*" she whispered, pushing the word out like a gust of wind. "I'm going outside to talk to Nate!"

"*Dorothy!*" she commanded, but Dory marched past Nate and down the aisle. "*Dorothy Hildebrand!* You come back here right now, young lady!" The woman propped her fists on her hips, but she seemed to know that she could not hold her daughter with mere words. When the door opened and slammed shut, she shook her head in short, rapid jerks.

"Ma'am," Nate said gently, "you ain't gotta be frettin' none 'bout me. I don't mean no harm to Dory. She done me a good favor once't."

The skin around Mrs. Hildebrand's eyes tightened. "What kind of favor?"

Nate looked down at the floor, hoping she might remove the accusatory glare from her eyes. When he brought his head up, he was disappointed.

"Ma'am, I got four little sisters at home. Naomi Jane is only a little younger than Dory. I look out for 'er, just like a big brother ought to. Makes me do the same for other girls like 'er." He nodded toward the door. "Now do you care if I go out an' talk with 'er?"

She stared past Nate out the front window and

inflated her cheek as she sighed. "Oh, go ahead! She's going to talk to you *somewhere*! It may as well be here where I can see her."

"Yes, ma'am," Nate said. He turned and walked out of the shop.

Chapter Thirteen

With her back to the street, Dory stood on the edge of the boardwalk, where it spanned the gap between the millinery and the funeral home. Stepping down to the ground, she fanned out the back of the white dress and sat, her feet planted together and her hands knotted in her lap as she stared down the alleyway. A price tag hung off the shoulder of the dress she wore.

Nate picked up the auger handle, walked quietly around her, and sat. He leaned the wood shaft against the wall of the funeral home and then removed his hat and set it on the boards between them.

"She thinks Lindy and I are supposed to be like her, wearing fancy clothes and smelling like garden flowers. She won't let us ride a horse, because she thinks it's not ladylike."

Nate stretched out his legs and crossed his boots at the ankles. "Well, I reckon she would'a thrown a fit if she'd seen Lindy in her undergarments out at the round rock."

Dory laughed, but her face hardened again. "Lindy only did that 'cause Billy Hill was there. She gets plain stupid around boys." She shook her head. "She doesn't even *like* Billy!"

Nate studied the toes of his boots and put some thought into what she'd said. But it was a hopeless effort. When it came to girls, there were just too many riddles.

"Henry Kirkpatrick apologized to me," Dory said quietly. "Did you know about that?"

Nate leaned forward and picked up an empty paper tobacco bag lying in the dirt. On the front was a profile of an Indian chief wearing a feathered war bonnet. All of it was painted in red and yellow. He crushed the bag into a tight ball and tossed it deeper into the alley.

"He tol' me he was goin' to, but I weren't sure," Nate replied. "Figured I'd ask you."

"Well, he did, but I'm not sure how serious he was." She squinted down the alley. "Why do you think he called me a *bitch*, Nate?"

Nate shrugged. "It's just a hurtful word, is all."

"I know what it means," she said, "but why is it hurtful? I like dogs. I wish I had one, but Mother won't let me. She says they're more trouble than they're worth."

"Y'all got chickens?" Nate asked.

She turned to him with a curious look and shook her head.

"We got a dog," he went on. He keeps the foxes and weasels out o' the chicken coop. My uncle George give 'im to us, and we named 'im *Checkers*."

She laughed. "How come *Checkers*?"

"It was my brother, William...he came up with the name. He said it was on account o' the dog always seemed to think for a while before he'd make a move."

Dory smiled. Behind them on the boardwalk, several people passed by without speaking, their footwear tapping on the boards as they strolled past.

"So, why's it a hurtful word?" Dory pressed.

Nate shrugged. "I don' rightly know. I just know people mean it in a bad way. One time I heard a pris'ner call my daddy *a son of a bitch*. When I asked Daddy 'bout it, he just said it was the way one man tried to rile up another'n."

Dory looked deep into Nate's eyes. "You made Henry apologize, didn' you?"

Nate studied his boots again. "We had a agreement. He said he would, an' I took 'im at 'is word. But I didn' know for certain till you tol' me just now."

"When he finished apologizing to me," Dory continued, "he asked me if *I* wanted to apologize for Naomi spitting on him."

"What'd you say to that?"

"I told him I couldn't apologize for someone else."

Nate nodded and rubbed his hands together slowly, making a dry, whispery sound. Then he stared into his calloused palms as if searching for a passage in a book.

"Listen, Dory...Lindy, tol' me you thought I'd asked you to go to the October dance."

Dory lowered her eyes to her hands in her lap. "I was just making her jealous."

"Jealous?" Nate said a little too loud. "She ain't got no int'rest in me."

Dory chuckled. "You're a boy, ain't you?"

Nate squinted down the alley and again wondered about the whims of females.

"You don't have to worry, Nate," she whispered. "I don't expect anything."

Nate sat forward and propped his forearms on his thighs. "I prob'ly won't even go."

"I know," she replied. "I might not go either."

Neither spoke as a heavy freight wagon from the quarry rumbled behind them on the street. Nate turned and watched the team of mules pull their load without complaint. The driver held the limp reins in one hand as he pushed a wad of tobacco into his cheek with the other.

"Listen, Dory," he said gently, "I'm sorry if you mistook my meanin' 'bout the dance."

"I didn't," she assured him. "You don't ever have to apologize to me, Nate."

Nate sat as still as a rabbit in the grass. He didn't know if he had been scolded or praised.

Across the thoroughfare behind them, a high, cackling laugh spilled out onto the street. The jangle of spurs and the sharp tap of boot heels on the far boardwalk stopped abruptly.

"Well, look a-here!" rang out a familiar voice. "The little runt what stole my saddlebags!"

When Dory turned to look across the street, Nate closed his eyes and gritted his teeth.

"Do you know him, Nate?"

Nate opened his eyes to the alley, but he did not turn. "'Fraid so."

The ring of spurs came closer until a boot stamped down on the board on which he sat. "Well, now! Last time I seen you, you were whisperin' in the ear of a mule-headed mare out at Snyder's. Now here you are a-courtin' a young filly who don't hardly seem o' age!"

When Nate said nothing, Dixie stepped closer, planted the sole of his boot between Nate's shoulder blades, and pushed hard, causing Nate to lurch forward by bending at the waist. Straightening up slowly, he remained seated, his eyes fixed straight ahead on the alley.

"Dory," Nate said quietly, "you'd better go back inside with your mother."

Dory turned to smile at Dixie. "This must be one o' those son-of-a-bitches we were talking about." She said this in a casual manner, as if she were commenting on the weather.

"Hoo-*whee!*" Dixie howled. "Well, ain't this'n gotta mouth on 'er!"

Dory remained cool and confident. "Nobody asked you to come over here and butt in."

Dixie laughed. "What are you? His mother? Cain't he speak for hisself?"

Nate leaned and whispered to Dory. "Go on inside... please."

Dixie snorted. "You just gonna sit there an' hide behind yore mama's dress, boy?"

Nate gripped the edge of the boards and took in a deep breath. His knuckles stood out like shards of white stone rising beneath his sun-browned skin.

"I want my goddamn saddlebags back, chief!"

Dixie placed his boot in the middle of Nate's back again, but this time Nate spun around so fast that Dory flinched and leaned away. Holding Dixie's right boot against his belly with both hands, Nate drove the saddler backward across the boardwalk, his momentum unstoppable. Hopping on one leg, Dixie twisted at the waist, trying to see behind him. His lone boot pounded on the boards as the spur rang out like a tambourine in the hand of a madman. Dropping from the walkway, he fell hard onto his back in the street, his shiny revolver tumbling from its holster and skittering across the dusty hardpan like a fish out of water. His hat lay upside down on the street next to him, its showy silver band two feet away and shining in the sun like mirrors.

Dixie lay stretched out in the street, his small teeth set in a grimace. He wore the same clothes Nate remembered from Mr. Snyder's paddock. His right arm stretched diagonally across his torso as he cradled his right elbow with his left hand. Across the street, in front of the billiards parlor, a man chortled, his deep guttural voice full of phlegm. He was a stocky man with reddish hair and a bushy mustache, and next to him stood Martin Tisdale.

Still holding his arm, Dixie sat up. "Yo're gonna pay for that, you lil' bast'rd!"

The red-haired man across the street stepped from the shade of the awning, leaned a shoulder into the post, and watched Dixie with interest. Tiz remained in the shadows. Several other men had gathered around them to spectate.

Dixie stood, picked up the nickel-plated revolver, and blew across the gun's cylinder. Nate stepped down into the street to stand between Dixie and Dory.

"You little shit!" Dixie hissed and snugged the gun back into his holster. "Yo're lucky you ain't wearin' a gun, boy!" He shifted his gaze to something behind Nate and broke into a smile. "Well, now!" He laughed. "Look who's all full o' piss and vinegar!"

Nate turned to see Dory wielding the auger handle over one shoulder, both her hands clutched to the shaft, her eyes blazing. "Dory," Nate said, "you got to go inside, do you hear?"

Dory didn't budge.

Unbuckling his cartridge belt, Dixie half turned his head to call behind him. "Bascomb?" When he got no reply, he twisted at the waist and put some iron into his voice. "Bascomb! Hold this for me!" Turning back to stare at Nate, he held out his pistol rig behind him and waited.

The man named Bascom lighted a cigarette, threw the spent lucifer into the street, and shook his head. "This is yore show, Brooks. I ain't got nothin' ta do with it."

Dixie's expression soured. "Tiz? Just hold the damned thing for me, will ya?!"

When Tiz was slow to respond, Dixie wrapped the belt around the holster and flung it underhanded. The belt uncoiled in the air, but Tiz managed to catch it.

Fuming, Dixie strode within a yard of Nate. "Let's see what you got, lover boy!"

As Nate crouched and readied himself, he heard Dory step down into the street behind him. "You're just a show-off with a big mouth! Nate will teach you some manners!"

Dixie scowled at her. "Shut up, you little whore, an' git back!"

Nate took a quick step forward and, putting all his weight into it, hit Dixie squarely on the nose, causing him to stumble backward and sit down in the street next to his hat. With his legs splayed out before him, Dixie steepled his hands over the bridge of his nose as blood dribbled onto his shirtfront.

"You broke my damned nose!" Dixie growled, his voice blurred inside his folded hands.

Nate stood over him. "You cain't talk 'bout her like that," he said in a low hum.

Dixie wiped his shirt sleeve across his mouth and got to his feet. "I'm gonna beat the Jesus outta you for that, you sonova—!"

Nate hit him again, this time connecting with the hard circle of bone around Dixie's left eye. Stumbling backward, Dixie stayed on his feet, but Nate followed and hit him in the other eye. When Dixie covered his face with both arms, Nate crouched and drove his fist up into the soft hollow just beneath the breastbone. A deep, wheezing breath escaped from Dixie's throat.

Still on his feet, Dixie clasped his hands to his bent knees and vomited into the street. Then he sucked in a gasping breath and watched his blood drip into the dirt.

"What's the trouble here?!" The deep voice that drew Nate's attention came from the doorway of the gun shop. Nate turned to see a sheriff's deputy standing on the boardwalk, his big hands closed into blocky fists and his brow pushed low over his eyes.

Chapter Fourteen

With a grunt of impatience, Gil Campo stepped down from the boardwalk onto the street. He was an ox of a man wearing a huge red and black plaid shirt with faded-blue suspenders stretched over his meaty shoulders and heavy torso. His baggy gray trousers were stuffed into his boots, making the material balloon around his lower legs. There was a comical look to the man that was offset by the bright badge on his chest and the gun belt strapped around his wide hips.

Campo walked to Dixie, stopping far enough away to protect his boots from any further digestive eruptions. "You sick or drunk?" he asked without a trace of sympathy.

Dixie remained bent over and raised one arm to swipe a sleeve across his mouth. "Ain't neither!" he growled. He straightened and tried to appear confident, but the effort was a futile one with the blood streaked on his face and the globs of puke clinging to his shirtfront.

Gil Campo puckered his lips. "Then you must'a got kicked by a mule, I'm guessin'?"

Dixie gently probed his nose with his fingers. "That sonovabitch there broke my nose."

When Campo turned, a smile flickered on his broad face, and he winked. "Don't see no sons o' bitches over that way," he said to Dixie. "Might can find a few over this way, though."

Nate glanced at the crowd across the street. The red-haired man was gone. Tiz, too.

"Why're you bleedin' an' pukin' on my street, son?" Campo said to Dixie.

Dixie straightened and widened his shoulders. "First off, I ain't yore son!" He pointed at Nate. "Whyn't you ask this fool why he attacked me!"

Gil pursed his lips. "Ain't no need for that. I know 'im, and he ain't the kind to be attackin' nobody 'less they's a good reason."

"You don' know *me*?" Dixie challenged.

"Yeah," Gil replied, "I know you, but that don't do *you* no good."

The muscles in Dixie's neck stood out like vines on a tree. "*He* attacked *me*!"

Keeping his eyes on Dixie, Gil turned his head slightly and spoke over his shoulder. "You start this ruckus, Nate?"

Nate stood relaxed with his arms hanging down by his sides. "Nos'r."

The deputy raised an eyebrow. "Then who did?" he asked, keeping his eyes on Dixie.

"Yo're lookin' at 'im," Nate replied.

Dixie's face flushed red. "You cain't just take his word over mine! I say *he* started this!"

"That's not the way it happened," Dory said and stepped beside Nate. She pointed at the mouth of the alley. "Nate and I were sitting there, mindin' our own business when he kicked at Nate from behind. Then he called me a *whore!*"

"*Dory!!*" came a strident voice from the millinery door. Mrs. Hildebrand bustled out onto the boardwalk with Miss Mayweather right behind her. "Who called my daughter by that filthy name?!" Her eyes darted back and forth between the three males standing in the street.

Campo plucked deferentially at the brim of his hat. "We'll git this straightened out, ma'am," he said, his voice now courteous and assuring. He took a handful of shirt at the back of Dixie's neck and turned him toward Mrs. Hildebrand. "I'm gone give this here jaybird a chance to 'pologize b'fore this thing gits all complicated an' took b'fore the judge."

Dixie tried to face the deputy, but Campo's grip held him in check. "*Apologize?!*" Dixie laughed and spat into the dirt. "Like *hell* I will!" He pointed at Nate. "That'n there stole my saddlebags right off my horse."

"That right?" the deputy asked with a smile. He turned to Nate. "Whatta you say, Nate?"

"Just that he's got a poor mem'ry. We traded bags. It was his idea."

The deputy nodded. "I'll choose to believe Nate about that. We still got this matter of a apology." He shook Dixie. "This is yore last chance, boy."

"I ain't no *boy* you fat tub o'—"

Campo shook him so hard that Dixie lost his voice. "Let's you an' me walk over to the coun'y offices and see what Sher'ff Peay has to say 'bout yore loose mouth."

Dixie thrust a finger at Nate again. "*He* attacked *me*, goddammit! Look at my face!"

"I'm tryin' not to," Gil replied and looked to Dory. "You say he kicked Nate first?"

Dory pointed again to the alley. "We were sitting right there talking with our backs to the street when this man put his boot right in Nate's back and pushed him hard."

The deputy turned to Nate. "You mind turnin' 'round so I can have a look-see?"

Nate pivoted and waited as the deputy approached his back. He felt the man's thick fingers flatten out the material on his shirt.

"I'd say that *there* is 'bout a perfect boot print." Campo announced. He looked down at Dixie's feet. "Just 'bout matches the size o' yore tiny lil' boot down to the stitchin'."

Campo clamped his big hand on Dixie's upper arm and started him down the street. When Dixie resisted, Gil shook him so hard that Dixie's hair fell over his eyes.

"You'd best simmer down, or I'll drag you by your spurs!"

"Well, at least lemme git my damn hat!" Dixie growled.

The big deputy walked Dixie to the hat and waited for him to fit the silver band to the crown. "Say, Nate, why don't you come by the office once yore bus'ness is all done here? Sher'ff might like to talk to you, too."

"Deputy?" Mrs. Hildebrand called out. "I would like to press charges against that man for insulting my daughter with his crude language."

As a courtesy to the woman, Gil tugged on the brim of his hat again. "Yes, ma'am. I'll pass that on to Sher'ff Peay. We got a ord'nance 'bout that."

Mrs. Hildebrand began pulling on a pair of white cotton gloves as she frowned at Nate. "I don't care for the kind of people with whom you associate, Nathan." Nate started to reply, but she wasn't finished. "*And...*I think you ought to socialize with girls your own age." Turning to her daughter, she made a quick come-hither motion with her fingers. "Come inside, Dorothy!"

"You're not being fair, Mother. Nate was—"

"*Now!*" Mrs. Hildebrand commanded.

Wearing a tired smile, Dory handed the auger handle

to Nate. "I'll explain it to her," she said and walked back into the millinery shop, her mother and Miss Mayberry right behind her.

———

After his visit to the hardware store, Nate loaded the new auger into the wagon and drove to the county offices, where he parked the rig in the shade of the old hickory tree. The leaves had begun to yellow, and a few early nuts lay in the street. He entered the side door he had once used on a regular basis when his daddy was sheriff.

Sheriff Peay sat at his desk scratching a pen across a sheet of dry parchment, the hollow sound like the quick panting of an overtaxed dog. The sheriff was a thick-set man with reddish-brown hair and a solemn, flat face that was mostly beard. His small, unblinking eyes shone with concentration. Even sitting, the man struck a noble pose, as if he were signing his name to a historical document.

The cellblock door was slightly open, and through the crack came the murmur of Gil Campo's voice explaining the rules that every prisoner was expected to follow. It was the same rite he had performed when he had worked for Nate's father.

"Nate, what brings you into town?" Sheriff Peay asked, his eye still on the paper before him. The low, monotonic timbre of his voice always reminded Nate of distant thunder.

Nate walked to the visitor's spot before the desk. "I came in to see 'bout a broke auger."

Sheriff Peay nodded. With a flourish of the pen, he signed his name and looked up.

"How is yore father?"

"Same as always, I reckon. He's just bought s'more cattle from over at Milam Coun'y."

"Buildin' a empire, is he?"

"Yes'r," Nate said. "Me and John Thomas are puttin' up a new fence on the north end."

John Peay had a way of smiling with only his eyes. "Which would account for the broke auger, I'm guessing." The sheriff set the pen in a Mason jar and its half inch of ink-tainted water. After screwing down the lid on the ink bottle, the sheriff laid the parchment aside to dry. In a slow but deliberate movement, he pushed both arms forward in the air to hike his shirtsleeves up his arms, exposing his hairy wrists, each as thick as a wagon tongue. Then he sat back in his chair and threaded his big fingers together over the lower buttons of his vest.

"So, how'd you get tangled up with this Brooks boy?"

"Just by accident," Nate said. "I never knowed him till 'bout a week ago."

"Want to tell me about it?" the sheriff said.

"You mean 'bout today?"

"Start wherever you want to."

Nate recounted his run-in with the three men at the Snyder ranch, omitting only the name of Martin Tisdale from the narrative. When he explained the happenings of the last half hour, he stressed how Dory Hildebrand had been insulted in front of him.

The sheriff nodded and raised his chin to face Nate directly. "Campo says he called the girl a *whore*. That right?"

Nate was grateful that Gil had already supplied the word "whore" to the story, so that he didn't have to say it in front of the sheriff. "Yes'r," Nate whispered.

John Peay glared at the cellblock door as if it had insulted him. "That boy's got a mouth on 'im, aw-right. Don't wanna seem to listen to nobody." He turned back to Nate with a twinkle in one eye. "Guess he prob'ly needed that broke nose. Bet he'll listen to *that*."

Nate frowned. "So, I ain't in no trouble for fightin'?"

The sheriff's chest heaved slightly, and a mild snort of air from his nose rustled the hairs of his mustache. "Not with me, you ain't."

Nate knew exactly what that meant. But he also knew that John Peay would not be the one to relate this story to Nate's father. Nor would Gil Campo. More likely, it would be some citizen who liked to spread such news.

The sheriff crossed his thick arms over his chest. "Well, it's clear to me who started this scuffle. And we got a law about profanity. We go easy on it with the drovers in the saloons, but when one of our higher class of people gits a earful, that's a diff'rent story. Brooks will stand before Judge Hughes and have a choice of jail time or a fine... maybe both."

Gil Campo entered the room and closed the cellblock door with his backside. "That boy musta missed out on manners from his mama. Ask me, he prob'ly needs to have his nose broke purty reg'lar." He frowned at the sheriff. "You want me to fetch a doctor for 'im?"

Sheriff Peay shook his head. "Let 'im bellyache awhile." When he looked back at Nate, he narrowed one eye. "Nate, you oughta think on bein' a dep'ty when you git a little older." He turned to Campo. "Whattaya think, Gil?"

Still standing by the cellblock door, Gil shifted his considerable weight and stuck his thumbs behind his suspenders. "Long as he don't take *my* job."

"How old are you now, Nathan," Peay asked.

"Fourteen."

Peay nodded. "Well, maybe in a coupla years. If I'm still sher'ff, yore chances would be purty good. Prob'ly make yore daddy proud."

Nate glanced down at his boots before answering. "I

plan on raisin' cattle. I reckon my daddy'll be proud o' that, too."

Peay arched an eyebrow. "You like all that work, do you?"

"I like workin' from a horse, but I might hire a man to lay in fencin'." Nate poked a thumb at the front door. "I reckon I oughta git back to that. Can I go now?"

The sheriff nodded. "Have at it, son. Go build that empire!"

Chapter Fifteen

He heard the bawling of the calves before he reached the front gate, and Nate knew that John Thomas and James were probably up to their elbows in blood and testicles. As he pulled the wagon up to the well house, Checkers trotted out from the barn, his tail wagging. Right behind him, John Thomas came out hauling a metal bucket in each hand. He trudged to the pigpen and emptied each bucket over the fence, inspiring a rough chorus of grunts and snorts from the two sows and their shoats.

When John saw Nate, he cleaned his hands on the front of his soiled apron and strolled over to the wagon. There, he laid his hands on top of the sidewall and peered into the bed.

"You git that at Davis's store?" he asked, looking down at the new auger.

Nate climbed down and scratched the dog behind its ears. "Yep."

"How much did that'n cost?"

Nate leaned on the sidewall. "He wanted nine for it. I got it for seven an' four bits."

John Thomas filled his cheeks with air and eased out a long sigh. "Daddy says I gotta pay half." He frowned and shook his head. "Davis wouldn' come down no more'n that?"

"He only come down four bits," Nate explained. "Mr. Cook give me a dollar for the axle."

John's face wrinkled with the calculation. "So I owe Daddy what? 'Bout three dollars?"

"And six bits," Nate finished. He rapped his knuckles against the spiral blade, eliciting a dull ring from the metal. "Mr. Davis said this'n'll last us a while, long as nobody tries to beat it to death with a tampin' rod."

John Thomas lifted his face to the sky and shook his head. "Well, what addle-headed pie-eater would be dumb enough to do that?"

Nate stared at the shining new tool. "They say a auger can bring out the worst in a man."

John Thomas nodded. "I've heard that."

"I'm gonna head out to the northwest corner and try it out," Nate said. "You done here?"

John Thomas's face wilted. "No. Got five more calves. It's goin' slow. James is lettin' me do all the cuttin' while he supervises. Says it's the family tradition."

Nate climbed up into the driver's seat. "Might be." He gave his brother a sympathetic nod. "I reckon William done the same to James."

John Thomas pointed at Nate. "An' one day I'll prob'ly be doin' it to you."

Nate shook his head. "'Xceptin' I won't buy into it, now that I know the game." He gave the Morgan a gentle tap with the reins. "See you at supper."

———

By the time Nate had finished tamping in his first post of the day, he spotted a rider coming in from the east, his ghostly-white quarter horse moving along at an easy walk through the belly-high Indian grass and bluestem. Between the lapels of his dark Prince Albert coat, Jack Champion's dress shirt burned like a white flame in the late afternoon sunlight. His face was dark in shadow from his wide-brimmed hat, but the lower part of his gray-white beard caught the light and identified him as clearly as a fresh brand.

When the father dismounted next to the wagon, Nate had wrestled the new auger a good two feet into the soil for the next hole. Backing off four turns, he pulled the blade free from the hole and prised away the curled chunks of mud with his gloved hands.

"How's she workin'?" his father asked in his soft Carolina voice.

"Works good," Nate said.

The man watched his son pour water into the hole, set the auger back in place, and muscle the handle through a few revolutions. "How much?"

Nate jerked the blade free, cleaned it, and set up again for the last half foot. "Came to seven dollars an' fifty cents."

The father took a grip on one end of the handle. Nate moved to the other end, and the two of them began working as a team. It was the first time in a year that Nate had seen his daddy engage in manual labor.

"Somebody set the cotton mill ablaze two nights ago up at Geo'getown," the father said. "With evah'body at the mill helpin' out, some rowdies cut out about thuh'ty head o' cattle from the Slash Nine. They drove 'em into the San Gabriel Riv'ah to cov'ah the tracks."

They turned the auger another half revolution before

Nate responded. "Anybody find where the cattle climbed outta the river?"

"Not yet, but they will. Been no rain up that way and they'ah ain't none 'xpected."

They pushed the handle through another full turn and reached the bright mark that Nate had scratched onto the axle with the blunt side of his knife blade. Nate watched his father straighten and gaze down the long line of fenceposts to the east.

"Word is...somebody saw the Tisdale boy up that way. He was with a rough-lookin' crowd that was aw-ready suspected o' rustlin' in Lampasas Coun'y. Seven of 'em makin' camp by the ri'vah the night befo'ah the mill burned."

"You mean *Martin?*" Nate asked.

Jack Champion did not bother to answer the obvious. Together, they pulled on the auger and dislodged it. Nate cleaned off the blade, adding the chunks of dirt to the fill pile.

"Are they certain it was him?" Nate said as he walked toward the wagon. "Wouldn' it be better to give 'im the benefit of the doubt? That's what you always tol' me."

Nate's daddy picked up the tamping rod and waited for his son to carry a new post from the pile stacked inside the wagon. After Nate dropped the post into the hole, he looked up to see his father staring at him, both hands gripping the rod. He looked like a messenger from God come to announce the advent of Judgment Day.

"Son, when yo'ah doubts about a man start pilin' up on a reg'lah basis, you need to take that into consideration."

Nate eyeballed the post for verticality, and then, as his father held it steady, he scooped dirt from the fill pile and stuffed it into the hole. When he began tamping with the rod, his father poured in a little water from the bucket.

"Martin has always been right considerate o' me," Nate said.

His father's expression remained stoic. "Bett'ah to know a thing than to not know it."

They worked in silence for a time, the father adding soil and Nate packing dirt with the rod. The sounds of the wind and the creek surrounded them like whispers from the prairie.

"Daddy, you 'member Dixie Brooks?"

Jack Champion nodded. "Knew his daddy when I was she'iff. Got drunk purt' near ev'ry Sa'rday, and spent the night in lock-up. He was a mean drunk. Always felt sorry for his boy."

"I had a little run-in with him today," Nate said.

The father looked up. "How's that?"

Nate leaned on the tamping rod. "He pushed a fight on me in town."

The old man sat down in the grass. "Bett'ah tell me 'bout it, son."

They sat facing one another with the clean smell of the freshly dug earth surrounding them. Nate told it from the beginning, starting with the incident at the Snyder ranch, following that with the insults spoken to Dory and the scuffle that followed on the main street in Round Rock.

The elder Champion was difficult to read, but when he snapped off a piece of buffalo grass and began chewing its stem, Nate knew that he had handled himself in a satisfactory way.

"I've always taught you to back away from trouble when you can, but sometimes trouble gets right in yo'ah face an' you have to deal with it. I reckon I'd'a done much the same as you, Nathan, but I fret about you settin' up a grudge with a man who ain't rational."

"I wouldn' say he's a man, Daddy."

Jack Champion plucked another grass stem. "Well, son, a gun don't know if it's in the hand of a man or a boy a-holdin' it. It'll kill eith-ah way."

They stared off at the hills on the southern horizon. The wind surged and moved across the land from west to east, pushing a broad, rippling wave of grass over the acres of meadowland stretching to the south. The reddening sun lent a fiery tint to the scene, like the uneven advance of a bright burn line smoldering across a piece of paper.

"What you need to think about, son, is that a aimless boy like Brooks don't know how to be a man 'xcept by usin' his gun. Now that you've put a dent in his pride, he's got no oth'ah way to prove himself but to go at you. I've seen too many like 'im. You cain't ignore this. He'll come at you again, and it'll be so the odds are with him."

Nate looked into his father's eyes. "Are you sayin' I oughta carry a gun, Daddy?"

Jack Champion closed his eyes and shook his head. "Lawd, but yo'ah sweet mama would shed te'ahs in her grave if I was to put a pistol into yo'ah hand." Opening his eyes, he allowed a mix of worry and sadness to show in his face. "You take aft'ah her, you know. You got that same gentleness about you, Nathan."

Nate propped his forearms on his knees and let his hands hang limp from the wrists. Staring down at the grass between his boots, he cleared his throat and tried to get his voice deep and confident...the way his brother William had spoken to their daddy.

"If yo're thinkin' I cain't handle people who—"

"No, son!" his father interrupted. "That ain't what I'm sayin' a-tall." He surprised Nate with a single airy laugh. "I know yo'ah tough as nails. I ain't worried the least bit about that. I just don't want you hurt...either by receivin' a bullet or by deliverin' one. Just ain't no call for somebody as young as you havin' to live with that. Or die with it."

Nate softened his voice. "D'you ever have to kill a man, Daddy? Since the war, I mean?"

The ex-sheriff turned his gaze to the hills. "No," he said flatly. "And that's somethin' I'm proud of." With his eyes hardened like glass, he looked at Nate. "Don't let this boy su'prise you."

Nate looked his daddy in the eye. "I'll be careful, but I don't reckon I can avoid 'im forever."

Jack Champion pulled the grass stem from his mouth and tossed it aside. "I think I might have an idea...somethin' that can nip this in the bud befo'ah it gets outta hand."

Chapter Sixteen

On Sunday, when the Champion family of twelve returned from church, Dixie Brooks was sitting alone on the edge of the front porch, carving a barkless stick with a folding knife. Ten feet away, Checkers sat unmoving, ears erect, his eyes fixed on the visitor. The dog turned briefly to the sound of the horses and wagon but then resumed his stoic vigil as if he were guarding a prisoner.

Wood slivers lay scattered in the dirt in a wide crescent before Dixie's boots, suggesting he had spent the better part of the morning here. He never once looked up at the approaching party, even as the family entered the yard. Keeping his head down, he continued shaving the stick, each stroke with the knife sending a sliver of wood arcing to the ground. His silver hat band shone like a small chain of polished coins.

As James and John Thomas unhitched the horses from the wagon, Nate and Dudley led the saddle horses into the barn, where they began brushing the animals dry. The other children ran to the house, hurrying past Dixie as if he weren't there. Nate's stepmother carried young Corelia inside, and behind her, Jack Champion walked hand in hand with two-year-old Calvin. The father and young son hesitated on the porch and watched the visitor for a time, but Dixie refused to look up. Jack and Calvin turned and went inside. The door closed, and Dixie continued to carve, the flakes of wood flying faster now.

A full minute passed. Through the barn's doorway, Nate watched Dixie drop the stick and close the blade on his knife. For another minute, he sat staring at the ground. Then he stood and ambled toward the barn, his spurs making a quiet *ching* with each measured step. Nate moved deeper into the breezeway to lead Peaches into her stall.

"Who is that fella?" Dudley said. "Looks like he's headed our way." Dud set down his brush. "I'll go out an' see what he wants."

Nate touched his brother's arm and stopped him. "It's me he's lookin' for," Nate said quietly. "I'll go."

The first thing that Nate noticed about Dixie was the pistol holstered on his hip. It was not the nickel-plated model with its ivory grips but an old model Navy Colt's dulled to a bronze gray with wooden scales on the handle. When he saw Nate approach, Dixie stopped halfway across the yard, leaned to one side, and spat. Gazing out the front gate, he flexed the tendons in his jaw.

"Sher'ff says I gotta come out here and talk to your old man b'fore I can claim my horse and guns and be shut o' this coun'y!" He ran the words together in a surly monotone.

Nate looked around the yard and frowned. "How'd you git out here?"

"How d'you think I got here? I walked! Now go git yore daddy, boy!"

Nate nodded toward the house. "You'll need to do that yoreself. Go knock on the door."

135

Dixie took a deep breath and expelled it in a rush. With a loud *ca-ching* from his spur, he kicked up dust with his boot heel and started back across the yard, his spurs ringing with each stride. Checkers stayed with him and then sat in the dirt when Dixie climbed the front steps to the house.

"I wouldn' wear that pistol, I was you," Nate called out to his back.

Stopping on the porch, Dixie propped his hands on his hips and let his head sag forward as if studying the toes of his boots. With a quick jerk, he loosened his cartridge belt and hung the rig over the back of a chair. Then he removed his showy hat and hung it over the butt of the gun.

Looking as vulnerable as a schoolboy summoned by his teacher, he stood before the door and cleared his throat twice. Then he knocked quietly three times.

When the door opened, Nate saw Naomi Jane look up at the visitor and wait for him to explain his presence. Nate could not hear the words, but within seconds his father appeared behind Naomi. Dixie straightened, shifted his weight from leg to leg, and delivered a greeting of some kind. Then the door opened wider, and Dixie entered. When the door closed, Checkers slunk under the porch and took up his regular station to watch over the yard.

"What's he doin' here?" Dudley asked, over his horse's back.

Nate picked up his brush. "Guess he *wasn't* lookin' for me."

John Thomas and James pulled the wagon to the rear of the breezeway and began distributing hay to the stalls. "I've seen that jackass in town," James announced to his brothers. "He'd rather find trouble than a shiny new dollar."

"That's the Brooks boy," John Thomas said. "You boys oughta steer clear o' him."

James snorted a laugh. "Yeah, he's a *Brooks*, but d'you know what he calls himself now?" He laughed again and answered his own question. "*The Texas Kid.*"

John Thomas cackled. "For real? What is he s'posed to be? Some kinda famous outlaw or somethin'?"

"What's he want with Daddy?" Dudley asked.

When no one volunteered an answer, Dudley stared at Nate.

Nate shrugged. "I ain't all that sure, but it's connected to me. Of that, I am sure."

John Thomas piped up. "Nate had a run-in with 'im in town. Put the hurt to ol' Dixie. Embarrassed the hell out of 'im. That about right, Nate?"

Before Nate could respond, the front door to the house opened and then closed. Dixie stuffed his hat on his head, strapped on his gun belt, and scuffed down the steps, the loose ringing of his spurs bringing Checkers out into the yard again. Nate set down his brush and moved to the open doorway to watch Dixie walk a straight line toward the front gate.

"You need a ride back into town?" Nate asked.

Dixie was quick to answer. "Hell, no! I don't need nothin' from you!"

Nate forked his hands over his hips and narrowed his eyes. "Yo're walkin'?"

"I walked out here, didn' I?!" Dixie snapped.

Nate watched him march out of the yard, through the gate, and onto the road that led to town. Not once did Dixie look back.

When their work with the horses was finished, the four Champion brothers started for the house together. Halfway across the yard, Nate veered to the west side of the house.

137

"Hey, Nate, ain't you comin' to dinner now?" Dudley called out.

Nate spoke over his shoulder. "Headin' for the privy. Be there in a coupla minutes."

When he came out of the outhouse, Nate saw his father standing on the back porch gazing at the cattle in the east meadow. He still wore his Sunday clothes, only now the top button of his collar was open, and the simple string tie was gone.

Nate stopped just shy of the porch and waited for his father to speak. When Naomi opened the backdoor, the elder Champion turned and waved her back inside. Only when the door closed did the old man begin.

"The Brooks boy will be leaving Williamson Coun'y in a couple o' days. Until he does, I want you to stay away from him, undahstood?"

"Where's he goin'?"

The father sniffed and fixed his gaze on the horizon. "He's got a job up in Denton Coun'y."

"Doin' what?"

"Oh," Jack Champion began, "usual kind o' ranch work...just like we do he'ah."

Nate tilted his head. "This your idea?"

The old man nodded. "Rememb'ah Dad Eagan? Sheriff up in Denton?"

"Nos'r."

"Well, it was a while back," his father explained. "He visited once an' took you on his knee and tried to teach you the fin'ah points o' bronc ridin'. Said you were a natu'al...be a champion one day." Jack Champion smiled. "You tol' him you aw-ready were a Champion! Anyway, he's hirin'. He needs men to run his ranch while he's pullin' sheriff's duties."

"Dixie signed on for that?" Nate said with a laugh.

His father's eyes scanned the hills again. "Sheriff Peay helped 'im a little with the decision."

"D'you really think he'll go?"

Jack grunted a laugh deep in his chest. "He'll go. Peay give 'im two days."

Nate narrowed his eyes. "Is this all on the up and up with the law?"

The ex-sheriff gave Nate a sober look. "If yo'ah lyin' dead out in the brush b'cause I waited to keep things legal, how could I live with that?"

Nate made no reply. They stood for a time looking out on the south pasture. A sparrow carried a few strands of dead grass in its beak and flew under the eave of the outhouse roof with an audible flutter of its wings. Within a minute, another bird arrived with a similar load. Without another word, the old man turned and went into the house, his back as straight as a fencepost. After a few seconds, Nate followed.

With everyone seated at the table, the room sounded like a yard full of chickens clucking. The father tapped a spoon to his coffee cup. At this signal, all heads bowed for the blessing.

"Lord, give us strength to look after one another. And each to look out for himself."

"And *herself*," Naomi added. "Amen."

Everyone laughed and soon the sounds of family chatter and the *clink* of serving spoons on porcelain took over the room. Nate pushed Dixie Brooks—*The Texas Kid* —to the back of his mind...but not out of it.

Chapter Seventeen

I t took three more weeks of planting fenceposts before Nate and John Thomas set a double-braced corner post at the northwest point of the Champion property. Now they started a line due south that ran away from the creek. The cottonwoods had yellowed, sending showers of pale fluttering leaves all around them each time the wind gusted. The late afternoon was pleasantly cool.

As Nate tamped dirt around a post, John Thomas started for the wagon with the auger. "That's all we're slavin' today," he proclaimed. "I got to git cleaned up for the dance."

Nate checked the sun. "Daddy know we're knockin' off early?"

John returned, snatched the tamping rod from Nate's hands, and marched back to the wagon, where he tossed the rod into the bed with the auger, making a racket on the sideboards. "He will when we git home," he replied with uncommon bravado. He latched the tailgate and climbed up into the driver's box. "Come on! Let's go!"

They bounced along the trackless prairie toward home, neither trying to speak above the buckboard's complaints. When they gained the road, John sent a ripple through the reins to speed up old Rube. Soon, he was trying to coax a whistling melody from puckered lips that had never produced a clear note. It was something John Thomas did, Nate knew, when he was nervous.

"Does Daddy even know yo're goin' to the dance?" Nate asked.

"No," John said defensively, "but I reckon he'll have to let me go when he finds out I'm takin' Sarah Netherlin. She's expectin' me to call on 'er at the hotel at seven."

Nate looked out at the bands of orange and pink in the eastern sky. "I hope yo're right."

John Thomas frowned. "Well, if he says I cain't go, I'll just go anyway an' deal with the punishment later. But I'm damned if I'll miss out on this chance with Sarah. B'sides, I spent a dollar on a corsage."

Nate turned quickly. "What's a *core-sarge?*"

John shook his head. "Some flowery thing doused in perfume."

Nate squinted. "Whatta you do with it?"

"You wear it!" John snapped. He patted his chest. "Right here."

"Why would you wont to?"

John turned to Nate and laughed. "It ain't for me! It's for Sarah!" He studied the road ahead again. "It's just one o' those things women expect, I guess."

Nate thought about that. "You reckon she'd go if you didn' bring 'er one?"

John's face closed down with that possibility. "I don' know! Hell, I guess! I mean, she'd be all dressed for it! An' she sure as hell wouldn' have no problem findin' partners for dancin'." He gave the reins a snap. "Come on, Rube! You can go faster'n that!"

When the Morgan did not heed the command, John Thomas whipped the reins with more authority. The old horse showed a little spark of indignation and snorted. When John started to send another whiplash through the ribbons, Nate put his hand on his brother's wrist.

"Go easy," Nate whispered. "We're almost there."

As they entered the gate, Checkers trotted across the yard to greet them, his tail wagging like a flagman for the railroad. As they gained the barn, John Thomas leaned to inspect the stalls.

"D'you see Daddy's horse in there?"

Nate turned to look. "Nope." Taking the reins from his brother's hands, Nate pulled the wagon to a halt. "Go on an' git ready. I'll take care o' Rube."

John jumped down and turned to Nate. "I wanna hitch up my sorrel to the wagon."

Nate threw a two-fingered salute from the brim of his hat. "I'll take care of it."

John squeezed Nate's ankle through the leather of his boot. "Thank you, brother!" Then he hurried to the house with Checkers leaping beside him like they were starting a game.

———

By the time John Thomas had rattled off down the road, Nate had finished brushing down Rube, filling the water troughs and doling out grain and hay to all the horses. Checkers had watched his every move. When Nate walked to the house, Checkers took up his sentry post under the porch.

As soon as he entered the front room, Nate heard his stepmother talking to Naomi in the kitchen. The conversation was about the baby's food preparation, and Naomi was complaining about having to take on the job. Tiptoeing through the house, he retreated to the room he shared with James, John Thomas, and Dudley. A strong, flowery scent filled Nate's nostrils. Looking around for the source of the unexpected aroma, he fixed his gaze on a white cloth bag hanging from the head post of John's bed. When Nate opened the drawstring, the cloying sweetness rose up to him like a fanfare of femininity.

He lifted out a light cardboard box small enough to hold a wren's nest. Opening the lid, he found a multicolored collection of ruffled satin fabrics sewn together and nestling a cluster of creamy white roses.

Carrying the open box into the kitchen, Nate came up on his stepmother's back as she pressed the heels of her hands into a roll of dough on the cutting board. Naomi stood on a stool next to her and worked a smaller wad on the countertop where flour was sprinkled all around her work area. Mary Champion instructed her in a low murmur as her shoulders heaved with the kneading.

"Ma'am?" Nate interrupted. Both females turned to his voice, their powdered hands held before them as if each them were holding an invisible object. "John Thomas took off for the dance in town. He took the wagon."

"I didn't know he was going," Mary said and frowned at the box. "What is this?"

"I reckon it's the cor-sarge he bought for Sarah," Nate ventured.

Naomi giggled. "It's not a *cor-sarge*, Nate. It's a *corsage*! Cain't you smell it?"

"'Course I can," Nate said. "Just 'cause I cain't say it don't mean I cain't smell it."

The skin on Mary's forehead tightened and creased with lines. "Who in heaven's name is Sarah?"

"She works at the Round Rock Hotel," Nate explained. "She ain't from 'round here."

Naomi snickered. "She's a *maid*," she said, pronouncing the word in a nasal drawl. "Cleans up after people. Sweeps the floors. Washes the sheets for people she don't even know."

Mary turned sharply to face her stepdaughter. "There's nothing wrong with keeping a place clean, Naomi Jane. Anyone who criticizes a young lady for holding down a decent job *might* be someone who has had everything handed to her on a silver platter."

Naomi pouted. "She's still a maid."

Mary's eyes caught fire and fixed on Naomi. She was only a decade older than her stepdaughter, but those ten years showed in her face like a roadmap of hard work.

"Naomi Jane, once we finish with this dough, do you know what you'll be doing?"

Naomi appeared unsure of her answer. "Bakin' the biscuits?"

"No," Mary said with a smile that contained no warmth. "The stove will do that. You'll be wiping up that mess on the counter, sweeping the floor, and washing the mixing bowl and spoons. And Ben's bed needs fresh sheets. All this before we eat."

Naomi had stopped breathing. "How'm I gonna do all that before supper?"

"Well, we could just call it *one* thing," Mary said. "*Being a maid.*"

Naomi swung around and let her anger pour out as she wrestled the dough.

"Is it aw-right if I fetch this to 'im?" Nate asked, holding up the flowery arrangement. "He'll be mighty disappointed when he figures out he left it behind."

Mary considered the box again. "I'll keep some supper warm for you, Nathan. Be sure to take your warm coat. It might turn cold time you ride back."

———

Peaches was high-spirited, seeming to draw energy from the crisp autumn air. Her hooves touched down so lightly on the dusty road, the sound seeming to be muted by the darkness. After clattering over the bridge into town, Nate turned off the main road and approached the hotel from the rear, where a Black man sat on the back stoop with a plate of food balanced on his thighs. He wore a white shirt with the sleeves rolled up, and beneath the cuffs of his trousers, his dusky ankles showed above a pair of battered, brown, button-up shoes. A gray coat lay neatly folded beside him.

"Howdy, Mistah Nate," the man called out. He pushed a piece of bread around the plate, sopping up the juices of his meal. Then he rushed it into his mouth as if there might be a chance that someone would deny him the pleasure.

"Hey, Mr. Jabby," Nate replied. "Still workin' for Mr. Kirkpatrick, I see."

"You knows you ain't got to call me dat," he complained, his voice lacking the usual whine of deference he practiced with other white folks.

Nate smiled. "Long as you call me *Mr. Nate*, I'm gonna call you *Mr. Jabby*."

Jabby picked up a leg of chicken, bared his big piano-key teeth, and tore off most of the meat in one bite. "What you doin' in town dis late?" he asked around a mouthful.

"Looking for my brother...John Thomas." Nate pointed to the hotel. "He's takin' Sarah to the dance. Have you seen 'im tonight?"

Jabby nodded deeply. "He take Miss Sarah in da wagon. Dey gone now."

"Well," Nate said, "reckon I'll head for the Masons' Hall an' find 'im there."

Jabby smiled as he chewed. "You find 'em easy. Miss Sarah got on dis purty yella dress. Mmmm-mm. Glow like

145

a sunflow'r." He pointed the bone at Nate. "You gone dance, too?"

Nate laughed. "I'd have to be pretty danged mad at a girl to dance with 'er."

Jabby frowned. "Nahhh! You be s'prised. Dancin' ain't so hard. You just let the music git inside you so's you can feel it, den yo're feet, dey knows what to do."

Nate nodded at the man. "Yo're a purty good dancer, are ya?"

Jabby waggled his head from side to side. "Ain't too bad. I tell you how you learn."

Nate stacked both hands on the pommel of his saddle. "Yeah? How's that?"

"Well, you gots to find a girl willin' to put on two pair o' boots. Dat's all."

Nate laughed. "That how you learned?"

"Oh...nos'r. *We* all learn with no shoes on. Dat way, nobody git hurt."

Nate smiled and nodded. "Smart."

"What dat smell, Mistah Nate? Dat you or Peaches smellin' like a rose?"

Nate patted his saddlebag. "Somethin' my brother forgot. He bought it for Sarah."

Jabby set his plate next to him on the stoop. "Dat remind me. I gots me somethin' to give to you." From the folded coat next to him, he produced several coins and held one out to Nate. "Dis for dat time you he'ped my boy, Eli, when Mistah Kirkpat's wagon broke down."

Nate shook his head. "Weren't no money involved in that."

"Yas'r, I b'lieve dey was. When y'all rig up a lever to jack dat wagon up, you brokes a sledge handle as I recall. Dat's da way Eli tell it."

Nate shrugged. "Things like that happen. I carved a new one from a broke plow handle."

"Yas'r," Jabby said, nodding. He continued to hold out the coin, showing Nate he no longer held claim to it. "But I reckon dat took you some time. An' you saved my boy a dressin' down from Mistah Kirkpat."

Not wanting to insult the man, Nate leaned and let Jabby press the coin into his palm.

"Now you go on an' find yo' bruddah. Just look for dat yella dress. You'll see."

Nate held back a smile "Yo're sayin' John Thomas is wearin' a yellow dress, too?"

Laughing, Jabby waved a farewell, and Nate started Peaches back toward Main Street.

Chapter Eighteen

Lining the sides of Mays Street were buckboards, high-wheeled buggies, spring wagons, and saddle horses that choked the thoroughfare down to half its regular breadth. On the boardwalks, the foot traffic flowed only one way. Everyone was heading toward the Masonic Hall.

Nate heard the music from two blocks away, a driving momentum of scratchy fiddles, strumming guitars, jaunty fingers on a piano, and the rapid-fire plucking of a banjo. Beneath all this came the heavy thunder of boots stomping on the Masons' hardwood floor.

When Nate reached the front of the building, the music surged from the dance room like an unleashed river crashing into the street. Spreading columns of yellow light spilled out of the four glass doors and stretched across the street. A crowd of forty to fifty people slowly funneled through the only open entranceway, where several women were stationed at a table to collect dance fees.

Nate spotted the Champion wagon in an alleyway. It had the appearance of a ragtag orphan, lost and out of place at this social event. Dismounting in the alley, he tied

Peaches's reins to a rear wheel rim and dug the box from the saddlebag.

After waiting his turn in line, Nate found himself facing Miss Mayweather at the pay station. The table was festooned in colorful ribbons and glittery decorations of silver and gold. Before Miss Mayweather was an open metal box filled with coins and dollar bills. Nate removed his hat and held it against his chest as he stepped to the edge of the table.

"That'll be ten cents," she said, her voice straining to speak over the noise blaring from the dance hall. "All proceeds go to the new schoolhouse. Any additional contributions will be gratefully received." She recited this in a dispassionate monotone and with a perfunctory smile.

"Ma'am, I didn' come to dance," Nate said louder than he had wanted to speak. "I just need to git this to my brother." He raised the cardboard box, hoping that the fumes radiating from it might be explanation enough.

The smile on her face hardened, and she looked to her right, where Mrs. Hildebrand was busy talking with a woman who leaned over the table to show off her earrings. Next to Mrs. Hildebrand stood Dory in a white dress with a blue lace collar. Her long blonde hair was pinned up on top of her head and woven with a white ribbon, all of which made her neck appear to be long and sleek like that of a fawn's. Dory pressed a small block of wood into an ink pad and then stamped the wrist of a man who offered his arm.

"Everyone has to pay," Miss Mayweather informed him. "Even if you don't dance."

"Yes'm," he replied and pulled out the coin that Jabby had given him.

Miss Mayweather made change for him and waved Nate down the table. "Dory will stamp you. That way, you can go out and come in all you want."

Mrs. Hildebrand put on a pained expression that etched a sunburst of lines at each corner of her mouth. Nate nodded to her as he passed by, but the woman just stared at him.

"Hey, Nate," Dory said, her smile moving up into her big brown eyes. Before he could speak, she took his hand, palm up, and pushed up his coat sleeve to expose part of his forearm. After pressing the wooden block into a black pad, she branded him with an ink mark and pulled Nate to the doorway, where Alice Kirkpatrick, Henry's little sister, checked the wrists of all who entered. Dory handed her the ink block with instructions to take over the stamping of arms.

Nate held up the perfumed box. "Dory, I just need to git this to my brother."

She snatched his hat from his hand and hung it on a wall peg. "Give me your jacket, too."

As he surrendered the coat, he looked out at the dancers. The great room was like a river in turmoil, churning and spinning in a foaming eddy full of familiar faces, people cutting loose on the dance floor in ways he had never before seen them move. John Thomas was nowhere to be seen, so he looked for a yellow dress.

"You know you have to dance with me just once," Dory whispered. "You promised!"

He bobbed the box up and down. "Can I git this to John Thomas first?"

Taking his hand, she led the way through the moving maze of bodies. Nate felt as if he had wandered into a foreign territory that used a language unknown to him. The band occupied the small stage at the back of the room. Standing in front, a caller with a megaphone delivered coded instructions to the crowd at regular intervals. All the dancers seemed somehow bound together by the steady pulse of instruments and the guidance of the caller. It seemed as if the music had unlocked the rites of a secret ceremony to which all had been privy long before this night. All except Nate.

"He's with Sarah Netherlin," Nate called to Dory. "She's in a yellow dress."

Dory pointed across the room. "That's Sarah right there!"

At the fringe of the mass of bodies, Nate saw a yellow dress twirling, spreading at the hem into a tipi shape. Nate recognized Sarah even before he realized he was looking at his brother partnered with her. Never before had he seen such an expression on John Thomas's face. John went through the dance gyrations so effortlessly, it was, for Nate, like watching a stranger who bore a strong resemblance to his brother.

When the music ended, the dancers stood in place and applauded. Most remained on the floor, as if eager for their next opportunity to dance, but John Thomas led Sarah toward the front of the room where several long tables were lined up end to end and covered with green tablecloths. Four large glass bowls of pink-red punch were spaced out on the tables, each holding a long-handled ladle for pouring. Platters of baked goods—cookies, cakes, and squares of shortbread—filled the spaces in between. Bunched together in the center was an arsenal of mismatched cups, mugs, glasses, and saucers. Mrs. Boyce, the wife of Nate's schoolteacher, stood behind a side table and collected money.

"I'll be back in a minute," Nate said, holding out one palm so she would remain there.

When Nate came up on John Thomas's back, Sarah was already smiling at Nate. John turned with a look of curiosity, which instantly gave way to a smile.

"What're you doin' here?" John said. As though to

verify Nate's presence, he reached out with one hand and squeezed Nate's upper arm.

Nate raised the box, and as he did, the smile on John's face widened, and his eyes shone with gratitude. Taking the box, John turned to Sarah and pulled Nate beside him.

"Look what Nate brought!"

Sarah smiled as she took the box. When she opened it, Nate was afraid she might cry.

"It's real nice," she whispered and handed it to John. "Will you pin it on?"

John's face collapsed into near horror. "It's for *you* to wear! Not *me*!"

She smiled sweetly. "I'm asking you to pin it on me. But don't poke me, okay?"

She took his hands and guided him through the process. When it was done, the corsage stood out on her yellow dress like a giant butterfly that had mistaken her for a flower. Nate wondered how she could breathe with all that fragrance so close to her face. And poor John Thomas. Now, he would suffer the smell, too, as they danced.

Sarah kissed John Thomas's cheek. "Thank you."

John's face flushed with color, making the whites of his eyes appear brighter. His mouth hung open without any hope of issuing a single word. Surprising Nate, John wrapped his arm around his brother's shoulders.

"I ain't likely to ever forget this, brother. Thank you."

Nate winced. "I ain't so sure you'll be thankin' me later. When you dance with 'er up close, yore nose is gonna be in the rose garden."

John Thomas smiled. "An' that'll be just fine with me!"

The musicians started up a slow ballad, with the raw wail of a harmonica establishing a melody. Nate watched Sarah pull John Thomas back onto the dance floor, where she spun to him and raised his left arm with her right. His other hand cupped her ribs, and together, they were swept away by the same invisible force that had put everyone else into motion.

As Nate watched, a small hand slipped into his and tugged him toward the swirling bodies. His first instinct was to resist, but when Dory looked back at him, he felt his willpower dissolve. She had let down her hair so that it fell around her shoulders. As she began to move her head with the rhythm of the music, her hair swayed from side to side and brushed her back.

"I don't know how to do this, Dory."

She stopped and turned to him, her expression confident and full of goodwill. "I'll show you. It's a waltz. It's just three steps over and over." She raised his right arm just as Sarah had done with John. Then she took his other hand and guided it to her back. All the while, the other dancers moved around them with the ease of cattle parting around a boulder.

"I'll mess up an' embarrass you," he whispered with some urgency. His eyes stayed on the vortex of bodies spinning around them, and he felt some measure of fear that he had never before experienced.

Dory laughed quietly. "You could never embarrass me, Nate."

"Well, what 'bout yore mama? I ain't s'posed to be with you. I promised her."

"Hush!" Dory whispered. "You promised this to me long b'fore you promised her."

She was already stepping to the music, and he shuffled his feet like a drunkard to keep up. "Dory, I'm tellin' I don't how to—"

When another dancing couple threatened to crash right into them, Nate had no choice but to sideslip with Dory to get out of their way. She used this momentum to keep him turning and flowing with the current of bodies.

His feet moved with hers, sometimes taking two steps to her one. Twice, he came close to getting tangled up in her small feet, but she seemed to know how to untie a knot even before it tightened.

"You count it in threes," she whispered and began to exaggerate her rhythm, accenting a dipping motion every third step. "*One*, two, three...*one*, two, three—"

He followed her moves, and his feet began to find the pattern. After a few revolutions he no longer had to watch his own boots to make sure they didn't trespass on Dory's shiny shoes, and this freed him up to look at Dory.

She appeared so comfortable inside all this movement. For her, the dancing was uncomplicated. As he studied her large brown eyes looking back at him, he sensed that she was enjoying this not only for herself...but also for him. At a certain angle in their turning, the lamplight reflected amber off her eyes.

Something indefinable flickered between them. Nate felt it in his gut. If there had been no music and footfall at that moment, Nate suspected there might have been a little crackling sound in the air. Like a spark jumping out of a wood stove. They both smiled at the same time, and Nate felt a gentle warmth spread throughout his body.

The harmonica player loosened up his melody, so that it was more difficult to follow the beat. But Nate kept up the rhythm with Dory. They were like a team. Two captains of the same ship, both turning and turning to keep themselves buoyant in the great roiling sea.

A flash of yellow drifted close, and Nate turned to see Sarah and John Thomas beside him, carried along inside the same current that had taken control of the room. John smiled at him, not like a big brother amused at his inexperience, but more like a fellow explorer who has bonded with him simply by their venturing into the same unknown.

Nate had walked this floor many times. There had been town meetings, auctions, Christmas celebrations, and school performances here. There had even been dances, but always, Nate had sat on the sides and watched from a distance as people he had known all his life revealed secret sides of themselves.

Now Nate was a part of it, moving across the floor with surprising efficiency, as he matched Dory's steps, stride for stride. When she leaned away and he reciprocated, only their firm grip on one another kept them upright. They shared an unspoken alliance. It was the first time he had felt an unimpeachable trust with someone outside of his family. This made the bond unique. And private. His very own. It expanded his sense of who he was. And somehow, Dory was a part of that new definition.

When the music came to an end, it was like waking from a dream—one that had suspended time. Now the clocks of the world resumed ticking. The crowd of dancers became a mob of clapping spectators, and the room filled with their chattering.

Nate and Dory remained in place, staring at one another like two people standing on opposite sides of a river with a noisy shoal between them. Then, the fiddle player spoke up loudly and announced something to the room, but Nate did not hear it. If Dory heard it, she did not acknowledge it. Nate cleared his throat and leaned toward her.

"Reckon I'd better git back home," he said.

Dory's smile surprised him. "I know," she said. "Thank you, Nate."

Nate looked around the room and then met her eyes again. "It's me oughta be thankin' you."

She tilted her head so that her long hair hung mostly

on one side. "It doesn't matter who says it. It goes both ways now without either of us having to speak at all."

He studied her face more closely, trying to see what might have changed since the last time he'd seen her, for she did look different. Older, perhaps. Certainly, more beautiful. But it was more than that. His aunt Hattie had once told him that as you get to know people better, you learn about what's inside them, and as you do, that inside part comes right out to the surface. It changes their outward appearance. A kind woman with a plain face can become quite attractive. A selfish man known for his good looks can turn repulsive to the eye.

"All we need is a little time, Nate," Dory whispered.

He could not think what to say to that. He just kept looking at her, memorizing her face.

Dory swung her hands together and clasped them at the front of her dress. "The years between us don't stay the same, you know. When we get a little older, two years won't seem like anything at all."

He tried to form a question on his lips, but he could not find the right words.

"*Dorothy!*"

Nate and Dory turned together. Mrs. Hildebrand stood six feet away, holding an empty wooden tray leveled before her. Her face reddened as she glared at Dory.

"You need to help with refreshments!" she said and nodded toward the lines of people crowded around the tables. Unfazed, Dory took the tray from her mother.

"It will be my one and only dance tonight, Mother." She swept an arm toward the room. "It's such a public place...what could be wrong about it?"

The woman's eyes were like hot coals. "I'll speak to you at home!" she huffed. "Now go help serve!"

Dory turned to Nate and smiled at him as if they were alone and miles out on the prairie. "Thank you for the dance, Nate. You did really well." She transferred the tray to her left hand and offered her right. Nate took it, and they simply squeezed as if testing the fit of their two hands. Then, surprising him, she pulled forward, rose up on her toes, and kissed his cheek. Nate imagined the colors of a rainbow flashing across his face.

Dory stepped back, curtsied, and then walked past her mother toward the crowd at the front of the room. Mrs. Hildebrand's cold eyes were waiting for Nate.

"I asked you to leave her alone!"

Nate propped his hands on his hips and let his head sag forward. When he looked up, she was still waiting for a reply.

"I didn' come here to dance, ma'am. I was just doin' a favor for my brother."

She huffed a sarcastic laugh. "So you and Dory just happened to meet by accident?"

"Ma'am, I didn' even wanna dance. I didn' know how. But Dory taught me tonight."

"Well, I hope you enjoyed it, because it's the last time you'll be with her!" Her face tightened like a sheet of rawhide drying in the sun. Nate had never received such a hostile look from a grownup in Round Rock.

"Ma'am, can you tell me what it is 'bout me that yo're so afraid of?"

Her head retracted an inch. "Are you that naïve, young man?"

Nate hesitated. "I don' know, ma'am. I don' know what that means."

Her mouth tightened to a humorless smile. "Do you know what it means to take advantage of a young girl? Can't you see the shame in that?"

Nate lowered his arms to his sides and stood erect. "I got nothin' but respect for yore daughter. If there's any shame here, it's that you cain't see that."

Mrs. Hildebrand crossed her arms over her stomach, and scowled. "So, *I'm* the one who should feel shame?"

Nate was shaking his head before she had completed her question. "I just meant—"

"If you're not a dancer," she interrupted, "then you might as well leave, mightn't you?"

Nate held out his wrist to show the ink mark. "I paid like ever'body else, ma'am."

Mrs. Hildebrand produced a small purse from somewhere and opened it to sort through some coins. "Here!" she said, making the word sound dirty. "Just take this and go." She thrust out her open hand palm up, a ten-cent coin lying flat against her shiny, pale skin.

Nate made no move to take the money. He simply looked into her angry eyes.

"G'night, ma'am," he said quietly and walked away. He felt her eyes on his back as he made his way to the front wall. After taking down his hat and jacket, he saw Dory watching him from the food table. He knew that there was apology in her face, but there was also something noble and strong. He wished he had a tintype of her wearing that very face.

Spring 1874

Round Rock, Texas

Chapter Nineteen

I t was twilight when Nate finished brushing old Rube. He latched the Morgan in his stall and then checked the yard, where Naomi Jane, Ben, and Dudley still squatted in front of the house. Taking turns, they shuffled around and stirred up dust as they thumbed marbles inside a circle scraped into the hardpan. Beside them, Checkers lay on his belly and ignored the game as he kept watch in the direction of the front gate.

Because these three had not been summoned inside to clean up for supper, Nate retrieved a brush from the tack room and lighted a lantern to hang in the breezeway. Leading Peaches from her stall with just his open hand cupped under her jaws, he settled her in the glow of the light and began brushing her neck in short, brisk strokes. When he reached her hindquarters on that side, she looked back and nickered.

"I know," Nate said, "I ain't forgot." He guided the stiff bristles of the brush around the sore that had become inflamed on her rump. "I'll put s'more salve on it when I finish brushin' you. How's that sound?"

At the scuff of boots in the doorway, Peaches turned

her head back to the front. Nate straightened to see his father standing in the barn entrance.

"That ol' gal ev'ah talk back to you?"

The lantern light brought out an ethereal glow from Jack Champion's white shirt. Bright as snow catching a beam of moonlight. His bare head showed a recent combing and a light sheen of pomade, giving his beard the wild look of a disheveled nest of silver and white threads. His usually stoic face was relaxed, and his eyes held a hint of amusement. It was the expression he wore when he talked to the men whose company he enjoyed. Like Uncle George or Mr. Snyder.

"Time for supper?" Nate asked.

The father shook his head. "Came out he'ah to talk with you. Whe'ah is John Thomas?"

Nate nodded toward town. "He cleaned up an' took off soon's we got back. He's takin' Sarah to see some kind o' play-actin' by them folks that come into Round Rock last week in that painted-up wagon."

"Shakespe'ah," his father said, as much to himself as to Nate. "How fah along are you two with the fenceposts?"

"We made the turn east at the southwest corner today."

The father nodded. "You reckon you've learned the plantin' o' posts by now?"

"Prob'ly do it in my sleep with my eyes closed," Nate replied.

His father smiled and then strolled into the interior of the barn. "I'm thinkin' yo'ah bett'ah suited for workin' with hosses. Wouldn' you agree?"

Nate widened his eyes. "That's *all* I wanna do! That an' work with the cattle."

Jack set his gaze on the russet saddle that straddled the gate to Peaches's stall. "Fuhst time William saved *his* money fo' somethin', he spent it on a blue muslin blouse with pearl buttons. Wasn't nothin' I could say to talk 'im out of it." The old man bounced once with a private laugh. "And James...he bought himself a beavah hat that he won't wear except to social events." He looked down and shook his head. "I reckon John Thomas will be a-spendin' his money on the Nethe'lin girl."

Nate said nothing. He had no idea where this conversation was going, but he did know that nobody was going to separate him from that new saddle. It was paid for, fair and square.

His father turned his keen eye on Nate and pointed a forefinger at him. "But you...*you* bought yo'self a workin' man's saddle."

"Yes'r."

Jack nodded as though the two of them had reached some kind of common ground. "That's what I wanna talk to you 'bout." He seemed to be watching Nate for some kind of reaction. The lantern light carved hard shadows into his face.

Nate turned Peaches around so that the light bathed the side of her he had not yet groomed. When he started stroking with the brush again, Nate's father cleared his throat, which every Champion knew was the preamble to serious talk.

"You remeb'ah Sam Strayhorn? Used to farm up near Florence? When I was she'iff, he was always aftah me 'bout a job. I fin'ly hired 'im part time for night duty, keepin' watch on the jail whenevah I had a pris'nah I knew was itchin' to break out."

Nate squinted. "He was a Ranger, wasn't he?"

His father nodded. "Had been at one time, so he said. But I didn' even take time to check on it. I just hired 'im 'cause he seemed like a man who would do what he said he would do." He laughed quietly to himself. "Then I found out that boy could track like a hungry Apache. I'd been usin' 'im to set in the office at night when he should'a been out leadin' my posses in the brush." He shook his head once and slowly blinked. "Waste o' talent, pure an' simple."

Nate kept up the brushing and waited to see where this speech was headed.

"Yo'ah aunt Hattie an' uncle Geo'ge got back today. You got a new cousin named *Euell*."

Nate's hand stilled on the paint's flank. "Euell," he said, trying out the word. "That a boy or a girl?"

"Boy," his father said. "They brought back a fine remuda o' hosses, too, ten o' which I'm takin' off they'ah hands. I'll be needin' somebody to train 'em. Now that you finished with those two o' Snydah's, thought you might take these on. Whatta ya say?"

Nate stopped brushing and looked the old man in the eye. "What about the fencin'?"

"Son, most anyone can set fenceposts. But I don't think they'ah's a man in the coun'y can train hosses bett'ah than you. Would you like to do it?"

Nate laid down the brush. "You ain't never asked me 'bout nothin' like this b'fore."

The father looked down at the dark dirt floor and smiled. When his head came up, the lantern light brought out a kindness in his eyes.

"You *tell* things to a boy, Nathan. But when he gets to be a man, you *ask*."

Nate swallowed to keep his voice from cracking. "I'd be proud to work the horses, Daddy."

The father nodded once and tucked his shirttails deeper into the waist of his trousers. "Figured I might hire you out to the Clucks, too. Yo'ah aunt an' uncle could use some help with their new stock. They'd be payin' you directly. How would that be?"

Nate shrugged. "I been doin' that for years 'round the coun'y. *You* know that."

The father nodded again. "Now you'll be workin' inside the family. Yo'ah aunt Hattie was yo'ah mama's favorite sistah, you know."

"Yes'r, I know."

The elder Champion let his gray eyebrows float upward. "Does all this suit you?"

"Suits me just fine. When do I start?"

The father cocked his head to one side. "D'you remem'ah the last post you sank today?"

Nate pictured the work site, where he and John Thomas had laid off for the day. "Yes'r."

The old man smiled. "That was yo'ah last post he'ah, son. I got oth'ah plans fo' you."

Nate thought for a moment. "Who's gonna work with John Thomas?"

The old man sauntered to the doorway and hesitated. The first stars were glittering above the horizon. The oil lamps inside the house burned now, and the yard was quiet.

"Figure I'll put Dudley on that," his father answered. "How do you think that'll go?"

"For Dudley...or for John Thomas?" Nate asked.

The father did not look amused. "Fo' the fencin'," he responded.

Nate shrugged. "Dud's gittin' purty strong. I reckon he'll do fine."

"Enough said, then." The old man turned in the doorway. "Let's go have us some supp'ah."

He waited while Nate put Peaches back in her stall, latched the gate, and blew out the lantern. Then they walked side by side to the house in silence, Nate matching his father's stride so that their boots on the hardpan took on the sound of a single man.

———

By the time the sun had risen enough to touch its golden rays to the idle blades of the windmill at the Cluck ranch, Nate stood with his forearms resting on the top rail of the main corral. As he surveyed the dark shapes of the horses clustered inside the fencing, the animals remained as still as gravestones, their silence interrupted only by an occasional flutter of nostrils or a quiet blow.

Only one light showed in a window at the house, and Nate knew that his aunt Hattie was in her kitchen preparing breakfast. It was a good bet that Uncle George had already been out to the barn to milk the dairy cow. Now, he was probably sipping coffee at the table and talking quietly with his wife. That was one of the ways they differed from Nate's father and stepmother, and it was an alliance that Nate had seen manifested in a dozen other subtle ways. They treated one another more like friends than husband and wife. Nate would rather spend time with them than any other couple he knew.

As the sunlight crept down the latticed tower of the windmill, the structure stood out against the fiery sky like a gigantic flower emerging from the land. Soon, the horses' smooth backs threw off a silver reflection, and the animals began to mill around, giving the appearance of fish weaving among themselves in shallow water. For a fleeting few seconds, the sun scorched the sky to a burnt-orange that seemed to capture the ranch like a sepia photograph. The horses turned their flanks to the welcome warmth of the light and grew still and contented.

The front door of the house opened with a high-pitched squeal from one of the hinges, and the dark silhouette of George Cluck moved to the edge of the porch. "I know I seen you somewheres b'fore. You kindly remind me o' one o' the Champion boys I knew. He was just a skinny kid who rode a purty little paint a lot like yourn."

Nate pushed away from the fence and crossed the yard toward his uncle. George Cluck smiled and laughed. He was known for his good heart and a sense of humor that could make a coroner laugh. But anyone who had ever seen the man riled knew that his eyes were the kind to look right through a man.

"You even walk like 'im a little," George said, keeping his performance going, "but yo're a sight taller and stronger-lookin' than that boy I remember. Better lookin', too."

"Welcome back, Uncle George," Nate said and scaled the two steps to the porch.

"Nate," George said, finally smiling. "By golly, you've growed like a weed." They clasped hands and pumped warmly, the strength in their grips telegraphing their mutual respect. "There was many a time on that trek I found myself wishin' you was along. I bet I said that to Dud Snyder ten times."

"How were the river crossin's?"

George closed his eyes and began shaking his head. "It was tetch an' go a few times. Red River was the worse. We had a helluva time gittin' across...both men and cattle."

"Did you lose many?"

"Men or cattle?"

Nate winced. "You lost some men?"

George held up two fingers. "Two."

Nate frowned. "In the river?"

George sniffed and looked out across the yard as if unwanted visitors had arrived. "Almost wish they'd drowned. They just stopped pullin' their weight, an' I had to let 'em go. I damned near didn' pay 'em their wages, but I couldn' go back on my word."

"What about the cattle?" Nate asked.

167

George sighed. "Lost a few in river crossings, a couple o' young ones in the Nations. Injuns prob'ly snuck off with 'em. The rest, we figured, must'a got spooked by lightnin' an' got lost." His face turned stony. "We 'bout lost the whole herd to a damn gang o' filthy saddlers in the Nations. That territory is crawlin' with outlaws."

"What happened?"

George huffed and glared at the hills in the east. "We stood up to 'em is what happened. They rode up on us bold as brass. Told Snyder to his face they was taking all the beef they wanted. I reckon they seen Hattie an' the children an' figured us for easy pickin's. But they soon learned the error in their thinkin'. We had two dozen men to their ten, and there wasn't none o' us afraid to use a gun." He cracked a grin. "That includes your aunt Hattie, too." He turned to Nate. "Ever see a woman with child load up a shotgun and set her mind to the business o' protectin' her family?"

Nate shook his head. "Nos'r...cain't say I have."

George turned back to the hills, his grim face set with an immutable truth. "Well, I can tell you it's a mighty convincin' message to a man on the wrong end o' that scattergun."

Nate could see how worked up his uncle was getting. The man was grinding his teeth and glaring out at a disappointing world. George sat down on the lip of the porch and propped his boots on the lowest step.

"I hear you brought home a new cousin for me," Nate said.

George's head came around quickly. "Sure did! Got me another boy! Euell."

The front door of the house opened, and the two older children rushed out onto the porch to crowd around Nate. Showing off all her teeth, eight-year-old Allie beamed up at her cousin. Emmet, a year younger, tugged on Nate's leg until he got the attention he wanted.

"Well, hey there!" Nate greeted and kneeled down to get on the children's level. Allie put her arms around Nate's neck, and Emmet tried to climb up onto Nate's bent knee, which had often served as a bucking bronco for the boy. "What'd y'all think o' Kansas?" Nate asked.

Allie made a face. "It's a *lo-o-ng* way up there...and a *lo-o-ng* way back!"

George laughed. "I reckon these two here, along with Minnie, was the youngest ever to go up the Chisolm Trail. An' I know for certain that Euell was the youngest ever to come down it." He gestured with his hand toward the house. "Folks in Ab'lene said Hattie was the first woman to make the trip up with a cattle crew." He shook his head and smiled. "And her carryin' a child in her belly. Was a doctor there who had me goin' for a while, sayin' the baby was gonna stutter on account o' the long, bumpy ride in a wagon. He had a good laugh about that one."

"Weren't true though, was it?" Nate said.

George's face wrinkled. "Naw...he was just funnin' me."

Allie tugged on Nate's sleeve. "Did you ride Peaches here?"

"Sure did," Nate said and pointed. "She's behind the barn."

Allie and Emmet ran across the yard, yelling Peaches's name and waving their arms. When they had disappeared around the corner of the barn, Nate turned to his uncle and tried to sound casual with his question.

"Did you really meet Wild Bill Hickok?"

George's eyebrows rose. "I did. Talked to him for about a half hour in a tobacco shop."

Nate stared at his uncle. "Well, what's he like?"

George pushed out his lower lip. "Likes cee-gars. I

know *that*. Talked me into buyin' one for 'im. Expensive, too."

Nate was shaking his head. "I mean, what kind o' person was he?"

George made a grunt deep in his chest. It was a sound he used to sum up his opinion on whatever topic was at hand.

"Kinda showy, I'd say. Dresses so you'll notice 'im." Got hair like a woman...down to here." He made a little slicing motion with the edge of one hand on the opposite shoulder.

Nate was all ears. "What'd you talk about?"

George cocked his head to one side and puckered his lips. "Well, at first, he was real quiet. I didn' think he was gonna give me the time o' day. But when he warmed up to me, we had quite a confab." George chuckled. "Well, it was mostly him a-talkin' and me a-listenin'. An' most o' what he said was...well...'bout *him*."

"Did he tell you 'bout any o' the scrapes he was in?"

"No," George said flatly. "Never came up. Mostly, he talked about how he wanted to make better money. He was on a long losin' streak with the cards, so he said, an' he assured me that wearin' a badge holds no reasonable hope for makin' a man rich."

Nate frowned. "But Daddy made purty good money as a lawman, didn' he?"

George raised an eyebrow. "Sheriffs keep a portion o' the taxes they collect all over the coun'y. Ain't so for a town marshal."

The door hinge creaked again, and Nate turned to see Hattie standing on the front porch. He stood and took in all five feet of her. Over her charcoal-gray dress she wore a pale blue apron stained with light-brown splashes of wheat flour. Little Minnie stood at her side with one fist bunching a handful of her mother's dress.

"Well, look at who's got to be a man while we were gone," Hattie said, her quiet voice like a whispery breeze slipping through the cracks of a house. Nate stood and hugged his aunt.

Like her sister, Nate's mother, Hattie was ninety pounds of generosity and practicality, all rolled into one. She was in her midtwenties and could run the ranch by herself if the need arose. Her stature was so slight that, when Nate hugged her, his arms formed a loose cage around her, the same way he arranged his fingers when he picked up a baby bird.

It was difficult to imagine this small woman holding a shotgun, much less shooting one, but there was a fire of determination in her, and she knew how to show it in her eyes. Nate had no doubt that those outlaws in the Indian Territory had felt the heat from her glare.

"Oh, but it's good to see your sweet face, Nate." Smiling broadly, she squeezed the sides of his shoulders and ran her hands down and up his arms.

"Now, Hattie!" George complained in the whiny tone of censure that he sometimes pretended with her. "You know that ain't the kind o' thing you say to a young man. You save all that for babies and womenfolk." He pulled little Minnie away from her mother and set her in his lap. "*Sweet* is for little girls. Like this little gopher right here."

"I'm not a gopher!" Minnie complained, pushing against his chest with her hands.

"Whatta you think, Nate? Don't she look like a gopher to you?"

George tried to turn Minnie to face Nate, but she buried her face in her father's chest. "Ain't you gonna say hello to Nate?"

Minnie giggled. Nate gently squeezed her little hand, but she withdrew it.

"Maybe I should meet Euell," Nate said softly. "He might talk to me."

"Inside," Hattie whispered. "He's asleep in the back room. Go in and wash up for breakfast, then go on in and see 'im."

George carried Minnie to the door and opened it. "I could eat a mule," he announced.

"Well, if you want to eat mule," Hattie said, "you'll have to cook it yourself."

George held out Minnie before him so he could see her face. With his strong hands under her armpits, she stopped squirming and dangled like a rag doll.

"What you say, Minnie-girl? You want some mule or will you settle for some eggs, a strip o' pork, and a biscuit?"

"Mule!" she said, the word bursting out of her and surprising them all. Laughing together, they moved into the warmth of the kitchen.

Chapter Twenty

Nate worked the pitcher pump while Allie, Emmet, and Minnie washed their hands. Then Emmet returned the favor for Nate. When Allie handed him a towel, she wore a hopeful smile.

"You wanna see the doll I found on the trail?"

"I do," Nate said. "But first, let me go an' have a look at this new cousin o' mine."

The three children followed him into the back bedroom that normally was the private domain of George and Hattie. The room had always been off-limits to the children for as long as Nate could remember, but now a low crib had been set up in the back corner, and the four visitors tiptoed like bandits across the creaky floor to peer down into a mire of wrinkled linens.

There wasn't much to see of the baby nestled in the soft folds of the sheets. One side of his face revealed a ruddy cheek, and on his egg-shaped head, sparse wisps of light-brown hair curled like Dudley's. It was too early to determine who Euell was going to look like. Nate thought all babies looked pretty much the same.

As they stood there as silent observers, George entered

the room drying his hands on a towel. Putting a wrist on Nate's shoulder, he leaned in to check on his infant son.

"He sleeps a lot," George volunteered. "Slept through most o' the trip from Kansas. Even with the wagon a-shakin' and makin' a racket like a tool box bein' dragged through a boulder field."

Nate shook his head in wonder. "He ain't no bigger'n a house cat, but already he's been to Abilene and crossed rivers I ain't never seen." Nate turned to his uncle. "I been to Austin once, and that there's the end o' my travel stories."

"Your day'll come, Nate, just like it did for William. You'll take off for parts unknown an' start seein' the size o' this world. Turns out there's a helluva lot more'n Texas out there."

They were quiet for a time, all their attention fixed on the sleeping baby. "I reckon that *there* is a *sweet face*, aw-right," George whispered.

Minnie spun to her father. "Mine is sweet!"

George touched a straight index finger to his pursed lips and bent toward her. "Shhh. Don't wake up yore little brother. Yo're right. Gophers are prob'ly at the top o' the sweet list."

"I'm not a gopher!" she insisted.

"Come on and get it while it's warm!" Hattie called from the kitchen.

The group walked quietly out of the room, across the hallway, and into the kitchen, where they arranged them-selves around the table by the window. When the food was served and the eating commenced, George spoke up as he spread butter on a biscuit half.

"Lotta folks in Ab'lene was talkin' 'bout Wyomin' and Montana, Nate. They say it's good cattle country up there. Good grass and water. They're bringin' dif'rent breeds 'o cattle to try out. Some from England. Some from Scotland. And France, too. Thing is, they're better eatin' than these stringy longhorns we push north."

"I heard 'bout Wyomin'," Nate said. "They say that country is easy on the eye, too. Got mountains there that look like they might be holdin' up the sky."

"Come a winter," Hattie said, "you might be singin' a different tune up there with your teeth a-chatterin' and your mustaches frozen into a horseshoe."

"Aunt Hattie," Nate said and placed his hands palms down on either side of his plate, "I might enjoy shiverin' in the cold for a change. I been sweatin' in the Texas heat so long I forgot how it feels to be dry."

George blew across the surface his coffee and sipped from the top. "Saw the Tisdale boy in town yesterday when we come in. Said he was thinkin' on tryin' his luck up there."

"John?" Nate asked. "In Wyomin'?"

George nodded as he set down his cup. "Thinkin' on it."

Hattie made the quiet humming sound in her throat that meant she had a different view on things. "He'll think about it some more when he's up there and the first winter sets in. I met a few women in Abilene who'd come down from Montana. I heard a story about a well freezing over with ice so thick it broke a bucket that was dropped for the purpose of breakin' up the ice."

George stopped chewing and stared at his wife. "Well, I don't reckon they got much've a bargain trading that for a Kansas winter. I seem to remember the blood freezin' in my toes in that hotel most nights." Using his fingertips, he carefully broke open another biscuit and buttered it. "That cold Kansas wind can hunt you down even when yo're underneath four blankets an' a sheepskin coat." He gave Hattie a sharp nod. "'Member that?"

She laughed. "I remember those toes of yours...trespassin' on my side of the bed." She gave him the knowing nod right back.

George winked at Nate. "Well, darlin', that's 'cause yo're such a warm human bein'." He smiled at his children as if they were in league with him. "And so purty, too," George added. Allie and Emmet seemed delighted to be included in the conspiracy.

"Is that when I look so pretty to you, George? When your toes are cold?"

"Cold or hot...it don't matter." He looked at her for a time. "Did I give the right answer?"

"Close enough," Hattie said and rose to fetch the coffee pot off the stove. When she sat again, Hattie spoke up in a cheerful tone. "That was good o' the Bolen girl to leave us some fresh butter." She turned her attention to Nate. "Did you visit while she and her husband were here?"

"Yes, ma'am," he replied. "Me an' Ben come over a few times in the last weeks an' prepared yore garden bed."

"Well!" Hattie announced through her natural smile. "I guess I'll need to take down a jar of my apples and bake a pie soon and invite the two of you over." Her face brightened, and her smile widened. "Oh! That reminds me!" She leaned toward Allie. "Allie-cat, go in my bedroom and bring me that skinny jar a-settin' on my dresser. Don't you wake Euell now, you hear?"

The little girl ran from the table and was back before Nate could scoop up his next forkful of eggs. Allie placed a five-inch-tall, narrow jar beside her mother's plate. Through the glass, Nate could see a white cloth wrapped around something. Hattie unscrewed the lid and removed the slender package of cloth, which she laid aside on the tabletop.

"Those are my bifocals," she explained. "I carried them in this jar to Kansas and back."

Then she upended the jar into her cupped hand, and a coin rattled out of the jar. It was an Indian head penny. Following the coin, a band of paper shaped like a flattened ring dropped lightly into her hand. The ring showed an ornate insignia of red, blue, and gold and was large enough to slip over a grown man's finger. Holding out her hand to Nate, Hattie smiled.

"Here...take these in your hand. They're for you."

Nate received the two items, frowned at them, and then looked at his aunt. "What's this?"

"That's a penny that Marshal Hickok held in his own hand. I thought you'd like to have it for a good luck piece."

George pointed at the ring of paper. "And that there is the band off the cigar I bought 'im. He left both at the tobacco shop. He dropped that one-cent piece but didn' bother to pick it up."

Hattie slid the jar closer to Nate. "Keep 'em in this if you want to."

Nate looked from aunt to uncle and then back to Hattie. "Thank you."

From outside in the yard came the sound of approaching hoof beats. The horse slowed and came to a halt at the front porch.

"Who is this now?" George wondered aloud as he got up from the table.

Nate heard him open the door and exchange a greeting with someone, and when the door closed, George reentered the kitchen with Dudley Snyder following close behind him. Mr. Snyder clamped a dark pipe in his teeth and left a trail of smoke in the hallway. He wore a denim work shirt and calf-skin gloves and looked like he had already put in half a day's work. Removing his hat and gloves, he dropped both on the small bench by the window and then stepped to the stove, where he rubbed his hands together briskly. Without his hat on, Snyder's ears appeared larger and flared outward from his head. Nate remembered hearing one of Snyder's ranch hands referring to his boss as "ol' buzzard wings." Now he knew why.

"Mornin', Miss Hattie," Snyder said and gave a general nod to the children. Then his eyes singled out Nate. "Howdy, Nate. You were next on my list o' people to visit."

Snyder wore his usual impassive expression. He was a thin, rugged man going on forty with a long face made longer still by a dark beard that hung from his jaws like a patch of scorched Spanish moss. His beaked nose hooked over a firm mouth. The thick, sweet smell of his smoldering pipe tobacco already dominated the room.

"Will you have some breakfast, Dudley?" Hattie offered.

He shook his head. "I ate hours ago. Might have some coffee, if you don't care."

While Hattie attended to the visitor's cup, Mr. Snyder stared at Nate and sucked in his cheeks as he drew on his pipe. "I see you come over an' got that little black colt?"

"Yes'r, I did. An' I took that new chestnut mare, too."

Snyder nodded. "Glad to hear that, 'cause if you didn' take 'er, I figured she was stole. Ramirez, the man I asked to look in on my place, didn't have a clue. Didn' bother to report it neither."

"I left a note for 'im on the barn door. I reckon he must'a missed it."

Hattie set a cup of coffee before Snyder, and the man set down his pipe long enough to sip off the top of the steaming surface.

"I seen yore pinto outside," he continued. "That's a purty saddle strapped to 'er. New, ain't it?"

"New to me," Nate replied. He watched Snyder

sample his coffee again. "Mr. Snyder, do you know a man named *Brooks*?"

Snyder nodded. "Milford Brooks...lived up near the ol' Hingus mine."

"Nos'r...I mean *Dixie*."

Snyder had started to drink again, but he stopped with the cup held an inch before his chin. "Carl Dexter Brooks...Milford's boy," he said, and the skin around his eyes tightened. "Took to callin' himself *Dixie* after his father died." Snyder scowled. "Got no use for that boy."

"So you didn' ask him to look in on your place while you were gone?"

Snyder looked up from his coffee cup and glared at Nate as if he had been insulted. "I did *not!*"

Nate pushed his plate forward and rested his forearms on the table. "He claimed you did. When I went out for the colt, he had yore mare tethered to the snubbin' post like he was tryin' to train 'er. But 'bout all he was doin' was a-beatin' on that horse with a whip."

"A whip!" Snyder repeated, his voice so cold and sharp that everyone at the table went still.

"That's why I took the mare with me along with the colt," Nate explained.

Snyder turned his head to stare out the window, his jaws flexing beneath his beard. "Who was with him?"

When the image of Martin Tisdale's face surfaced in Nate's mind, he stared into his plate. "There was a man 'bout yore age, I reckon. An' another'n 'bout Dixie's age."

"If anything," Snyder returned, "I would'a told Dixie Brooks to stay *off* my ranch! I don't want him within a rope's throw o' any o' my horses. Was the mare hurt?"

Nate shook his head. "Nothin' that would show. But she didn' care for that whip one lick, an' neither did I. That's when I took charge o' her."

Mr. Snyder nodded once as if they'd sealed a deal. "How're those two horses comin' along?"

"I worked with 'em all winter. They're in fine shape. The mare is gonna make you one good cow pony."

A gleam of respect shone in Snyder's eyes. "I'll pay you double what we agreed on." He glanced at Nate's empty plate. "Can you step outside with me?"

Surprised, Nate gathered up his plate and napkin and walked them to the washbasin. Snyder sipped more coffee and then stretched to settle his cup upon the wood stove. When he stood, Snyder gave a crisp nod to Hattie.

"I'll just keep my coffee warm here, Miss Hattie." Then he turned his business eyes on George. "Nate an' I won't be but a coupla minutes. Then I wanna talk to you about the horses we brought back."

"I'll be right here a-plannin' out my day," George said and raised his cup like a toast.

Chapter Twenty-One

Just beyond the end of the porch, Mr. Snyder's roan gelding stood content to be tied to the railing in the sunlight. Wispy clouds of steam accompanied her breathing and quickly dissolved in the air. The sun had risen high enough to flood light into the corral beside the barn. Content to soak up the morning rays, the new remuda of horses stood nearly motionless. A little breeze carried dust across the yard, and the windmill seemed to rouse from its night's rest by facing into the wind and starting up a slow rotation of its blades.

Snyder stepped down from the porch, walked to his horse, and untied two straps behind the cantle of his saddle. Nate waited on the porch and watched the man turn to him with a brace of saddlebags draped over one hand. The leather was warped, stiff, and somewhat bleached by the sun. Each bag showed a number of penny-sized bullet holes.

"Found this up a tree at my place. One of my men fetched it down. Yore name was wrote on the inside flap." He reached into a bag and brought out a pair of pliers and moldy leather gloves.

"Those are mine, aw-right," Nate said and took the bags. "Reckon these're bullet holes?"

Snyder stared at the perforations in the leather. "Don't know what else they could be."

Nate stuffed the pliers and gloves back into a bag. "While I fetched the colt from the barn, Dixie cut these bags off my saddle. When I come out, I spotted 'em up in the cherry tree where he'd throwed 'em. So, I took his. Cut 'em off his saddle while he was a-sittin' his horse."

Snyder couldn't help but laugh. "That there's the difference in a bawlin' jackanape like Dixie Brooks an' a young man like you. One playin' the fool behind another man's back...and the other'n lookin' a man in the eye to handle bus'ness." He stared at Nate as if he expected some kind of reply.

Nate nodded to the bags in his hand. "I reckon he shot 'em up out o' spite."

Snyder frowned and shook his head. "I'm gonna have me a talk with that boy."

"He ain't 'round here no more, Mr. Snyder," Nate said, draping the shot-up saddlebags over a shoulder. "My daddy sent 'im packin' up to Denton Coun'y."

Snyder forked his hands on his hips. "What's he doin' up there?"

Nate shrugged. "Cowboyin', I reckon. He's workin' on the sheriff's spread up there."

Snyder looked off to the north. "Ask me...that boy could use some whippin' hisself." He huffed a laugh without a trace of humor. "And I wouldn' mind if was me that did the whippin'." After a time, he seemed to clean the slate of his mind. "So, tell me s'more about the chestnut and the colt."

Nate welcomed the change in direction. "The mare perks up when I strap on a saddle, and she takes to the bit like a slice o' apple. She's smart...got good legs and sharp instincts...can cut left an' then right like a rabbit. Like I said, she'll make a good cow pony. The colt is already circling in the paddock usin' three gaits an' makin' the change-up just by my voice. He's eager to please if you know how to ask 'im...an' stubborn if you don't."

Snyder nodded. "You bring 'em out to my place, an' we'll settle up. I might have s'more work for you if you want it. I'll be takin' some o' these here off o' George's hands." He nodded toward the corral. "Maybe eight or ten."

"Yes'r," Nate replied. "I can work with 'em."

Snyder squinted one eye. "You know yore way 'round a Winchester?"

Nate hesitated. "Sir?"

"Can you shoot?"

Nate tried to read the man's face to see where this was going. "I can shoot."

Snyder pulled a short rifle from the scabbard mounted on his saddle. Then he fished out a box of cartridges from his saddlebag.

"Here!" he said and held out a Winchester carbine and the box of shells. "Load this. I'll go tell George we're gonna make some noise out by those trees." He nodded across the north pasture.

When he returned from inside the house, Mr. Snyder took back his Winchester and pointed to the shot-up saddlebag hanging across Nate's chest. "Can we use that as a target?"

Nate looked down at the parched leather. "I ain't got no use for it now."

They walked out the front gate and turned to the sound of hoofbeats coming up the road. Nate's older brother, James, came on at a canter on his skittish bay mare. When he reined up before them, he tugged on the front of his hat brim and gave Mr. Snyder a nod.

"Mornin', sir. Welcome back."

Snyder returned the nod. "James," he said.

James shifted his gaze to the weathered saddlebag hanging over his brother's chest. Then, his eyes fixed on the rifle.

"Where're you goin' with that carbine?"

"I reckon we're 'bout to do a little shootin'," Nate said.

Snyder pointed at James's saddle scabbard. "Bring yore rifle an' join us."

James dismounted and drew his old Henry from its sheath. "What're we shootin'? Prairie dogs?"

Mr. Snyder pointed at the weathered bags hanging over Nate's shoulder. "We're gonna try'n punch a few more holes in these old bags."

James sidled up to his brother and felt the stiff leather of Nate's old bags. "What the hell happened to these? They're yores, ain't they?"

Nate shrugged. "Yeah...used to be."

James fingered one of the bullet holes. "Well, who the hell shot 'em?"

Nate avoided the question by asking his own. "What're you doin' here anyway?"

"Daddy sent me," James replied. "He wants you to round up some strays down in those arroyos where we found that dead mule coupla summers ago."

Nate lifted his chin to point at his brother. "How come you didn' take care of it?"

"I'm headed to Georgetown to talk to a buyer for some o' those horses yo're to break."

"I don't *break* 'em. I try'n teach 'em how to tolerate the people who own 'em."

Mr. Snyder started away toward the gate and called over his shoulder, and the brothers hurried to catch up with him. After they had crossed the yard, James leaned to

Nate and whispered over the swish of their boots in the grass.

"What's this all about?"

Nate shrugged. "I ain't got no idea."

When Snyder stopped walking, he pointed to the edge of the forest. "James?" he said. "How far do you make it out...from here to those trees?"

James squinted at the distance. "Oh...maybe a hun'erd yards?"

In his mind, Nate was picturing a row of fenceposts spaced across the grass all the way to the trees. Each post stood ten paces from its neighbor, and each pace measured almost a yard.

"I see it as eighty," Nate volunteered.

Mr. Snyder glanced at Nate, allowed a subtle smile, and then looked back at the distance in question. "'Eighty' is the way I figure it, too," he said. He pointed toward the trees again. "Nate, see that dead shrub b'neath the tall oak? Hang the saddlebags on its branches, then git back here."

Nate jogged down to the barren shrub. There, he jammed the bags over a fork of the slender trunk so that the front bag showed its full silhouette facing out to the meadow. Once he'd tested its snug fit, he turned and ran back to the others.

Mr. Snyder levered a cartridge into the chamber of his carbine, the metallic sound well-oiled but crisp and seeming out of place there, where the only other sound was the gentle blow of the wind sweeping over the grass. High in the trees, the branches swayed, and their leaves rustled. Low in the forest, where the leather target waited, there was no movement at all.

"Let's see what we can do from here," Snyder said.

Taking a wide stance, he raised the rifle, set the stock against his shoulder, and tilted his head over the sights.

The explosive discharge seemed to shatter the air around them. Right away, the bullet slapped into wood some-where in the dark of the forest. A plume of gray smoke billowed forward and began to peel away with the wind. To the left of the target, a branch of the dead bush hung down, broken and swinging like a pendulum. The saddle-bags remained in place.

"Hmmh," Snyder huffed deep in his chest and cocked the lever again, this time more forcefully, as if he were just now getting serious about hitting his mark.

When the gun went off the second time, another limb snapped off and tumbled into the branches below. As the smoke cleared, the target hung exactly as it had before.

"Give it a try, James," Snyder suggested and lowered his rifle. "Maybe you can put the fear o' gunpowder into that old piece o' warped leather."

When James fired his Henry, nothing changed down-field. There was not even a sound of impact from the bullet. Even before the smoke had drifted off, he worked the lever and aimed again, his lips pressed into a tight line and his open eye shining like a silver coin in sunlight. The report of the Henry came quicker this time, and the results were the same.

"Those bags are laughin' at us, boys," Snyder ribbed. "Here, Nate. Give 'er a try."

He held out the Winchester by its forestock, and Nate took the weapon. Taking a step away from his compan-ions, he stared downfield at the bags, levered a round into the chamber, and seated the butt of the rifle against the rounded muscle in his shoulder.

With the gentle squeeze of his forefinger, the rifle roared and kicked his shoulder back a good two inches, but there was fluidity in the movement, as though Nate had willingly received the jolt and absorbed it without surprise. When the smoke lifted, he saw that the leather had been pushed deeper into the shrub. The bag had twisted to one side, so its outline was smaller now.

"Bet you cain't do that again!" James challenged.

Nate's elbows spread wide as he cocked the lever again. All the while, his eyes remained fixed on the target. Without hurry, he leveled the rifle, squeezed, and took the quick recoil in that same smooth manner. This time, the bag had been pushed back into shadow.

"Damn, Nate," Snyder chuckled. "Don't you miss?"

"Here!" James said and pushed the Henry onto his brother. "Do it with *that!*"

Nate returned the Winchester to Mr. Snyder, took his stance again, and went through the same motions with the Henry. When he fired, the bag jumped deeper into the shrub so that it was barely visible.

"Bet you cain't hit *that!*" James brayed.

Nate cocked the rifle on its way up to his shoulder. The gun fired almost as soon as it was seated. The bags tumbled out of the branches and fell from view behind the meadow grass.

Snyder chuckled as he shouldered his rifle. James glared at the bare bush as if it had somehow betrayed him. Nate tapped on his brother's arm and held out the Henry.

"Where the hell'd you learn how to shoot like that?" James asked and took back his rifle.

"Same place you did. From William."

James narrowed his eyes. "I only 'member the one time you shot with us."

Nate nodded. "You 'member how I did?"

James pushed out his lower lip. "As I 'member, you got off a few lucky shots."

Nate smiled down at the grass. When he brought his head up, he'd scaled down the smile to a friendly grin.

"After that, William worked with me alone. Said you'd stay mad if I kept outshootin' you."

James's face squeezed down. "He said that?!"

Nate nodded. "Yep."

James studied the rear sight of the Henry from two different angles and then tested the notched plate with his fingers as if he might find it loose. "I got to git on to Georgetown," he said in a gruff voice. Turning, he threw a hasty wave of goodbye at Dudley Snyder. "I got to git goin', Mr. Snyder." Without waiting for a reply, James hurried off through the grass in long, swift strides. As Nate watched his brother make his way back to the main yard, he felt Mr. Snyder's hand clasp his shoulder.

"I wont you to do more'n train horses for me, Nate. There's a pack o' ki-yotes been badgerin' my chicken coop. I ain't got the time to deal with it. While yo're workin' with the horses, I wont you to keep a eye out for them bandits and—when you can—send 'em straight to hell. I'll pay fifty cents for each one kilt."

Nate pivoted, cupped his hands around his mouth, and yelled to his brother's back. "James!"

James stopped and turned, his stance defiant. "What!" he barked.

"Come on back here!" Nate called out. "Mr. Snyder's got a job for you!"

James said nothing but remained in place.

"Now, wait a minute!" Snyder muttered to Nate. "I'm askin' *you* for this work."

Nate looked Mr. Snyder in the eye. "I ain't got the temper'ment for it, sir. James will be better at it. He's a better shot when it's just him an' nobody else a-watchin'."

Snyder's eyebrows squeezed together to make a peak over the bridge of his nose. "I don't follow, son. You got somethin' agin killing ki-yotes?"

Nate smiled just enough to soften his answer. "It just ain't in my nature, is all."

Snyder narrowed his eyes and ran his tongue around

the inside of one cheek, as if he were expecting the punch line of a joke. When Nate continued to hold the smile on his face, Snyder cocked his head to one side.

"Yo're ser'ous, ain't ya?"

"Yes'r, I am."

Slowly, Snyder began to nod. "Well...lemme go talk to yore brother, then."

Chapter Twenty-Two

After Pedro Ramirez and his two brothers arrived on horseback at the Cluck ranch, they cut out the eight horses of Mr. Snyder's choosing and started them north toward the Snyder ranch. Then Nate and his uncle George divided the remainder of the remuda, ten to go to the Champion ranch and sixteen to stay with the Clucks. The ten were herded into a holding pen, leaving the Cluck's stock in the big corral. There, Nate threw a rope over the dodging head of a light-brown mustang with white spots on its flanks. This one, he led to the round paddock behind the house.

And so it began.

While his uncle settled back into a rancher's life after his long absence, Nate worked the rest of the morning, bringing three horses closer to the bond of trust between man and animal. Occasionally, George stopped by the paddock to stand quietly behind the fence to watch his nephew at work. Then, as silently as he had arrived, he would slip away and return to his routine.

Like so many of the other older boys in the county, Nate had been excused from attending school due to the spring roundup time. An hour after noon, Billy Hill reined up outside the paddock on his daddy's big dapple gray, propped his right boot over the pommel of his saddle, and folded his arms across his narrow chest.

"Figured I'd find you here," Billy said, keeping his voice quiet for the sake of the horse Nate was working. "I saw the remuda come through yesterday. You gonna break the whole lot?"

"Ain't gonna *break* nothin'," Nate said. "Try'n' to teach 'em some trust."

Billy looked out into the grasslands and squinted. "You ain't seen a steer with a twisted right horn out this way, have you? I been lookin' for 'im 'bout two hours."

Nate shook his head. "Nope."

Billy pointed with his chin toward the west pasture. "D'you reckon Mr. Cluck would care if I covered his range out there. I need to find that damned rascal. Daddy says don't come home if I ain't got it."

Nate shook his head. "Go look all you wont. I'd help you, but I got my hands full."

The roan mare on Nate's lead rope trotted like a circus horse, and Billy watched her circle around the paddock, with Nate moving in a smaller circle around the snubbing post. Nate's eyes remained dedicated to the roan, but each time Billy appeared in his vision, Nate could see that the boy had something on his mind.

"You hear 'bout Lindy?" Billy said, trying to sound casual. "Her parents are sendin' 'er off to a boardin' school somewheres. Her an' her little sister."

The next time Nate's rotation faced him toward Billy, Nate asked, "Why's that?"

Billy shrugged. "To git smarter'n the people 'round here, I reckon." When Nate's back was turned again, Billy fired another question, this time with a little break in his voice. "Have you been sparkin' Lindy?"

Nate turned with the roan but twisted at the neck to see Billy. "Have I *what*?"

"You heard me," Billy returned.

Nate held his gaze on Billy until his back was turned again. "No!" he called over his shoulder.

Billy waited as the roan came around again. "You ain't lyin'?"

Nate waited until Billy came into view again. "No, I ain't lyin'."

On his next revolution, Nate saw Billy gazing out at the pasture. "Well," Billy mumbled. "Guess I heard wrong."

"Guess you did!" Nate called out, putting a little censure in his tone.

The roan swung her head toward Nate and slowed her gait. He knew that the horse was responding to mixed signals. Tugging lightly on the rope, he talked the horse down to a walk.

"Whoa, now...who-o-o-oa."

The roan came to a stop, snorted, and picked up a foreleg to scrape its hoof on the hardpan. Once...twice...three times. When the animal settled, Nate faced Billy and watched the boy spit on his fingertips and rub at something on his boot.

"So, you ain't seen hide nor hair?" Billy asked.

Nate frowned. "We talkin' 'bout the steer?"

Billy let his head sag. "No. Lindy."

Nate walked toward the roan, coiling the rope as he did. When he was just a yard away, he stopped, and the roan turned her long neck to study him with a dark eye. Holding out his hand, Nate waited for the curious animal to stretch to him and smell his scent. Then he backed away carefully, feeding out the rope, letting it lie idle in the dust.

"I ain't seen nobody from school in a week," Nate said

and waited to see if there would be more questions. Billy kept polishing his boot. "Where're they headed to? Austin?"

Billy's hand stopped its rubbing, and his eyes fixed on Nate like the heads of ten-penny nails. "France!" he said, pushing the word out with decided animosity.

"France!? You mean like...'cross the ocean?"

Billy's mouth curled as if he'd bitten into a lemon. "Yeah!" he groaned. "*That* France."

"When are they leavin'?" Nate asked.

Billy shrugged. "Coupla days, I reckon," he replied, keeping his eyes angled down. Then he looked up quickly. "So, if you ain't been courtin' Lindy, how come people are sayin' her mother told you to stay clear o' her daughter?"

Nate stared back at Billy. "Reckon you'll need to ask the mother."

"I'm askin' *you*, dammit," Billy spat out. "Just tell it straight out, Nate!"

Nate remained composed, but the look he gave Billy was gauged to stem the flow of his careless words. "I cain't tell you what's inside another person's head, Billy. So let it go!"

Billy returned his attention to his boot. When Nate saw that the boy was not going to meet his eyes again, he flicked his wrist and sent a ripple out the rope as he made a *chick-chick* sound with his tongue against his back teeth. The roan started circling again, following the repetitive path inside the fence. After the horse had completed two laps, Billy swung his foot back to its proper side and booted into his stirrup.

"Guess I'll go on an' look for that steer," Billy called out and prodded his gray across the yard and into the west meadow.

When Billy was far out into the pastureland, Nate called for the roan to stop and walked her to the barn.

There, he combed and brushed her until her coat was dry to the touch. Then he led her into a stall.

"How many does that make?"

Nate turned to see his uncle George standing in the doorway with a long-handled hoe propped over one shoulder. The man pushed back his hat from his forehead and waited for an answer.

"Four," Nate replied. "All I'm doin' right now is lettin' 'em git to know me."

George nodded and hung the hoe on a pair of wall pegs. "How 'bout some water?"

Nate closed the stall gate and followed his uncle to the well house. Inside the little shed, the shade and the cool air from the well were a welcome relief from hours in the sun. Nate took off his hat and set it on the stacked stone wall that encircled the mouth of the well.

George gave the hat a hard look and then turned an amused eye on Nate. "Can I share some useful information that I have acquired from my many years o' becomin' a wise old man?"

Nate ran his fingers through his damp hair. "I'm listenin'."

George picked up Nate's hat and hung it on a peg next to a coil of rope on the wall. "Never set yore hat on the well wall." He held up a hand like a man taking an oath. "I know the difficulty in fishin' one out." He laughed. "Took me a week. Hattie said our water tasted like *hat* for a month. But that was just her remindin' me that a man who loses his hat might be owed a little ridicule."

Nate laughed and nodded. "I'll keep that in mind."

George cranked the windlass and set the bucket on the wall. Taking turns with the ladle, they drank in silence and soaked up their sanctuary from the heat. George hung the ladle on its nail and wiped his mouth with his sleeve.

"Accordin' to my nose, Hattie has baked a rhubarb pie. I think she plans to spring it on us. Wanna go see?"

"I'm gonna need to take off, Uncle George. I gotta coupla things need tendin' to b'fore dark. Me an' my brothers will come back tomorr' and drive our ten horses over to our ranch."

George nodded. "Go on an' do what you need to do, Nate. I'll see you boys tomorr'." He hitched his head with a concerned slant to his eyes and then held his poker face as steady as a burled knot on the side of an old oak tree. "We'll just hope there's some pie left for you boys."

———

It was late enough in the afternoon that Dory and Lindy should have had time to walk home from the schoolhouse. Nate rode Peaches to the outskirts of town, where the Hildebrand's two-story home was perched upon its juniper-covered knoll. The house overlooked Brushy Creek on one side and on another, a grassy plain that washed up against a spine of low hills to the north. To the south sprawled the rooftops of the business section of Round Rock.

Extending along the south side of the house, a trellis supported a screen of red rose vines. In front of the trellis stood a sculpted figurine of stone—a small woman tilting a jug over a larger-than-life mussel shell. A trickle of water poured from the mouth of the jug into the shell, making a burbling sound that kept up a continuous monologue in the open yard.

The false window shutters of the house were freshly painted white against the gray-green limestone from the quarry. The roof was shingled with white oak shakes, the orderly pattern as distinctive as the scales of a coachwhip. Two stone chimneys rose up on opposite sides of the house, each showing a capped metal flue at the top. The front porch was fortified by a row of balusters ornately lathed and glistening white from heavy layers of paint. Every feature of the home seemed overwrought with impractical expense.

Even the wooden outbuilding in back showed the handiwork of an accomplished carpenter. Though empty now, this shed was large enough to accommodate a carriage and a few horse stalls. Mr. Hildebrand was the only man Nate knew who regularly chose a carriage over a horse as his transportation into town each day. It was less than a quarter mile to his office from here, but Nate guessed that driving a buggy had something to do with being an insurance salesman and attending to the appearances that were required of that profession.

At the front of the house, Nate tied Peaches to the newel post at the bottom of the steps. Giving notice of his arrival, he scuffed his way up the five steps, cleared his throat loudly, and knocked on the paneled door that was painted the same pristine white as the balustrade. Right away, the sound of footsteps inside grew louder until the door swung open and revealed Mrs. Hildebrand in a dark-blue dress with white collar and cuffs. Her hair was piled on top of her head and pinned in place at several strategic points. In the flash of an instant, her face went from curiosity to disappointment.

She partially closed the door until her billowy dress filled the gap, effectively blocking passage into the house. "What do *you* want?" she said quietly.

Nate had forgotten to remove his hat, so he did so now and held it against his chest with both hands. "Hope I'm not disturbin' you, ma'am."

Tightening her mouth into what looked like a painful knot, she looked older than he remembered. A spray of lines fanned from each corner of her mouth, giving her the appearance of someone brittle and starting to crack.

"What is it you want?" she said, this time her tone more insistent.

"Wonder could I talk to Lindy an' Dory, ma'am?"

Now she narrowed her eyes, and two more lines creased vertically above the bridge of her nose. "I thought we had an understanding about that."

Nate lowered his head and nodded and then looked her squarely in the eyes. "Yes, ma'am. And I have honored your wishes. I just come to say goodbye to 'em. I heard they are leaving Round Rock for a boardin' school. Is that true?"

The door swung open wider, and Dory squeezed past the dark-blue blockade. In her stocking feet, she had come up quietly, surprising both of them. Mrs. Hildebrand was irked.

All through the winter, Nate had seen Dory only from a distance at school, usually when he played ball with the boys, and she watched from the sloped schoolyard where the girls spread their blankets. Up close like this, he could see how she had changed. She was taller and her shoulders wider. Her blonde hair covered her shoulders and reached almost to her elbows. Her face was still defined by the clean, youthful lines of an ivory cameo, but she had lost the simplicity of a child's features and gained a kind of quiet and confident bearing along with the grace of her movements. Like a fawn transformed into a doe.

"Hey, Nate!" Dory greeted. Her expression was luminous, almost canceling out all the gloom in the mother's scowl. "Did you come by to visit?"

"Come to say g'bye to you an' Lindy."

Dory looked up at her mother. "Mother? Aren't you going to invite Nate inside?"

Like a hound catching a scent, Mrs. Hildebrand raised

her nose in the air, revealing two thin webs of skin that hung down from her chin and connected to her neck. She clutched Dory's shoulders and pulled her back into the folds of her dress.

"It's getting close to suppertime," the woman said tersely, her chin just above the top of Dory's head. "I need you to set places at the table."

Like a candle flame snuffed out by a gust of wind, Dory's face lost all its light. "Mother, can't we just talk a little bit?"

"You can talk right here," the woman insisted. She widened her stance to show that she was not leaving the doorway. Behind her, footsteps tapped in the hallway. When the door swung open wider, Lindy pushed her way to the front.

"Nate!" she said with a smile. "What in the world are you doin' here?"

Nate rotated his hat a few degrees and glanced at the mother to see if she would deny him the right to speak. When she only glared back at him, Nate cleared his throat.

"I wonted to say g'bye to the both o' you. Billy tol' me how yo're goin' off to school."

Lindy put on a sulk. "We didn't get any say in it. We *have* to go!"

"It's for your own good, young lady," said Mrs. Hildebrand. "You'll be the first—"

"Neither one of us wants to go!" Lindy shouted over her mother's droning voice.

Mrs. Hildebrand's head turned as if jerked by a rope. "That will be enough of that! We've been all through this! Do you know what other girls would give for an opportunity like this?"

"Then pick two of *them!*" Lindy yelled.

Mrs. Hildebrand made a show of composing herself.

"It's one of the finest girls' schools in Europe. And Paris is the cultural center of the world. There's no place like it."

Dory looked up at her mother. "But you haven't even been there."

The mother stiffened and sniffed. "I'll see it when I come to visit you."

"Don't bother," Lindy mumbled. She turned and walked away, the heels of her shoes stabbing the wood floor as she retreated to the back of the house.

Mrs. Hildebrand forced a smile and presented it to Nate like poison. "It was nice of you to come by," she said, her voice rising and falling in a meaningless melody. "Now, these girls have things to do." She pulled Dory back and began closing the door.

"What about summer?" Nate asked hurriedly. "They'll be back then, won't they?"

The mother hesitated with her hand on the doorknob. "They'll be starting school late, so they'll be attending in summer, too. They'll have some catching up to do." She made a quick nod as a final gesture. "Goodbye," she said in a clipped voice.

Dory managed to push her way into the shrinking space in the doorway. "Goodbye, Nate."

Nate tried to offer a proper farewell to her, but Dory was mouthing a silent word to him, exaggerating the movements of her lips like the way people do when they speak to the elderly. *Win-dow,* she mouthed and pointed over her shoulder toward the back of the house.

When the door closed in his face, Nate stood looking at the pristine shine of its white paint. Then he plopped his hat on his head, walked down the steps, and slipped the knot on his reins. After climbing into the saddle, he took the paint at a walk, turned two corners of the house, and came up on the back side just as the window at the far end opened.

Dory's head parted the folds of green curtains, and she waved Nate over, stacked her forearms on the windowsill, and waited for him to approach. When he reined up before her, she extended a hand to Peaches, and using the backs of her fingers, she stroked the soft velvet on the front of the horse's muzzle.

"She's still the prettiest horse in the county," she whispered.

Nate nodded once. "I reckon so."

She leaned to one side and smiled. "That saddle looks good on her, Nate."

"It's the one I was savin' my money for," he said.

Dory nodded. "I know." Then her smile dissolved as her eyes slanted with the sadness that people wear at funerals. "I'm sorry 'bout my mother, Nate. She doesn't know you, and she won't listen to what I have to say about you."

"I've followed her wishes," he said quietly. "I ain't even talked to you at school."

She lowered her eyes. "I know."

Peaches snorted and shook her head, rattling the hardware of her bridle. Dory checked the room behind her and then leaned closer to Peaches.

"You be quiet, girl," she whispered. "We're supposed to be having a secret rendezvous."

From deep inside the house, they heard Lindy's voice making some kind of protest. When the mother's sharp rebuke intervened, Lindy said no more. Then came the angry stamp of shoes on a flight of stairs. The sound climbed to the second floor, and then a door slammed. After that, all was quiet.

"Maybe you'll like a big town once you get there," Nate suggested. "My mama—my real mama—was fond o' goin' down to Austin for these flower festivals they got there."

Dory's eyes softened. "Do you remember her, Nate?"

He nodded. "Sure. I was only five when she died, but I ain't likely to ever forget 'er."

Peaches shifted her weight and whipped her tail at the flies landing on her haunches.

"I wish I could stay here, Nate," Dory said in a voice so despondent it made him ache for her.

"Why d'you reckon she's sendin' the two o' you there?"

"It's on account o' Lindy," she said. "I heard Mama and Daddy talking about it. They found out she's been seein' a man who's too old for her...someone they do *not* approve of."

"Who?" Nate replied.

"I don't know his name. They think she needs to learn some manners or something, and they're afraid she'll hate them if they send her by herself." She shook her head slowly. "Lindy already hates them."

Nate looked off toward the sound of the creek, but it was not visible through the junipers. "Well," he said and met her brown and amber eyes, "it's a raw deal...'specially for you. But maybe there'll be somethin' over there that you'll like. You never know how things'll turn out."

Even as he spoke, he felt the emptiness of his words. Dory stared at him as if she had heard none of it.

"I'm going to write to you, Nate. You don't have to write back if you don't want to. I just know it'll help me to be able to talk to you." She raised her eyebrows. "Will that be okay?"

He looked down at his hands stacked on his pommel and imagined all the ribbing he would get from Dudley and Naomi and John Thomas if letters were to arrive at the Champion ranch addressed to him in the fancy script of a female.

"I ain't so good with letter-writin', but I reckon I can give it a go."

When she smiled, it was like watching the sun peek out from behind a sky troubled by dark clouds. He straightened in the saddle and nodded in the direction of his ranch.

"I got to round up some strays that split off from our herd. Reckon I better get to it."

Dory's moist eyes shone brighter now, as if all the afternoon light were trying to gather in a place too small to contain it. "I'll be older next time you see me," she said in a dead-earnest voice. He was afraid she was about to cry.

Trying to stem her tears before they could sink into his heart, Nate managed a gentle laugh meant to put her at ease. "I reckon I will be, too. Some things just cain't be avoided."

When she did not smile, he wished he had not spoken at all. From deep in the house, Mrs. Hildebrand's strident voice called out like the cry of a hawk.

"Dorothy?! Come in here! I want to talk to you!"

Dory reached behind her and then held out a small, leather-bound book through the window. "This is for you, Nate," she whispered.

"What is it?" he asked.

"It's something I bought for you."

He dismounted, dropped the reins in the dirt, and hooked his hat over the pommel. Stepping closer to the window, he took the book and felt its fine leather covers. On the front was a painted image of a horse—a pinto with light and dark splotches of brown against its dominant white. Gently, he ran the fingertips of one hand over the painting and felt its raised texture on the leather. When he realized that the horse's markings were similar to Peaches's, he guessed that she had done the artwork herself. Opening the book, he thumbed through the pages and frowned.

"There ain't no words!" he told her.

Dory smiled. "It's for you to write in."

Nate felt his face tighten up as if a drawstring had been pulled around it. "But what do I write?" His eyes roamed over her face, and he realized he was trying to commit a perfect image of her to his permanent memory.

"Just write about yourself...each day, if you want to."

Nate closed the book and held it in his hands as if she had handed him a baby bird that did not yet know how to fly. "You mean...just sit down an' write whatever comes to mind?"

"If it helps, you could do it like you're writing to me. You know? Like a letter."

He screwed up his face with a question again. "But not post it?"

Her smile softened to the kind he imagined that an angel might wear. "Maybe you'll let me read it one day, Nate."

Narrowing his eyes, he began a slow nod to show he was considering such an ingress into his private life. If he would talk to anyone about his innermost thoughts, he knew that person would be Dory.

"I guess," he said and looked into her doe eyes again. It was odd to him that at this moment, she seemed like the older of the two of them.

"Here," she whispered and reached for the book. When he surrendered it, she turned to the back of the pages and turned the book around so he could see. "This is my address at the school, if ever you feel like sending me a real letter."

Mrs. Hildebrand called again from the kitchen. Dory closed the book, but she did not extend it to him.

"I have to go," she said.

Now, her face showed nothing but sadness. When he held out his hand for the book, she made no move to give it back to him, so he stepped closer. Taking hold of the leather covers, he felt her firm grip on the book and waited for her to relinquish it. When she leaned out from the window, the book itself seemed to draw them closer. Dory's head tilted ever so slightly as she touched her lips to his. Her mouth was soft and welcoming, and he felt as if he had connected to something holy and secret. Something uniquely his own. He knew this moment would stay with him forever. Like a scar. But one that held only good memories.

When she pulled back, her teary eyes stayed on his as she backed through the green curtains. Then he watched her fingertips hook over the sash of the window to slide it down. The curtain stilled, and he heard her soft footfall moving away from him out of the room. Nate was left with the feeling that he remembered when his father had sat down with him and his brothers to explain that their mother had died.

After securing the book in his saddlebag, he donned his hat, gathered his reins, and led Peaches around the corner of the house to start back the way he had come.

Letters

10 Rue des Pierres
Paris, France
May 29, 1874

Dear Nate,

A week in a stagecoach to Houston ought to be a punishment for criminals. We had dust for every meal, and the bones in my body came unglued from all the bouncing on those hard seats. Daddy hired a lady going back to her home in France to escort us. She was as miserable as we were. If she had not been paid already, I think she would have quit the trip in Elgin and walked back. Her name is Miss Bevard. Lindy calls her Miss Beaver-lard to her back.

I thought the train ride to New York would never end, even though we flew across the land like we were all on horses that never got tired. It was smooth riding, but that was 10 days of being caged up with people you would never want to meet. Fat salesmen who sweated and smoked cigars and talked too much. Loud families with children you'd like to spank. Prissy old women with bad breath. Men wearing their Sunday clothes who thought they were too important to talk to anyone else.

It turns out the railroad part of the journey was nothing compared to crossing the Atlantic. The ship was called Oceanic but Lindy named it Nauseanic, because we were sick as two dogs that had eaten rat poison. Those were Lindy's words. Miss Bevard vomited on someone's valise in the dining area. She was not well thought of by the passengers.

You can't believe the ocean. Every direction I looked into the distance, all I could see was the faraway line where water meets the sky. And the waves are like bullies trying to push us around. It was a big boat, but in the rough water with waves crashing all over the deck it was a nightmare. We just stayed in our room and moaned about how sick we were and prayed the ship would just go down and take us with it. Miss Bevard did not disagree.

Nine days of this. We arrived at Liverpool on a Monday, but my stomach still thought it was on the ocean until Wednesday. I don't know how we survived a week on that water.

On a train again, we traveled for 3 days to London and from there sailed out the Thames River, which everyone on the boat pronounced Tims. Anyway, we crossed over the Channel to France on a big paddle-wheeler called the Queen. Only 2 hours for that trip to Calais. From Calais we took a train for the last part of the journey all the way to Paris. That took 3 ½ days. I have to tell you, Nate—as much as I miss Texas—I dread the idea of going through all that again in the other direction.

I don't think I'm going to like this school. I don't speak French, and that's all that comes out of their mouths here. I'm taking a course to learn their language, but the teacher does not like us to use English. She knows it but will hardly ever use it. I guess she expects me to read her mind.

And you can imagine what it's like to sit in a literature class where all they speak is French. I'll probably fail everything until I can learn parler francais. That means to speak French.

Lindy hates it here. They won't let us go out from the campus except in groups with teacher escorts. Lindy gets mad a lot and gets in trouble. I think she <u>wants</u> to fail everything so they will kick her out. That's okay with me, because Daddy would never let

her make that trip alone. If she comes back, I
come, too.

Only two things good can I tell you about this
place. One is that they have a stable not far from here,
where students can take riding lessons. That was the
first course I signed up for. The other thing is that for
the first time I am getting lessons in painting, and I
have discovered that I love it even more as I learn
about it. I'm not talking about painting a barn. This is
painting on canvas to make portraits and still-lifes
and landscapes. Like the horse on your leather book.
I'm learning a lot about colors and how they work
together. And I like this teacher. Her last name is
Chevalier. She says art has no language barrier. It
speaks every tongue. I like that.

I hope you will write me back and tell me what
you are doing. I missed seeing you over the last
months I was in Texas, but at least then I knew you
were close by. Over here the missing is something else
altogether. I don't want to lose our connection, Nate.
So please write.

Give Peaches a big hug around her neck for me.

Yours,
Dory

———

August 30, 1874

Dory,

I got your letter but I have not had any news that
seemed worth writing about until now. I'll get to that.
First I should tell you all is good in Round Rock with
the exception of Mr. Henderson at the Sentinel. Looks

like our newspaper is going out of bizness. I don't know why. Seems like there is always news to print and people want to read about it. Daddy says its on acount of the econamy. Which I cannot explain. Anyway I will miss the paper ever time I have to build a fire in the wood heaters or in the kichin stove or when I wrap up my noon meal before going to work.

I seen your mother and father in town last week and both look the same as last time I seen them, so I guess they are doing all right. Your mother was at Miss Mayweathers store again and your daddy was waiting outside in his carrige. That old sorrel mare that pulls it is favoring a swole up fetlock and I showed that to him. He thanked me, but I don't know if he knew who I was. I asked about you and Lindy but he did not say much.

There is talk of a railroad coming here. It might not be for a few years but some survayers for the Great Northern have been looking at land to the south and east of town. If that happens it shood make traveling back here a little easier for you.

My brother John Thomas is planning to get hitched to Sarah who works at Mr. Kirkpatricks hotel. They are talking about moving to the Arizona Territory. He says he is all done with ranching. I don't know what else he can do but he seems set on going.

Now my news. I have had my hands full of work with green horses. For my uncle George for Mr. Snyder and ours here. I guess word spreads because I got more jobs around the county. Then I got offers from all over. Leander, San Marcos, and Kerrville. Even Waco. One came from Lampasas but this is not a good time to go there. Lots of killings going on. I

*been so bizy I missed racing Peaches at the July 4
festiful.*

*You know how I like working horses, but I like
working from the back of one better. Mostly I want to
work with cattle. Which is why I will start to turn
down a good many horse jobs. I like working our own
cattle but I like hiring out to see new places too. When
I get the time I do some cowboying for a couple a
spreads in nearby counties. Daddy says it is all right
long as I am caut up with work here at our place.*

*My brother James is learning how to take over
most of our daddys work as ranch manager and with
John Thomas going away that leaves me to head up
the work details. I guess you could say I am foreman
now. Maybe the youngest one in the county.*

*Well that is my news. I wish you well in learning
how to talk like a France lady. Its good you found a
way to ride over there. I'm wondering if those France
horses require that language from their riders. I'm
betting they wood understand you either way. Its how
you say it that is important. They listen to your boots
and to your knees too. And the way you sit or lean.*

*I never painted nothing before less it needed a
good coat to keep the rain off. Maybe one day I will
get to see something you painted.*

Nate

And tell Lindy hello for me.

10 *Rue des Pierres*
Paris, France
September 24, 1874

Dear Nate,

I was so happy to get your letter yesterday. I know
you will think this is silly but I tried to smell Texas on
the envelope. And maybe a little scent of Peaches. But
it just smelled like paper.

I am proud that you are a foreman now. That
means that people trust you and know you will get a
job done. Of course people already knew that about
you, but now it is official.

My time with horses is half of the best part of
being here. Sometimes we get to ride outside of town
through farmlands that are no longer in use. Our
riding teacher goes along but she is much nicer than
the teachers at the school. I have made a good friend
who rides with me. Her name is Sabine. Just like the
river at home. She helps me with my French too. She
says I ride like a *voleur de grands chemins* leaving the
scene of a crime. I found out later that means a high-
wayman. That's like a stage robber.

The horses here are tall and have long legs and
most of the girls have to use a stool to reach the stirrup. I don't. Over here people like to do fancy things
with horse tails. Weaving them like Miss Mayweather
does with her hair. The saddles are real skimpy on
leather but the rest of the tack is pretty much like
home. I have seen a lot of different breeds of horses
here but none of them are as pretty as Peaches.

The other best part is my art class. I am working
on a painting of the view from my dormitory window.
If I can get Sabine's father to take a picture of it, I can

send it to you. He makes his living as a photographer
in Paris.

Lindy has been sent to the *directrice de l'école*—
headmistress—six times already. All the girls think of
her as a troublemaker. The only friend she has made is
another troublemaker named Lya. Lindy is getting
bad grades and does not even try to get along with her
teachers. She says she and Lya slipped out one night
but they did not get caught. I tried to talk to her but
she will not listen to me. All she talks about is leaving
this place, but she never talks about going home.

She did tell me about the man she was sneaking
out to see in Texas. She called him Tis or Tizz. That is
all I know about him except that he is a lot older than
her. I know she writes to him but I don't think he
writes her back because Lindy and I share a mailbox
and I always check it early as soon as the mail
comes in.

I am picking up a few French words every day but
I still have to ask people to talk slow and repeat everything. Sabine is the only one who does not laugh at
me. I guess people are the same everywhere. Some of
the girls try to get me to talk so they can make fun of
the way I sound. One teacher told me my voice was
like *mélasse* and that it needed to be more like water. I
looked that word up in my book. It means molasses. In
school I have to write my name as Dorothée.

I have grown some, Nate. About an inch. And I
am stronger. We have a game time called *heure de
gymnastique* twice a week and it is held in a room
with lots of soft mats and these bars you can climb on.
We have to do cartwheels and back walkovers and
these flips called *appuis renversés*. If I was to perform
these on the street at Round Rock, I would probably
be sent to one of those places they keep crazy people. I

like the bars. I was the only one who could pull myself
up to my chin five times. Since I did that, a few of the
girls have been nicer to me.

I was homesick when I first got here but I am
doing better now. Riding and painting have helped a
lot. But getting a letter from you helps the most. If you
write again, I have a favor to ask. Would you send to
me something of yours that I could keep to remember
you by? It doesn't have to be anything real special, but
it would be nice if it was something you valued. Not
in terms of money, but more like something that has
some personal meaning to you. You decide what
that is.

Give Peaches another hug for me and please write
to me again when you feel like it.

Yours,
Dory

———

November 19, 1874

Dory,

There is a reason that so much time has gone by
since I last wrote to you. When school started up in
September I was coming back through town on my
way home and your mother come out of your daddys
office and waved me over. She told me to come inside
and sit which I did. Your daddy was there but he left
the room. I think he was embarrassed. He remembered
me and told me I was right about his carrige horse. He
thanked me. Your mother had a speech ready for me
and delivered it like a circuit judge talking to a prisoner. I'll just cut it short and say it was a order for me

not to write you again. I don't know how she knew
but I did not lie to her when she asked.

I reckon it aint you who told her so I figure there
are only two ways she knows that we write. Could be
the post office here letting her know or it is someone at
your school who sorts the mail. Your mother made me
promise I would not write you but I figured I owed
you this last one to explain.

I reckon I will see you when you come home for
Christmas.

Nate

PS You are probly wondering about the cigar band I
put in the envelope. It's the thing you wanted me to
send you. I will tell you about it one day.

Also in case you are wondering—my little sister
wrote out the address on this letter so my handwriting
would not show. She made up the name in the top left
corner too.

10 Rue des Pierres
Paris, France
December 4, 1874

Dear Nate,

My parents are not letting us come home for
Christmas. Sainte Chapelle gives the students one
month to spend the holidays with their parents.
Daddy says that the trip takes so long that coming and
going would take more time than we have. And
because we are so behind in our schoolwork. That's
because we can't understand what our teachers are
saying. Mother wants us to spend Christmas here in
France with a tutor to work on our French lessons.
The headmistress has already arranged this with
Sister Ines, who talks deep like a man and hits the
back of my hand with a straightedge if I don't give an
answer that pleases her.

Lindy is so mad she has decided to go on a talking
strike. She won't utter a word to anybody unless she
and I are alone where nobody else can hear. Then she
has plenty to say. She has learned to curse like those
men who work in the quarry at home. Even in French.
It is the curse words she wants to learn first. I do not
see how Sister Ines will take to that.

I did not intend to write a letter so full of disagree-
able subjects, so let me tell you about the horse that I
ride. He is called a French Trotter and his name is
Audacieux, which means bold one. I call him Audie.
They say he used to race pulling a one-man cart.
When he retired from racing his owner gave him to
the school. He loves to run in the fields and sometimes
on the paths he breaks into a fast stiff-legged walk.
The teacher says that he is remembering his old days

on the racetrack. He is a good horse but he would not
be able to keep up with Peaches herding cattle.

I am almost finished with my painting. My art
teacher wants me to use a few bright colors to pull the
scene out of its gray mood, but I don't see the school's
main yard that way. For me—most things tend to be
gray right now.

Thank you for sending the cigar band. It's perfect.
I coated it with candle wax so it would last. I get a
warm feeling every time I look at it. I will always
keep it, unless, of course, you ever want it back.

Nate, even if you decide to stop writing to me
because of your promise to my mother, I will continue
to write to you. I do not care what my mother thinks.
She gave up her right to control me when she shipped
me off to this place.

Take care of yourself. And Peaches too.

Yours,
Dory

July 1878

Chapter Twenty-Three

After a three-day stint of rounding up cattle scattered along Cowhouse Creek and driving them to their owner at the Bar 9 ranch near the Brazos, Nate and Billy Hill were homeward bound, trekking due west toward Round Rock through a dry and trackless boulder field that people called "the Indian Rocks." The place was so called due to rumors of Comanche rituals held there as recently as five years ago.

As they traveled, Billy kept up a constant, one-sided conversation that rambled on and on and suffered from a lack of direction. Nate tolerated the long-winded waste of words by scanning the landscape. He was determined not to miss one of the few springs that sustained travelers in this arid terrain. So far, Billy had not spotted a one, but there seemed to be a tacit understanding between them: Billy provided entertainment; Nate looked out for their livelihood.

When Billy reined up and paused in his narrative to take a drink from his canteen, Nate stopped with him. Both horses blew and snorted and settled down from the redundant rhythm of the journey. As Billy tilted back his head and drained his canteen, Nate shielded his eyes with a hand flattened before his hat brim as he studied the broad plain that stretched before them. The glare of the sun dotted the chaparral with bright speckles of silver and painted the rocks around them with a reddish-gold.

"You smell that?" Nate asked quietly.

Billy wiped his mouth with his shirtsleeve, his pinched eyes above his arm scanning the land. He lowered his arm and stopped breathing.

"Smell what? I don't smell nothin'."

Nate concentrated on the wind. Feeling a light touch of current on his left cheek, he looked to the south. "Woodsmoke," he said and stared at the stand of trees they had skirted for the past couple of miles. "And there's some other scent mixed in...somethin' sharp an' rank."

Capping his canteen, Billy frowned and scanned the edge of the forest, his head turning left and right like a compass needle searching for true north. "You see anythin'?"

Nate shook his head. "You ever think 'bout Comanches still bein' out here?"

"This far south?" Billy challenged.

Nate shrugged. "All this used to be theirs, you know."

"Well, it ain't theirs no more!" Billy argued.

Nate arched an eyebrow. "Might be some Comanches don't agree with you on that."

They sat their horses and let their eyes take in every facet of the land. It was the longest stretch of silence Billy had allowed since starting their journey home.

"What makes you think it might be Comanches?" Billy whispered.

Nate shook his head. "Didn' say I did."

Billy winced and stared open-mouthed at Nate. "Well, why in hell'd you bring up the Comanches for?" He sounded angry when he spoke, but Nate could see the uncertainty in his eyes. "Maybe we should'a been quieter," Billy whispered.

Nate laughed. "You been jabberin' since we left the Brazos. I doubt we could'a heard a pots and pans peddler takin' his wagon through here."

Billy scrunched up his face in a scowl. "Aw, hell, you know me. I just like to talk, is all."

The wind shifted, and once again, the acrid scent of woodsmoke washed over them. "There it is again!" Nate whispered. "Smell it?"

Billy lifted his nose in the air. "That there's burnt leather," he volunteered. "An' I oughta know, 'cause I burned up a good boot last winter tryin' to dry it by a fire."

From their right came the clatter of hooves of a lone horse coming down the slope, not a stone's toss away. Turning to the sound, Nate reined Peaches around to face a man approaching them on a white-socked chestnut mare. The rider's loose body rocked from side to side as his horse picked its way through the rocks and brush. He was dressed in a tan blouse and open gray vest. Under the brim of his dusty hat, he wore a stern expression and a bushy brown mustache that drooped like a permanent frown. His eyes fixed on Nate and Billy and never blinked.

Stopping in front of the two boys, the stranger blocked the narrow trail and said nothing as he studied Nate up close. Then he shifted his focus to Billy, but right away, his gaze returned to Nate.

"What're you boys doin' out this-a-way?" He asked the question in a no-nonsense monotone. The thick timbre of his voice grated like gravel crunched beneath a boot heel.

"We're just on our way home," Billy volunteered, his voice higher than usual.

The man lifted his chin toward Nate. "Whatta *you* say?"

Nate looked into the stranger's light-blue eyes but

relaxed his focus to let his peripheral vision assess the whole of the man. A blued revolver was holstered at his right hip, but his hands remained before him, gripping his reins in a relaxed fashion.

"Like he said," Nate replied, "we're headed home."

The man's face showed nothing at all. "An' where's that?"

Nate nodded west. "Round Rock."

The mustachioed man straightened. "You boys live in Round Rock?"

"Not in the town," Billy was quick to say. "We live outside it on our ranches. Nate's is on Brushy Creek, and mine is out toward the Onion Branch."

"Who's the sheriff in Williamson now? Is it still John Peay?"

Billy shook his head. "Sher'ff Strayhorn."

The man examined them from hat to boots. "I see you boys ain't fixed for trouble." He hitched his head like a regret. "Run into the wrong man out here an' he'll git the drop on you." He pointed to the rifle scabbard attached to Nate's saddle. "What you got in there? Looks like a old Henry?" He chuckled deep inside his chest. "'Bout the time you pull that thing halfway outta that scabb'rd, you'd be lookin' into the muzzle of a man's pistol." He cocked his head at an angle and squinted. "Ain't you boys got side arms?"

"We got 'em," Billy lied. "Just don't wear 'em all the time." He gestured toward Nate. "B'sides...Nate, here, is a crack shot with his repeater."

The man's mouth knotted into what might have been a private smile. "That so?" he said, letting Nate see the amusement in his face. Nate said nothing.

"Coupla years ago, he got second in the shootin' match on the Fourth o' July," Billy bragged.

The man leaned again and seemed to study Nate's horse. "That paint o' yor'n looks like she might be fast."

Billy cleared his throat. "Nate's won the—"

"Fast enough!" Nate interrupted and gave Billy a hard look. Nate leaned forward and stroked Peaches's neck. "She's trained as a cow pony mostly."

The stranger eyed Peaches. "How much you take for 'er?"

"Wouldn' sell 'er for no amount," Nate answered without hesitation.

The man smiled, turned his reins around his pommel twice, and pulled a small leather pouch from the pocket of his vest. Laying a curled piece of paper in one palm, he sprinkled tobacco from the pouch, rolled the paper, and ran the edge along his tongue. When the seal was to his liking, he took the cigarette in his mouth and let it hang downward from his lips so that it bobbled up and down when he spoke.

"No amount, huh?" When he smiled, the loose cigarette leveled out before him. "Never know'd nothin' that couldn' be bought for some price."

Striking a lucifer against the buckle of his cartridge belt, he cupped the flame with his free hand and lit his cigarette. After taking in a long draw, he blew a stream of smoke that hovered in the still air before him and then came apart like rotted fabric.

"How 'bout on a trade?" he suggested and nodded down at his own horse. "This here chestnut, and I can throw in maybe ten dollars." When he saw no reaction from Nate, he added, "An' I gotta old cap and ball Remington I could prob'ly part with."

Nate shook his head. "No amount," he repeated. "This horse and me...we're partnered up solid."

Holding his cigarette between thumb and forefinger, the man took a draw again and blew a double stream of smoke through his nostrils. He nodded as though he were accepting one more disappointment in his life.

"I can see that," he said, his voice carrying an unexpected sincerity.

"Hell, *I* might wanna trade," Billy butted in. "What kind o' Remington we talkin' 'bout?"

The stranger appraised Billy's dapple gray with a glance and shook his head. "Offer's just for the paint."

No one spoke as the man took another draw on his cigarette. This time, when he exhaled, the cloud of smoke drifted toward the slope whence the man had come. Once again, Nate smelled the mix of woodsmoke and scorched leather wafting from the trees. He turned his head to Billy, but he was speaking for the benefit of the man blocking their way.

"We need to git home. I got work to do."

A branch snapped at the edge of the forest and turned every head that way. A lone rider emerged from the woods on a powerful gray stallion. Even before Nate could make out the rider, he recognized the horse. When the new arrival moved from the shadows into full sunlight, his hat band shone like a chain of silver coins. With his stringy blond hair hanging to his shoulders, the rider jerked up on his reins and raised a hand to block the sun from his eyes. Right away, he pulled up a bandanna to cover the lower half of his face.

"Barnes!" the masked man yelled. "He wants you back at camp!"

The high-pitched voice clinched it for Nate. It was Dixie Brooks.

With his mouth hanging open, Billy squinted at the man on the gray. Turning quickly to Nate, Billy started to speak, but Nate was waiting for him, staring into Billy's eyes with a silent message. Nate shook his head in tiny increments, the movement so slow and deliberate that

Billy closed his mouth and turned back to the sound of the gray as horse and rider disappeared into the shadows of the trees.

The man named *Barnes* showed no indication that he had heard his name called out. He flicked ashes from his cigarette and studied Nate's paint again.

"Damned good-lookin' horse," he reaffirmed and shook his head. He stuck the cigarette into his mouth, leaned on his pommel with one arm, and cocked the other arm elbow-up as he propped his free hand on his thigh. "What if I said my horse plus thirty dollars? What would you say to that?"

"Same answer," Nate replied without delay. He nodded past the man's shoulder toward the trail ahead leading west. "Mister, I got obligations to git to." He flipped his fist over and poked a thumb at Billy. "My friend does, too. Will you clear the way?"

As if he had heard none of what Nate had said, Barnes remained in his relaxed pose and produced a crooked smile as he continued to admire Peaches. Then he straightened and tapped his heels into the chestnut's sides. The horse balked but stutter-stepped off the trail into the brush, where the man reined around to face Nate again.

"You know who I am, boy?"

Nate made a quick decision not to lie. "Just that yore friend called you *Barnes*."

Barnes looked at Billy. "How 'bout you?"

Billy shrugged. "I thought he called you *Bob*." Billy nodded toward the woods. "What're y'all burnin' back there, anyway? Smells like burnt leather."

Barnes's smile widened. "You boys git on along now."

Nate urged Peaches forward at a walk, and Billy followed. The two of them were quiet as they slowly put distance between themselves and the stranger. When the trail widened a bit, Billy prodded his horse to gain Nate's side. Turning in his saddle, Billy checked their back trail.

"He's gone," Billy whispered and faced forward again. "Damn! For the last half minute, I was 'bout half scare't o' gittin' a bullet in my back!"

Nate said nothing.

"That feller that showed up...an' pulled up a mask... weren't that the Brooks boy that got throwed outta school back when yore oldest brother was around?"

Nate kept his eyes straight ahead. "It was."

"What do you reckon they're doin' out here?"

Nate shook his head. "I thought it best not to ask."

Billy kept staring at Nate as though he needed more explanation. "Did *you* think we might git shot?"

Nate pursed his lips. "I considered it. For all I know, we still might. That man Barnes could be gettin' up ahead o' us to ambush us."

Billy reined up and fell in behind Nate. "I'll let you ride up front. You got better eyes than me."

Chapter Twenty-Four

They had traveled less than a mile beyond the rocks when Billy twisted around in his saddle and peered out over the chaparral they had crossed. "Nate!" he called out in a stiff voice. "There's someb'dy comin' up hard behind us! It ain't Barnes. Rider's on a buckskin, looks like."

Nate reined up and turned in his saddle. The rider was chewing up the distance between them as if he had a war party of Comanches on his tail. The man was leaning forward in the saddle, but now he straightened and raised an arm high in the air.

"Better git out your rifle," Nate advised and turned Peaches around. He slid his Henry from its sheath, worked the lever, and held the gun poised before him where he could quickly swing the stock to his shoulder.

Billy walked his horse in a half circle and stopped to form a flank at Nate's side. He pulled out his daddy's Winchester and held it down by his side with one hand on the shank of the stock.

"That ain't the same feller, is it? Maybe on a diff'rent horse?"

"Not 'less he changed clothes, too," Nate said.

When the man was fifty yards out, he cupped a hand beside his mouth. "Don't shoot, boys! It's me, Nate! Tiz!"

Twenty yards out, Martin Tisdale slowed his mount to a trot, the buckskin blowing and heaving her chest as she bobbed her head up and down. White froth foamed at the corners of her mouth and hung in strings that dangled and swung with the movement of its head.

"Ain't that John Tisdale's brother?" Billy whispered.

Nate lowered the hammer on his rifle. "Yeah," he said. "Sure is." After setting the hammer on safety, Nate inverted the rifle, stuffed it back into its scabbard, and watched his old friend approach.

Tiz wore a big smile as he reined up beside Nate, stirrup to stirrup. As if he had dressed in a hurry, his faded-blue blouse was only half tucked into his trousers. His sand-colored hat was the same Nate remembered from the day they had raced for money in the west pasture. Now the hat sported a hawk feather jammed into the band at a jaunty angle.

Tiz offered his hand. "How the hell are you, son?" He gripped Nate's hand and shook it with such vigor that Nate's head bobbled on his shoulders. "They told me two riders had come by, and when they described yore paint, I figured it to be ol' Peaches there."

"Been a while, Tiz?" Nate said. "You been well?"

When they released hands, Tiz leaned away and eyed the length of Nate. "I been aw-right, I guess. Looks like you done growed some! You look fit as a racehorse!"

Nate gestured with his hand toward Billy. "You 'member Billy Hill?"

Tiz plucked the front of his hat brim. "We ain't met, but I know yore name."

Billy's eyebrows rose. "Yeah? How's that?"

Tiz put on his smile again. "Lindy Hildebrand."

Billy's face sobered. "How do you know *her?*"

Tiz laughed. "Well, we got to know each other purty damn good b'fore her mama sent 'er off to t'other side o' the world."

Billy swallowed. "You was courtin' 'er?"

With a fingertip on the underside of his hat brim, Tiz pushed his hat back to an angle that revealed a pale band of skin high on his forehead. "As much as could be allowed, considerin' she was a pris'ner in 'er own house."

It was clear that Billy wanted to ask more, but he seemed to withdraw into himself. Raising his rifle, he guided the muzzle into the mouth of his saddle scabbard and pushed the weapon deep into its pocket. Then he just stared out into the wide expanse of the prairie as if he wanted to spit at something.

Tiz chuckled under his breath and smiled at Nate. "How's ever'thin' in Round Rock?"

"Railroad's finished laying tracks through town. That's what ever'body's talkin' 'bout."

"I heard that," Tiz said. "That's gonna mean a lot more money comin' through there."

Nate said nothing to that. He nodded back toward the Indian Rocks.

Who're you with back there, Tiz?"

Tiz turned his head and squinted toward the rocks as though he might spot one of his company from there. "Just some boys I run into up in Denton Coun'y. I guess you recognized Dixie Brooks back there."

"Who's this Barnes fellow?" Nate asked.

Tiz's face wrinkled. "He tol' ya his name?" he asked, his voice rising with surprise.

"No," Nate said, "but Dixie come out o' the trees and called it out."

Tiz laughed and shook his head. "Damn! Sounds like Dixie!"

"So, who is he?" Nate pressed. "This Barnes fellow?"

Tiz shrugged. "Just a out-o'-work Texas cowhand. Didn' give ya a hard time, did he?"

"Just a little pushy, I'd say," Nate replied.

Tiz shrugged. "Well," he drawled, "that's just the way he is."

Nate waited to see if there would be more, but Tiz busied his hands with the buckskin's mane, needlessly flipping the dark hairs to one side or the other. "What're y'all doin' out this way, Tiz?" Nate asked.

Tiz arched his eyebrows. "I could ask the same o' you."

Nodding toward Billy, Nate crossed his wrists before him and relaxed in his saddle. "Me an' Billy been roundin' up cattle for a man over on the Brazos."

"Oh-h-h," Tiz fairly sang. "So yore pockets are full o' wages an' you decided to take a route as lonely as a church on a Sa'rday night." Tiz laughed. "An' who do you run into but Seaborn Barnes." The amusement in Tiz's eyes was like a dancing flame struck on a lucifer.

"What's wrong with him?" Billy snapped.

Tiz laughed again. "Well, nothin' 'xcept he's a road agent of the highest order."

Billy frowned. "Then why didn' he rob us?"

Smiling, Tiz shook his head. "There ain't no figurin' Seaborn. I reckon you caught 'im in a rare mood."

"Why're *you* ridin' with him?" Nate asked.

Staring down at the reins in his hands, Tiz began weaving his head left and right. "Well, me and Seaborn and Dixie and a coupla others all ride for the same man." He glanced at Nate and then turned his head quickly to look south. "Ain't nobody you'd know."

Billy spoke up. "We might? We know 'bout every rancher in Williamson Coun'y."

Tiz frowned into the sun and thought for a time.

"Well," he finally said, the single word full of apology, "it ain't really somethin' you boys need to know."

Nate watched his old friend comb the buckskin's mane again. "Tiz, what are y'all up to?"

Tiz's troubled eyes bored right into Nate's. "Maybe you boys oughta just forget about seein' us. Can you do that?"

When Nate did not answer, Billy spoke up. "Y'all are fixin' to rob someb'dy, ain't ya?"

Tiz lowered his head and kept up the pointless flipping of the buckskin's mane. After taking in a deep breath, he purged the air in a rush and then looked from Billy to Nate.

"Listen to me now," he began, his voice all business. "Them boys back there wanted to make sure you two could never mention us to anyone. You know what I'm sayin'?" The skin tightened across his forehead. "I told 'em I knew you, an' I'd take care o' things...that I could depend on you to keep quiet."

Nate kept his voice calm. "What is it we need to keep quiet about?"

Tiz shifted his gaze out to the prairie and pulled at his upper lip with a tooth. Finally, he breathed in and out quickly and looked at Nate with earnest curiosity.

"Cain't you just forget you seen us?" A pained look seized Tiz's face. "Look...I was told to git yore word on this. Either that or make sure you'd stay quiet."

Billy's face reddened. "What the hell's *that* s'posed to mean?!" He started to rest his hand on his rifle butt but thought better of it. Tiz's pistol was holstered on his hip, but he showed no interest in taking it out. He glanced at Billy and made a dismissive wave of his hand.

"Leave off on that, son. I ain't no killer."

The three of them sat their horses in an uneasy triangle. The silence of the prairie was absolute, making the creaking sounds of their saddle leather seem a conversation unto itself. When a breeze picked up out of the south, the dry leaves of a nearby yucca rattled with hollow clacking sounds. Nate listened to it as if the land itself were laughing at the folly of the men who passed over it.

Tiz stacked both his hands on the horn of his saddle and leaned forward on stiffened arms, his head bowed like a man engaged in private prayer.

"We're all friends here," Nate advised quietly. He waited for Tiz to look up. "We'll make a deal with you, Tiz. You ride back with us now to Round Rock...go out to yore brother's ranch and lay low...and we won't mention yore name should somebody ask." Nate turned to Billy's anxious face. "You aw-right with that, Billy?"

Billy snorted and spat off to one side. "Well, he ain't *my* friend, but...if that's what you wanna do—"

"I cain't just ride off with you," Tiz whispered, his head shaking as he spoke.

"Why not?" Nate challenged. "You aw-ready got a mile start."

Tiz shook his head as though embarrassed. "I need the money," he moaned.

"You mean...you need somebody else's money," Nate said.

Annoyed, Tiz nodded back toward the Indian Rocks. "I cain't just leave Dixie. Him and me sorta partnered up."

"What is it y'all are plannin', Tiz?"

Lowering his eyes, Tiz shook his head again. "Lord, don't ask me that, Nate." When he looked up, his eyes were pleading. "But I can tell you this...I don't never plan to hurt nobody."

"Hmm," Nate said, making a humming sound deep in his throat. "Can you say that 'bout Barnes and the others?"

Tiz frowned like a man who believed that the world had somehow wronged him.

"Well, can you?" Nate pressed.

Tiz began to shake his head. "I reckon not," he admitted.

Nate waited to let Tiz's reply hang in the air for a while. "I reckon there's a right and a wrong somewhere in all this. An' I figure you know which is which. Am I right?"

Tiz looked away. "Reckon I do," he murmured.

Nate took off his hat and fingered the moist sweatband. Without looking up, he spoke to Tiz in the same gentle voice he used with horses.

"You need to git out o' this arrangement right now. It's the only way I can be quiet 'bout seein' you. I'd have to tell your brother, John, you know."

When Nate looked up, he saw Tiz staring at the sky in the east, where the scarlet and gold colors of the sunset seemed to have been assigned to the wrong horizon. Worrying his lip with a tooth again, Tiz looked like a man suffering through the misery of a stomach cramp.

"Aw, hell," he groaned and stared at the distance he had just covered. "I still got to go back for Dixie." He turned to let Nate see the conviction on his face.

"Is that your word on it?" Nate asked.

Tiz looked Nate in the eye. "It is."

Nate nodded. "Aw-right. We cain't wait on you, so I'd 'preciate it if you'd come by our place on your way out to John's. Can you do that? I need to know you got out o' there aw-right."

"Yeah," Tiz said, "I can do that."

Chapter Twenty-Five

After removing saddle and blanket from his horse, Nate brushed down Peaches, fed her grain and hay, and led her into her stall. Checkers sat by the door and watched the entire grooming. Nate crossed to the tack room door, opened it, and faced the dog. Then he patted his hand three times against the side of his trouser leg.

"Come here, Checkers," he whispered. "I got to lock you up tonight."

Head down, the dog obeyed and jumped over the threshold. Inside the room, Checkers curled his tail under and made short, pitiful wags under his belly. Nate laid out a blanket on the floor, and the dog stepped onto it, circled twice, and plopped down. Nate kneeled and scratched him behind his ears.

"Cain't have you barkin' up a storm when a stranger comes a-callin' tonight. I'll bring you some water."

After latching the door, Nate took a step into the yard and checked on the house. All was quiet, and the windows were dark. He delivered Checkers's water bowl and then headed for the house, hoping to find something to his liking left over from supper. He hadn't eaten since morning. Easing the door open, he entered quietly and listened.

It was dark inside, but right away, he sensed someone's presence in the room. A crisp scratching sound came from across the room, and a yellow flame flared near the hearth. The sound of it was like a sudden rush of wind or water heard at a distance. The flame settled to a sedate, teardrop shape, illuminating the white beard and face of Nate's father as he leaned in his chair and lighted the lamp on the side table. The wick took the flame, and the shield dropped in place, pushing a halo of soft yellow light across the side of his father's face. Nate pulled the door closed until the latch clicked.

"I was just about to wake up James an' John Thomas an' the three of us come a-lookin' fo' ya," his father said.

He was sitting in the leather chair where, each night after supper, he smoked his pipe and read the newspaper. The rims of his eyes showed some pink color, and the loose skin below made fleshy hammocks that made him look older than he was.

Nate took off his hat and stood before his father. "Sorry, Daddy. We ran a lil' late, an' I didn' have no way to let you know."

Jack nodded, his stiff white-and-gray beard brushing against his chest. "I und'ahstand that, son. But I want all of you boys to stay close to the house fo' the next few days. I need you he'ah workin' with those new mustangs."

Nate laid his hat on the hearth and sat next to it. "What's goin' on, Daddy?"

The elder Champion picked up his pipe and ran his thumb around the rim of the bowl several times. Then he set the pipe back on the table.

"I don't want you tellin' anybody about this, do you he'ah me?"

"Yes'r," Nate promised. He leaned forward, propped

his forearms on his knees, and threaded his fingers together, his attention on his father complete.

Jack Champion settled back deeper into his chair and reclined his head against the backrest. He closed his eyes long enough to gather his thoughts, and then he turned his old sheriff's eyes on Nate.

"Sam Strayhorn paid me a visit this mo'nin'. Brought me some news. Somethin' he thought I oughta know about."

"The sheriff came out here to the ranch?"

The old man nodded. "I reckon you been hearin' about this Bass gang? Last ye'ah they held up a Union Pacific train near Ogallala. Stole a fortune in gold coin. Lately, they've hit the Texas Pacific a coupla times up around Dallas."

"Yes'r," Nate said. "I heard about 'em at school. Lot o' the boys talk about Sam Bass like he's some kind o' hero or somethin'. Lee Moore does."

The ex-sheriff shook his head. "Lee Mo'ah might change his mind if Sam Bass was to stop him on the road and ask to see the inside of his pockets. Bass is just one mo'ah reprobate who ain't got the mettle to make a livin' the honest way." He scowled and hissed a stream of air through his teeth. "Hero!" he huffed. "Some people say the same thing about Jesse James—that he's some kind o' righteous bandit standin' up fo' the South—but these people don't know what they'ah talkin' about. Outlaws like these are the scum o' the earth. Vicious and full o' hate. They place no value on a human life if a man stands between them an' the money they want."

"Yes'r," Nate agreed. "I know 'bout men like this."

The old man nodded and then went very still. His eyes bored into Nate the way an auger digs into the soil. Raising his right hand a few inches from the armrest of the chair, he punched his forefinger down three times onto the leather upholstery.

"Sam Bass and his gang are right he'ah in Williamson Coun'y. They'ah plannin' on robbin' the bank in Round Rock."

Nate stopped breathing for a moment. "How d'you know all this?"

"The Rangers caught one of 'em a while back, and they convinced 'im to turn on Bass an' relay his plans so a trap could be set. Rangers ah scattered all ovah town now, an' Strayhorn has called up all his deputies for full-time duty till this gets settled."

Nate tried not to believe that it was Sam Bass hidin' out near the Indian Rocks. It was hard to believe that Tiz was desperate enough to ride with someone like Bass.

"When's this gonna happen?" Nate asked.

The father shook his head. "Don' know. They'ah waitin' to get info'mation from the info'mant." He raised a vertical finger in the air and bobbed it toward Nate, something he did to give importance to whatever words he was about to say. "Nobody in this family leaves the ranch until this is ovah. Do you und'ahstand?" This tone in the old man's voice was the law at the Champion ranch—one that brooked no questions, no opinions, and no disobedience.

"Yes'r," Nate whispered.

When Jack pushed up from his chair, Nate stood. "Daddy?"

His father stopped and turned, and to Nate, the silence in the room was like that gentle squeeze on a trigger just before gunfire erupted. "Me an' Billy smelt woodsmoke out at the Ind'an Rocks. There's some men set up camp out there."

Jack's eyes caught fire in the lamplight. "How many?"

Nate sighed. "Don' know for sure. One of 'em stopped us an' tried to buy my horse."

Jack narrowed his eyes. "Buy it...or take it?"

"He was ready to pay cash on a trade for his horse. 'Course I wouldn' agree to it."

"Did you git his name?"

"Someb'dy yelled out to 'im from the trees...called 'im *Barnes*."

"Any mention o' Sam Bass?"

"Nos'r."

The father thought for a moment and then nodded once. "I'll let the she'iff know." Then his eyes softened. "Have you had anythin' to eat?"

"Nos'r.

"Mary left you a plate on the stove," Jack said. "I'm goin' to bed, son."

After his father had closed his bedroom door, Nate entered the kitchen and transferred the plate of warm food to the sideboard, where he ate standing up, finishing off the meal in less than a minute.

Slipping quietly out the front door, he stepped down from the porch and sat on the front step with his boots on the ground. Above the yard, the stars spread across the sky as thick as sparks rising from a pine bonfire. Thinking of Tiz, he stared toward the road beyond the gate and listened for the sound of hoofbeats that he was afraid might not come.

"Come on, Tiz," he whispered to the night.

After twenty minutes, he stood to go back inside and was surprised to find a stiff feather pinned into a crack between the boards of the door. A hawk feather. He pulled it out and twirled it between his thumb and finger. Its white blotches caught the starlight in flashes, reminding Nate of the signals the soldiers sometimes sent using mirrors.

"Good man, Tiz," he said aloud.

He walked quickly to the barn and opened the door to

the tack room to find Checkers standing in the center of the floor, looking eager and wagging his tail.

"Come on out, boy. Yo're back on duty."

The dog ran out the door and made for the yard. By the time Nate had returned to the house, Checkers had settled in under the porch. Nate entered the house, took off his boots, and tiptoed to the room he shared with James, John Thomas, and Dud. He set his boots by the door, stripped off his clothes, and slipped into his bed.

"Hey," came James's whispery voice from the back corner of the room. "You just now gittin' in?"

"'Bout a hour ago," Nate whispered.

"You talk to Daddy?"

"Yeah, he knows I'm home."

"How'd it go over on the Brazos? You make some decent wages?"

"I did," Nate said.

James huffed a laugh deep in his chest. "How 'bout Billy? He pull his weight?"

"He did fine," Nate whispered. "Didn' git paid as much, but he don't know that."

James laughed again, and then both brothers went quiet. The bedroom window was open, and a cool breath of night air crept across the room. From the east pasture, Nate heard the tear of grass, a snort, and the grinding of molars.

"Daddy tell you the news?" James whispered.

"'Bout Sam Bass? Yeah. We were just talkin' 'bout 'im."

Nate heard James turn in his bed, the leather straps under his mattress creaking like dozens of knots tightening in a sequence. "I wouldn' mind bein' there to see those boys face the Rangers, would you?" James said. "The way I hear it, they ain't likely to go easy. There'll be a fight."

Nate could hear his brother's escalated breathing as he

241

waited for a reply. At the front wall of the room, John Thomas snored quietly, oblivious to the conversation. Dud, too, was gone to the world.

"Maybe so," Nate said.

Nate closed his eyes to the dark, and though the image of the darkness was unchanged, it made him feel as if he were in a more private place. "Don't reckon I'd ever wanna go out o' my way just to see people try an' shoot each other."

After several seconds of quiet, James made a humming sound in his chest. Nate heard him settle back into his bed, and they spoke no more. When his weary body seemed to sink deeper into his mattress, Nate let his mind follow the same path to take the freefall into sleep.

Chapter Twenty-Six

By midafternoon, Nate had worked in the paddock with four of the mustangs, introducing each to a bridle and the willingness to circle in the direction of Nate's bidding. The horses showed promise as cow ponies, and each had earned a name according to its temperament, coat, or quickness to learn: "Frowner," "Think-About-It," "Preacher," and "Coffee."

The day had been hot, and the long shadows of late afternoon brought a welcome relief. At the well house, Nate emptied half the bucket into a wash pan, took the pan into the yard, and cleaned his hands, face, and neck with the cool water. Then, leaning forward from the waist, he poured what was left in the pan over his head and back. When he straightened and began combing his fingers through his scalp, he saw the mail wagon making its way from town.

"Tug" Blevins sat in the driver's box and worked the ribbons over his two draft horses as if he were late for a delivery. As the wagon bounced and banged over the rough road, its flat canvas canopy rippled like water running over a shallow shoal. Nate raised one arm as a distant greeting, but Tug did not return the gesture. Instead, he turned his team through the Champion gate and rattled into the yard. Checkers came out from under the porch barking up a storm, so Nate walked to the dog and calmed him with gentle strokes along his flank.

"Say, Nate!" Tug called out, "d'you hear 'bout the shoot-out in town?" He reined up his team and brought the wagon to a stop in the middle of the yard.

Tug was about to burst with his news. Straightening up from the dog, Nate walked to the wagon. Two mail bags were stacked behind the seat in the bed, one sack labeled for "Georgetown" and another for "Taylor."

"What happened?" Nate asked.

Tug's eyebrows pushed low over his eyes, and his fleshy forehead pleated with the thick, rounded mounds of flesh. "All hell broke loose on the street is what happened! Deputy Grimes got hisself kilt deader'n hell! Shot five times, so they say. And another deputy from Travis Coun'y took a bullet to the chest! He prob'ly ain't long for this world! But he got off a shot and hit one man in the hand. And they was—"

Nate pushed his hand, palm out, to stop Tug's nervous jabber. "Who was doin' all this shootin'?"

Tug's eyes widened. "They's sayin' it was Sam Bass and his boys. One of 'em got shot right'n the head. Feller dropped like a turkey shot out the air. Texas Ranger did that. Turns out they was Rangers all over town a-waitin' on 'em. One Ranger, he come a-runnin' out the barber shop with shavin' soap all over his face, and he made it damned hot for them boys. Chased after 'em afoot and shot one through the body right here." With some difficulty, Tug twisted around and poked a finger into the swell of fat just above his left hip. Then he twisted the other way and tapped a finger to his rib cage. "Come out 'bout right there. They's sayin' that'n was Bass hisself."

"So, they got 'em?" Nate asked.

Tug raised a plump forefinger. "Just the one...the feller with the hole in his head. Bass and another'n started to git away—ol' Bass a-reelin' in the saddle and his partner tryin' to prop 'im up. When Bass fell off his horse, his pard come back for 'im, helped 'im mount again, and held off the Rangers to boot!" Tug shook his head. "That kid couldn'a been much older'n you, Nate, but he stood his ground and got Bass outta town." Tug shrugged. "If it *was* Bass."

"You mean they escaped?" Nate said.

Tug pointed northwest out the gate. "Way I hear it, they headed out toward the Tisdale place. Mr. Tisdale, Senior was gone to Georgetown with John, but the missus was there by herself and scared half to death, what with all the blood. She said the man who was all shot up was wontin' some water, but she was afraid to accommodate 'em. So they rode on. North, so she said."

Nate looked north across the road, ran one hand through his wet hair, and flung droplets of water into the dirt. "How many are out lookin' for 'em?"

Tug laughed. "There ain't *nobody* out a-lookin' for 'em! Ever'body's afraid Bass has got a army out there a-waitin' to ambush any posse that might take up the chase."

Nate frowned. "The Rangers ain't trackin' 'em?"

Tug shook his head in a slow, deliberate arc. "Ain't *nobody* goin' after *them* boys!"

Nate felt a hot bubble of anger rise inside him. "They kilt one o' our deputies, an' we just let 'em ride away?"

Making an elaborate shrug, Tug shook his head again. "The Rangers are gittin' men together. They say they'll start to trackin' in the mornin'."

Nate propped his hands on his hips and stared in the

direction of town. "Well, what was it all 'bout? Were they tryin' to rob the bank or somethin'?"

Tug made a doubtful face. "Nobody seems to know for sure. It all just happened so quick-like. These boys was in Koppel's Store. Plenty o' people saw 'em—Rangers and sheriff's deputies—but nobody knew who they was. Grimes thought he saw a coupla pistols on one of 'em, so he walked into the store to confront the man. That's when it all blowed up."

The door to the house slammed shut. Nate turned to see his father standing on the porch.

"I got to git goin'," Tug said. "You tell yore daddy what I just tol' you. Just figured y'all would wanna know." He gave Jack a nod. "You take care now, Nate."

Tug started to send a little snap through the ribbons, but he paused with his hands before him. "Oh, yeah! Nate! Almost forgot!" He grunted as he leaned forward to reach inside a wood crate beneath his seat. "This come in for you on the train yesterdee. I tol' Elwood I'd drop it off for you on my way to Georgetown."

Tug's round, fleshy face stretched like rubber when he produced a big, toothy smile. He held out an envelope covered with the colorful stamps that Nate remembered from Dory's letters. It had been years since he had received a letter from France.

"Looked important to me," Tug said and winked. "Female handwritin' and all. Figured it deserved a special deliv'ry!"

Nate studied the flowing cursive address that rendered his name. In the top left corner was the type set return address for Dory's school.

Tug's team of horses seemed anxious to go, but he held them back with a strong grip on the reins. "You know, it's a funny thang. I watched Elwood sort through the Round

Rock mail as I tightened the rope on one o' my bags that had loosened up on the train ride. I just happ'ned to see 'im toss your letter into the "city pile," and so I spoke up. He seemed mighty embarrassed 'bout it. When he set it aside on the counter, I just scooped it and said I'd hand-deliver it to you. Said I was goin' right by your place anyway. Then Elwood...he seemed all agitated like he didn' know what to say."

Nate stared at the letter and frowned. "It's from a friend o' mine over in Paris, France. I ain't heard from 'er in over a year." He raised his eyes to the mail carrier and tried to keep his voice friendly. "Do you reckon Elwood might hold back some o' my mail? Maybe redirect it to somebody who asked 'im to do that?"

Tug pursed his lips. "That'd be breakin' at least two fed'ral laws that I know of. Hell, he could go to jail for a long time for such shenanigans." Tug lowered the reins and leaned his stout forearms on his knees. "Elwood can be a weak-kneed sonovabitch. You want me to look into it?"

Nate shook his head. "I don't wanna git 'im in trouble. I think the trouble is somebody else!"

Tug's eyebrows came together in a peak over the thick bridge of his nose. "Who'd that be, Nate?"

Nate shook his head. "I'll take care of it, Tug. I 'preciate you lettin' me know."

Tug nodded and settled himself in his seat by bracing his boots on the front of the driver's box. "Aw-right, Nate. You take care now, and y'all keep a lookout for them damn killers till the Rangers git off their asses and git their job done."

The mail wagon turned a half circle and rolled toward the gate, the harnesses jangling like loose spurs and the canvas support ribs rattling enough to wake the dead.

Nate stuffed the envelope into his blouse and walked back to the house where his father waited. Checkers walked ahead of him and slunk underneath the porch.

"What was that all about?" Jack asked.

"The Bass gang came into town today. There was some shootin' in Koppel's Store that spilled out into the street. Deputy Grimes was kilt. And another deputy from Travis Coun'y got shot, too."

Nate's father looked away, and the muscles in his jaw tightened. "Caige Grimes," he muttered. "Young fellah. Used to be a Range'ah." He turned back to Nate. "Did they catch 'em?"

"Nos'r. They killed one and wounded Bass. Bass an' another one got away."

Jack's stony face showed no change, but his eyes smoldered. "Got away?" he huffed.

Nate shrugged. "Nob'dy wanted to go after 'em. They were afraid Bass had more o' his gang hidin' out there just waitin' for the law to show up."

The father said nothing. The air whistled through his nose as he glared at the east pasture.

"Daddy, they killed one o' our deputies. Why don't we go after 'em? We could git Lee Moore an' his daddy, the Koppel brothers, John Tisdale, and some men from the quarry."

Jack Champion shook his head. "I am not the she'iff anymo'ah, son. It's not my job, and it ce'tainly is not yo'ahs. An' you don't wanna be invitin' yo'ah friends into a situation that could git them killed. That kind o' thing can stay with you and eat you up from the inside." He began to nod. "The Range'ahs have prob'ly sent out somebody to scout fo'ah an ambush."

Nate looked down at the porch's floorboards and crossed his arms over his chest. He shook his head once and brought up his face to show his disappointment.

"Well, can I at least ride over to the Tisdale ranch to check on 'em?"

The old man looked to the west. The sky was a rusty-gold color that was sharpening to scarlet. The long shadows of the hills pooled like dark water over the fiery grass.

"No," the father said, "yo'ah gonna stay close. Besides, it's too late in the day."

"Daddy, those men have prob'ly waded across the Lampasas River by now."

Jack leaned in an inch or two and put a hand on Nate's shoulder. "The most impo'tant word in that statement of yo'ahs was 'prob'ly.'" The old man shook his head. "You don't stay alive on 'prob'ly,' son. You got to think with a cool head and a openness that allows fo' what *could* happen. Not what you *want* to happen. Do you und'ahstand the diff'rence?"

"Yes'r, I do," Nate replied. "But somebody's got to ride out to the Tisdale ranch."

The elder Champion dropped his hand from Nate's shoulder. "Why is that so impo'tant?"

"Tug said Bass an' another man showed up out there an' frightened Mrs. Tisdale. John and his daddy were gone to Georgetown. Somebody needs to check up on 'er...make sure she's aw-right."

The ex-sheriff lowered his brow as he looked north in the direction of the Tisdale ranch. "Well, I s'pose we'll have to go an' see that she's aw-right. Go inside an' tell James and John Thomas they'ah goin' with us. I'll ask Mary to pack us some food. You boys saddle up and get the big gray ready fo' me. We'll want two lante'ns fo' the trip back. They'ah's a good-sized moon tonight, but it won't rise until well aft'ah midnight."

Nate stared at his father. "I didn' know you kept up with the moon, Daddy."

Jack almost smiled. "Old habit," he explained, "from when I was she'iff." He pointed to the door. "Now go get your broth'ahs." When Nate turned to go inside, his father added, "Ev'ahbody pack a rifle, too. And a box o' shells."

Holding the door open, Nate nodded and then hurried inside to fetch his brothers.

Chapter Twenty-Seven

The four Champions rode north for the Tisdale place, each with a rifle propped across a saddle just behind the horn. Staying on the main road, they took their horses at a relaxed gallop until the darkness thickened around them and reduced the trail to a faint, starlit glow of sandy soil that cut through the scrub and grass.

"Light up yo'ah lante'n, John Thomas," the father ordered.

John Thomas was quiet until the horses settled to a walk. "The horses can still see the road, Daddy."

"It ain't fo' the hosses," his father replied. "It's to show who we are...an' who we ain't!" He reined up his horse, and the others gathered around him. "We don' know fo' ce'tain if men are out a-lookin' fo' these kill'ahs. If we shine a light, we won't be taken fo' outlaws."

"Well, hold on a minute!" John Thomas complained. "I cain't find my lucifers."

As they waited, Nate prodded Peaches closer to the gray. "Daddy, are you thinkin' the Rangers put out the word 'bout not followin' Bass to trick 'im?"

It was too dark to see the old man's face. When he spoke, his voice was a private whisper intended for Nate alone.

"I'm actin' on what *could* be, son."

Nate could feel his father's attention fixed on him the same way his schoolteacher waited for him to answer a question. "Yes'r," he replied.

John Thomas struck a lucifer and set it to the lantern wick. When he lowered the shield a circle of light spread among them, but beyond that glow, the land was rendered pitch black.

"Kinda makes us a good target, too, don't it?" Nate said.

His father said nothing to that. He motioned for John Thomas to approach.

"I'll carry that," he decreed and took the lantern from his son. "You boys, follow behind me...just outside the light."

———

When they reined up in the Tisdale's yard, the father turned down the wick on the lantern until the flame was as small as the quick of a thumbnail. Together, they studied the house. All the windows were dark except for one. Nate knew this one to be the parents' bedroom.

"Nathan?" Jack said quietly. "How well do you know the Tisdales' hosses? Would you recognize any that don't belong?"

"Yes'r, I b'lieve so," Nate answered.

The father held out the lantern. "Take this an' check they'ah stalls."

Nate dismounted, took the lantern, and moved quietly toward the barn. Inside, he raised the light at each stall gate to inspect the livestock within. In the first two stalls, he recognized John Tisdale's sorrel and the father's bay. In the third stall, he found Tiz's buckskin nosing at a swatch of dry hay strewn about a back corner. The only other animals in the barn was a stout Belgian draft horse showing gray around the muzzle and two milk cows.

When Nate walked back to his party, he reported his findings. The father took the lantern, turned up the flame, and cupped his free hand beside his mouth.

"Hello, the house!" he called out. "It's Jack Champion!"

Right away, the lighted window went black. The glow from the Champion lantern dimly illuminated the front porch and a small half circle of the hardpan yard. Outside of that, there was only darkness. Nate propped a boot on the bottom step to the porch, stilled himself, and listened.

Within seconds, an inside light filled the rectangle of window closest to the front door. When the door opened, a lighted lamp floated out from the front room, followed by a man wearing a light shirt that hung outside his trousers. The light shone from below and cast eerie shadows across the man's face, giving him a demonic appearance.

"Mr. Champion? Is everything all right?"

Nate recognized John Tisdale's voice. In his stockinged feet, John stepped silently to the edge of the porch, his lamp throwing a large shadow that followed behind him. Then, the elder Tisdale came out the door with a shotgun extended before him.

"That you, Jack?" John's father called out. He stopped beside his son and shifted the shotgun diagonally across his torso like a soldier on sentry duty.

"Me and three o' mah sons," Jack Champion replied in a soft voice. "I apologize fo' callin' on you so late. We thought it best to check on things up he'ah."

"We're all right," John was quick to say.

Nate's father nodded. "I guess y'all got wind o' what happ'ned in Round Rock today. The mail carri'ah told us that some o' the Bass gang stopped by he'ah and frightened Amanda."

"Well, you're right on both counts," Mr. Tisdale reported. He tilted his head toward his son. "John and I were in Georgetown and didn't know nothin' 'bout it till we got home. A bloodied man showed up with a young feller, and they asked for water. Amanda shut up the house and loaded this here shotgun and herded our young'ns into a backroom. The two strangers must'a just moved on, 'cause she didn' have no trouble with 'em."

"Well, that's good to know," Champion said. "So, she's aw-right?"

"She's fine," Tisdale sighed. "One o' the Moore brothers come out to check on 'er an' told 'er 'bout what happ'ned in town. He said one o' the gang was kilt an' another shot up pretty bad. It must'a been Bass that got shot, 'cause the other feller was just too young to be Sam Bass. Anyway, we're on guard and doin' fine."

All the while that the two fathers conversed, Nate watched John Tisdale's nervous eyes. They looked everywhere except at Nate.

"We won't trouble you any mo'ah," Jack said. "Y'all have a good ev'nin'."

"I thank you for your kindness in comin' out," Mr. Tisdale said.

When Jack Champion reined his big gray around, James and John Thomas did the same. Standing at the foot of the stairs, Nate watched the Tisdale elder walk back into his home toting the shotgun. With only a quick glance at Nate, John turned to follow his father.

"John?" Nate whispered and climbed the three steps up to the porch.

John stopped and looked back. Pulling the door

almost shut, he approached quietly in his stockinged feet. Nate brought out the hawk feather and offered it to John.

"What's this?"

"B'longs to Tiz," Nate whispered. "He aw-right?"

Before opening his mouth, John glanced at the other Champions moving toward the front gate. "He's all right," he said quietly. "Thank God he came in when he did." John's face softened. "Thank God you talked some sense into him." He raised his chin toward Nate's father and brothers out in the dark. "They don't know?"

Nate shook his head.

John shifted the feather to the hand holding the lamp and reached out with his free hand to Nate. His eyes were teary as the two friends shook hands.

"You probably saved his life," John whispered.

Nate glanced at the house and wondered where Tiz was hiding. "Did Bass come here lookin' for him?"

John shook his head. "I don't think they knew whose place this was. They just wanted water." John narrowed his eyes. "Who else knows about Martin?"

"Just Billy Hill and me know. Billy won't say nothin'."

John looked down at his stockinged feet and shook his head. When he brought up his face, he seemed to have aged ten years.

"It would kill Daddy if this got out. He wouldn't be able to face his friends."

Nate nodded his understanding but said nothing.

John lowered the lamp and set it on the boards. Widening his stance, he crossed his arms over his chest, the hawk feather extending to one side.

"If Martin can't settle down and work the ranch with me, I'm thinking it's time for him to leave home...maybe leave Texas." His sober eyes fixed on Nate to watch for a reaction. When Nate said nothing, John unfolded his arms and leaned with a hand on the doorframe. "Daddy doesn't deserve this."

"Where would he go?" Nate asked.

"Somewhere it ain't so damned hot all the damned time!" The rough voice in the doorway surprised John, who pushed off from the house and turned around, his foot rattling the lamp shield. Fully dressed and carrying a pistol in his waistband, Tiz walked out onto the porch, faced his brother, and propped his hands on the sides of his hips. "I can sign on with a crew drivin' cattle north. I know o' two outfits fixin' to leave b'fore the month is over." He snatched the feather from John, sat down heavily on the bench against the house, and stretched out his legs, crossing his boots at the ankles. There, he slumped back against the wall and frowned at the feather as he twirled it between a finger and thumb.

John's face darkened like a cloud full of rain as he stared at his half brother. "Anything you want to say to Nate?"

Tiz shrugged and watched the spinning feather. It was Nate who broke the silence.

"You made the right decision, Tiz. Did you come in alone?"

Tiz glanced at his brother as if he knew John would answer. "No," John quipped. "He brought that cocky rooster, Dixie Brooks, with him, but I sent that boy packing. I've got no use for him, and the sooner Martin feels the same way, the better things will be for all of us."

Tiz scowled. "You ain't got no call to judge my friends!"

John took a step toward Tiz. "I do if I see you knocking on hell's door with that jackass!"

Tiz squinted his eyes. "Whatta you care who I ride with?!"

John kicked his brother's boots with his stockinged

foot. "I care about my daddy, who is trying to look out for you and your mother, but you're too self-absorbed to see what you could have here as part of this family."

Tiz hissed a sharp stream of air through his teeth as he laughed. "Well, maybe I'll just make ever'body happy and start over in Wyomin' or Montana or someplace that don't feel like livin' in a hot skillet."

"Maybe you *should!*" John shot back.

For an instant, Tiz's angry face showed a flash of surprise as he stared back at his brother. Then, without another word, he stood, flung open the door, and strode inside the house, leaving Nate and John in an awkward silence.

Out in the dark, the scratchy rhythm of katydids could be heard from the stand of trees beyond the road. A brief flutter of wings came from the chicken coop, but they paid it no mind. Nate tried to think of something proper to say, but a soft clop of hooves came from somewhere near the front gate.

"Nate?!" John Thomas's whispery voice was a mixture of curiosity and impatience. "You comin'?"

"Reckon I better go," Nate said quietly. He moved down the steps and mounted Peaches. John leaned from the edge of the porch and offered his hand again. Leaning from the saddle, Nate took his hand, but this time, John held on and looked deep into Nate's eyes.

"Thank you, Nate. You're a good friend." He jerked his head back toward the house. "When my mule-headed half brother comes to his senses, he'll thank you, too." John released Nate's hand, picked up the lamp, and went inside.

When Nate and John Thomas caught up to their family, James was carrying the lantern and talking to his father, who rode on his left flank. John Thomas took up a place beside his father, while Nate brought up the rear of the party.

Nate thought about Tiz hiding in his own house from his neighbors. There seemed to be something shameful in it, knowing that four old friends had ridden six miles through the night to check on the welfare of his family and then returned along that same six miles to reach their beds to get some rest before the next day's work.

But it was hard to be angry with Tiz. He was the kind to give you his only blanket on a cold night if you were shivering under your own bedding. Then, the next day he might laugh about almost freezing to death, at which point he would turn the story toward fantasy and relate his adventure of curling up with a she-bear and her cubs in a den he happened to stumble upon.

It was clear to Nate that John Tisdale felt a dedication to protect Tiz, even though he was a half brother. Nate admired that—one trait among many others that made John stand out from most men.

Nate stared at the backs of his father and two brothers as they shifted from side to side with the rhythm of their horses' easy walk. The three brothers were bound by the blood of the same mother and father, which connected them by an innate sense of looking out for one another. This same bond extended to William, Dudley, and Naomi Jane, who shared that same lineage. And though he would do anything for his new siblings and their mother, Nate sensed a vague, unspoken line that separated those who were born from Nate's mother and those who weren't. There was no friction in this division, just an awareness of differences in blood, which, to Nate, seemed like a tacit truce that all had agreed upon in order to meld them into one family.

As the lantern lit their way along the dark road, all was still around them. There was no breeze except for the one that came from riding a horse. The heat of the day continued to rise up from the road. Nate took off his hat, arched his neck, and looked up. Stars were scarce with a gauzy cloud cover slowly scudding across the sky, and like his daddy had predicted, the moon had not yet risen.

Tiz was right about one thing, Nate thought. *Living in Texas was like tiptoeing through a hot fry pan.* He fanned his face with his hat and settled in for the ride home. No one in the party spoke for the remainder of the trip. Twice, he watched John Thomas nod off and jolt awake so as not to fall off his horse. Finally, James leaned out and slapped him on the back so hard that John Thomas yelped like he was shot. He got so mad at James that his boiling blood kept him wide awake for the remainder of the ride.

Family love, Nate thought. *It works in strange ways.*

Chapter Twenty-Eight

Because he offered to groom his father's horse, Nate was the last one of their party left in the barn. With both Peaches and the gray brushed down, fed, and watered, he sat on the stoop of the tack room to pull up a stocking that had bunched under his heel. When he leaned forward to tug off the boot, he heard something crackle under his blouse.

Pulling out the forgotten letter, he studied it by the light of the lantern hung above him. Even with the envelope wrinkled, he could see that Dory's flowing cursive had matured. The words stretched across the paper as if she had ruled lines on the envelope before writing.

Using his knife, he cut open the top of the flap. Then he removed a single sheet of folded paper and opened it in his lap.

École des Arts Sainte Chapelle
10 Rue des Pierres
Paris, France

June 24, 1878

Dear Nate,

It has been five years since I received a letter from you. I suppose you are honoring your word to my mother. But if not, if there is another reason, I would like to know. Even if you have found yourself a girl to court back there in Texas, I want you to tell me. You can say anything to me, and I will always listen and try to understand.

As I have written in my last few letters to you, I feel like a prisoner in this school. I never would have dreamed that my parents would abandon me to a place like this. In a letter I wrote to you three years ago, I told you that they visited here just after Lindy ran off, and yet they say they do not have the funds to furnish a trip home for me. I've begged them to send money so that I could arrange my passage back to America, but they say I must wait until I finish school next year.

No one knows where Lindy is. After that first and only letter she sent me, I have heard nothing. But the last thing she wrote in that letter was not to worry about her, because she said she knew how to be happy even if our parents did not. She sounded so strong-willed that I have decided to take her word and not worry about her. She's probably living in luxury somewhere with a duke or a marquis or the King of Spain, for all I know.

I don't know why people go quiet with the ones who love them. I don't even hear from my father anymore, other than my mother writing me and saying that he sends his love. I don't have a real incentive to go back to Texas. If I heard something from you to change my mind, I would come. But since I don't *hear from you at all, I will probably stay here and share a studio with a few artists who are making a name for themselves in Paris. I have sold three paintings in one of the galleries here, which is why I was invited to work in the studio. I am told that I have a promising future.*

Nate, if I don't hear from you after this letter, I will not bother you with more missives. I will assume that you want it that way. Please know that whatever you decide, I will always be your friend and grateful for the little bit of history that we share. If you do have a girl who has caught your eye, she is very lucky and must be quite a young lady.

I will always wish the best for you, Nate. And as always, give Peaches a hug for me.

Dory

Chapter Twenty-Nine

B y early afternoon on the next day, the broil of the sun was relentless. In the pastures that lay in sight of the house, not a steer or cow was to be seen. Nate knew the cattle would be huddled in the shade of the willows and cottonwoods at the creek. In the corral, the remuda crowded into the northeast corner in the shade of the sycamores that grew just outside the fence

There was no wind. The blades of the windmill had not stirred all day, and its latticed tower stood in a silent sulk, useless as an armed soldier without a battle to fight. Since midmorning, Checkers had lain under the front porch of the house and could not be coaxed from his dark retreat.

From the center of the paddock, Nate circled a honey-colored palomino mare. He held the lead rope in a loose arc and turned with the horse as he sidestepped around the snubbing post. With the heat dulling the horse's senses, Nate sent an occasional ripple up the rope and called out a gentle command to remind her of the crisp gait he wanted.

Out on the Onion Branch Road, a rider came out of

the north at a full gallop. It had to be Billy Hill. He was always running his horse too hard. A cloud of dust rose behind his dapple gray and hung low over the land like a smoke trail of pink and gray. Crossing over the main road, horse and rider came through the Champions' gate and raced around the barn to the paddock, where Billy reined up hard on the lathered gray.

"Nate!" Billy called out. "D'you hear the news?"

At this sudden interruption, the mare-in-training broke stride and shied away from the fence. Nate tried to turn her back to her appointed direction, but she would have none of it. Facing him with her ears pinned back, the mare stretched the rope taut and balked, her eyes wide and white-rimmed.

"Nate!" Billy persisted. "They caught Sam Bass!"

Walking toward the frightened mare, Nate carefully pulled the rope hand-over-hand as he approached. "Whoa-oa-oa, now girl," he murmured, the words humming in his throat. When he reached the mare, he untied the rope from the halter and stroked her neck. Her ears went erect, and she blew. For a moment, it looked as though she would stand for being touched, but then she bolted with a snort and began running circles of her own design, repeatedly interrupting her gait to high-step and shake her head from side to side.

"Nate! D'you hear what I said?"

Without looking away from the mare, Nate raised a forefinger as a semaphore, telling Billy to hush and be patient. He watched the palomino until she settled into a sassy trot, her pale mane dancing on her neck and her plume-like tail arching in a show of dignity.

"Nate!" Billy squawked. "Sam Bass is in Round Rock right now...dyin' with a coupla bullets in 'im."

Nate gave Billy a sidewise glance. "I don't reckon it'll mean much to this mustang. I'm trying to put her mind at ease. It don't help none to be a-yellin' like you got a scor-pion in yore boot." He pointed to the barn. "Meet me inside."

By the time Billy had dismounted, tied his horse at the water trough, and stepped into the shade of the barn, Nate was seated on the step of the tack room, his hat sitting upright on a wood crate next to the door. His wet hair was plastered to his skull, and the cooler air in the barn spread over his scalp like a baptism of river water.

"All kinda people been out lookin' today," Billy began, "tryin' to pick up Bass's trail. Jim Tucker an' another boy in the posse had rid right past 'im, them thinkin' he was one o' the workers on the new rail line. And by God, it was Sam Bass, hisself...sitting back against a tree...bleedin' like a sonovabitch. Bass even called out to 'em so they wouldn' pass him by."

"What about the other one?" Nate asked. "Tub Blevins said there was a feller with Bass."

Billy shook his head. "It was just Bass they found. He was by hisself. He talked a bunch, but he wouldn' say nothin' 'bout the rest o' his gang." Billy slid Nate's hat to the edge of the crate so he could sit.

"He didn' put up a fight?"

Billy pulled in his lips and shook his head. "They say he didn' have no fight left in 'im, all shot up like he was."

"Is he in jail now?"

"They put 'im in that old shack down the street from Cooke's livery. They're sayin' he'll be dead b'fore dark." Billy sighed. "Tell you what...it's a good thing yore friend Tiz didn'—"

"Unh-uh!" Nate interrupted and thrust a open palm toward Billy. "You cain't say nothin' to nobody 'bout him. You understand? Not even to me! I want you to forgit 'im!"

Billy winced as if Nate had spoken in Chinese. "Aw-right, aw-right! Keep yore shirt on."

Nate lowered his voice to a whisper. "He quit them just like he told us he would. He come by here last night to let me know."

"Well." Billy laughed. "it's for sure that feller Barnes didn' quit. He got shot dead right in the street. Bullet went clean through his head." Billy tapped a finger to his temple and made an airy sound with his mouth—his version of a bullet flying through the air. "A damn Texas Ranger come a-runnin' out the barbershop with soap all over his face and shot that man Barnes dead."

Nate nodded slowly. "So, you seen all this yoreself?"

Billy lowered his head and swung it left, then right. "Well, I didn' actually see it, but I got it from Lee Moore. He was right there and saw it all from the boot shop across from Koppel's Store. He painted a picture of it near to perfect in my head, so I might as well'a seen it."

Far to the south, a deep rumble of thunder rolled across the sky. Nate looked out the barn door at the solid blue of the firmament. Though he could not see the windmill, he heard its blades start to turn slowly. The loose axle started its rattle until it smoothed out to a steady hum.

Billy stood, walked across the bay of the barn to Peaches's stall, and leaned his back into the gate. "Hey, you 'member that smell o' burnt leather out at the Ind'an Rocks?"

Nate stood and stretched his back. "Yeah, I 'member."

"Well, I went back out there today an' found where they'd camped. Guess what I pulled outta the ashes o' their campfire?"

Nate almost laughed at the bright anticipation on Billy's face. "What?"

Billy's eyes widened. "I found what they was burnin', is what!" He positioned his hands before him like a man about to play a concertina. "A canvas bag 'bout so big... with a leather bottom and leather trim around the lip." He lowered his hands, never taking his eyes off Nate. "Guess what was stamped into the leather at the top?"

Nate waited and lifted both eyebrows.

Billy spoke slowly, enunciating each letter with a touch of drama. "*T*...*P*...and *R*." He shrugged. "The rest was burned away." He kneeled, swept away some hay, and drew a curly figure in the dirt with his forefinger. "Between the *T* and the *P* was one o' those." He pointed at the mark.

Nate stared at the drawing. "Texas and Pacific Railroad."

"Damned right," Billy snorted. "It's one of them bags they carry in their mail cars. Prob'ly was filled with money b'fore they burned it."

"Or mail," Nate suggested. "Like you said, it's a mailbag."

Billy frowned. "What would they want with mail?"

"People send money through the mail sometimes," Nate said. "Last month a man down in Dripping Springs sent me thirty dollars in cash that way...for some horse work I did for 'im."

Still kneeling, Billy stared down at the letters. "You figure they was goin' to rob the train down this way?"

"Got no way to know that," Nate replied. He bent and grabbed his hat. "Billy," he said in a tone that got Billy's attention, "you got to swear you'll never mention Tiz in all this."

Billy's face wrinkled as if he had been accused of a crime. "I ain't gonna say nothin'!"

"I got to hear you swear it," Nate pressed.

Billy tilted his head and squinted. "For real? Long as we knowed each other?"

Nate nodded.

Billy stood, forked his hands on his hips, and pushed his mouth to one side of his face. "Aw-right! If that's what you need. I swear it."

Nate stood and offered his hand, and they shook on it. "What'd you do with the bag?"

"Nothin'." Billy laughed. "It ain't the kind o' thing you wanna keep for a souvenir, you know? Be hard to 'xplain."

Nate fitted his hat to his head. "Sheriff Strayhorn might would wanna see it,"

Billy spewed a rush of air that made his lips sputter. "Well then, he can just go out there an' find it for hisself!"

Outside the barn, the gray nickered, and Billy's eyes angled that way. "I gotta git back. I tol' my daddy I'd clean out all our stalls b'fore dark."

They walked together out into the sun, where the dapple gray stood patiently by the trough. Streaks of dust-coated sweat were layered on the horse's flanks. Her head hung low.

"I'd hate to be yore horse," Nate said.

Billy turned and narrowed one eye. "Why's that?"

Nate hitched his head out of sympathy for the mare. "You run 'er too hard in this heat."

Billy pushed at the air between them. "Awww...horses are built to run. B'sides, she ain't never complained once."

Nate nodded toward the fatigued animal. "She's complainin' right now. You just cain't hear it."

Before Billy could reply, both he and Nate turned to the steady rhythm of a horse out on the road. A heavy-set man on a dark bay came trotting through the gate.

"That's Gil Campo!" Billy announced.

As the deputy approached, he greeted the two boys by plucking at the brim of his hat. "Yore daddy at home, Nate?"

Nate pointed to the house. "He's inside workin' on the books."

Campo eyed the remuda in the corral and then fixed his attention on the palomino isolated in the paddock. "You trainin' all these, Nate?"

"One at a time," Nate replied.

Campo studied the animals and pursed his lips. "If I was a horse...you'd be my choice." He winked at Nate. "I hear you never beat 'em."

Nate looked at the glassy-eyed palomino staring back at them. "Don't do no good to hurt somethin' if yo're tryin' to earn its trust."

Campo nodded. "You boys hear 'bout Sam Bass?"

"Sure did!" Billy chirped up. "Can anyb'dy go into town an' have a look at 'im?"

The deputy looked down at his hands gripping the reins, and then he brought his eyes up to Nate. "Bass died 'bout a hour ago. Looks like we'll be shed o' train robberies for a while anyway." He shifted his gaze to Billy. "I reckon you can go in an' look at 'im if you wont to."

The front door to the house slammed shut and turned everyone's attention that way. Standing on the porch, Jack Champion spread his feet and slipped his thumbs into his waistband. He wore a white, long-sleeved blouse and gray trousers. Instead of boots, he was shod in a new pair of brown shoes that Nate had never seen.

"You fellers take 'er easy now," Campo said and took his horse at a walk to the house.

"I guess Round Rock is gonna be famous now," Billy said to Nate. "We'll always be able to tell people we come from the place where Sam Bass met his bloody an' bitter end."

Nate stared at Billy for a time. "Maybe you oughta think 'bout bein' a writer for a newspaper. You could write about things like a 'bloody an' bitter end.'"

Billy snorted. "I'll see you later, *amigo*." He climbed into the saddle. "Hey," he said, gathering his reins. "If I

269

finish up my work early enough, I'm gonna ride into town an' see what a famous outlaw looks like. You wanna go?"

Nate shook his head. "I reckon he'll just look like a dead man."

Billy's face brightened. "Yeah, but how many dead people have you ever seen?"

A flash of memory brought back to Nate the image of his mother lying in her bed as if she were asleep. Nearby stood his father talking to the doctor in whispers as if they were afraid they might wake her. Nate had walked to the side of the bed and touched her hand. She was still warm, but he knew that hand would never reach out to him again.

"You can tell me 'bout it later," Nate said and gave the gray a light slap on the rump that started the big horse toward the gate at a walk.

Billy dug in his heels and coaxed the beleaguered gray into a trot. As soon as they were through the gate, Billy growled a command and used his boot heels again, and the horse broke into a gallop.

Nate walked to the porch and stepped up into the shade, where Gil Campo was still struggling with a proper greeting for his former sheriff.

"Well, they're doin' fine, Sher'ff," Campo said. "We got another'n on the way. I'm hopin' for a boy...one better lookin' than me if God will show us any mercy."

"Don't need to call me *she'iff* no mo'ah, Gil. Just call me *John* or *Jack*...I respond to eith'ah one."

"Well," Gil said and pushed out his lower lip. "I reckon I can do that."

Jack Champion opened the door and stood back. "Come on inside whe'ah it's cool'ah."

As Campo shuffled inside, Nate stepped beside his daddy. "Can I set with the two o' you? I'd like to hear this."

The father thought for a moment and then nodded. "Come on in, son."

Nate took off his hat and hung it on a wall peg. The three men stood facing one another at the center of the room. Through the open kitchen door, they could hear Nate's stepmother repeatedly tapping a bowl with a stirring spoon. Jack Champion walked to the back of the room and closed the door. When he returned, Campo widened his stance and cleared his throat.

"We found Sam Bass up past the Tisdale ranch in a little side pasture that nudged into some woods. He was purty bad shot up from yesterday. We took 'im back to town, and the doc worked on 'im, but he said it was hopeless. Bass died 'bout a hour ago. There ain't no trace o' t'other feller. We reckon he's headed north. Sher'ff Strayhorn figured you'd wanna know."

"And yo'ah satisfied the dead man is Bass?" the ex-sheriff asked.

Campo nodded deeply. "Oh, yeah...we're sure. That feller, Murphy—the one who rode with them boys and worked a deal with the Rangers—he identified both dead men."

"Did Bass talk any befo'ah he died?" asked Jack.

Campo shrugged. "Nothin' useful. He told us he *ordered* the boy who was with 'im to skedaddle. Said the boy didn' wanna leave 'im, but Bass made 'im. Wouldn' give a name." Gil snorted. "Whoever that boy was, there was more to him than just bein' a outlaw. When Bass got shot off his horse in town, he couldn' remount. So, this young feller comes back under a hail o' rifle fire from the Rangers and gits Bass back into his saddle. Then, on their way outta town, this young feller spots the little Kirkpatrick girl a-climbin' in a tree out front o' her house, and he reins up long enough to call out to 'er. Tells 'er to go inside so she'll be safe."

Jack made an affirming sound deep in his chest. "Well, I guess they'ah's *some* good in ev'ahbody." He looked Gil Campo in the eye. "But let's rememb'ah they killed Caige Grimes."

The three remained quiet for a time, as though to honor the fallen deputy. The spell was broken when Naomi came into the room carrying a sewing basket pressed against her belly. When the three males turned to look at her, she read the solemnity on their faces and turned around to go back the way she had come.

"What about this man Muh'phy?" Champion asked. "Did he give up the boy's name?"

Campo nodded. "Frank Jackson, so he said. Said this boy Jackson saved *his* life when Bass suspected Murphy o' bein' a Judas. Bass was ready to kill Murphy, but the kid talked him out of it."

"Where was Murphy during all this shootin'?" Nate asked.

Campo squinted up at the ceiling boards as though he were recalling the words to a half-forgotten song. "Well... let's see...he said the four o' them come into town to look things over before they'd rob the bank on the next day. That's why they were at Koppel's Store, right next to the bank. Murphy gave Bass some story 'bout havin' to stop off at a privy, and he'd catch up with 'em. What he was really doin' was to git off a message to the Rangers 'bout the bank holdup a-comin'. Then the rest just happ'ned like it did. Grimes noticed these boys carryin' weapons into the store, and so he went inside to investigate. Then the whole thing just blew up." Campo chuckled. "I reckon if Murphy had been with 'em just then, he'd 'a found it purty hot out on the street. He was damned lucky, I'd say."

"So what happ'ns to Murphy now?" Nate wanted to know.

Gil shrugged. "I don't rightly know. He's in cust'dy

right now, but I guess he'll go free. That was the deal. His ol' man is sick an' prob'ly dyin'. He says that's why he made the deal."

Campo sighed, as if he had reached the limits of his talking endurance. But he hadn't.

"Tell you one thing," the deputy went on. "I betcha Murphy'll be lookin' over one shoulder the rest o' his life... watchin' out for that kid."

In the silence that followed, Nate began to wonder how Tiz would take this news about Murphy. Jack offered his hand to the deputy.

"Tell the she'iff I'm grateful for keepin' us info'med."

Campo bowed his head as they shook. "Yes'r, I will." Then he hitched up his cartridge belt and opened the door.

As the two men filed outside, Nate hurried back to his bedroom and slipped from the bookshelf the letter he had written last night. He strode back to the front room, molded the envelope inside the crown of his hat, and stepped out into the heat of the day. The two Champions watched from the porch as Gil Campo mounted his big bay.

Checkers poked his head out from under the porch floorboards, twisted his neck around to see Nate and his father standing side by side, and then backed into his shady post again.

Sitting his horse, Campo nodded once to Jack and then cracked a grin for Nate. "Teach them mustangs some manners, Nate. Might be I'll wanna buy one off you."

Father and son watched the deputy take his horse across the yard and through the front gate. When Campo reached the main road, the bay broke into an easy lope, heading east toward town. They watched until horse and rider disappeared behind the pale-green willows at the seep.

"I need to git a letter to the post office today," Nate said and studied the profile of his daddy's face. "It's important."

Only a few years ago, Nate knew, his father would have questioned him about dropping his work for such an errand. But Jack Champion just gazed at the east pasture and nodded.

"Maybe you can pick up some t'bacco fo' me. Just a small tin. You know my brand."

"Yes'r," Nate replied.

The father started to turn away. "Let me get you some money."

"I got some, Daddy," Nate said and looked his father in the eye. "I'll need to stop out at John Tisdale's place, too. I might be a few hours."

After ten seconds of silence, the old man nodded again and opened the door. "Just let me know when you get back, son." He went inside and closed the door.

Nate walked to the barn to saddle Peaches.

Chapter Thirty

When Nate entered the post office, Orvis Elwood was standing behind his counter, carefully dribbling ink from a bottle onto a stamp pad. When the balding postman glanced up and saw Nate, his fingers twitched, and ink spilled onto the polished wood of the countertop.

"Oh, hell!" the man murmured under his breath. Both his hands dripped ink as he set down the bottle and bent low behind the counter. Bringing up a stained cloth, he began cleaning his fingers and the countertop at the same time.

"Well!" Elwood huffed. "Now I'm going leave a smear on every letter I touch today!"

Nate spotted a stepping stool and a bucket of soapy water sitting on the floor below the front window. A rag was draped over the bucket's rim. The top half of the windowglass was clean, while the bottom half showed a dusky patina of gray-brown dust.

Detouring by the window, Nate snatched up the moist rag and wrung it out. "How 'bout this?" he said, walking the rag to the counter.

Mr. Elwood took it and began a more vigorous attack on his ink-stained hands. "I'll be right with you," he said distractedly and hurried into the backroom. The tap of his footsteps was soon replaced by the slamming of cabinet doors and the clinking of bottles.

When he returned to the front room, his hands were stained as dark as the paw pads of a ferret. By the postman's sour expression, it was clear to Nate that the man was irked at having an audience to his mishap. He laid down a fresh cloth, leaned in, and began scrubbing the counter.

"Help you?" Elwood said, trying to hide the irritation in his voice.

"Mr. Elwood, I come to ask you a question," Nate said, speaking to the bald spot on the man's lowered head.

Keeping his eyes on the task at hand, Elwood grunted, "What is it?"

"Ain't there a law that says you got to deliver every letter that comes through here?"

Elwood shook his head but did not look up. "I don't *deliver* the mail," he was eager to point out. "I sort it out and make it available for people to pick up here. Sometimes the mail carrier might deliver if convenient, but that is *his* choice. If a letter sits here for more than two weeks, I put a notice in the newspaper." He stopped rubbing the counter and worked his elbow in a circle from the shoulder. "If no one claims it within a month, it is returned to the sender."

For being given such a simple question, the man was like a burst dam in giving his answer. Before Nate could rephrase his question, the talkative man had caught his breath and started up again.

"The only exceptions, of course, are Fort Bliss and Fort Hood. We pack up their letters and packages and send them by the mail wagon. Once the mail goes inside the forts, it's out of our hands. The military is responsible for it."

Nate watched the man give his arm another rest and then recommence scrubbing with his other arm. The bald circle on top of his head was now dotted with pearly beads of sweat.

"Ain't there a law that says you cain't give one man's mail to another'n?"

Elwood shrugged his head to one side and kept rubbing. "It's common practice to let a man or a woman collect a neighbor's mail and carry it to the proper recipient."

Nate waited for the man to look up at him, but the postman would not give up his battle with the ink stain. "What 'bout you keepin' letters that I intended to go to France...an' then you handin' over them letters to the Hildebrands?"

The circular motion of the man's hand stopped, and he looked up to meet Nate's eyes. Elwood's face slackened, and his lips parted to form a perfect O. Closing his mouth, he swallowed, bringing life to the protruding lump in his throat, which rose and fell like a fishing bob.

"Who did you say you are?" he asked, his voice rising to a falsetto.

"I'm Nathan Champion."

The postman's eyes grew large as hens' eggs, and the damp skin on his face paled. "I'm sure I don't know what you mean," he mumbled and began rubbing again.

Nate kept his voice calm and even. "I reckon you do."

Elwood suddenly looked up with a cordial smile. "You're the one who breaks horses, aren't you?" When Nate did not fall for the diversion, the postman wet his lips with his tongue and abandoned all pretense of amenities. "What is it you need, Champion?"

Nate leaned on the clean half of the counter, his forearms stacked side by side, hands cupped to elbows. "I'm guessin' it's Mrs. Hildebrand who's put you up to all this."

The postman averted his eyes so quickly, he may as well have confessed. Standing straight as a hat rack, he rested his ink-stained fingertips on the edge of the counter and frowned at the space between his hands. He looked like a piano player whose memory had failed him in the middle of a song.

"Mr. Elwood, I want the letters that I write...to go where they're intended...and the letters that come in for me to go into my hands...*not* Mrs. Hildebrand's."

Elwood closed his eyes and exhaled a long sigh. "She gave me no choice in the matter." He grimaced as he eyed the front door. "She just stormed in here one day and demanded that all letters dropped off here—the ones addressed to go to either of her daughters in France—have to go through her first. She claimed that her girls' school allowed no personal mailboxes. Only the parents can get packages in. That's what she said."

"That don't make no sense," Nate said flatly.

Elwood shook his head. "I know it doesn't, but her husband is a friend to the postmaster general in Washington, and he could get me fired, she said." He shook his head and made a pained expression. "She insisted that any letter coming here from France that is addressed to you... it's got to go through her first."

Nate stared at the man's fearful eyes. "How do you figure that to be legal?"

Frowning, Elwood shook his head. "I don't," he admitted quietly. "I just do like she says." His eyebrows came together, peaking above the bridge of his nose in a pleading slant. "I can't afford to lose my job, you see."

Nate let his eyebrows float upward. "Seems to me you could lose it by what you done."

The implied threat seemed to undo the miserable

man. He pulled in his lips, closed his eyes, and began to shake his head in a slow arc of contrition.

"Mr. Elwood, you work for Hattie Cluck, right?"

Surprised, he opened his eyes. "Of course. She is the postmistress for the county."

Nate smiled to soften the coming blow. "Did you know she is my mother's sister?"

Elwood's face froze as if he'd been slapped. "Oh, my lord! I'd forgotten that!"

Nate maintained a friendly tone. "Mr. Elwood, whatta you think *she'd* say 'bout all this?"

Elwood frowned down at his stained hands, studying them as if his palms were an open book of blank pages. He began shifting his weight from one leg to the other and back.

"She said this was all on account of her daughter being so young," he explained, glancing at Nate to check his reaction. "I have a daughter, too, you see. So, I know what it means to want to protect them." He presented Nate with an expression that fairly begged for mercy. "As a father, you just do whatever you can, you know."

"Does Mrs. Hildebrand have all the letters that should've gone to me?"

The postman made a helpless gesture by spreading his hands before him. "Whether she's still got them, I couldn't say." A hopeful light came into his eyes. "I did express my reservations about it all, but she assured me the letters would get to where they belonged." He shrugged. "I had to take her word, you see." A film of moisture covered the wretched man's eyes, reflecting light coming in from the front windows. He licked his lips. "Are you going to tell your aunt?"

"I ain't decided yet," Nate replied. "But I plan to have a talk with Mrs. Hildebrand."

"But Mr. Champion," the man whispered as he leaned

over the counter. "This may not be a good time. She was here this morning...quite upset...I could tell she'd been crying."

"She git some bad news?"

Elwood shook his head. "Not from me. I had mail for her, but she arrived here distraught and teary-eyed."

Nate removed his hat and pulled out the letter to Dory. He laid the envelope on the counter, and the postman's eyes followed his movements as if watching a magician's sleight-of-hand performance.

"I want this letter to go to France," Nate said clearly. "Do you understand?"

Elwood stood very still, like a man having his verdict read aloud by a jury. Lowering his eyes, he nodded with the barest movement of his head.

"And the next time a letter comes in with my name on it, I 'xpect you to put it in my hand an' nob'dy else's."

"Yes, sir," Elwood promised.

Nate pointed to his letter. "Now I wanna watch you put that where it belongs!"

Elwood frowned at the letter as he lifted it with the fingertips of both hands. "You'll need a five-cent stamp," he advised and looked up at Nate as if he had said the wrong thing. "But I'll be glad to supply that!" he added.

From a drawer, he brought out a green and white stamp, which he ran across his tongue and pressed to the envelope. Flashing a nervous smile at Nate, he turned and walked it to a canvas bag hooked to the wall and dropped it in. Then he looked to Nate for further instructions. When Nate turned to leave, Elwood came around the counter and followed him to the door.

"I hope you won't report me to Mrs. Cluck," he said in earnest. "And please, if you do talk to Mrs. Hildebrand, I beg you...don't tell her that I mentioned her name?"

With the door half open, Nate turned to let the man see the conviction in his face. "B'fore I make any promises to you, I'll see how things go now that we've had this lil' talk."

The postman stepped forward and offered his blackened hand. His face was the picture of optimism.

Having never refused a handshake, Nate met the man's grip and found his hand warm and clammy but enthusiastic.

"Thank you, Mr. Champion," Elwood gushed. "Thank you for understanding."

When they released hands, Nate made a conscious effort not to wipe his palm on his trouser leg. "Mr. Elwood, you seem to think that a secret pact has been made b'tween us. Kinda like you did with Mrs. Hildebrand. Like I said, I'll see how things go."

Nate walked out and crossed the street to where Peaches was tethered in the alley beside the dry goods store. He untied the reins from the awning post and glanced back at the post office door. The postman still stood there, watching him. When Elwood raised a hand in farewell, Nate nodded once, hopped into his stirrup, and swung a leg over his saddle. As he rode west on the street, he felt the postman's eyes fixed on him like two fingers pressed into the back of his neck.

———

The sun had but a few hours before it would dip into the trees at the west end of town, but still, the heat was like a pile of blankets thrown over the hill country of central Texas. Nate let Peaches choose her own speed for the climb up to the Hildebrands' house. When they reached the edge of the clearing, he dismounted and tethered the paint in the shade of the trees. There he hung his hat over the saddle horn, tucked in his blouse, and raked his fingers through his hair. He walked across the open ground and climbed the steps to the front porch. There, he knocked on the door three times and then stood back with his hands propped on his hips.

The door crackled when it opened. Instead of Mrs. Hildebrand's commanding silhouette or her husband's plump and innocuous presence, a short, slender woman with coffee-colored skin stood in the doorway. Nate dropped his arms and felt his anger evaporate.

"Beth'ny? What're you doin' here?"

When the old Negro woman smiled, her teeth shone like the polished ivory keys of a miniature piano. She wore a white apron that reached from neck to knees, all but covering a faded yellow shift beneath. Her thin, dark arms were still corded with a sinewy strength, and she stood as erect and as light on her feet as a fourteen-year-old girl.

"Well, Lawd, Lawd! Would you look at who come a-visitin'?"

Her hair was grayer than he remembered and as wispy as cottonwood down. When she stepped out onto the porch and opened her arms, Nate bent at the knees to meet her embrace. He kissed the side of her face below her sharp cheekbone, and her skin was cool and dry and smelled as clean as freshly washed linens dried in the sun. She wrapped her wiry arms around his neck, pulled his cheek against hers, and made a pleasant humming sound deep in her throat, as if she had just sampled something delicious in the kitchen.

"What in da world bring you he'ah to dis place, Lil' Pony?" Bethany asked in his ear.

"I need to have a talk with Mrs. Hildebrand. Is she home?"

Bethany gently pushed him back to arm's length and shook her head. "A boy bring a telegram an' she rush out wit'out even sayin' one word to me. She even saddle up a hoss wit'out any help an' ride off." Bethany put on the false-scolding face that he knew all too well. "Why ain't you come out to my house to see me, Lil' Pony? It been way too long, an' I gettin' too old to make dat trip out to yo' ranch."

As part of the game, Nate hung his head in shame before giving her an earnest smile. "It don't mean I don't think 'bout you, Beth'ny. There's hardly a day goes by that I don't remember somethin' 'bout you that makes me smile."

She closed her eyes long enough to nod once. "Well, dat's good! Dat mean you don't recall all dem lickin's I give you fo' bein' so rowdy and sassy."

Nate laughed. "Beth'ny, you ain't never even swatted at a fly, much less laid a hand on me. You never even spanked Dud, who prob'ly needed it at least twice a day."

She giggled. "Well, it like somebody once't tol' me 'bout da hosses...you ain't never gonna win dey's trust if all you do is beat on 'em."

Nate's grin stretched across his face. "Where'd you ever hear somethin' like that?"

Her smile spread into her eyes. "Lil' baby boy I use to know. He could talk to dem hosses, an' dey talk right back to 'im."

Nate played along and scratched at his cheek. "Think I've heard of this feller."

Dropping her act, Bethany reached out and took Nate's hand. "It so good to see you, Lil' Pony. I miss da way we liked to sit on da front po'ch an' watch ol' man sun lay down at da end o' da day, close his eye, an' go to sleep. You rememb'ah dat?"

Nate squeezed her hand. "I do." He hitched his head with regret. "I just wish Daddy'd kept you on. The house ain't never been the same without you."

She folded her arms across her flat chest and offered a sad smile. "Lil' Pony, when yo' mama died, yo' daddy juss need a woman to clean house an' fix da meals an' do laundry an' he'p out with da chi'ren. When he find Miss Mary, he didn' need me no mo'. Simple as dat."

"Well, you sure helped us," Nate said.

She chuckled. "Wasn't you needin' dat help. Yo' mind was aw-ready took up with da hosses. Soon's you were able to pull on yo' boots by yo'se'f, you was gone out to da barn an' I didn' see you again till dinn'ah-time. The lookin' aft'ah was fo' John Thomas an' Dudley an' Ben an' Naomi Jane. Mostly Naomi. How *is* dat lil' firecrack'ah?"

Nate laughed. "She's still a firecracker, I reckon."

Bethany stepped backward through the doorway and stood aside. "Come inside whe'ah it ain't so hot, Mistah Nate."

Nate stood his ground. "*Mister?!* You ain't never called me that b'fore."

She swept a slender hand toward him. "Well, juss look at you. Yo' gots to be a man."

"Beth'ny," he said and took her shoulders in his hands, "you can call me *Nate* or *Little Pony* or just about anythin' you wont...but I ain't a *mister* to you. You an' me are friends." He squeezed gently. "More like a mother an' son really."

When she smiled, wings of wrinkles fanned from the corners of her eyes to spread across her temples. "You rememb'ah how we talked 'bout yo' mama sometimes?"

"I sure do. Weren't for you, I wouldn' know half o' what I do know 'bout 'er. Daddy still don't much talk 'bout 'er."

She took his hands in hers. "Maybe he don't talk, but

he ain't forget. You gots to rememb'ah he want you to love yo' new mama. He *owe* dat to Miss Mary. It ain't easy steppin' into a new fam'ly like she done. Dat's why he keep dose ol' feelin's shut inside, Lil' Pony."

"I reckon so," Nate said in a whisper.

Bethany smiled, took a step back, and looked him over from head to boots. "Guess I shouldn' call you *Lil' Pony* no mo'. You done growed outta dat." She narrowed her eyes at him. "How ol' is you now?"

"I'll be twenty-one in September," he said and shrugged. "But I ain't really no bigger than most sixteen-year-old boys in the coun'y."

The kindness in her eyes was like the welcome glow of a lamp in the window of a house. "Well, yo' mama—Mizz Naomi—she was small, and you take aft'ah her. But she seem to stand tallah dan most women. Men, too." Bethany flattened a hand over her heart. "She had somethin' powerful strong right he'ah." Keeping the heel of her hand on her chest, she patted herself three times. "She a special lady. I knew her from da times y'all's church he'p out Mama after my daddy died. Yo' mama was a angel, Nate. You got some o' dat in you, too."

"I wish I could'a known 'er better," he said quietly.

Bethany's smile hardened as she shook her head. "Well, you know well as anybody we don' always git what we want in dis world." She nodded toward the hallway behind her. "Git on in here outta dat heat."

Nate stepped over the threshold and waited as she closed the door. The pungent smell of roasting meat brought back memories of his early childhood.

"Thank you, Beth'ny. You were a gift to me an' my family."

The dusky skin on her face flushed to a darker shade. She raised a hand and pressed it firmly against Nate's chest.

"Dem gifts go two ways, you know. Yo' daddy needed help an' paid me well at a time I needed dat. An' I gots to know all o' you." She closed her eyes and patted his chest once. When she opened her eyes, they were moist and full of light. "'Specially you."

Chapter Thirty-One

She led the way into a high-ceilinged room with a sofa, three chairs, and a long pecan-wood table set back from a limestone fireplace. The entire room was darkened to a permanent twilight by the curtains closed over the windows. Nate stood at the center of the room, feeling the expensive woven rug under his boots. He turned in a slow half circle as he examined the decor. One wall was shelved with books, while the others showed off framed paintings and small, dark, polished, wood cabinets that contained little square drawers for storing tiny objects like buttons and needle and thread, or so he guessed.

"Dis be da coolest room in da house," Bethany said. "Do you want somet'in to drink?"

Nate shook his head and continued looking around the room. "How'd you come to be workin' for the Hildebrands?"

"Mistah Hildebrand come to me," she said and laughed under her breath. "I t'ink he need rescuin' from his wife's cookin'."

"How is it...workin' for them?"

She barely cracked a smile. "Fo' him? He fine to work fo'. He pay good. But I don't see much o' him. He stay right busy at his office in town." Her eyes angled away to the curtained front windows, and she shook her head slowly. "But Mizz Hildebrand...she a diff'rent story." Bethany turned to Nate and narrowed her eyes. "Why you wantin' to see *her*?"

Now it was Nate's turn to stare at the curtains. "Just somethin' I need to git straightened out."

Bethany swept a hand toward the furniture. "Well, whyn't you just sit down and make yo'self at home. I gots to finish up da cookin' b'fo' she git back."

Nate lifted his arms a few inches from his sides and looked down at himself. "I'm too dirty to sit. Why don't I come back an' help you in the kitchen."

Bethany's graying eyebrows lowered. "I t'ink she 'xpect her guests to sit in he'ah. An' she 'xpect *me* to be da one a-workin'...not *you*."

The rattle of wheels and the jingle of a harness came to them from outside. "Dat sound like da buggy now," Bethany said and moved to the front window. Barely parting a curtain with one hand, she leaned her face close to the crack. "Dey both in da buggy. Her hoss is tied behind." Letting the curtain fall back in place, she started for the hallway. "I gots to go out an' take care o' da hoss an' buggy."

Nate started after her. "I'll help you with that."

Bethany stopped and turned in front of the door. "You bettah let me go. Dat's what dey pay me fo'." Slowly, she pushed both palms toward him. "You juss wait right he'ah, aw-right?"

When she had walked outside, Nate moved back into the dimly lit room and faced the hallway where the Hildebrands would enter the house. As he waited, one of the paintings on the wall caught his eye. The image leaped out at him, and a chill rippled up his spine like ice water defying gravity. In the picture, a lone horse stood in a field of yellowing grass. Behind the animal was a massive live oak tree spreading its muscular limbs and branches like an explosion of growth caught in a photographer's flash.

Though the tree took up the greatest space on the canvas, it did not dominate the scene. The piebald horse drew the eye in. It was a pinto. The splotched colors were perfectly rendered to match the unique pattern of Peaches's coat. The horse was in the same pose as the one painted on the book that Dory had given him, the difference being that this horse in front of the oak was more skillfully proportioned. The artist had included a ray of late afternoon sun that touched the flank of the animal, making the patches of white as bright as the starched collar of a Sunday morning preacher. It was Peaches, down to her all-white mane, unkempt forelock, and feathery white tail with a streak of rust-brown running down one side.

Nate stepped closer to the painting and saw that it changed as he neared it. The dabs of color no longer seemed as detailed as they had appeared from a distance. Now, the brush marks of paint were more like haphazard pieces of a vague puzzle that had gone slightly out of focus. Up close, the applications of paint only suggested an unfinished picture of horse and tree and grass. Leaning to the bottom right corner, he made out a small, dark-green signature hidden in the yellowing blades of grass. *Dorothy Hildebrand,* it read.

His eyes panned up to the framed picture above this one. He could see that this painting utilized the same style of brushwork, but the subject could not have been more different. Buildings and houses, grassy yards and gardens, cobblestone streets and walkways. A few individual trees were spread out in isolated spots within the jumble of manmade scenery. All of it was painted from above, as though the artist had been suspended in air. The signature in green was identical to the one on the painting below it. It had to be the painting from Dory's dormitory window.

From outside came an angry exchange of words, and Nate feared that Bethany was on the receiving end of an upbraiding from both of her employers. The heated outburst came to a climax with a vicious outpouring from a strident male voice.

"You're the one who insisted! Or have you forgotten that?!"

Nate moved to the window and parted the curtain just as Bethany had. The Hildebrands faced one another on the stone walkway, each glowering at the other. The man suddenly turned away and stormed toward the house, his face flushed with anger, and his raw, teary eyes rimmed in red.

Mrs. Hildebrand looked like she might yell to his back, but instead, she lowered her head, buried her face in her hands, and began to sob. With her elbows tucked into her stomach, she hunched forward, and her shoulders began to shake to the rhythm of her wailing.

Behind her, Bethany took the Morgan by its cheek strap and led horse and carriage toward the shed in back. A saddled red dun mare followed, its reins tied to the back of the carriage. Nate backed away from the window and waited.

Mr. Hildebrand hurried through the front entrance, lugging a small leather carrying case in one hand. With his other hand he pinched the bridge of his nose between his eyes. Leaving the door open behind him, he marched past the parlor entrance without seeing Nate. Further down the hall, he turned and began climbing the flight of stairs that led to the second floor. As he ascended, his shoes scuffed the steps like a coded message of defeat. When he reached the upper level, his footsteps moved slowly to the back of the house, where a door slammed shut. This sound spread through the building like the closing shot on a battleground.

When Mrs. Hildebrand entered the house, she paused in the hallway to untie the strings of her blue sunbonnet. She wore a light cotton dress that matched the bonnet and black button-up boots. Nate watched her through the parlor entrance as she removed the hat and set it on a small table beneath a wall mirror hanging at the level of her face. Sniffing wetly, she stared into the mirror and swiped at the tears on her cheeks with her fingers, until her eyes fixed on Nate's image in the reflection. She lowered her hands quickly and turned as if to verify what her teary eyes had seen in the mirror.

"What are *you* doing here?" she demanded, pinning him with the sharp, predatory glare of a hawk.

"I come to have a private talk with you, ma'am." He stepped into the parlor doorway and gestured toward the room behind him. "Can we do that in here?"

Folding her arms across her stomach, she put her heels together, as though she were rooting to the hallway floorboards. Her eyes were wet and weary, and her lips knotted so tightly that a sunburst of lines etched the skin around her mouth.

"Don't you know the courtesy of making an appointment instead of barging into people's homes?! This is not a day that we want any visitors!"

"I didn' barge, ma'am," Nate replied. "I knocked on yore door polite-like, an' a nice lady let me in."

Her angry face gave way to confusion. "What lady?!"

291

As they stared at one another, Bethany entered the hall from outside. Without a word, she closed the front door and walked between them, keeping her eyes straight ahead. She passed quietly down the hallway and turned right into the kitchen.

"Her," Nate said and pointed in the direction Bethany had gone.

Mrs. Hildebrand's face flinched as if she'd had a hank of hair plucked out of her scalp. She leaned forward and lowered her voice to a haughty whisper.

"Don't you know you don't call a nigra woman a *lady*?" Instead of waiting for an answer, she cocked her head sharply to one side. "What is it you want? Why are you here? Today of all days!"

Nate remained calm before the woman's hostile eyes. "I come for my letters." He said this quietly, but the simplicity of his request seemed to hold her in check.

"I'm sure I don't know what you mean," she snapped and lowered her arms to her sides. Her hands balled into small fists and pressed into the cotton material where it flared from her waist. She raised her chin and looked down her nose at him as though willing him to leave.

"I just come from the post office," Nate went on. "Had a talk with Mr. Elwood. Now, I've come out here to get what's mine."

As she stared at him, her breathing escalated, making a thin whistling sound in her nostrils. She spun a quarter turn and pointed to the front door.

"I want you out of here now!" she ordered. "Do you hear me? Now!" She crossed her arms tightly over her midsection and began shaking her head in tiny increments. "Of all the days for you to push your way into my house!"

Nate held his ground. "I wont the letters that were

s'posed to come to me...*and* the ones I wrote that were s'posed to go to France."

She looked down at herself and brushed at her dress with her hands, but Nate saw nothing there for her to bother with. When she looked up, her mouth was a grim, straight line.

"Mr. Elwood told me all 'bout what you done," Nate said, as casually as he might have commented on a horse's color. "It breaks a fed'ral law to steal somebody's mail."

For just a moment, she looked like a frightened child trying to hide her lie. Then she cleared her throat and worked up some bravado.

"I have nothing of yours! Now leave!"

Nate raised one arm and pointed to the wall next to the parlor entrance. "What 'bout that?"

Frowning, she started to step forward for a look, but she caught herself. "I want you gone from here! Can't you hear me?!"

Nate did not move. "I wont my letters."

When she stiffened and refused to talk, Nate nodded toward the painting of the pinto standing before the spreading oak. "I reckon that there was packaged up with my name on it, too. Am I right?"

She licked her lips and swallowed. "I don't know what you mean!"

"Yes, ma'am, I think you do. You stole my mail goin' out...an' comin' in." He raised his arm to point at the other painting. "I can understand Dory sendin' you the paintin' of the city," he said agreeably. Then his arm levitated to the picture of the pinto below it. "But not that one. That there's a paintin' of *my* horse." When she started to speak, Nate cut her off. "I know what you been doin', an' I know how you scare't Mr. Elwood into helpin' you."

She pointed at the front door again. "Get out!" she

said, raising her voice. "You can't come here and accuse me of things you know nothing about!"

Nate did not budge. "I ain't leavin' without what b'longs to me."

The livid woman looked ready to burst. "I have nothing that belongs to you! *Nothing!* I don't care what Mr. Elwood at the post office says!"

Nate nodded as if what she had said was interesting. "My aunt will prob'ly care."

Mrs. Hildebrand's brow lowered. "Who?"

"My aunt," he said. "Harriet Cluck. She's my mother's sister an' the postmistress here."

"You've already spread this lie to your aunt?" she asked, her voice now higher pitched.

"Not yet," he replied. "Not b'fore I give you a chance to make things right."

After closing her eyes for a moment, she walked past him into the parlor and stood by a window. There, she drew back the curtain so that she could gaze outside. A thin blade of afternoon light cut across her, carving her out of the darkness with a bright line tracing the profile of her face. Looking through the glass, she seemed empty, depleted of her anger, her shoulders sagging, one arm limp at her side, and her other hand gripping the curtain as if it were her last hold on to life.

"It doesn't matter anymore," she whispered. "Tell anyone you want." She kept staring out the window as if she had fallen into a trance. Tears welled in her eyes and spilled over, running down her cheek to the soft angle of her jaw.

"You don't know what it is to be a mother," she said, surprising Nate with the fullness of her voice. Her words echoed off the windowglass, giving her the sound of someone speaking in a limestone cavern. She began shaking her head slowly. "A mother has to protect her daughter from men who could ruin her life. You were too old to court her. You must know that." She turned to look at him, and for the first time since she had walked into the house, there was no hostility in her eyes. "Not that it matters now."

"I ain't been a-courtin' her or anybody else, ma'am. I reckon Dory an' me have got to be friends. 'Cause that's what I consider her...a friend...an' a good one."

She forced a minimal smile and turned back to the window. "A man can transgress and be forgiven his sins, but a woman is dishonored forever. And for a woman, it takes away from her all that she could have been."

Nate did not know that word "transgress," but he sensed that it was a shameful thing. "I ain't been nothin' but honor'ble with Dory, ma'am, and you ought not judge me diff'rent."

She took in a deep breath and let it out as a sigh. "A mother has the right *not* to take a chance on her daughter's reputation."

"Did you ever think to ask *her* 'bout me?" he asked in earnest.

"No," she said, glancing at him briefly, showing him that she could be honest, too. When her attention was fixed on the yard again, her jaw clamped down hard, raising a bulge of tendon beneath her flaccid jowl. "We never talked about such things as that."

"Why not?"

A film of tears covered her eyes again, gathering light from the window. "It doesn't matter," she mewled. "It's too late now."

She turned to glare at him, and her eyes spilled teardrops that ran down her face. When she turned back to the window, she pulled a white handkerchief from a pocket of her dress and pressed alternately into each eye several times. When she returned the linen to the pocket, her hand came out holding a crumpled yellow paper. Bowing her head, she began opening its creases and folds until she could flatten the paper on the wide windowsill. There, she ironed the wrinkled page with the flat of her hand, pressing it out with repetitive strokes.

"It ain't never too late to try an' fix what's wrong, ma'am," Nate said. "Otherwise, it's bound to git worse. You know Dory's gonna find out what you been doin'. Ain't it better for her to hear 'bout it from you?"

She was quiet as she read from the paper. Each time she breathed in deeply, the air made a quiet, shuddering sound in her throat. It was like the soft wingbeat of a small bird. Other than that, the room was so quiet that Nate could hear the faint humming of a hymn coming from the kitchen. He knew Bethany's voice as well as he knew his own, for her stories had escorted him into sleep on many a night when he was a young boy.

"Ma'am?" Nate said. "You know it's only right that you give me those letters...an' give Dory the ones I wrote to her. That might go a long way in patchin' up any problems that the two o' you got."

"No," she replied, forcing the word out of her constricted throat. "I can't do that!"

Nate kept his voice gentle but firm. "Sure, you can."

Closing her eyes, she shook her head in tight, little jerks. "I burned them," she blurted out and began to cry in earnest. "I burned *all* of them."

While she sobbed, the rest of the house seemed to hold its breath in reverential silence. In the kitchen, the humming had stopped. Nate looked around the room and fixed his attention on the cleanly swept fireplace, wondering if this was where she had destroyed all his letters. The woman seemed to be contrite now, but all his sympathies went to Dory. She had probably written him many times over these years, and as far as *she* knew, he was purposely ignoring her. When he thought of the painting, he cringed. She had not received even a thank-you.

"Did you read 'em?" Nate asked. "The letters?"

She lowered her arms, straightened her back, and swallowed. "I read the first two from Dory but none from you. I didn't *want* to read your words."

Nate huffed a quiet laugh. "I wish you had. Then you'd know somethin' 'bout who I am."

Surprising them both, a gentle voice spoke up from the hallway. "Mizz Hildebrand...you can trust Nate to be a gen'leman. I knows dat as well as I knows da sun gonna rise in da mo'nin'."

Bethany stood just outside the room, her narrow shoulders back and her hands clasped together below her chin. She looked like an angel offering up a fervent prayer.

Despite her tears, Mrs. Hildebrand managed a fearsome scowl. "Are you in the habit of listening in on the personal conversations of the people you work for?"

Bethany's beatific smile was unfazed by the woman's criticism. "No, ma'am. But when a house be as quiet as dis'n is, you cain't he'p but he'ah what's said in da next room." She lifted her eyebrows. "Y'all's words been echoin' down da hall like peoples talkin' in a cave."

"Well, that doesn't mean you have the right to butt in!" Mrs. Hildebrand snapped. "I can't see how this is any of your business!"

"No, ma'am," Bethany agreed. "But I t'ought I could be o' some he'p. I knows dis young man well as I knows my own chi'ren. I t'ought I might ease yo' mind some, 'cause dis man he'ah would treat any woman with respec'. I know dat to be true. He treat me dat way since he a lil' bitty boy...an' I's a Black woman."

Mrs. Hildebrand turned away and swiped at her cheeks with the flat of her hand. Though she got her crying under control, she seemed flustered about what to say.

"Well, how is it you two know each other so well?"

"Beth'ny helped raise me when my mother died," Nate volunteered. "To tell the truth, she became my second mother."

The woman studied her housemaid intently through her teary eyes. "Do you have daughters?"

"Yes'm. I gots two...eighteen and twen'y-fo' year old."

"Married?"

Bethany smiled and nodded. "Da oldest. She awready make me a gran'mama."

Mrs. Hildebrand sniffed wetly. "What about the younger one? Don't you try to protect her from men who might take advantage?"

Bethany smiled. "She old enough now to be smart 'bout t'ings like dat. But I know what you mean. Was a time I took a go-o-o-d long look at who was sniffin' 'round my front do' askin' fo' my daughtah." She nodded toward Nate. "But I tell you what, ma'am," Bethany said, letting her smile harden to conviction. "I juss wish some young man as upstandin' as Nate Champ'n be da one to come a-knockin' at my lil' girl's do'."

Mrs. Hildebrand glanced quickly at Nate and then buried her face in her hands again. "I can't undo what I've done," she murmured. "All those letters are ashes now."

"You could write Dory an' tell 'er what you done," Nate suggested.

When her hands came down this time, she stared at Nate for so long that he feared she had drifted off into some kind of deranged state of mind. Stepping forward, she extended to him the wrinkled yellow paper. As soon as he held it, he recognized the Western Union masthead.

"She's gone," she managed to say in a raspy whisper.

Nate frowned. "What do you mean? Gone where?"

Turning her back to Nate, she moved to the window and pushed aside one of the curtains. For a long time, she just stared through the windowglass and stood as still as the furniture in the room. It surprised Nate when she spoke, her voice full now as it echoed off the glass.

"The first telegram came early this morning," Mrs. Hildebrand explained. "The school insisted that we contact them immediately. I went into town to get John, but he was busy with a client. So, I went alone to the telegraph office, sent off a message, and waited." She turned at the waist and waved a hand toward the paper in Nate's hand. "And *that* came!"

Bringing the telegram closer to his face, Nate strained to decipher the rumpled message as he read aloud. "To Madame Hildebrand. Regret to inform you. Body of Dorothy Alma Hildebrand found last night on—"

Nate felt a sudden, weightless void open up inside his gut. "Body!" he blurted out, as if challenging the paper itself. Looking up quickly, he waited for Mrs. Hildebrand to explain the mistake of what he was reading, but she turned back to the window and remained quiet.

Nate turned to Bethany, but there was none of the usual light radiating from her kind face. She looked at him as if she were trying to soak up his pain and take it as her own. When a tear broke from her wet eyes and coursed down her cheek, she closed her eyes as if she knew of some refuge where it was possible to escape the miseries that befell people's lives.

Nate felt a heavy pressure build in his throat and behind his eyes, and the details of the dusky room around him began to blur. It was like trying to see out a window pummeled by a slanting rain. He tried to swallow away the hardness in his throat, but it was like trying to down a smooth river stone the size of a hen's egg.

"Keep reading," Mrs. Hildebrand croaked in a dry voice.

Unsure that he could coax a single word out of his throat, Nate wiped his eyes with his sleeve and looked at the telegram again. After rereading the first line in silence, he cleared his throat roughly and swallowed.

"...Found last night in Champ de Mars on banks of Seine, short distance from Exposition Universelle. American ambassador Edward Noyes to contact you." There was more to read, but Nate skipped down to the last line to silently read who had wired this terrible message: *My condolences. Will keep you informed. Cap. Adrien Pelletier, Investigating officer, Paris Gendarme.*

Nate squeezed his eyes shut and lowered the hand holding the telegram. A flurry of images passed through his mind: talking with Dory on the round rock at Brushy Creek...watching her hug Peaches around the neck... dancing with her that one time at the Masonic Lodge. Then, his mind created a picture of her standing before an easel, dabbing colors onto canvas with a brush, rendering the scene of oak, grass, and horse as a gift she would mail across an ocean.

Nate fixed his teary eyes on the back of Mrs. Hildebrand's head, only now seeing the hasty manner in which she had pinned up her hair. "But she cain't be dead!" he said, feeling the futility of his words even as he spoke them. He looked to Bethany for some help, but her eyes remained closed as she silently mouthed a prayer.

"There ain't nobody who would wanna hurt Dory!" Nate argued. "Why would they? It's gotta be a mistake somehow!"

When Mrs. Hildebrand turned around, there was not a trace of the haughty woman Nate had come to know. After being at war with the world around her, she was a down-trodden soul who might never find comfort again in this life. Nate remembered this hollow-eyed look on his own father's face when Nate's mother had been lowered into the earth.

"They could'a made a mistake, couldn' they?" he said.

The woman shook her head. "It's all there in the telegram. They found her school identification card in her purse. And the scar on her foot from the time she was stepped on by the carriage horse. One of her teachers went to the morgue and verified it. It was Dory."

Mrs. Hildebrand hugged herself, clasping each hand to the opposite upper arm. Lowering her head, she stared down at the expensive rug beneath her feet.

"They found something odd on her...something they think might have been left by whoever attacked her." She shook her head. "It makes no sense to me." She looked up at the paintings to her left and spoke in a dreamy voice. "It was the paper band from a cigar. It was on her finger like a ring. It had been hardened somehow...soaked in something that made it firm."

Nate felt a chill pass through his body and then disappear, as if a ghost had walked right through him. "Candle wax," he whispered. "That was from me."

Her face wrinkled, and her red-rimmed eyes fixed on his. But rather than ask a question, she merely closed her eyes.

They were quiet for a time. Bethany had covered her eyes with one hand to silently weep. Mrs. Hildebrand opened her eyes and stared past Nate at the semi-dark room, seeming to focus on nothing at all.

Up to this point, Nate had reacted to his own loss. He felt as if some part of his future had been snatched away from him. Now he began to take in the tragedy through the eyes of this woman who had tried to bar him from her family's life. Crawling into her skin, he caught the briefest glimpse of an abyss filled with permanent pain.

Losing a child, he considered, must be the worst kind of hurt.

"Ma'am, I cain't git the words together to tell you how I feel." Her vacant expression did not change, but he continued in a soft whisper. "She was a good friend to me, but she was yore daughter. An' I reckon that tears away a big part o' yore heart. I just wish—"

Without finishing his thought, he looked down at his scuffed boots that had trespassed into this woman's carefully groomed world. When he raised his head, she was still staring into the void.

"I reckon I *should* go," Nate said and moved quietly past both women into the hallway. He walked out the front door and closed it with barely a sound. As he moved across the open ground, the fancy house behind him seemed little more than a hollow vault of grieving. A silent sarcophagus holding its misery up here on this hill, separate from the rest of the world. When he reached Peaches, he pushed his hat onto his head, untied the reins, and led the paint on foot to the carriage path that curved down the slope of the hill.

"Lil' Pony?!"

He stopped and turned to the house, where Bethany carefully descended the front steps, leading with the same leg for each step. Gripping the handrail with one hand, she carried under the other arm what looked like a serving tray draped inside a white bedsheet. As she came toward him through the yard, she gathered the loose ends of the sheet to keep the linen out of the weeds and dirt. By the time she reached Nate, she had the package wrapped neatly. Her cheeks were streaked with the shining tracks of tears.

"She say to give dis to you. I gots some twine he'ah to bind it wit'."

Handing the wrapped package to Nate, she pulled

from her apron pocket a ball of brown string and began looping opposite corners in figure-eight patterns until the sheet was firmly bound.

Through the linen, he could feel the stretch of taut canvas that barely yielded to the press of his fingertips. Nate knew what he was holding. Without the fancy frame he had seen on the wall, this package was the right size for Dory's painting.

"You gots a knife wit' yo'?" Bethany asked.

He brought out his knife. When Bethany took over holding the gift, he cut the cord.

"She must'a t'ought mighty highly of you, Lil' Pony."

Putting his knife away, Nate shook his head, glanced at the house, and nodded toward the closed curtains in the front windows. "No, I doubt she could ever think anythin' like *that*."

Bethany smiled. "I ain't talkin' 'bout her. I talkin' 'bout Mizz Dory. She a mighty special one. When I knew her, she didn' have many friends dat was her age. She was awready ahead o' dem by a long ways."

"Yeah," he breathed. "I know. I was older'n her by more than two years, but in some ways she was ahead o' me, too. She always said the difference in our age would change when we got older."

"It would have, fo' sho'," Bethany agreed.

Nate adjusted his hat forward and back but returned it to its original position. "I always liked 'er," he said. "Liked 'er a lot." He raised one shoulder and let it drop. "But I reckon it was bound to be more'n that with enough time."

Nate felt his face grow warm. A sudden pressure built up behind his eyes, until the dam broke, and warm tears ran down his face to confirm what he had said.

Bethany reached out and cupped her cool hand to his cheek. "My Hoddy...he 'bout fo'teen years olde'n me. He smokin' cig'rettes b'fo' I was walkin'." Raising her eyebrows, she nodded. "Yo' daddy is thi'ty years olde'n yo' new mama."

He wiped at his tears and stared into her loving eyes. He felt no embarrassment about crying in front of her. If anything, he knew that he and Bethany had tightened their bond on this day.

"Climb up on Peaches an' I hand dis up to yo'," she said.

Nate mounted, took the painting, and tucked it under one arm.

"I t'ink dis da onliest way da Mizzes know how to say she sorry."

He nodded and gazed at the house. The door stood open from Bethany's hurried exit, but there was no sign of Mrs. Hildebrand.

"She say anythin'?"

Bethany shrugged. "Just to run dis out to you b'fo' you leave." Her eyes took on a pained expression. "She t'ink it best if you don't come out he'ah no mo'." She turned her head and eyed the house. "She in d'ere cryin' like a baby right now."

Nate stared at the parlor windows. "Will she be mad at you for lettin' me in?"

Bethany took in a deep breath and let it ease out. "Dey ain't no tellin' what she gone do wi' me." She shook her head and made a wry smile. "She humbled right now. But come suppah-time she prob'ly snap at me 'bout over-cookin' da greens or puttin' too much salt on da meat." She laughed silently. "It ain' no easy task tryin' to please her all da time."

"How late do you stay here?" Nate asked.

"Till I gets da dishes done aftah suppah."

"How do you git home? Ain't it dark by then?"

"Hoddy come to git me in da wagon. Den I go home

an' fix suppah fo' my owns fam'ly." She patted his leg and delivered her warmest smile. "I gots to get back an' see to my cookin'." She began backing away, and her sweet smile turned into a toothy grin. "Even wit' all dis bad news, Lil' Pony...did my soul a heap o' good seein' you today."

She turned and walked up the hill, her shoes crunching on the sand and rock and her yellow dress skimming the tops of the weeds. When she reached the steps, she scaled them as nimbly as a schoolgirl. Then the door closed, and she was gone.

Chapter Thirty-Two

It was twilight when he reached the Tisdale ranch. Lights burned in several windows of the house. In the corral a remuda of horses stood as still as a tintype image. Nate reined up before the front porch and listened to the complete quiet.

"Hello, the house!" he called out.

He sat his horse for half a minute before the door cracked open. Nate could see a dark head silhouetted against the dimly lighted room. When John Tisdale opened the door wider, Nate saw that he carried a repeater rifle in one hand.

"That you, Nate?"

"Sure is," Nate replied, "I was hopin' to have a talk with you...private-like. Could you come out?"

Lowering the rifle beside his leg, John stepped out onto the porch. "We were all just sitting down for supper." He glanced across the yard. "Meet me in the barn. I'll just need a minute." He started back inside but hesitated. "Is everything all right? You don't look yourself."

Nate shrugged. "I'm aw-right."

John continued to study Nate from hat to boot heels. "What's that you got there?"

Nate looked down at the package under his arm. "A picture," he replied.

John frowned and nodded at the same time. "You mean...like by a photographer?"

Nate shook his head. "It's a paintin'. Like by a artist." He hitched his head toward the barn. "I'll wait for you out there."

When John disappeared inside, Nate reined Peaches around and walked her across the yard. Behind the barn, he dismounted and propped the covered painting against the building's oak siding. Then he tied Peaches near a rain barrel out of sight from the house. After hanging his hat on the horn of his saddle, he dipped his hands into the barrel, making a bowl of his hands. Leaning over the water, he scrubbed his face and the back of his neck and then ran his fingers through his hair.

With streamlets of cold water trickling down between his shoulder blades, an image flashed in his mind. A sunny day at the round rock in Brushy Creek...he, standing in the water and Dory climbing onto his shoulders to be carried to the bank.

A flood of emotions washed through him. Regret. Loss. Confusion. Anger. The coming apart of what might have been. The finality of death. It all came together like a great slab of stone come to bear down on him. He felt his knees weaken, and this forced him to grab the rim of the barrel to keep himself upright.

"Dory!" he whispered aloud, surprised at the wounded mewl in his voice. He broke into a series of racking sobs as he leaned over the barrel. With his head lowered, Nate's tears dolloped onto the surface of the water like notes plucked from the strings of a muted fiddle.

He felt his heart shrink inside him, like the wrinkled telegram Mrs. Hildebrand had wadded into a ball inside her fist. Worst of all was knowing that Dory had died, thinking that he had abandoned their friendship. She had made the painting for him, crated it up, and shipped it to Texas, all without a word of appreciation from him. Without even an acknowledgment that it had safely arrived. He thought of the leather-bound book she had given him. It lay hidden in the chest of drawers in his bedroom. She had wanted him to write in it, but he not scratched a single word on its pages.

"Nate?" John said, his questioning voice coming from the corner of the barn.

Nate leaned forward and washed his face again. Then he straightened and buried his eyes in the crook of his arm, drying himself with his shirtsleeve.

"Gimme a minute," he whispered, still holding his bent arm over his eyes.

When he believed he had purged his tears, he walked around the corner of the building and entered the dark bay of the barn. Inside, John was a black silhouette standing at the front stall where his sorrel mare was kept. Across the bay, two horses hooked their heads over their stall gates and stared at Nate as if awaiting an explanation for his presence. One was Tiz's buckskin.

Nate moved across the bay from John and sat on the stoop of the tack room. John turned to face him and leaned back against the stall gate. The sorrel nickered, moved to the front of the stall, and extended her head over the gate. Nate leaned back against the tack room door and rested his hands in his lap.

"Everything all right over at your place, Nate?"

Nate gave his friend an earnest nod. "Yeah, we're all fine."

John was in no hurry. He ambled down to the stall

where the dairy cow stayed, returned with a small three-legged stool, and sat in the middle of the breezeway facing Nate.

"Where's your painting?" John said in an upbeat voice. "Don't I get to see it?"

Nate poked a thumb over his shoulder toward the back corner of the barn. "It's out yonder by the rain barrel." When John held onto his look of anticipation, Nate said, "You really wanna see it?"

"Of course, I do."

Nate clasped his hands to his knees and pushed himself up. "I'll fetch it."

When he returned, John was hanging a lighted lantern from an iron hook nailed to the tack room wall. Nate unwrapped the package and propped the painting against the tack room door, revealing the scene of horse and tree and meadow. He turned to see John's reaction.

"My god." John laughed. "This is excellent!" His voice was breathy and full of admiration. He pointed at the painting. "That's Peaches!"

Nate nodded. "Yeah, that's her."

John's eyes roved all over the picture as if he were reading words hidden inside the colors. "Who painted this, Nate?"

"One o' the Hildebrand girls painted it," Nate said, and instantly, he was ashamed that he had not used Dory's name.

John leaned closer to the picture. "The one that Martin was courting?"

Nate closed his eyes and shook his head. "The younger one...Dorothy." He cleared his throat and swallowed. "But ever'body called 'er *Dory*."

When he spoke her name, Nate felt his throat tighten. The pressure was hard and unforgiving on the back of his palate, as if another stone had lodged there. His face warmed, and a fresh supply of tears threatened to pour from his eyes.

"Dory?!" John said. His brow lowered over his eyes as he turned back to the artwork. "But she's only a little girl, isn't she?"

"Prob'ly was last time you saw 'er," Nate replied. "She's been in France for four years."

John nodded. "So she went to that school, too...the same one they sent her sister to?"

"I reckon it was a rare case o' the younger sister lookin' out for the older," Nate said.

John's eyes pinched. "Did Martin have anything to do with them being sent away?"

Nate shrugged. "Don' know nothin' 'bout that," he said, "but Dory bein' over there might have somethin' to do with me."

John's eyebrows rose. "How do you mean?"

"Me an' her were friends, but her mother took it to mean somethin' more."

John's gaze angled out across the yard. "Four years," he mumbled. "She'd be what now? Sixteen or seventeen?" With a little laugh of surprise, he turned to Nate. "She'd be a young lady now, Nate."

Nate began re-wrapping the sheet around the canvas. "I reckon she would. Kinda hard to see that in my mind. You know what I mean?"

John cocked his head to one side. "She didn't send you a tintype?"

As he bound the linen with the twine, Nate pictured a pile of gray ash in the hearth of the Hildebrands' parlor. "If she did, I never got it."

Nate propped the package against the wall and sat on the stoop again. "I come out here to tell you somethin' I figure you need to know." Nate watched his friend lose his smile and steel himself for bad news. "One o' Sam Bass's men—fellow named *Murphy*—he made a deal with the Rangers a while back. Told 'em 'bout the plan to rob the bank in Round Rock. In exchange for that, he was to go free."

In the light of the lantern, John's face shone like alabaster. "So, this Murphy fellow knows Martin," he said in a flat tone.

Nate nodded. "I reckon he'd have to. They were all camped out by the Ind'an Rocks."

John stared at Nate, his eyes burning as steady as candle flames on a church altar. "Do you think he would give up my brother...even though Martin did not take part in the fight?"

Nate shook his head. "Got no way to know that. All I know is he gave up ever'body else's name...even Frank Jackson, the one who got away." Nate shrugged. "If he's that free with names, stands to reason he'd tell the Rangers 'bout yore brother, don't it?"

Frowning, John closed his eyes and leveled his hand against his forehead, squeezing his temples with thumb and fingers. "This man, Murphy...did they let him go?"

Nate shook his head. "Not yet. Gil Campo come out to our ranch an' said they got 'im in the jail right now. He'll prob'ly have to testify in court b'fore they can release 'im. I guess they figure he's safer in jail after turnin' Judas on Bass...'specially with this Frank Jackson loose."

John took in a lungful of air and expelled the breath slowly. "This changes things," he said sharply. "If this man, Murphy, talks about Martin—and why shouldn't he?—my brother will go to jail, and the Tisdale name will take on a whole new meaning in Williamson County." He gave Nate the kind of solemn stare that people use at funerals. "This will cut my daddy to the bone, Nate!"

Nate remained quiet for a time, letting John sort out

his thoughts. John turned in profile and stared out the doorway at the darkening yard and the grassland beyond.

"Maybe you could ask yore brother if Murphy would name 'im," Nate suggested.

John huffed a dry laugh. "I guess a man bargaining for his life might give up just about anybody!" He stood and walked to his sorrel's stall, where he stacked his forearms on top of the gate. The mare turned to him, touched her muzzle to John's shoulder, and blew gently from her nostrils. John was so deep in thought that he paid no attention to the horse.

"Damn it!" John said, his voice like the growl of a dog. He turned quickly to face Nate, and the mare jerked her head up, snorted, and backed away. "I knew it would come to something like this!" John hissed. "I guess a part of me has been waiting on this for a long time."

"What're you gonna do?" Nate asked.

John narrowed his eyes and wiped the back of his hand across his mouth. "For starters, I'm going to see that he gets out of this part of the country. He needs a job he can stick to. I might know of someone in the Montana Territory who can take him in."

"When would he leave?" Nate pressed.

John breathed out a heavy sigh. "Soon. Before the sheriff comes out here and starts asking questions." He let his head sag forward, raised one hand, and pulled at the skin on either side of his chin. "Hell, he'll need to leave tonight! Soon as he can pack up!"

"Do you reckon Tiz was in on any o' Bass's other rob'ries?" Nate asked.

John sniffed. "I don't know," he sighed. "Don't think I want to know!"

"What will you tell yore daddy 'bout Tiz leavin' so sudden-like?"

As John thought about his answer, the front door of

the house opened and closed. Footsteps tapped down the stairs and then softened on the bare dirt yard.

"Daddy knows all about what kind of life Martin is drawn to," John explained, "but we won't tell him where Martin is headed. I'll get Martin to write a letter, and then I'll post it from somewhere south of here, so Daddy can show it to people and make it look like he's struck out for Mexico."

A sound at the doorway turned both their heads at once. There stood Tiz, looking his carefree self and wearing a crooked smile on his face.

"Who the hell's strikin' out for ol' Mexico?"

Chapter Thirty-Three

Tiz leaned a shoulder against the doorframe and crossed one boot in front of the other, as he folded his arms over his chest. His eyes stitched back and forth between his brother and Nate.

"You're packing up and leaving here tonight," John announced.

Tiz lost his smile as his face went slack. Pushing away from the doorframe, he straightened and lowered his arms.

"To Mexico?"

John shook his head. "We're going to make it look that way, but you're heading north."

Tiz lowered his brow and frowned. "What's the hurry? Why tonight?"

John widened his stance and propped his hands on his hips. "I guess you know a man named *Murphy*?"

Tiz nodded. "What about 'im?"

John kept his eyes on his brother. "Tell him, Nate."

Nate cleared his throat. "A deputy come out an' talked to my daddy 'bout Sam Bass. That fellow Murphy, who rode with you boys...he'd aw-ready turned on you. He told

314

the Rangers all 'bout yore plans to rob the bank in Round Rock."

Tiz narrowed his eyes and mulled over the information. Then he revived his smile and shook his head.

"Murph? Hell, he wouldn' do that!"

"He's down there at the jail right now," John broke in. "Probably spilling his guts to the Rangers. Can you think of any reason he would leave you out of the story?"

Tiz looked down at the dirt floor and thought. "Just a few days ago, Bass accused Murph o' bein' a informant, but the rest o' us wouldn' b'lieve it, so Sam finally let it go."

John huffed a self-satisfied laugh. "You see what I mean about an outlaw having no real friends."

Tiz met his brother's gaze, and the two of them seemed to engage in a silent, ongoing debate dredged up from conversations past. "They better have plenty o' guards 'round Jim Murphy," Tiz announced with a sneer. "Long as Frank Jackson is loose."

"What do you think Jackson will assume about *you?*" John asked.

Tiz frowned. "Whatta you mean?"

"I mean," John went on, "what's he going to think about a fellow who dropped out of his gang the day before they walk into an ambush by the Texas Rangers?"

Tiz laughed. "Hell, Frank wouldn' think that 'bout me?"

John looked into his brother's eyes. "He didn't think that about Murphy either, did he?"

Tiz just laughed and shook his head.

"I don't see anything funny about this!" John snapped. "Now we know there are two people who can name you as being part of the Sam Bass gang! One of them might yet give up your name. He's named everyone else in your sorry crowd."

"So, what if he did?!" Tiz balked. "I didn' have nothin'

to do with that shoot-out. I weren't even there. B'sides, even if he gave me up, it's his word 'gainst mine!"

John closed his eyes and pinched the bridge of his nose. When he opened his eyes again, he looked vulnerable, as if he had just awakened from a deep sleep.

"Sounds to me like the Rangers are putting a lot of stock into what Murphy is saying. He's desperate for his freedom and doesn't mind who he has to send to jail to get that freedom."

Tiz pushed at the air with an open hand. "Aw, me an' Murph got along just fine."

"And you're willing to bet your life on that?" John challenged.

No one spoke for a time. Through the barn's big doorway, Nate could see the pinpoints of stars in the eastern sky. The horses were quiet. There was only the chirr of crickets out in the pasture, their sounds like the moving cogs of a hundred windmills facing into a stiff wind.

"Even if Murphy stays quiet," John said, regaining his composure, "you've got Frank Jackson to worry about. He might suppose you were in cahoots with Murphy and got out to save your own sorry hide."

Tiz shook his head, but he looked doubtful. "Me an' Frank got along just fine, too."

John sat down on the stool again. "He was probably friends with Murphy, too," he said, his voice solemn and unforgiving. "But I doubt Jackson is feeling any of that friendship now."

Tiz looked down at his boots. Then his head came up with hostile eyes.

"Why're you two gangin' up on me like this? I didn' take any part in that damned street fight in Round Rock!" He pointed at the ground. "I was right here!"

Quick as a jack-in-the-box, John stood up, his whole body stiff and his chin extended toward Tiz. Holding his fierce gaze on his brother, he raised one arm to point at Nate.

"And you have that man there to thank for it!" He lowered the arm and took two steps toward his brother. "Martin, don't you see that Nate and I are probably the only real friends you have in this world? We're trying to help you."

Looking more angry than gracious, Tiz lowered his gaze to the ground again.

"If you *had* been a part of that shoot-out," John went on, "I would take you to the sheriff myself. Caige Grimes was killed that day just for doing his job!"

"I know it!" Tiz mumbled, his voice as meek as a scolded child's. When he showed his face again, there was a pleading slant to his eyes. "But it still weren't me done the killin'!"

John rubbed his temples again and shook his head like a dog throwing off rainwater. "Do you think a jury would care about that? The people of Round Rock will consider anybody in the Bass gang to be guilty of that murder." He stiffened his hands before him, the fingers splayed, as if he wanted to grab Tiz's head and shake him. "Martin, you're going to have to start over somewhere...take a new name... and choose any way but the way you were headed. Do you hear me?"

Tiz worked his tongue around the front of his teeth and then turned his head and spat a speck of food off to his side. "Well, where the hell am I s'posed to go?"

John threw his arms out to his sides. "Anywhere you can stay out of trouble...if such a place exists."

In the silence that gelled around them, they heard the door to the house close. "John?" a cracking voice called from the porch.

John looked from his brother to Nate. "It's Daddy," he whispered. "Both of you...stay here." He walked out of the barn and called out right away. "Right here, Daddy! Martin and I are just checking on the horses."

"Your food's gettin' cold!" the old man announced. "Those horses will still be there after you eat."

"Yes, sir!" John replied. "We'll be right in!"

Reentering the barn, John stopped in front of Nate. "Will you have a meal with us?"

Nate shook his head. "I 'preciate it, but I need to git home."

John offered his hand. Nate took it and was surprised at the strength in John's grip.

"We'll always be beholding to you, Nate. You probably saved my brother's life." He turned his head to Tiz, as though expecting him to speak. Tiz sniffed and looked away.

When Nate stood up, John put a hand on his shoulder. "My brother is too mule-headed to say it, but he thanks you, too." Turning to leave, John spoke to Tiz over his shoulder. "Let's go, Martin. Daddy's waiting."

After John started for the house, Tiz and Nate stood alone in the glow of the lantern, each looking anywhere but at the other. Tiz spat off to one side and then cleared his throat.

"I reckon he's right," he conceded. "I might *be* dead if you hadn' showed up out there." He nodded out the doorway, where the Indian Rocks lay far to the east.

Nate watched Tiz try to hide his embarrassment by keeping his eyes fixed on the darkness. "Reckon you would've gone with 'em to rob the bank?"

Tiz turned at that. He seemed surprised at the question. But he could not look Nate in the eye for long. Using the side of his boot, he began scraping up a little mound of loose, black dirt and forming it into a miniature wall.

"Prob'ly would've," Tiz admitted and nodded twice to confirm it. "Me an' Dixie had to take a oath that we'd stick through it." He kicked a hole in the little wall he had built and snorted an airy laugh through his nose. "'Course, we broke that oath anyway by runnin' off like we did in the night."

Nate waited for Tiz to look him in the eye. "You'd steal from yore neighbors? People who've known you all yore life?"

Tiz scowled. "It ain't like that! Banks got *in*sur'nce to back 'em up. There ain't nobody in Round Rock would be caught holdin' the short end o' the stick. Just the bankers would. And who gives a damn about bankers?"

"That don't make it right," Nate said, "but I guess you know that aw-ready."

Tiz kicked at the dirt wall with his boot. "I know it!" he snapped, seemingly annoyed by the truth. Calming himself, he brought up a contrite face. "But I wouldn'a used a gun on nobody innocent, not like Bass or Barnes would."

"Maybe," Nate said, "but you cain't really know what you'd do when things git outta control. What if a citizen threw down on you an' started to shootin'?"

Tiz lowered his brow. "Well, then he wouldn' be innocent no more, would he?"

Nate kept his face blank. "What if it was me?"

Widening his eyes, Tiz looked hard at Nate. "You'd shoot at me?"

Nate shrugged. "I might not know it was you."

Tiz laughed. "Why the hell not?"

"You'd be wearin' a mask, wouldn' you?"

Tiz slapped at the back of his neck. Then he examined his hand and flicked something away with his thumb.

"Aw, come on now, Nate! Would you horn in on a bank holdup like that an' risk gittin' shot yoreself?"

"I would," Nate said without hesitation. "At least I would in Round Rock."

Tiz's face wrinkled like a wrung-out rag. "What the hell for?" he whined. "I aw-ready tol' you...it don't hurt nobody. The *in*sur'nce would—"

"I don' know nothin' 'bout that *in*sur'nce," Nate interrupted. "But it's still stealin' another man's money, plain an' simple."

Tiz bowed his head and busied himself with the dirt again, tamping it down with his boot. He held a frown on his face, but Nate could see the uncertainty in his eyes.

"I think you figured some way to convince yoreself that stealin' from a bank is fair game," Nate said quietly. "But deep down, you got yore doubts 'bout that. Am I right?"

Tiz kept his eyes on the dirt as he shook his head in a series of quick jerks. "You just don't understan' how it works." He looked up at Nate. "Nobody has to git hurt in this business!"

They stared at one another so long that the silence around them became oppressive.

"You know," Nate said, "Caige Grimes was 'bout the same age as you, the diff'rence bein' he had a wife an' children. Now, the wife has no husband, and the children have no father."

Tiz stopped the movement of his boot. He took in a deep breath and eased it out.

"Hell, I knew Caige," he whispered. "We went huntin' together a coupla times. I'm sorry he was kilt, but I had nothin' to do with it."

Nate said nothing. He just watched in the lantern light as Tiz bent forward and picked up a scrap piece of baling twine. Tiz wrapped it around one finger, unwound it, and wrapped it again.

"I got to go inside," Tiz said and tossed the string into the dirt. "I ain't finished my supper." He flashed an impotent grin and nodded once as if all were settled. Raising the lantern shield, he blew out the flame, leaving the two friends in the dark. Tiz turned to leave.

"What 'bout Dixie Brooks?" Nate said to Tiz's back. "Where's he gone to now?"

Tiz stopped and turned at the waist. "Why do you need to know *that*?"

Nate shrugged. "When it comes to Dixie...it's better to know than not know."

Tiz hesitated only a moment. "I got no idea where he's at."

"You takin' him with you?"

Tiz blew a flutter of air through his lips. "John wouldn' have it. He cain't tolerate the boy."

"But you can?" Nate asked.

Tiz shrugged. "He ain't so bad. Just got a lotta piss an' gunpowder in 'im." He lowered his voice. "He had it purty rough as a kid." It seemed that Tiz wanted to say more, but after a few seconds he lifted his chin to Nate. "I better go in." He turned and walked out of the barn.

Nate picked up the painting and exited through the front door to find Tiz standing in the middle of the yard. When Nate stopped, Tiz walked back to him and stopped five paces away.

"I don' mean to be such a ass, Nate. I know I owe you my thanks. John's prob'ly right. Weren't for you...guess I'd be dead right now." He huffed a dry laugh. "If I'd been with 'em that day in town, I'd'a got caught up in that shootin', sure as hell."

They were the most sincere words Nate had ever heard spoken by Martin Tisdale. Now there was a softness in his voice, and Nate fully expected Tiz to crack a joke and cover his vulnerability. But Tiz stepped forward and extended his right hand. Nate shifted the painting to his left hand, and they shook.

"I'm just glad you got shut o' them when you did," Nate said.

Tiz nodded, propped his hands on his hips, and then went very still. "I might not be seein' you again, Nate. There's no tellin' where I'll end up."

For several seconds, they listened to the ratcheting sounds of the insects in the fields.

"You take care o' yoreself, Tiz," Nate said quietly.

Tiz looked down and pushed a clump of dirt aside with the toe of his boot. When he brought his head up, the starlight gave Nate a last picture of his friend to remember.

"Yeah...you, too." And with that, Tiz turned and walked across the yard to the house he would soon be leaving. Nate watched until the door closed and Tiz was gone from sight.

Chapter Thirty-Four

After crossing the small branch that marked the southern extent of the Tisdale ranch, Nate entered a wooded section of the trail, where he rode through a darkness so complete that he relied upon Peaches to find their way. Just as he emerged from the forest to the open, starlit sky, a horse and rider swept out of the brush on his left, taking Nate by surprise and causing Peaches to snort and pick up her pace. It happened so quickly that Nate's reach for his rifle was a wasted effort, as he found himself looking into the muzzle of a shining, nickel-plated revolver.

Mounted on a muscular gray with a dark mane, Dixie Brooks matched Nate's speed so that the two moved along side by side, their stirrups almost touching. Under the starlight, Dixie's hat band threw off glints of silver, and his garish smile showed a set of small, white teeth.

"Hold!" Dixie growled, and right away he broke into a cackling laugh.

Nate pulled back on the reins and watched Dixie wheel his big gray around in front of Peaches, until the two men faced one another. The gun now hovered above the gray's ears, its barrel trained on Nate's chest. The horses snorted and nickered and rattled their bits. Once they had settled, the high-pitched sawing of night crickets filled the air.

"Well, hello there, chief!" Dixie crowed. "You have the honor of bein' waylaid by The Texas Kid." He laughed again and poked his gun barrel toward the bundle under Nate's arm. "What's that yo're carryin'?"

"Nothin' that's any bus'ness of yores."

When Dixie canted his head and cocked his gun, his eyes seemed to catch fire. "I asked you what're you carryin'!" he said louder.

"It's a paintin'," Nate mumbled.

Dixie bobbed the gun toward Nate's saddlebags. "You got anythin' to eat?"

Nate shook his head. "I'm headin' home for supper right now."

Dixie's face hardened and his eyes turned mean. "I need some goddammed food!"

Nate gestured with his hand down the road. "You can come with me an' eat a meal, if yo're of a mind. It's all I got to offer."

Dixie scowled. "I ain't lookin' for no favors. I'd rather steal from you than take yore charity."

"That don't make no sense a-tall," Nate said.

The crickets sang on, indifferent to the confrontation on the road. Dixie's gray steed shifted on the wagon ruts in the dirt, but the nickel-plated gun held steady on Nate.

"What were you doin' at Tiz's place?"

"Takin' news to John. Why do you care?"

Dixie ignored the question. "That pious sonovabitch? What does he need to know? I thought he aw-ready knew ever'thin'." He laughed in a series of hisses. "What *news* was so important for you to ride up here this time o' night?"

324

"Tiz can tell you."

"Well, Tiz ain't here, is he?!" Dixie taunted. "So, I'm askin' *you!*"

Nate stared into the dark and wondered what Dixie's reaction would be if he were to find out about Murphy. Dixie kicked his horse forward beside the paint and pressed the muzzle of his gun into Nate's ribs.

"Don't be makin' nothin' up, goddammit! I'll know if you do."

Nate leaned both hands on his pommel and turned to face Dixie. "You boys had a traitor among you," he said quietly.

Dixie's smooth face wrinkled. "Whatta you mean?"

"One o' your gang helped lay that ambush by the Rangers in Round Rock."

Dixie's expression turned savage. "Who?!" he demanded. "It was Murphy, wasn't it?"

Nate nodded.

Dixie clenched his teeth and growled, the tendons in his neck standing out like taut ropes stretched under his skin. "That goddammed sonovabitch!" He pressed his gun hard into Nate's ribs. "Yo're gonna go wrap up some food for me an' bring it back here."

Nate shook his head. "I offered you a meal...but I ain't gonna deliver it for you."

Dixie produced a jack-o-lantern smile. "Well, that's exactly what yo're gonna do, boy! Bring somethin' that'll keep for a while...somethin' to git me through the next coupla days."

Nate almost laughed. "That ain't the best plan I ever heard."

Dixie scowled. "What?!"

Nate shrugged. "What's to keep me from just stayin' at home once I git there?"

Dixie's jaw knotted repeatedly, and his nostrils flared

each time he inhaled. Tightening his mouth into a smug vee-shape, he pointed his revolver at the package under Nate's arm.

"I'll keep *that* here with *me*...till you git back."

Nate felt a little spark of heat snap inside him, like a lucifer scratched into a flame. The idea of Dixie Brooks holding Dory's painting disgusted him. It was sacrilege. When Dixie reached for the package, Nate jerked it away and held it at arm's length, where Dixie could not touch it.

"That the way you wanna play it, chief?" Dixie leveled his cocked gun at the painting and fired, the explosion deafening so close to Nate's face. The skin on his forehead, nose, and cheeks stung from the spray of powder burn. Tossing his package into the barrow ditch beside the road, Nate grabbed the barrel of the gun with both hands, wrenching it so as to bend Dixie's finger backward in the trigger guard. When Dixie cried out in pain, Nate put all his weight into purposely falling between the two horses, pulling the gun and the young outlaw with him.

When they hit the ground, Nate had complete control of the weapon. Dixie had fallen under his own horse, and he began yelping like a whipped dog. The gray had panicked and was stepping all over him, forcing Dixie to scramble away on hands and knees. As soon as he was clear, he sat in the road, and using his left hand, cradled his right to his chest.

"*God...damn!*" Dixie screeched, baring his teeth and squeezing his eyes shut as he pumped his body forward and back like a rocking chair.

The two horses backed away from the injured man, their reins dragging in the dirt. Peaches came to a halt and nickered, but the gray turned and trotted down the road like she'd had her first taste of freedom. Nate stuffed the shining revolver into the waistband of his trousers. Then he picked up his hat, stuffed it on his head, and walked to his horse.

When he was close to the ditch, Nate saw a thin, red circle smoldering brightly on the sheet wrapped around the painting. A lazy string of smoke twined upward into the air above it. Nate kneeled, spat on his fingertips, and wet the burning ring until the red was extinguished and the smoke ceased to rise.

Still holding his injured hand, Dixie sat in the road and moaned as he rocked forward and back, forward and back. Next to him lay his hat, its crown crushed almost flat by the gray's hooves. The showy metallic band was broken into several pieces, its silver conchos scattered like a handful of coins dropped in the dirt.

When Dixie saw Nate looking down at him, he rose above his suffering long enough to snarl at Nate. "You broke my goddammed finger, you bast'rd!" Then his eyes fixed on the pistol at Nate's waist, and his face turned demonic. "You better gimme my gun, you lil' sonovabitch! By God, nobody takes my gun!"

Nate said nothing. He led Peaches back to the trees. There, he tied her to an inch-thick sapling. When he turned back to Dixie, the young outlaw was still glaring at him and holding his hand to his chest.

"Now that you scared off my damned horse, you can just go an' fetch 'er for me!" Dixie ordered. "That's a damned expensive mare an' she's carryin' a good saddle and rifle!"

When he got no reply from Nate, Dixie extended his left arm and pointed his forefinger at Nate as if he were sighting down the barrel of a gun. "If I didn' have this stoved up hand, I'd tear you apart right now! I'd kick yore ass from hell to Sunday!"

Nate stared down at the troublesome braggart. Without a word, he pulled the revolver from his waistband, opened the loading gate, and slowly clicked the cylinder through a full revolution as he ejected the cartridges one at a time into the palm of his hand.

Dixie frowned. "What the hell're you doin'?!" His voice had risen to a higher pitch.

With an easy swing of his arm, Nate tossed the ammunition out into the dark, where it rained down on the ground in scattered *thumps*. Then he reversed the gun, taking it by the barrel, and slung the pistol on a high arc in the same direction he had thrown the bullets. For two seconds an eerie quiet fell over the road. Even the crickets had stopped chirping. Then the silence was broken by the sound of the pistol crashing into the brush some distance away.

"You goddammed bast'rd! D'you know how much that gun cost me?!"

Opening his saddlebag, Nate fished out his pigging string and fashioned a sliding loop at one end. This he slipped over his right wrist, and then he whipped the free end of the rope around his waist and knotted it one-handedly, binding his right hand against his torso.

"What the hell are you doin'?!" Dixie scoffed.

Nate slowly raised his left hand, waist-high, palm up, and curled his fingers to beckon Dixie. "Git up!" he said, his voice so quiet that, for a moment, Dixie stopped breathing to hear whatever else he might say.

When, after several seconds, Dixie had not moved, Nate leaned to him, grabbed his shirtfront, and jerked him up until he got his legs and stood on his own.

"I'm sick o' yore mouth," Nate said plainly enough. "We both got only one arm, so why don't you commence with all that *kicking-me-from-hell-to-Sunday* you were talkin' 'bout."

Dixie held his damaged hand against his wiry midsection. "Yo're just wantin' a edge on me when I'm hurt."

"There ain't no edge," Nate returned, nodding toward his own bound wrist. "There's just you bein' a cow'rd when you ain't got that showy gun to flash around."

Dixie lowered his head and let his shoulders slump, as if he were declining any offer to fight. Then, quick as a wink, he took a short skip forward and kicked at Nate's privates. Nate pivoted his hips, caught Dixie's boot, and lifted it so high that Dixie's supporting leg came off the ground. He crashed onto the road, landing on the back of his head. Groaning, Dixie rolled slowly onto his side, and clamped his good hand to the back of his neck.

"Damn it all!" Dixie rasped. He let go a savage growl and then glared at Nate with his lips pulled back from his teeth. "You sonovabitch!" Scrambling to his feet, Dixie assumed the position of a one-armed pugilist and began to move around Nate, his bent left arm held out before him, his fist circling in the air. "Come on, you sonovabitch! Let's go!"

The words had no sooner left Dixie's mouth than Nate lunged forward and delivered two quick jabs, one to Dixie's mouth and the other to his nose, each punch solid and deliberate. The blood that ran from Dixie's nostrils appeared black in the starlight. Still on his feet, he seemed to expect a "time-out" while he recovered from the blows, but Nate moved in again and threw a powerful cross that knocked Dixie down sideways to land hard on his shoulder.

Stunned, Dixie sat up and gently probed his nose with his fingertips. When he inspected his hand and saw the abundance of blood, he roared something unintelligible, got to his feet again, and ran at Nate like a crazed animal.

Nate feinted right and then stepped to his left as Dixie almost fell in trying to keep up with him. Just as Dixie stumbled past him, Nate unleashed a powerful blow in front of Dixie's ear, knocking the boy off his feet again.

When Dixie tried to cushion his fall with his injured hand, he screamed in pain, rolled to his side, and drew himself into a ball on the road.

Mewling like a calf, Dixie shut his eyes so tightly that his face appeared to shrink. Each time he inhaled, the air hissed through his clamped teeth. Then, when he exhaled, his cheeks inflated and pushed the air out with a hollow sound.

"I can keep knockin' you down ever' time you care to git up," Nate said.

Dixie looked up and fumed. "I ain't done!" he snapped in a hoarse voice.

Nate waited. When Dixie got to his feet again, he managed a garish smile, each of his teeth now outlined by a thin frame of blood.

"Just let me catch my breath," Dixie said. He bent his knees slightly, leaned forward from the waist, and clasped his good hand over his knee as he let his head sag from his shoulders. His breathing was deep and scratchy, and his wounded hand trembled as he held it tucked into his belly.

When he stood upright and propped his good hand on his hip, he began to walk a circle around Nate as though he were considering his next tactic. Nate turned with him the same way he worked with horses from a snubbing post. After a quarter revolution, Dixie suddenly broke into a dash toward Peaches, his legs churning, and his boots clawing for purchase in the sandy road.

Nate caught him just as Dixie grabbed the narrow shank of Nate's rifle stock. Clamping his arm around Dixie's neck, Nate wrenched him away from the rifle and ran him across the road with Dixie bent over and flailing to keep his feet beneath him. Flinging him into the brush, Nate remained at the edge of the road and watched the loudmouthed saddler plunge into a cluster of "horse crippler" cactus. Dixie's scream could have chilled the soul of an undertaker.

"*Shit!*" Dixie yelled, his voice in a panic. "Goddammit! Git me outta this!"

Screaming and cursing, he tried crawling out on all fours, crying out like a child whichever way he moved. Finally, with a deep growl from his chest, he heaved himself up and tumbled into the road. There he lay very still on his back for ten seconds. His hands were streaked with blood, and the forefinger of his right hand was bent at an unnatural angle. Slowly and deliberately, he rolled to his left side and drew his knees up slightly. Then he began sobbing.

Nate stood over him and waited for The Texas Kid to purge his misery. When the young outlaw was able to get control of himself, Nate spoke to him in a matter-of-fact tone.

"You should'a taken me up on my offer to have some supper."

Dixie turned his head to show a face streaked with tears. Every part of him appeared defeated, except his eyes, which locked on Nate like the muzzles of a loaded shotgun in the hands of a madman.

"I'm gonna kill you," Dixie whispered. "That's a promise."

Chapter Thirty-Five

Nate untied the rope around his waist and freed up his hand. As he stuffed the pigging string back into his saddlebag, he heard the *clop-clop* of horses' hooves coming from the south. Peering down the road, he saw a horse emerge from the dark. It was Dixie's gray.

Then a second horse appeared behind the gray, and Nate was surprised to see his little brother, Dudley, approaching on his roan. Just behind Dud came James on his bay. Dud held a coil of lasso that he had dallied around his pommel. Its loop end had been thrown over the gray's neck and snugged tight just behind the jawbones.

"We found this'n 'bout a half mile back down the road," Dudley explained. "It was headin' south, so me an' James figured we oughta bring it this way to see who it might'a throwed." He tugged on the rope. "Whoa, now, big'n!"

James reined up beside Dud and stared at Dixie lying in the road. "Well, I guess we know who got throwed," James said.

Nate fastened the flap on his saddlebag and watched

his brothers get an eyeful of Dixie's wounds. "What're you two doin' up this way?" Nate asked.

Dudley unwound the rope from his saddle horn and began pulling in the slack to shorten the gray's tether. "Daddy sent us to find you. He's all lathered up 'bout you bein' so late."

James kept his gaze on Dixie. "What's happened here, Nate?"

Nate nodded toward Dixie. "This joker waylaid me. Wanted to rob me."

"Of *what*?" James asked. "Did he think you carried money around with you?"

"He was after food," Nate explained. "Then...I guess he was after me."

"You two been fightin'?" Dud asked.

Nate walked to the gray and slid out a Winchester repeater from Dixie's saddle scabbard. "Yeah," he said. "Me and him...and some cactus."

Moving to the far side of the road, Nate gripped the rifle by the barrel and slung it out into the dark in the same direction he had thrown Dixie's pistol. It clattered among some dry branches and rustled a bough of leaves just before thudding to the ground.

"He ain't to be trusted," Nate explained as he crossed back over the road to Dixie's horse. Taking hold of Dud's rope, he tugged the loop off the gray's neck and let the rope fall into the dirt. Dudley began coiling the rope into even loops.

James winced at Dixie's bloodied clothes. "He gonna be aw-right?" he murmured to Nate.

Nate led Peaches to the ditch and picked up Dory's painting. "He'll live. Just leave 'im be."

James frowned. "We ain't gonna help 'im?"

Nate looked James in the eye. "Told me he had plans

to kill me," Nate said in an even voice. "So, we're leavin' 'im here just like he is."

James's eyes pinched. "Who the hell is he?"

Nate filled his lungs with the night air and let his breath ease out slowly. "Carlton Dixon Brooks. Went by *Dixie* till recent. Now he calls hisself *The Texas Kid.*"

At the sound of his newly chosen moniker, Dixie turned and glared at Nate. The message in his eyes was pure venom.

Dudley prodded his roan closer to Dixie and leaned to get a better look at him. "That right?" Dud said, resting his forearm across his pommel. "You wanna kill my brother?"

Dixie's lips drew back from his blood-streaked teeth. "Yo're goddammed right I do!"

Dudley casually slipped his carbine from its scabbard and propped the butt of the stock on his thigh. "You ain't too smart, are you?" Then he added in a comic drawl. "*Texas...Kid.*"

"Dudley!" James snapped. "Put that away!"

Dud kept his eyes on Dixie. "Don't make no sense to leave 'im alive," he said loud enough for his brothers to hear. "Not when he admits he's gonna kill Nate." He turned to James. "How're you gonna feel if he does that?"

"Dud, it ain't yore job to execute a man!" James argued. "We'll take 'im in to Sheriff Strayhorn an' let the judge decide it."

Dudley reined his horse closer to James. "When a man threatens to kill you...you got a right to keep that from happ'nin'. You cain't count on the law to protect you!"

"Dud?" Nate said. "It's my call. We're gonna leave now. Put yore rifle away."

Dudley didn't blink as he stared at Nate. "It's a fool thing to do!" he cautioned.

Nate nodded. "Then it'll be *my* fool thing. Now put the rifle away."

Dixie had gotten to his feet. As the Champion brothers argued, he sidled toward his horse and laid his arm on the gray's rump just behind his bedroll. When Dixie's hand slipped into his saddlebag, Nate caught the movement. He tossed the painting to the ditch again, swung up on Peaches, and kicked his heels into her flanks.

"*Look out, boys!*" Nate yelled. "*Hyah!*"

Peaches charged ahead, leaping into action from a standstill, as Nate reined her in a straight line for the gray. Dixie had pulled out an old, dark-gray revolver and now struggled to cock the hammer with his blood-slicked left hand.

The paint's chest collided with Dixie, smashing him against the gray with the sharp *smack* of flesh and leather. The gray squealed and whinnied and stumbled sideways, as Dixie fell beneath the hooves of both animals. The pistol—fully cocked—lay on the ground, a dark shape silhouetted against the lighter shade of the sandy road. Nate coaxed Peaches into a slow, high-stepping walk that blocked Dixie's access to the gun.

The gray turned hostile and tried to bite Peaches, and in the process stepped all over Dixie with her steel shoes. Three times he yelped as he tried to crawl out from under the horse.

The crisp ratchet of a rifle lever was followed immediately by another. James sat his bay with his rifle butt firm against his shoulder. Dudley had his rifle leveled on Dixie, too. Nate dismounted and snatched up Dixie's pistol. After easing down the hammer, he heaved it out into the night with the other guns.

"What the hell's wrong with this jackleg?" Dud asked. "He's beggin' to git hisself shot!"

Dixie's bloody shirt was in tatters. An open gash on his forehead bled profusely. He lay spread-eagled in the road with cactus thorns still tangled in his clothing.

James lowered his rifle. "Why's he wanna kill you, Nate? What's wrong with 'im?"

"What's wrong with 'im?" Nate repeated. "Well, he's got a broke finger, broke nose, busted lip, an' a coupla loose tooth. His horse 'bout stoved in his head. Add to that 'bout a hunerd cactus spines."

Taking up the gray's reins, Nate led the horse off the road into the weeds. There, he gave the animal a smart slap on the rump and watched her trot away ten yards and then stop as if unsure what to do next. Then she seemed to realize the freedom she had once again gained, and she trotted out toward the open prairie.

Nate walked to barrow ditch and picked up Dory's painting. Tucking it under his arm, he returned to Peaches and one-handedly pulled himself up into the saddle.

"What *is* that?" Dud asked.

James twisted in his saddle and waited. He wanted to hear Nate's answer, too.

"Paintin'," Nate mumbled. He hitched the package a little higher into his armpit and nodded down the road. "Let's git home."

James led the way, and Dudley started off behind him. Nate reined Peaches closer to Dixie, pulled up, and looked down on the pitiful sight of The Texas Kid. Dixie looked back at him, his face distorted into a countenance of pure hatred.

"I'll see *yore* blood soon enough, you sonovabitch! You hear me?!"

Nate said nothing for a time. When he did speak, his voice was low and calm, causing Dixie to raise his head off the ground to better hear him.

"Yo're gonna hear me now. I'll say this just once, so you better listen good."

Dixie strained to keep his head lifted off the ground, but it was too much for him. His head dropped back into the dusty road while his eyes remained fixed on Nate.

"Yo're a tiresome fellow," Nate said. "I have just barely tolerated what comes out o' yore mouth. An' I don't care to fight you no more. You don't never seem to learn the lessons that git pushed right into yore face."

When Dixie started speak, Nate thrust his free arm out and pointed at him. "I ain't finished!" he said, his voice now hard as steel. Lowering his arm, he cleared his throat and returned to the calm manner in which he had begun. "You've threatened my life. My brother, Dudley, was right. Most men would kill you for that and receive a pat on the back from a jury."

Nate paused to let the words sink in. Dixie closed his eyes tightly as if a pain had flared up somewhere inside him. When he opened his eyes, there was still hatred burning in his face.

"I'm givin' you this one chance," Nate continued. "Git out o' Williamson County for good, 'cause I ain't gonna let you take my life from me. From this night on, if ever I see you around here, I *will* kill you."

Dixie's face sobered for an instant. Then another stab of pain racked him, and he looked away to scowl at the night.

The first breeze of the night came out of the trees, stirring the leaves in the forest into a susurrus of a thousand whispers. Nate faced into the wind and closed his eyes, letting the cool air wash across his skin.

When he started for home, Peaches took off at a crisp trot. He could see James and Dud waiting for him fifty yards down the road. Their horses were turned in profile, and the two brothers sat facing one another, relaxed in conversation. Behind him, Nate heard Dixie cough up phlegm and then spit. Of her own volition, Peaches sped up to an easy gallop and covered the distance quickly.

By the time Nate reached his brothers, they had turned and prodded their mounts to match his speed. They rode three abreast for only a few seconds before they heard Dixie's high-pitched voice screech like a hawk.

"You better be watchin' for me, Champion! By God, that's *my* warnin' to *you*!"

The Champion boys rode on, their horses shoulder to shoulder like a synchronized unit.

"I'm gonna kill you, you sonovabitch!" Dixie screamed louder. "You hear me?!"

Dud turned his head and stared at the side of Nate's face. "I still think we're makin' a mistake, Nate. It'd be smarter if we left him dead out in the brush."

Nate started to speak, until Dixie yelled out again, this time at the top of his lungs.

"I'll kill *all* o' you Champions, by God! Yo're all dead men! Ever' one o' you!"

Dudley snorted a laugh. "D'you notice how he gits braver the farther we ride away."

"Still, you got to watch out for 'im," James counseled. "He may be a cow'rd, but a cow'rd is just the kind to git hold of a gun to settle his differences with a man. Long as he don't have to face 'im, that is. You hear me, Nate?"

Nate nodded. "I'll be keepin' my eyes open."

"Hunh!" James returned. "We'll all be keepin' our eyes open for that snake."

Chapter Thirty-Six

As the moon rose, the road before them began to give off a silvery light, making an easy trail to follow in the night. When their path melded with the wide cattle trail, the Champion brothers slowed their horses to a walk to negotiate the uneven hoofmarks gouged into the hardened mud.

"Well, Nate," Dud said, breaking the long silence they had kept for the past miles, "are you gonna tell us what that was all about back there?"

Nate looked straight ahead as he answered. "Some people just carry trouble with 'em wherever they go. An' Dixie Brooks has a pow'rful callin' to be a genuine desperado. Ever' time I've been 'round 'im, he gits my blood a-boilin'."

Dud frowned. "So, you had a run-in with 'im b'fore?"

"Coupla times," Nate replied.

Dud kept his eyes on Nate. "And did you git the better of 'im ever' time?"

Nate took in a deep breath and purged it before answering. "That ain't hard to do." He turned a solemn expression on Dudley. "I don't take it light, if that's what yo're wonderin'. I know I got a enemy. I'll keep a sharp lookout."

When Dudley spoke again, his voice carried a rare tone of sincerity. "Yo're gonna need more'n a sharp lookout, brother." Dud fingered a lock of his roan's dark mane and flipped it from one side to the other. "Maybe it's time you started carryin' a pistol, Nate. I know yo're plenty good with that rifle o' yores, but it don't clear leather as fast as a pistol. Maybe you oughta ask Daddy to loan you the use o' his sher'ffin' pistol...that ol' 'sixty-six Army Colt's."

Nate shook his head. "That ain't likely to happ'n."

"What...the askin' or the loanin'?"

"Both," Nate said.

They spoke no more until they reached the Champion ranch. Checkers came out to greet them and followed them into the barn, where the brothers tended to their horses by the glow of the lighted lantern. When they were done, James snuffed the flame, and the trio walked together to the house, with Nate carrying his wrapped gift under his arm.

As they ate a cold meal in the kitchen, their father appeared in the doorway of the dining room. He stood in his night clothes and fixed a questioning gaze on Nate.

"You all right?" he asked in his soft drawl.

"Yes'r," Nate replied. "Sorry to be so late." He waited for the inevitable questions, but his father seemed content to see his sons gathered together and eating.

"I'll talk to you in the mo'nin'," the elder Champion said. Then he turned and walked back the way he had come. They heard his bedroom door close softly, and then the house was quiet again. Dud and James turned to each other, each making the same expression of surprise, their eyebrows bobbing up and then relaxing.

After cleaning up, the three brothers retired to their shared bedroom, where John Thomas was so deep in sleep, he could have been a corpse. The brothers began peeling off their clothes in preparation for sleep. Nate was first to slip into his bed and turn his back to the room. He had closed his eyes for less than a minute when someone sat down beside him on his mattress. Turning, he found Dudley holding a blue cloth bag in his lap. As Nate watched, Dud loosened the drawstring and brought out a Colt's Navy model, .36 caliber. He held it in the flat of his hand and offered it to Nate.

"Feel this'n. It's lighter an' better balanced than that ol' cannon o' Daddy's."

James approached in his sleeping gown and leaned in for a look. "Where the hell'd you git *that*?"

Dud did not answer. Nate sat up, took the weapon, and appraised it by little weighing motions of his hand. He felt the gun's compact craftsmanship and agreeable heft.

"Where *did* you git this, Dud?" Nate said and looked his little brother in the eye.

Dudley smiled. "Bought it in Georgetown from Mr. Taylor at the mercantile. He give me a good price on it, since there ain't nobody much buyin' cap-an'-ball no more."

Nate studied the working parts and the smooth finish of the metal. The gun appeared not to have seen much use.

"Daddy know 'bout this?"

Dud laughed. "Whatta *you* think? *He's* why I bought it in Georgetown."

James chuckled. "Well, let's hope Mr. Taylor an' Daddy don't cross paths."

Nate turned the pistol over to examine its other side. "How come you was to buy it?"

Dud shrugged. "We're all gonna need one, ain't we? Might as well be sooner'n later."

"Well, I don' know 'bout *all* o' us." James laughed. "Let's pray Naomi don't git a hankerin' for one anytime soon."

The three brothers laughed quietly and then went silent as they returned to admiring the gun. Dudley patted the Colt's with his hand, as if he were saying "goodbye" to it.

"You keep that'n with you for a while, Nate." He picked up the bag and stretched open its mouth to show the contents. "Here's ever'thin' you need for loadin' and cleanin'." He set the bag on the mattress next to Nate. "You know how to use a cap-an'-ball?"

Nate nodded. "William taught me."

Dudley grinned as he nodded at the Colt's. "That there's the same kind o' gun Hickok used, you know."

That got Nate's attention. "How'd you know *that*?"

Dud shrugged. "I read all them dime novels you used to hide in yore dresser drawer."

Nate frowned. "Whatever happ'ned to all those?"

Dud pointed to his bed. "I keep 'em in that box under my bed with my leather tools." He raised a hand, palm out toward Nate. "Now b'fore you start yellin' at me, I saved 'em from the burn pile, when our stepmother was hell-bent on cleanin' an' throwin' out anythin' that weren't practical or nailed down."

Nate laughed. "Guess I owe you then."

Dudley's eyebrows lifted. "Does that mean you want 'em back?"

Nate shook his head. "You keep 'em. Maybe one day you can pass 'em down to Ben." Nate turned to show the earnestness in his face. "All them stories 'bout Hickok... they ain't true, you know."

"I know that!" Dud snapped a little defensively. "Not

all of 'em, anyway. But there ain't no reason they'd lie 'bout the kind o' gun he used." He pointed at the pistol and its bag of accessories. "Go ahead an' put all that away somewhere. If Daddy catches you with it, it's *yore* problem not mine. Aw-right?"

Nate secured the pistol and cloth sack under the head of his mattress. When he turned back to Dud, he offered his hand, and the two brothers shook.

"I 'preciate it," Nate said.

Dud winked. "Our secret, brother." He turned to James. "All of us."

Nate leaned back on an elbow. "Uncle George shook hands with 'im, you know," Nate said. "Hickok, I mean. Met 'im in Abilene. Said he was kinda showy the way he dressed. Carried his pistols in a red sash!"

"Yeah, I know," Dud said. "Uncle George has told me *that* story so many times, I feel like I was there with 'im." A wistful look came over Dud's face. "Whatta you reckon it would be like to be so famous that ever'body knew who you were and gave you a wide berth on the sidewalk?"

"Prob'ly a lonely life," Nate said.

Dud put on his smile of admiration. "I reckon *you* got to be sorta famous now...at least in our part o' Texas...for yore horse trainin', I mean. You ain't lonely, are you?"

Nate felt the void of losing Dory open inside him again. This time, the emptiness expanded beyond him until it was like holding on with his fingertips to the edge of a bottomless crevice, where the world had unaccountably opened its jaws and tried to swallow him. His gut went light with a fear he had never known. It was not the fear of the falling. Nor was it the fear of the unknown that waited for him in that deep, dark hole. It was knowing that he would fall alone. Without Dory. And without ever knowing the woman she had become.

"I ain't famous, Dud," Nate mumbled.

Dudley laughed. "I ain't so sure 'bout that."

"If Nate *was* famous," James said, "he'd prob'ly be the last one to know 'bout it."

Dudley narrowed his eyes as if a foul smell had come his way. "What the Sam Hill does *that* mean?"

James smiled. "I'll let you think about that one, little brother."

Dud rolled his eyes. "You cain't be famous an' not know it. That don't make a lick o' sense. An' b'sides, what good is it to be famous if you don't know you are?"

Now James gave Dud a look. He started to say something but closed his mouth without a sound.

Dud smiled. "I'll let *you* think about that one, big brother!" Then he lightly bumped Nate's leg with the back of his hand. "What about it, Nate? You ever git lonely?"

James chuckled. "Dudley, ain't you ever watched 'im work the horses? Nate would rather work alone doin' that than be the judge at a apple pie bakin' contest."

Dud slapped a hand to his belly. "Now, there's a job I could handle!"

"Yeah." James laughed. "You are a top hand at eatin'. I'll give you that."

Dud nudged Nate's leg again. "What about it, Nate? Ever git lonely?"

"First off, I ain't alone when I work with a horse. You cain't discount the horse from that assessment. And second, bein' alone an' bein' lonely ain't the same thing."

Dud pointed at Nate. "Now, *that* one I git! But you didn' answer my question. You ever git lonely?"

Nate turned to Dud. "Never thought I did. Not b'fore. But now I ain't so sure."

In the morning, while the aromas of eggs, bacon, and freshly baked biscuits spread through the house, Nate and his father stood on the back stoop, shoulder to shoulder as they gazed out on the south pasture. Nate related the events of the previous night, and Jack Champion listened without interrupting. The father's stoic face showed no reaction, even as Nate described wrestling Dixie Brooks's weapon away from him. When Nate finished the story, his father said nothing and continued to stare out over the grassland.

"I didn' start the trouble, Daddy. I just had to handle it as best I could."

His father nodded once, took in a deep breath, and eased it out as a sigh. Turning to Nate, he laid his hand gently on his son's shoulder.

"After we eat, I wanna see you in my office."

"Yes'r," Nate replied.

After squeezing Nate's shoulder once, Jack Champion started for the door. "Let's go have some breakfast, son."

All the family was gathered in the dining room, and the conversations mixed like a confluence of multiple rivers crashing into one another. Throughout the meal, however, nothing was said about the three brothers returning home so late. Even Naomi Jane did not ask questions about it, though she most certainly would have heard her brothers come in.

When he had finished his meal, Jack Champion walked into the kitchen and remained there for ten minutes. Nate could hear his low voice delivering a long narration to his stepmother, throughout which Mary remained silent, other than the tap of pots and pans as she cleaned.

When Jack returned and sat at the head of the table again, he tapped a fork against his empty coffee cup, the dull ring sufficing to quiet everyone at the table. He set down the fork, flattened his hands on either side of his plate, and made eye contact with each of the children.

"We'ah gonna need ev'ahbody helpin' around he'ah today. Mary an' I wanna put a new coat o' whitewash on the house while we got this dry spell."

Nate looked at Dudley...and then at James. All three knew what this was about. The rooster and the hen wanted to keep the chicks close to the coop today. Somewhere out there was a weasel named "Dixie Brooks."

"John Thomas," the father continued, "you and Dudley and Ben gather up the brushes an' the turpentine from the tool shed. They'ahs rags in that box on the back stoop. James, you fetch the cans o' paint. They'ah behind the feed sacks in the tack room. Salt's in the kitchen pantry." He turned to Naomi. "Naomi Jane, do you wanna paint or work with yo'ah mother in the kitchen?"

Surprising everyone, Naomi spoke up without any hesitation. "Kitchen!" she announced.

Mary looked Naomi's way and stared, her coffee cup suspended before her. "I think you should help with the painting, Naomi. I'm going to help, too."

"Yeah, come on, Naomi," Dudley said. "The more hands with a brush, the quicker it'll go."

"Dudley is right," Mary said. "The job will get done faster."

She looked up quickly, her dark eyes fixing on Dudley like the muzzles of a shotgun. "Last time I helped," she carped, "you whitewashed more of me than the house!"

Dud frowned and laughed at the same time. "Well, you must'a just got in the way."

The skin around Naomi's eyes tightened. "Like hell!"

Mary's head snapped around quick as a snakebite. "Naomi!" she scolded. "Clear the table and clean up your mouth, young lady! You can just do all the breakfast cleanup by yourself!"

Naomi stood and began moving around the table, casually gathering up the plates and silverware. When she stood across the table from Dudley, she flashed a wicked smile and then carried her load into the kitchen.

Chapter Thirty-Seven

Nate returned to his bedroom to change into his old boots for the sloppy task of painting. Dudley sat on his bed, his boots already switched. Dud leaned forward, his forearms propped on his knees, and stared at the package wrapped in sheets behind Nate's bed.

"So, when do we git to see this paintin'?" Dud said and pointed across the room.

Nate toed off his boots and began tugging on the other pair. "I was thinkin' o' hangin' it on the wall there tonight."

Dud nodded. "D'you git it at the Tisdales?"

Nate shook his head. "I brung it from town."

Dud tilted his head and frowned. It was clear he was not done with his questions.

"So, what's it a paintin' *of?*"

Nate stood and stamped his old boots against the bare wood floor. "It's just somethin' I'm gonna hang on the wall over my bed," he said, trying for a casual tone.

Dudley slid back further on his bed and leaned his back into the wall. Smiling, he propped one boot over the other at the ankles and crossed his arms over his chest.

The top boot swung from side to side like the wagging tail of a dog.

"Aw-right, now I know where it's gonna hang. But what is it?"

Nate felt his face go warm. "It's a picture o' Peaches," he murmured.

Dud's face brightened. "Peaches!" He laughed. "Who'd you git to do that for ya?"

"Didn' *git* nobody. It just got done without the askin'."

Dud laughed again. "Well, who painted it? Is it any good?"

"Yeah," Nate said. "It's good."

"We got us a painter in Round Rock?" James asked from the door. He came in, sat on his bed, and began wrestling off his boots.

Nate shook his head. "This painter ain't in Round Rock," he said quietly. "She painted it a long way from here. In Paris, France."

Nate saw that Dud's smile had turned a tad mischievous. "*She?*" Dud said and looked at James. "Did he say *she?*"

James arched both eyebrows. "He said *she,*" he confirmed, fairly singing the words.

As Nate changed his shirt, he tried to gather the words that might end his brother's inquisition. When his head popped through the collar of his old work shirt, he saw Dud grinning at him and wagging a finger the way a schoolteacher does.

"I heard Lindy Hildebrand has been over at some school in France," Dud said, putting a little melody to his words. "Wouldn' be her, would it? I didn' think you an' Lindy was that good o' friends."

Nate tucked the shirt's tails into the waistband of his trousers and kept his eyes down as he smoothed out his shirtfront. "Her sister," he said.

The smile on Dud's face relaxed, and his eyes pinched enough to crease wrinkles into his smooth brow. "You mean the one they call *Dory*?"

Nate looked up and resigned himself to the simple truth. "That's right," he said.

For several seconds, no one spoke. Then Dud cleared his throat.

"Yeah, I 'member her," Dud said. "How old is she, anyway?"

"It ain't what yo're thinkin'," Nate said in a flat tone.

Dudley shrugged. "I weren't thinkin' nothin'," he said, keeping a straight face.

When Nate looked at James, the older brother held out both palms to Nate. "I weren't thinkin' nothin' neither."

Dud and James stared at the white sheet of linen bound around the painting. The room was quiet. Nate could hear the wind outside teasing the windmill into staggered turns.

"Can we see it, Nate?" Dudley asked in the tender voice that he rarely used since his childhood years.

Nate shrugged. "Go ahead, if you want to."

Dud pushed up from his bed, crossed the room, and sat on Nate's bed. He reached back for the painting and laid it across his knees. When he felt of the burn hole in the sheet, he looked up at Nate, his face wrinkled with a question.

"Dixie Brooks," Nate said, answering the question before it was asked.

Dud's brow tightened. "Bullet?"

Nate nodded.

Dud loosened the string, unwrapped the package, and laid the linen aside. Taking the canvas by its sides, he held it at arm's length and retracted his head to take in the full picture.

"You got to look at it from a distance," Nate explained.

Dudley reached back, propped the painting upright on the mattress, and leaned it against the wall. Then he crossed the room and stood next to James, where the two of them stared open-mouthed at Dory's work.

"Damn!" Dud breathed. "She's good!" He laughed. "That's Peaches aw-right! Right down to that crazy stripe on 'er tail."

James inflated his cheeks and quietly released an airy whistle that swooped upward and then trailed down. "She's better than good," he whispered. "That girl is an artist."

The three brothers stood before the painting as if they had entered an empty church and paused to admire a window made up of colorful sections of glass. Nate spotted the bullet hole down in the grass, where it did not significantly interfere with the scene. He thought he might stuff a wad of dried grass into the hole as a way of repairing the damage. He imagined Dory smiling at the idea.

"I'll be outside in a few minutes," Nate said as he turned. "I got to go an' see Daddy."

Jack Champion sat at his desk, entering figures in a ledger that was open before him. Looking up at Nate's entrance into his office, he set his pen in its stand. Then he leaned to blow across the page. After letting the ink dry for a time, he closed the black cover of the book and pivoted in his chair. The oil lamp burning on his desk cast a soft light onto his nest of a beard, making the gray hairs shine like silver threads. Nate stood in his usual spot on the rug, spread his boots, and waited.

"Which direction did the Brooks boy go aftah yo'ah confrontation?"

Nate pursed his lips and shook his head. "He didn'. We just left 'im there in the road."

After stroking his beard for a time, Jack Champion nodded. "I want you an' James to ride into town this mo'nin' and tell evah'thing to the she'iff."

Nate kept his face expressionless as he thought about the repercussions of reporting to Sheriff Strayhorn. If Dixie was arrested, the loudmouth might tell how he had partnered up with Tiz. With Murphy still in the jail, it would be just a matter of time before Tiz's connection to Sam Bass might be uncovered.

"I'd rather just handle things myself, Daddy."

The father's deep-set eyes bored into Nate. "What about the next victim this boy waylays?"

"I ain't so sure he's a common thief," Nate said. "Seems more like he's just got some kinda grudge 'gainst me."

The old man's eyes hardened. "They'ah's a reason we have men with badges, son."

Nate held his father's gaze. "I'd rather handle it on my own."

A twitch of impatience flashed across the old man's face. "Son, if that boy—"

"Daddy," Nate interrupted. "I wish you'd trust me on this."

Jack Champion closed the hand on his desk into a fist, opened it again, and let go with a long sigh. "And I wish *you* would trust *me*. It's bett'ah to get this on the reco'd now. If the Brooks boy thinks he can get away with this kind o' thing, he'll just keep pushin' his luck."

"He ain't got away with nothin', Daddy," Nate said and raised an arm to point north. "He's prob'ly still out there right now without a horse...his face all bloodied up... his finger broke...his guns all scattered in the brush...an' he's stuck full o' cactus spines."

Jack sat back in his chair and idly combed the fingers

of one hand through his beard. A faint wheeze whistled through his nose each time he exhaled.

"I don't discount the threat, Daddy. I'll keep myself sharp. But I ain't gonna let the likes o' him change the way I live my life. I won't give 'im that kind o' pow'r over me."

Jack looked long and hard into Nate's eyes, and Nate stared right back at him, not challenging his father with defiance but trying to assure him of his capabilities. This facedown stretched out for half a minute until the father slowly began nodding his head.

"I can see yo'ah mind's made up on this."

"Yes'r, it is."

The old man turned his head and stared at the ledger book lying closed on his desk. When he looked back at Nate, his face seemed more relaxed and open.

"Yo'ah a man now, son, an' I'm bound to respect that. I und'ahstan' what yo'ah sayin' about not givin' this boy pow'ah ov'ah you. But a gun is a pow'ah unto itself, an' you have *got* to respect that." He opened the center drawer of the desk and pulled out a light metal box that might have been a tin for cookies. "I'm gonna count out fo'ty doll'ahs fo' you, son."

Nate frowned. "Sir?"

The father opened the tin and took out a small stack of bills. After wetting his thumb on his tongue, he dealt out four notes of legal tender onto the desktop, like a man about to play a game of solitaire. Then he picked up the bills and held them out to Nate.

"I want you to go to Mist'ah Maddox's sto'ah and pick out a new Colt's pistol fo' yo'self. Yo'ah gonna need ammunition, a cah'tridge belt, a holst'ah, and a cleanin' kit."

Nate had to rerun his father's words through his head to be certain he had heard correctly. Simply out of obedience, his hand reached forward of its own volition, and he took the money.

"You'll want the fo'ty-fo'ah calib'ah so you can carry the same ammunition for the pistol and yo'ah rifle. Don't get a self-cock'ah. With a single-action, you'll be mo'ah likely to hit what you aim at."

"I can help pay for it, Daddy. I been savin' the money I make on trainin' horses."

The old man reached out and closed Nate's fingers around the money. "These ah gifts, son. It's yo'ah time now to have 'em. I did the same fo' William, an' I'll do it for yo'ah oth'ah brothers when the time comes."

Nate swallowed. "Yes'r. But shouldn' James and John Thomas come b'fore me?"

"All in good time," Jack said. He turned back to his desk and opened the book. "You an' James can pick up on the whitewashin' when you get back."

Nate watched the side of his father's face as the old man studied the numbers in the ledger. Reaching for his pen, Jack dipped the nib into the inkwell.

"Daddy? Are we paintin' the house 'cause you want ever'body stayin' close to home? Is this on account o' Dixie Brooks?"

Jack Champion kept his eyes on the open page and held his poker face. "It'll do the house some good. I know Mary will appreciate it. Yo'ah mama used to insist on it ev'ah few ye'ahs."

Nate watched his father dip his pen into the ink again. In this moment he felt that he understood the man in ways that he had never before considered. Jack Champion had lost his wife—Nate's mother. Nate thought he might ask about how a man gets past such a loss, but when he opened his mouth to speak, he could not bring himself to say Dory's name out loud, lest he break down into tears in front of his father.

"Daddy, a man named Mooney over on the San

Gabriel River is puttin' together a big herd o' cattle that he plans to run north come next spring."

Jack nodded as he scratched the pen across the paper. "This is Ab Mooney yo'ah talkin' about?"

"Yes'r. He's asked me to sign on with 'im as head wrangler. I'd be in charge of the remuda he'll take along. I'd like to do it. Like to see that country up north. Do you reckon you can spare me?"

The old man stopped writing and lifted his face to stare at the shelf of books before him. Setting the pen back in its stand, he threaded his fingers together on the desktop and turned his head toward Nate.

"Son, I know you wanna see what lies out beyond Texas. It's only natu'al." The father huffed a quiet laugh through his nose. "But I can tell you...ain't much to see in Kansas but a lotta open space and grass." He cocked his head to one side as if in regret. "I read in the newspap'ah they'ah shuttin' down some o' the cattle trails that run through the state. It's a qua'antine against the tick fev'ah."

"Mr. Mooney is not headin' to Kansas, Daddy. He's plannin' to sell off his herd in the Wyomin' Territory. Said he's aw-ready got a contract with the army at two of the forts up there."

Jack's eyes glazed over as if he were deep in thought. "Wyomin'," he said plainly, as though trying out the word on his tongue. "Always did wanna to see that country myself. They say it'll take hold of a man an' won't let 'im go."

Nate said nothing to that. The silence in the room drew out, but both father and son seemed comfortable in this quiet. It was as if they had reached some tacit new agreement between themselves. The clock ticking in the parlor seemed already to be marking the time Nate had left in Texas.

"So, yo're sayin' that it's aw-right for me to go?"

The father stared at the son for what seemed a long time. "I'm sayin' yo'ah man enough to make yo'ah own decisions now."

"But you can git along without me here?"

The father pursed his lips and raised his chin. "Yo'ah brother James will stick close. He's already runnin' the ranch an' learnin' the books." Jack Champion put on a smile that he rarely showed. "It doesn't mean I won't miss you, son. Yo'ah as good a hand at the ranch as any man I've known, and you got a gift with the hosses. *No* man can replace you in *that* job, but it's no su'prise to me that you wanna spread yo'ah wings a little." Slowly, he swept an arm around the room. "You'll always have a home he'ah, you know."

"Yes'r," Nate replied. "I know."

The two Champions continued to look at one another. It was the first time that Nate had ever considered himself to be on equal footing with his father...now that they had both lost persons so dear to them.

"If you go to Wyomin', son, that land just might nev'ah let you go." Jack raised his hand and held it out. Nate stared at it for several heartbeats. It was a gesture never before offered from father to son. Not to Nate, anyway. He had seen his daddy shake hands with William on the day he had left home.

Nate placed his hand inside the gentle grip of his father's. They squeezed just enough to telegraph their unspoken love for one another as their hands moved slowly up and down to consummate the ritual.

"Whatev'ah you do with yo'ah life, Nathan...I know I will be proud of you."

"I hope I've lived up to yore expectations, Daddy."

Jack smiled beneath his bushy beard and mustaches. "Mo'ah than I could've hoped fo'ah, son."

The old man released Nate's hand, and he seemed to

revert back to the stoic father that he had always been. Picking up his pen, he found his place on the page and began scribbling numbers.

"You two get back from town as soon as you can," Jack said. "Then the rest of us won't have to listen to John Thomas's complaints about havin' to paint the house without you."

"Yes'r," Nate said and walked out of the room.

Before going outside to find James, Nate returned to his empty bedroom and beheld Dory's painting still on display against the wall. A strange mix of beauty and loss filled him, and all at once he felt a great longing, while at the same time, he experienced a sense of completion at having become the man he was meant to be.

Propping his foot on the head post of James's bed, he stuffed his father's money down into his boot. When he let the foot drop to the floor, he crossed the room to the chest of drawers, kneeled, and pulled out the drawer that was his. Taking out the leather-bound book that Dory had given him, he thumbed through the blank pages and felt the stir of air on his face from the papers as they fanned before him. It felt as soft as a breath. He imagined Dory's mute voice trying to talk to him, reminding him that he should put his own words into this book.

He closed the book and looked down at its leather binding, touching his fingertips to the small painting of the horse centered on the front cover.

"I'll start writin' when I leave on the cattle drive," he whispered aloud. "I promise."

Securing the book under his clothes folded in the drawer, he felt around the bottom until he found the Indian head penny that his uncle George and aunt Hattie had given him. The one that Hickok had dropped on a floor in Abilene. Turning the coin to look at both sides, he determined to give the penny to Dudley as a keepsake. Then, one day, maybe Dud would pass it on to Ben.

He slid the drawer shut, stood to his full height, and left at a brisk pace to go find James. There was a degree of excitement about a brand-new Colt's revolver waiting for him in town, but at the same time, he sensed the change that was coming with it.

The gun was nothing more than a tool, he knew, but by strapping it on, a whole new set of rules was about to descend upon him. It had to do with how men interacted with other men. The words they chose to use. And the words they avoided. The stakes were going to be higher now. Wearing a gun meant that differences between two men might be settled by drastic means. It was a little like signing up for a war and accepting a state of constant jeopardy.

But he also knew that, unless one chose to be a preacher or a doctor, it was part of being a man. He figured it would always be that way as long as there were men like Dixie Brooks in the world.

A Look at Part Two:

Nate the Wyoming Story

The captivating tale of history's best-kept secret continues in this Western fiction duology—showcasing one of the Old West's most heroic figures.

When Nate Champion strikes out to Wyoming Territory and discovers the allure of the Powder River Basin as an ideal location for raising cattle, he builds up a bankroll by hiring out to the cattle companies already established there. Earning a reputation as a top hand, a uniquely gifted horse trainer, and a man of his word, he becomes one of the few men in the territory whom small ranchers can trust.

After the Wyoming Stock Growers Association begins eliminating small ranchers through ghastly executions, the classic battle lines form between the rich man and the commoner. Because Nate is trusted, he becomes a rallying point for the oppressed—leading to his name topping a list of inconvenient ranchers whom the barons want to see removed from the face of the Earth.

Read along as, amid sweeping landscapes and historical turmoil, Nate Champion's legacy unfolds in a fictitious narrative that resonates as a crucial chapter in American history.

AVAILABLE AUGUST 2024

About the Author

Mark Warren teaches primitive survival skills at Medicine Bow, his nationally renowned wilderness school in the Southern Appalachians. His trilogy *Wyatt Earp: An American Odyssey* was honored by WWA's Spur Awards, The Historical Novel Society, and the 2020 Will Rogers Medallion Awards.

In 2024 Warren's book, *A Last Serenade for Billy Bonney,* won the New Mexico-Arizona Book Award for Best Historical Fiction. He is a 2022 Georgia Author of the Year recipient for his book *Song of the Horseman.* His novel, *Indigo Heaven,* his Western parody, *The Westering Trail Travesties,* and his short story, "The Cowboy, the Librarian, and the Broomsman," are all Will Rogers Medallion Award winners.

His other books include *Two Winters in a Tipi, Secrets of the Forest, Last of the Pistoleers, A Tale Twice Told, A Copperhead Summer,* and *Moon of the White Tears.*

www.ingramcontent.com/pod-product-compliance
Lightning Source LLC
Chambersburg PA
CBHW010823250626
47169CB00010B/2931